starlighter

Dragons of Starlight

starlighter

Bryan Davis

ZONDERVAN.com/
AUTHORTRACKER
follow your favorite authors

To download discussion questions for this book, please go to
www.zondervan.com/starlighter

We want to hear from you. Please send your comments about
this book to us in care of zreview@zondervan.com. Thank you.

ZONDERVAN

Starlighter
Copyright © 2010 by Bryan Davis

This title is also available as a Zondervan ebook.
Visit www.zondervan.com/ebooks.

Requests for information should be addressed to:

Zondervan, *Grand Rapids, Michigan 49530*

ISBN 978-0-310-71836-9

Cover design: Jeff Gifford
Interior design: Carlos Eluterio Estrada

Printed in the United States of America

10 11 12 13 14 15 16 /DCI/ 22 21 20 19 18 17 16 15 14 13 12 11 10 9 8 7 6 5 4 3

To Amanda—

Thank you for giving me the idea for this story. Your imagination sparkles like starlight, and you are more precious to me than any gem, whether in the heavens or on the earth.

one

lood match. The words echoed in Jason's mind as he stood at his corner of the tourney ring and gripped the hilt of his sword. Like a beating drum, the announcer must have repeated that phrase a hundred times, as if the potential for bloodletting might whip the crowd into a frenzy.

Jason scanned the two-hundred-plus onlookers. Seated in the surrounding grassy amphitheater during the warmth of midday, they offered no cheers, no applause, just a low buzz signaling a rising anticipation. Jason Masters, a peasant boy, had advanced to the finals and faced the obvious favorite, Randall Prescott, son of the governor of all Mesolantrum. And with the final round came new weapons and new rules, designed to pose a fresh challenge to a young warrior's expertise and courage.

Drawing his sword closer, Jason looked at its tip. The referee had fitted a blocking circle within a half inch of the end, ensuring that his jabs would not inflict a mortal wound. Of course, a blow to the face could rip out an eye, but such an attack would immediately disqualify the offender. No one wanted that to happen, no matter how much he disliked his opponent.

Randall paced at the opposite corner, looking smug as he slid his big feet across the dirt floor. Being the son of the governor, he had been provided with the best equipment and was trained by some of the finest swordsmen in Prescott's domain.

Yet not *the* finest. Jason looked up at the royal box where Governor Prescott sat. His bodyguard stood next to him, always watchful, always ready to defend the governor against attack — *the* best swordsman in the land, Jason's brother Adrian Masters. From his soldier's uniform to his polished leather boots, dark gray trousers, and flowing, long-sleeved forest green shirt, he looked very sharp, especially with the sword and belt attached to his hip. Training with him had provided Jason with all he needed to succeed this far in the tournament, but would it be enough to defeat Randall?

A young woman sat on Prescott's other side — Marcelle. She was still wearing her gray tourney britches and white shirt, both stained with sweat, and had her auburn hair tied back, supporting a laurel leaf crown. She played the part of the new adult champion quite well.

Jason tensed. "Played the part" was right. She shouldn't be the champion. If only Adrian would be as concerned about truth as he was about chivalry —

"Now hear the rules!" the referee bellowed. A tall man with a black beard and a swarthy complexion, the tourney's lead referee, stood at the center of the ring and looked at Jason and Randall in turn. His deep voice continued. "Honor and integrity will be your guide, as always, but in this match, the contest will end the moment one of you draws blood, and that contestant will be declared the winner. Be warned, however, that any blood drawn above the shoulders will disqualify the assailant.

"The judges will tally points, as usual, but the points will not matter in the outcome unless no one draws blood before four minutes expire. In the absence of blood, the point totals will be used to determine the winner, as in all your previous matches."

As the referee droned on about the usual rules of engagement, Jason searched the peasant section. His father and mother sat together, his father alternately cracking his knuckles and pushing back his thinning gray hair, and his mother biting the nails at the ends of her roughened fingers. Meredith, the carpenter's wife and Mother's best friend in the peasant commune, sat nearby, leaving one empty seat in between.

Jason let out a sigh. That seat was for Meredith's daughter, Elyssa, who had once been his best friend. Their friendship had waned as he began attending warriors' school and she started working at the governor's palace. It was a shame—she was really a good friend. If she were still alive, she would be cheering him on.

The referee nodded at each contestant. "The final rule is simple. All manner of cunning is allowed, but you may never leave the ring." He then backed out of the way and shouted, "Let the battle begin!"

Randall charged toward the center with his sword out in front, obviously looking for a quick strike. Jason ran to

meet him and blocked his thrust. The two blades rang out
and then screamed as metal slid against metal.

Jason pushed with his legs. Randall was stronger,
heavier. Staying locked for very long would be a big
mistake.

With a burst of strength, he shoved Randall back, but
before he could jump safely away, Randall swiped his
blade across Jason's sleeve. The material tore, and the
point nicked his skin.

The crowd roared, the nobles with cheers of approval
and the peasants with moans of lament.

While Randall pedaled back, pumping a fist, Jason
stared at the wound. The referee ran over and grasped
Jason's arm. Both studied the superficial scratch, Jason
breathing heavily as he silently begged, *Don't bleed.
Please don't bleed.*

He twisted his neck and found Adrian. The governor
was standing and applauding furiously, while Adrian stood
stoically at his side. Adrian laid a hand on his heart and
mouthed, "Listen to your heart." He then moved his hand
and pointed at his head, this time mouthing, "But use
your brain."

Jason nodded. They had long ago mastered lip reading,
finding it helpful for communicating during the Counselor's
long sermons at Cathedral.

After a few seconds, the referee raised a hand and
shouted, "There is no blood! Let the match continue!"

Randall stood near his corner and waved his sword.
"Your turn, Masters." His voice carried a mocking tone.
"Make your move."

Padding slowly toward his opponent, Jason watched
his eyes. *Listen to your heart*, he repeated in his mind.

Listen to your heart. His heart said that it was about time a peasant put one of these high-minded aristocrats in his place, but his brain said that matching muscle with Randall would be a fool's game. Like it or not, Randall was bigger and stronger. Exploiting Randall's biggest weaknesses—lack of speed and cunning—would be his only hope. And it had already been two minutes. If four minutes expired, the judges, all from the noble classes, would award Randall the win no matter how well either contestant performed.

Jason drew within a sword's lunge and stopped. Using the tip of his sword, he scratched several letters in the dirt. He then nodded at Randall and spoke in a matter-of-fact voice. "I made my move."

"What?" Randall tilted his head. "What did you do?"

"I wrote it here." Jason pointed at the marks. "Can't you read?"

Setting a hand on his hip, Randall chuckled. "Do you really think I'm going to fall for that old trick? I'm not as stupid as—" Jason lunged, jabbed Randall in the thigh, and leaped back. Blood immediately oozed from the wound and soaked his pant leg.

As the crowd roared again, Randall glared at Jason. His face flushed almost as red as his blood. The referee grasped Jason's wrist and lifted his arm in the air. "The winner and champion of the youth division!"

Jason gave Randall the traditional contestant's bow and spoke in a smooth tone. "The writing says, 'Never drop your guard.'"

Like an explosion, Randall burst from his corner and charged with a pronounced limp, shouting, "You little conniver!"

The referee pushed Jason out of the way and caught Randall in his arms. "Control yourself, Randall. Do not play the fool in front of your father and the entire domain. The rules allowed for the cunning Jason employed, so you will have to accept the outcome with dignity."

Still flushed, Randall drooped his shoulders and backed away.

"Your swords, please," the referee said, holding out his hands.

Jason laid his hilt in the referee's palm, and Randall did the same. Randall offered a quick bow and strode from the ring. Barely limping now, he stalked through a gap in the amphitheater's circle, allowing him to quickly duck out of sight.

"Jason Masters!"

Jason turned toward the voice. Governor Prescott stood in the ring, holding a crown of green laurel leaves, Adrian and Marcelle at his side. Wearing a grim expression, Prescott extended the crown with both hands. "Bow, please."

Keeping his eyes on Adrian, Jason bent at the waist. With his lips thin and tight and his cheeks flushed, Adrian looked embarrassed. Had Marcelle said something that wounded his pride?

When he straightened, Jason mouthed the words, "What's wrong?"

"Ask me later," came the silent reply.

"And now ... " Prescott spread out his arms, laying one on Jason's shoulder and one on Marcelle's. "Let us honor the warrior champions in the adult and youth divisions!"

The peasants stood and cheered, while the aristocrats sat and applauded politely. Jason guessed they were not excited about Marcelle's victory. Even though she was the daughter of a nobleman, she had never been popular with the elite. Her outspoken ways saw to that.

She took Jason's hand and shook it warmly. "Congratulations, Jason." She glanced back and forth between him and Adrian. "It was a pleasure to watch a son of Edison Masters do battle in the final round. I'm glad to see that you're courageous enough to face an opponent who might be able to defeat you." With a final smile directed at Adrian, Marcelle walked out of the ring and into the crowd descending the amphitheater steps.

Adrian set a hand on Jason's back, his fingers flexing. No doubt he was angry. "You'd better go home as soon as you can, Jason. I'm sure Mother and Father will want to congratulate you."

Jason turned just in time to see his parents leaving. Of course, there was no law against peasants coming into the ring, but approaching while the governor stood there would be frowned upon.

While Governor Prescott spoke to an elderly noble, Jason leaned close to Adrian and whispered, "Will you be home for a while, or are you going out on one of those dragon-hunting missions again?"

"Shhh!" Adrian nudged Jason with his elbow. "I'll meet you at home this evening. We have a lot to talk about."

"Okay. I'll see you then." As Jason walked between two sections of grass-covered seating areas, he took the crown of laurels from his head and looked at it. Somehow it didn't feel quite right, like something was missing. Sure, it was great being recognized as the best young swordsman in Mesolantrum, but having matching crowns with Adrian would have been a lot better. If only he hadn't withdrawn!

As Jason passed a massive oak, two male peasants huddling under the boughs suddenly stopped their whispered
conversation. Jason nodded, recognizing them as two of
Adrian's friends from another commune. They nodded in
return. Something made of parchment protruded from
the front pocket of the closer man.

Quickly turning his head, Jason strode on. Most of
Adrian's friends were believers in the Lost Ones and the
dragon world, and the hidden parchment likely meant that
a new issue of the *Underground Gateway* was circulating.
That would explain the whispers. Since the newsletter
had been forbidden by the governor, the believers never
openly talked about it. Important or not, the paper wasn't
safe to carry around.

"Safe," Jason muttered to himself. With the exception
of the tournament, all of life had been too safe. Work,
study, eat, sleep, and then do it all over again the next day.
What a boring existence! But slaying dragons? Rescuing
slaves? Now that would break up the monotony.

He glanced again at the men. Both had turned their
backs to him. Were they reading the newsletter? If they
had a copy, might Adrian have one?

Jason let a smile grow on his face. Even if the stories
were nothing more than fairy tales, just reading them
would take him on an adventure, something that would
make his sword training feel worthwhile. So far his life
had been nothing but lessons, training, tournaments, and,
of course, his tasks in the commune. Since the governor
allowed one guardian warrior in each commune, being
chosen to train for that duty was supposed to be a great
honor, but what had all the hours prepared him for? To

chase away an occasional wolf … or something more exciting?

Jason picked up his pace and hurried toward home. The answers couldn't come soon enough.

Koren blinked open her eyes. As she lay on her thin mat, her tired muscles complained about the previous day's labors, hauling felled trees so the men could build new rafts for the stone movers. Such labor was usually reserved for the young men, but they had been called to the number two mining pit to help the older men open an especially productive vein, so the stronger girls had been summoned for raft duty.

In the glow of a single candle burning in one corner of their cramped room, she looked at Natalla and Petra, her fellow orphans, still sleeping on their mats between her and Madam Orley. They, too, were exhausted. Madam, of course, was too old to help with the trees, but she had completed the girls' labors while they were gone. At her age, that was quite a task.

Clenching a fist, Koren sat up. What those slave-driving monsters wouldn't do to get their precious pheterone! Even whipping young girls to get the last measure of strength from their worn-out bodies!

She cradled her chin in her hands and sighed. None of that mattered. Slave drivers or not, they were in charge, and she and the other humans had no choice but to obey them. Dawn would arrive in less than an hour, and chores wouldn't wait. Arxad was more patient than her previous masters, but his expectation that slaves should obey promptly was the same. He would want his breakfast on time.

Koren crawled over to Natalla's mat and shook her. "Wake up. It's time to get to work. Arxad will want fresh meat this morning."

"Mmmm?" Natalla rolled to her stomach and hid her face. "Tell him to go out and kill a squirrel."

"Madam purchased two stags from the merchant last night." She shook Natalla again. "We have to butcher them before reading time."

Natalla's pillow muffled her voice. "Read now. Butcher later. I'm listening."

Rolling her eyes, Koren reached under her own pillow, withdrew a small book, and laid it open in her palms. She flipped to page forty-one and, keeping her voice low, read her two paragraphs out loud, glancing at Natalla every few seconds to make sure she was listening. When Koren reached the end, she repeated the final sentence, "You will recognize love when you see someone sacrificing himself for the sake of a pauper."

Koren shook Natalla yet again. "Were you listening?"

Natalla sat up, grinning. "You will recognize love when you see someone sacrificing himself for the sake of a pauper."

"You clown." Koren shoved Natalla's foot with her own. "But do you know what it means?"

"I think so." Natalla's brow bent. "Are we paupers?"

"Of course not." Koren picked up a hairbrush from a nearby desk and pointed it at Natalla. "Except for the promoted slaves, we have one of the best Assignments possible."

"Then who is a pauper?"

As she brushed her hair, now down to the middle of her back, the way Arxad liked it, Koren let her mind wander from home to home, thinking about all the possible Assignments on Starlight. Finally, her thoughts drifted outside to the walled-in fields of dry grass and pebbly soil where the unfortunate children toiled while waiting for the Traders or the Separators to decide their fate. With a sigh, she said, "The cattle children are paupers."

"So we're supposed to sacrifice for them?"

Koren tapped on the page with her brush. "That's what it says."

"But how? How can a village slave help someone in the camp?"

Koren closed the book and caressed the old leather cover. "I'm not sure, but someday I'm going to find a way to help them. Someone has to."

"You'll get in trouble."

Koren grinned. "Only if I'm caught."

"I think I have it memorized," Natalla said, reaching for the book. "Stephan is next. He'll memorize his part quickly. You can count on that."

Koren laid the book in Natalla's hands with a mingled sense of relief and loss. The book of the Code was a precious thing, and while in her possession it was her responsibility. If her master found it, every human on Starlight would lament its destruction. And keeping it out of Arxad's sight for much longer wouldn't be easy.

As her fingers slid away from the treasured book, Koren made a face. "Tell your brother that if the bees are hostile, I might need some help today."

"Don't get stung!" Natalla swatted at imaginary bees flying around her head.

"I won't." Koren stood and hoisted Natalla to her feet. "Come on. I have an idea."

"An idea? What?"

"The beehives are near the cattle camp. Maybe I can sneak a meal inside, at least a hunk of bread."

"But there are dozens of children," Natalla said, "and you might get trapped in there."

"I know, but if we're going to sacrifice for the paupers, we need to start somewhere, and helping them one at a time might be the only way."

two

*J*ason stared at the message flashing on the side of the silvery tube. *Deposit genetic material for access.*

Now this was different. Why would Adrian have a Courier's message cylinder concealed under their bedroom floor? Marcelle wouldn't be communicating with him, not after Adrian's latest refusal to battle her in a tournament. And she certainly wouldn't encrypt it with a genetic identification filter. She wasn't one to worry about who heard what she had to say.

Kneeling as he held the tube, Jason looked at the hole in the floor he'd made while searching for the newsletter. Adrian often kept a copy hidden under the wooden panels, but a Courier's tube was used only for official communications from Governor Prescott or his staff. Surely Prescott would have nothing to do with the covert operations of the Gateway.

Jason rose and looked out the door. The hall was empty. Now, with harvesting and school hours finished for the day, Adrian would return from the castle soon. He wouldn't mind that his brother had been snooping around for the latest newsletter. After all, Adrian had long wanted Jason to accept the teachings of the Gateway and join their ranks, but maybe this tube was meant to be secret. Yet why would that be? Since Adrian was the governor's ceremonial bodyguard, he wouldn't have to hide official communications at home. And who could have sent it?

Shaking his head, Jason laid the tube back in the hole. There was no doubt about it; Adrian's secretive ways had shifted from abnormal to bizarre.

Jason scanned the room, letting his gaze drift from the arched entry to the two thin sleeping pads on the wooden floor. Without pillows or blankets, the beds, if anyone would call them that, had only wadded blue sheets on top, not much protection from the cooler nights that season three had recently ushered in.

As if on cue, a breeze blew in from an open window, brisk, damp, and smelling of wood smoke. Jason stepped over the beds and stuck his head through the window. Outside, a thin mist veiled the governor's castle and the forested hill it sat atop. Somehow the white curtain made the castle seem distant, as if it would take more than the usual hour to make the journey on the forest path and up the grassy slope.

At the foot of the hill, the fog completely shrouded Jason's two-story school. It had been clear earlier in the day. Perhaps the quick change portended a late-night storm. The smoke in the air proved that many were preparing for a cold, wet night.

A loud *thwack* caught his attention. To the right, his father swung an axe and split a short log down the middle, raising another sweet, percussive note. It was a welcome sound, an annual passage of sorts. Harvest labors would soon end, and a season of shorter days, book reading, and more intense battle training would begin.

As Jason watched, his father carried a double armload of wood toward the shed, limping heavily, as always. Why hadn't he asked for help? With his eyes fixed straight ahead and his brow low, he seemed worried about something. Maybe he wanted to be alone.

Extending his arms, Jason pulled the shutters to a partially closed position, leaving enough of a gap to provide light for the room. The wall to his right caught his attention, as it often did. Adrian's mural of the planetary system decorated the once-white plaster. He had drawn the configuration from data gathered at the governor's observatory, where a triad of sky scopes watched the dark heavens each night. Because of Adrian's fascination with the legends surrounding the location of the mythical dragon world, knowing how the planets took their steps in the cosmic dance had become part of his obsession.

In the center, Solarus hovered with orange flares streaming from its more reddish surface. Eighteen planets, some large and some small, orbited the central point, each one scattered from one side of the wall to the other and frozen in place at various distances from the red star.

Jason touched the fourth large planet from Solarus, Major Four ... home. Adrian had added stunning detail, including a relief map of Mesolantrum on the face that showed the Elbon River and the oceans that bordered their country on three sides.

Moving his finger across the wall and past Solarus, Jason mumbled each planet's name out loud until he reached a dark sphere directly opposite Major Four. He stopped and planted his finger on its center.

"Dracon," he said out loud as he leaned closer. Adrian had drawn no details on its surface, only a vague sketch of a dragon. It figured. No sky scope had ever located Dracon, so a sketch of a mythical beast seemed appropriate.

As he shuffled back to the hole in the floor, he spotted a hair floating in the still-swirling air. He grabbed it and let it dangle in front of his eyes. Long and light brown, this was obviously Adrian's. *Perfect.*

He reached down and picked up the tube. About a foot long and as thick as his wrist, it was shorter and thinner than the old model, but the screen on the side was the same size as always, a square the length of his thumb.

He slid open the small metal door next to the screen, the hatch for the genetic material. The moment he dropped the hair in, the screen would display acceptance, allowing him to look through the end of the tube to view the video message.

As he suspended the hair over the hatch, he looked at a drawing propped on the desk, a portrait of himself and Adrian crossing swords. Guilt weighed down his heart. Strange or not, Adrian had done so much for him—teaching him everything about being a man, from battle training to treating a woman with honor and respect. When Father had tried to teach the same lessons, they had bounced off Jason's mind, but Adrian's words seemed so much easier to grasp.

He looked down at the spot where the tube had lain. A scrap of parchment lay there, a piece of the Code. With the last known copies of the great book burned by

Prescott's men, only a few remnants survived, and this quarter of a page would stay hidden until a better man took the governor's place.

Although too small to read from this distance, the words on that ancient parchment reached into his mind and spoke with Adrian's voice. *If you wish others to treat you and your belongings with respect, then let respect for them flow in your thoughts, your speech, and your deeds.*

Jason dropped the hair on the floor and set the tube back in the hole. He couldn't do it. No matter how bizarre Adrian's recent behavior had become, there was no excuse to pry into his business.

Rapid footsteps approached. Snatching in a breath, Jason used his foot to slide the floor panel back into place. Adrian marched into the room, his wake drawing in the warmer air from the fireplace down the hall. Looking at Jason, he cocked his head. "Are you searching for something?"

With steely eyes, a tanned, angular face, and a three-inch height advantage, Adrian posed in his familiar interrogative stance, making it impossible, as usual, to win a stare-down contest.

Jason averted his gaze and slid his foot across the floor panel. "Yeah, I thought you might have picked up the latest communiqué." He refocused on his brother. Now he could maintain a stare. That *was* the reason he had come in, but the Courier's tube had made him forget to pull the newsletter from the cache.

"I have it." Adrian dropped to one knee, pried up the flooring plank, and withdrew a single page of parchment from the hole. "No news," he said as he handed it to Jason. "Just the usual rumors with a different twist."

"No rumblings of rebellion?" Jason asked.

Adrian shook his head. "Until we find the portal, not many people are willing to risk their lives for a hopeful dream."

Turning away from Adrian, Jason glanced at the bold header line — *The Underground Gateway* — before reading the small print. For months this rumor rag had been another of Adrian's obsessions, and since the stories occupied so much of his big brother's time, Jason wanted to keep up to date.

He read through the newsletter, the usual collection of tales about long-lost ancestors being taken captive by dragons to another world. The lead story quoted Uriel Blackstone's prophecy describing the elusive portal and how finding it would bring about freedom from slavery for the Lost Ones as well as liberation from oppression for those who rescued them.

With the governor's dictatorial rule becoming more tyrannical, the latter part of the prophecy always sparked Jason's imagination. What a thrill it would be to use his sword to shatter the bonds! And for many of the Gateway believers, the potential for overthrow provided more of an impetus than did the thought of rescuing slaves. And why not? No one knew the poor wretches in the other world, but everyone certainly knew of the injustices here in their own world.

After finishing the article, Jason gave the hole in the floor a sideways nod. "Why do you have a Courier tube?"

Adrian picked it up and slid the panel back in place. "A message from someone who has a new clue, a much more promising one than usual."

"To the portal? Are you going to try to find it?"

"I'm packing now." Adrian pulled a duffel bag from an alcove in the wall. "I'm heading into the wilderness at sunset. Two decoys will draw the guards away from me, so I should have a clear path."

"Can I—?" Jason clamped his mouth shut. He couldn't ask to go with him right away. It would be too quick, too eager. "I mean, can you just quit your job? What will Governor Prescott say? What will Father say?"

"I already asked for leave to"—he gave Jason a wink—"further my training. And the governor approved the replacement. Father approved as well."

"Really? Who is the replacement? Marcelle?"

Laughing, Adrian mussed Jason's hair. "No, not Marcelle. She hates ceremonial positions. Besides, when she finds out she wasn't chosen for the mission, she'll be as hot as a firebrand. If the governor even mentioned my name, she might kill him herself."

Jason murmured under his breath, "She's not as good as you anyway."

Adrian gave him a friendly punch on the arm. "Always the encourager, aren't you?"

"Well, it's true. Everyone knows it."

"Her crown says otherwise." Adrian's face tightened, but it quickly relaxed again. "She's a superlative fighter, and you know it."

Jason caught his brother's grimace. He was more distressed by his own decisions than he was letting on. Yes, Marcelle was good. But she wasn't the best. Jason let his shoulders sag. If his brother weren't so chivalrous, he would have had a chance to prove his superiority. When he entered the tourney ring for the final-round battle with Marcelle, he didn't even bother to approach the referee and take his sword, and he didn't utter his famous line: "In honor of the lady's expertise, I surrender."

This time, she said it for him before he could open his mouth, and her tone didn't exactly mirror Adrian's usual geniality. Although her sarcasm was enough to be noticed by everyone in the crowd, only a few likely caught the gleam in her eye. Her gaze followed Adrian as he left the ring, and her expression reflected a deep, albeit frustrated, respect. Even with the intense rivalry, neither Jason nor Adrian could deny her gifts or her decency.

Jason eyed Adrian's sword and belt. With a polished, ornate scabbard, it looked like a costume sword, but he knew better. Although it had yet to see a battle or even a sparring contest, it was a superior blade, forged by Qualyn himself. "So who's the substitute bodyguard?"

Adrian unbuckled the belt and extended it to Jason, sword and all. "You are."

Stepping back, Jason waved a hand. "Oh, no you don't! You're not saddling me with that job."

"Why not? You're perfect for it. You have the strength and skills, and you're young enough for Prescott to boss around."

"That's my point. You know what Prescott will do. He'll force me to be friends with Randall."

"It's about time you faced up to it. Dealing with difficult people is part of becoming a man." Adrian pulled Jason back and wrapped the belt around his waist. With a quick tug, he fastened it in place. "There," he said as he straightened the sword at Jason's hip. "You look great."

Jason glared at the belt. "What do looks have to do with it?"

"Everything." Adrian grasped Jason's shoulders and pushed them back. "Prescott craves attention. That's one of the reasons he wants a muscular young man at his side. Just keep a confident posture and you'll be perfect. It's not like the old days. Being a bodyguard now is more show than substance. The only guarding I ever did was to chase away a stray dog that didn't like Prescott's odor."

Jason pinched his nose. "The dog was right. Prescott eats too much garlic. When he gave a speech at school, I had to sit on the front row. I thought I would need a breathing mask."

Adrian laughed. "You'll get used to it."

"What about school? I can't just quit."

"You'll be tutored with Randall."

"Tutored with him!" Jason frowned. "This gets worse and worse."

"It's not all bad news," Adrian said. "You'll get to train with a photo gun. You can't bring it home, of course, but I know you've been aching to use one."

Jason let out a quiet humph. Only castle guards and the highest elites were allowed to own the powerful guns. Adrian and Father dismissed them as new, untested gadgets—inaccurate and unreliable in battle. A sword, spear, or bolt from a crossbow could pierce the wielder of a photo gun before he could charge up his weapon, and it was often slow to recharge after firing, making the warrior vulnerable. Still, it would be fun to give one a try, and then Randall wouldn't be able to boast any longer about knowing how to use one.

Jason grinned. "How often did you see Randall while you were on duty?"

"Pretty often, but after what he did at the tournament, he'll probably make himself scarce for a while."

Jason fingered his new sword's hilt. "So what am I supposed to do? Just show up at the castle?"

"At sunset. Report to Drexel at the main gate. Just ignore his uppity attitude. He won't bite." Adrian pulled a sword belt from the storage alcove and began strapping it on. "The invocation for the new Counselor is tonight, and you will be at Prescott's side from start to finish."

Jason noted Adrian's hands as he fastened the belt and sword into place. For some reason the more rugged leather in the belt and the nicks on the sword's hilt made the sinews in Adrian's hands look stronger, tighter, as if he had cast aside the gaudy pretense of costume weaponry and was now putting on the real Adrian Masters.

"Just remember," Adrian continued, "although we disagree with most of his policies, when it comes to our country, Prescott is a patriot, so he is due your honor and respect."

"You mean he's a pig, but an honorable and patriotic pig?"

Adrian scowled, but his tight lips trembled, stifling a laugh. "I think being a bodyguard will be good training for you. You'll find out soon enough what I mean. And don't forget—Prescott will have a hernia if you mention the Underground Gateway, even if you just joke about it. You know the law."

Jason rolled his eyes. "I know."

While Adrian packed his duffle bag with clothes, Jason thought about the latest anti-Gateway proclamation.

Prescott's herald read the scroll in the village square. From thenceforth, no stories recounting the old dragon myths had been allowed, nor any mention of the Underground Gateway. Violators were subject to punishment, the first offense bringing three days of public exposure in the pillory. A second offense brought three months in the dungeon.

The problem in Prescott's strategy, however, was simple. The more he tried to suppress the stories, the more it made people believe they were real. Why would anyone in the government be so adamantly opposed to an obvious myth unless it were true? What were they hiding?

Since the law took effect, membership in the Underground Gateway had tripled to almost fifty, in spite of the strict secrecy oaths and the threat of facing Adrian—or worse, Marcelle—if anyone chose to violate the covenant. But the oaths seemed to be working. It appeared that Prescott had no idea their ranks had grown.

Adrian picked up the Courier tube and stuffed it into his duffle bag. "I can walk with you as far as Miller's Spring."

"No supper?" Jason asked.

"I have to travel light and fast." Adrian hoisted his bag over his shoulder. "When I reach the boundary, our people will provide what I need." Giving Jason a smile and a wink, he added, "And you'll have plenty to eat at the invocation."

Jason laid a hand over his stomach. "I can live with that."

"Let's say good-bye to Mother."

Jason followed Adrian out the doorway and into the community room. His mother sat on a wicker bench, a pillow beneath her for cushioning. She was talking to Meredith.

Dressed in breeches and bonnets, they were both dirty from harvesting the crop of corn, late beans, and early potatoes. With evening approaching, they would soon wash in the bath house before going to the kitchen to prepare their commune's meal while the men continued their labors. Since many had taken an hour or two off to watch the tournament, they had to hurry through their chores in order to finish before nightfall. As a younger male, Jason was expected to help with the meal preparation, but his assignment as Prescott's bodyguard would allow him to be excused.

Jason glanced at the new belt around his waist. Maybe this position wasn't a bad idea after all.

When Adrian approached his mother, he lowered himself to one knee and bowed his head. Surprised at his brother's formal pose, Jason nevertheless copied it, still clutching the newsletter in one hand.

Her graying hair falling from her bonnet, his mother stood and gestured for Adrian and Jason to rise. With glistening gray eyes peering out from the midst of dark, loamy smudges, she forced a smile. "Adrian, will you be joining the hunting party tonight?"

Adrian glanced at Meredith, who had also risen. "Yes, Mother. The prey is too great a beast for only two, so they have requested that I accompany them."

Blinking nervously, Meredith wiped her hands on a once-white apron. "Is it a mountain bear you seek?"

Jason looked at Meredith's hopeful eyes. Hers, too, glistened. Maybe she and Mother had been talking about

Elyssa, captured and dragged away by a mountain bear well before harvest began. These bears had been known to keep humans captive for months before killing and eating them. Able to speak word-like grunts, they found the company of captive humans entertaining, at least for a while. The myths said dragons did the same, but the dragon stories were likely just embellishments of the mountain bears' ways.

Adrian gave Meredith a kindly nod. "As always, Mistress Cantor, we will search for any sign of Elyssa. With her cleverness, I am sure she has devised a way to signal her whereabouts."

Removing her bonnet and letting her gray hair spill down to her shoulders, Meredith looked away, hiding her tears. "And no one is better able to find her than you, Adrian."

Jason tried to gauge Adrian's expression. Why would he say that to Meredith? Was he really planning to look for Elyssa while he was in the wilderness? He shouldn't raise false hopes. A teenager couldn't survive that long in a bear cave. Ten days, maybe, but not fifty. As Adrian said, Elyssa was clever—so clever one of the clerics had accused her of being a Diviner, but she had avoided the consequences. Her mother had convinced the governor that Elyssa's perception skills were merely the result of an innate intelligence, which was probably true. Still, her cleverness couldn't guarantee survival in the rigors of the wild. She wasn't a warrior maiden, certainly not like Marcelle. Not even close.

Now weeping, Meredith strode toward the kitchen area. "I had better start a fire and clean up."

When she was out of earshot, Jason shifted his gaze back to Adrian. "What was that all about?"

Adrian looked at his mother. "Shall I tell him or let Father do it?"

"You tell him. Your father doesn't wish to see you until you return. You know what he says about good-byes."

"Yes," Adrian said, nodding. "I know. And I will tell him very soon."

Jason looked at their somber expressions. Neither wanted to repeat their father's lamenting words: *The last time I said good-bye to a son, he never returned.* No. Another reminder of Frederick would reopen wounds still too raw to expose. After all, it had been only one harvest since Frederick went on his journey, less than two years. Their hopes for his return had been dashed only thirty days ago when Adrian found Frederick's distinctive cap near the boundary on the north side. It was a three-corner style with a long purple feather through the band, dirty and torn. He had gone on the same journey Adrian would now attempt.

Jason's mother touched his sword. "Adrian told me of your new position. Your father and I are very proud of you. I wish we could go to the invocation and see you at the governor's side."

Offering a sad nod, Jason looked at the floor. Communal villagers would never be invited to an invocation. Being poor, they would forever be servants, their backs fit for bearing loads, their muscles fit for plowing furrows in unbroken ground, and their warrior skills fit for defending the softer bodies of the elite and spilling blood in their stead.

She kissed Adrian on the cheek. "Do not let doubts from the home front rise in your heart. You know that your father and I believe in your quest, though he cannot speak the words to bless your journey. May the Creator be with you."

"And with you, Mother." Adrian hugged her. "I will find the Lost Ones. I swear it."

When they broke the embrace, they stared at each other for a moment, neither one saying a word. Unspoken emotions seemed to flow from heart to heart like a flood.

Jason pondered his brother's words. *The Lost Ones.* For some reason the old fables sounded so real now. Adrian believed them. His mother believed them. His father, though he no longer mentioned them, believed them as well. If three of the wisest people in all of Mesolantrum took the stories seriously, why would everyone in school think they were nonsense?

Tears welling, Adrian patted Jason on the back again. "Let's go. You have to get there by sundown, or Prescott will make you work without pay."

Their mother waved. "I will see you tonight, Jason. Take care."

Adrian opened the heavy oak door and strode out. When they were both outside, he leaned a shoulder against the door and pressed it until the latch clicked. Such a heavy barrier was necessary to keep out the cold during the post-harvest season and to bar the night predators during the warmer days, though no sign of mountain bears had been seen since Elyssa's disappearance that fateful morning at the end of second season.

Deep scratches marred the ground the morning Meredith discovered Elyssa was missing, taken from her room in the middle of the night. The scattered and torn clothing and broken jars had told the rest of the story. Elyssa had put up as much of a fight as she could. Everyone guessed that the bear had caught her by the throat. Otherwise, someone in the commune would have heard her scream.

At least that was the report the constable wrote. To this day, Adrian doubted the details. He claimed he would have smelled the beast or at least heard a jar breaking. Being a light sleeper and trained in survival, he always woke up at the slightest provocation. The tracks looked real, but it didn't make sense that a bear could steal away a young woman without notice.

Adrian hiked up his duffle bag and marched toward the forest path. As Jason followed, Adrian spoke quickly. "I told Mistress Cantor that we would search for any sign of Elyssa, but when I said *we*, I meant you. As I have ranted many times, I don't think a bear took her. Just today I caught Governor Prescott whispering her name to Drexel as I walked into the court. They seemed annoyed at my sudden appearance, but since I am forbidden to speak without being asked for my opinion, and since my journey cannot be delayed, I was unable to inquire further. So I need you to—"

"Adrian!"

From the forest's edge, their father hurried toward them. Carrying his axe and hobbling as quickly as the old battle wound in his leg would allow, he seemed agitated, but not angrily so.

"Come," Adrian said, pulling Jason into a quick jog. After a few seconds, they met their father near the woodshed, just a spear's throw from the forest.

Breathing heavily, their father looked at Adrian. His wrinkled brow shadowed his dusky eyes, and his gray hair swept from left to right, tossed by a cool breeze. From his stocky legs to his barrel chest to his broad shoulders, his body quivered with emotion. "I wanted to tell you something." He paused, and, though his habitual grip on his passions seemed to choke the words in his throat, his wide eyes said it all. Love poured forth.

Adrian grasped his father's forearm tightly. "You have nothing to fear. I will honor you in all I do, your wisdom, your vision, and your legacy. We are not saying good-bye, for I take your heart and your passion with me. I will find the Lost Ones and restore them to our world."

With powerful arms, their father embraced both brothers, then, without another word, he turned and strode back toward the forest, his head low and his shoulders shaking.

Adrian pulled Jason again. "Come. We must not watch his grief." They strode along the path, maintaining silence until they reached the edge of the forest. When the arching boughs of the manna trees created a blanket of shadows over their heads, Adrian spoke up. "I want you to search for any record of what Prescott knows about Elyssa. It won't take you long to learn your way around the castle. As bodyguard, you'll have free access to any wing. As long as Prescott is at leisure in his office or entertainment room, he won't need you, and he has been spending a lot of time at leisure in recent days."

"Do you have any more clues?" Jason asked. "The castle is huge. I can't just snoop through every hall and chamber."

Adrian reached into his bag and withdrew the Courier's tube. "Watch the message," he said, handing it to Jason. "There is a cryptic puzzle in the words. When you hear it, you'll recognize it. I need you to solve the puzzle."

Jason took the tube and glanced between it and the newsletter. A puzzle to solve? The mysteries were mounting.

"And don't let Prescott see the Gateway parchment," Adrian continued. "I don't want to have to spring you from the dungeon when I return."

Tucking the tube under his arm, Jason folded the newsletter and stuffed it into his hip pocket. "Prescott won't see it. I'll eat it first."

Adrian plucked a hair from his head and pushed it into Jason's palm. "You'll need that for the genetic key. Be sure to keep watching the message, even after you think it's complete. There will be a long pause. You'll know it's finally finished when he says, 'The rest will be up to you.' Then erase it immediately."

"The rest will be up to you." Jason closed his hand around the hair. "Got it."

When they reached the glade that marked the upwelling of Miller's Spring, Adrian stopped in the spongy grass that bordered the spring's flowing creek. He laid a hand on Jason's shoulder. "My brother, I know you have doubted the stories Frederick and I have taught you all these years, and I have offered you no solid proof. But you have honored your family by working with us as if you were a true believer. Soon, however, you will reach a crossroads that will force you to decide to either believe in or betray our cause. You will find that you can no longer stand outside the tourney ring."

Jason let the words repeat in his mind. *You can no longer stand outside the tourney ring.* Isn't that what Adrian had done? When it was time to fight for the honor of his family and every commoner in the forestlands, hadn't he decided to stand outside the ring and allow a noblewoman to claim the crown? The word *hypocrite* tried to push through Jason's tightening throat, but he swallowed it down. It wasn't true, no matter what others claimed. Not only that, treating his older brother with such disrespect would violate the Code.

"You're right." Jason grasped Adrian's wrist in a warrior's clasp. "Even though the legends sound like storybook fables, I will keep my mind open. But as long as I live, I will never betray you or our family, no matter what happens."

Adrian pulled Jason close and kissed his forehead. He whispered, "Good. Because if you betray us, I'll walk all the way back from Dracon and introduce you to a mama mountain bear who has lost her cubs."

With that, Adrian marched away from the path, following the stream into the woods. Shadows quickly swallowed him, and he disappeared.

As he stared at the trees, Jason shoved the hair into his tunic's small inner pocket. This was no time to let emotions choke his resolve. He had a job to do: two jobs, one for Prescott and one for Adrian. He had to get going.

The mysterious tube still in his grasp, he splashed across the shallow water. When he reached the other side, he broke into a run, careful to keep his new sword in place. He could listen to the message later. For now, he had to make sure he arrived at the castle before sundown.

three

*J*ason gazed at his reflection in the parlor's mirror. The new uniform, a duplicate of Adrian's gray trousers and forest green shirt, looked and felt good. His mother would approve. She always said that this shade of green went well with his brown hair and eyes. And with the addition of a long black cloak, the outfit was complete.

An elderly servant, a grandfatherly type with a hefty paunch, bowed as low as his belly would allow. "Is there anything else I may do for you, Master Jason?"

Jason smiled and shook his head. Whenever adults called him by that title, he had the urge to tell them they had it backwards—Jason Masters, not Master Jason. "Thank you, Mortimer. But please, just call me Jason."

"As you wish." He bowed again. "His Lordship is tarrying in the parlor with a special guest, so he will not need you until he is ready for the ceremony. Kindly wait here for a summons."

"I will." As soon as Mortimer exited the room, Jason grabbed his wadded clothes from a bureau and withdrew the Courier tube. After finding the hair in the pocket, he inserted it into the hatch. Instantly, new letters appeared on the screen. *Genetics verified.*

He raised the tube to his eye and looked inside. A video played, accompanied by audio, loud enough for him to hear but likely too quiet for anyone else to pick up, unless the eavesdropper looked over his shoulder.

A tall, lean, middle-aged man with salt-and-pepper hair and goatee stood in a forest, clutching Frederick's tricornered hat. As the man held it up he said, "Adrian, you gave me this hat to analyze, and I have very little to tell you beyond what you already know. Bear hunting is perilous, and I fear that your brother has fallen victim to an especially dangerous variety. As you suspected, the blood on the band was not his. The genetic markers indicate a variety from a distant region, one that neither you nor I have ever ventured into. Yet your brother mentioned many times that he wished to go there to hunt this species.

"Of course, all mountain bears are intelligent, but these appear to be especially crafty. I fear that one has visited our region and placed the hat here in order to lure us to his lands. He likely wants us to come there in order to provide more captives for him and his clan. And, as you long suspected, there is a bear in our midst, one that hides his own guilt by concocting stories about other bears stealing innocent girls. If you find the bear among us, you will find his captive. The key to his secrets never leaves him, for even as he sleeps it rests upon his heart."

The man placed the hat against his chest. "Because I honor your brother so highly, I urge you to hunt the bears and rid the world of the danger."

The screen went blank. Jason kept his eye in place, waiting for the next part. Whoever this guy was, he veiled his words skillfully, and anyone who found this tube and managed to break the genetic key would think the message had ended. The idea was simple, but brilliant.

After nearly a minute, another man appeared on the screen, but with his back turned, Jason couldn't identify him. He carried no weapons but wore a tricornered hat on his head. Could he be Frederick?

The man was looking at a tall stone fence covered with thorny vines, near which a little boy stood, picking up stones and putting them into a big pail. Dirty, rail-thin, and bare-chested, he hoisted the pail into his wiry arms and shuffled away with it, his feet bloody.

As soon as the boy walked out of view, the man, gaunt and unshaven, turned toward the screen.

Frederick!

Jason's heart raced, thumping so hard he could barely hold the tube in place. He glanced at the dressing room entrance. No one was around. All was silent. Focusing again on the video, he tried to calm his heart. *Settle down. Just listen and learn.*

His eyes wide and his tense face dampened with sweat, Frederick spoke with an agitated voice. "Adrian, if every prayer of mine is answered, you will get this message. Hear me, my brother." He licked his lips and swallowed. "It is all true. Every story is true. I have seen the dragons. I have met the Lost Ones. I do not have time to explain everything, so I simply beg you to come. Attempt the passage in the way I explained before I left home, and we will work together to rescue the lambs from the wolves. I cannot leave, for I fear that I will not be able to return to this world. I must stay and help them for as long as I can."

Frederick swallowed again. Passion throttled his voice. "I hope to be here to greet you when you make the passage, but if the dragons learn of my presence, you will likely not see me again. For now, I can only bring comfort to the Lost Ones. The rest will be up to you."

The screen went blank again.

His hands shaking, Jason jerked toward the bureau and dropped the Courier tube back on the wad of clothes. His heart continued pounding. Sweat dampened his armpits. Although no dragons appeared in the video, Frederick would never lie about something like that. The legends had to be true.

He pulled the folded newsletter from the pile of clothes and read the words greedily. Now they seemed alive. They were no longer fairy tales; they were eyewitness accounts blazing across his mind, as true as his mother's most solemn promises.

More than one hundred years ago, a dragon by the name of Magnar came from a world they called Starlight and captured several families of humans. No one knew the makeup of the victims, but based on missing persons reports, most guessed that they included ten to twelve adults along with a few children. Magnar took his victims to Starlight through a strange underground gateway, and they disappeared in a flash of light. About a year afterwards, one of the younger men, Uriel Blackstone, escaped.

He told his story to the authorities, but they thought his tale was a fanciful version of an abduction by a group of mountain bears. They dismissed it as the fruit of a vivid imagination. Later, when Uriel grew bolder and began publicizing his story, the authorities prosecuted him and locked him up, first in the dungeon, then in the insane asylum. Although no member of the Gateway had been able to locate Uriel's grave, by all accounts, he died at the age of seventy-seven, alone and in chains.

That imprisonment, however, did nothing to stop the rise of believers in Uriel's claims. In fact, the persecution helped to raise doubts about the government's version of the story, especially among the families of the missing. While in prison, Uriel wrote his now-famous prophecy, which emboldened the faithful and drew into their fold those who hoped for an end to their oppression, and the Underground Gateway, a secret society of people dedicated to finding the truth, was born.

"Excuse me. Jason Masters?"

Jason swung his head toward the door. A young man stood there, his body ramrod straight, his hands behind him, and his uniform pressed. The loose sleeves and pant legs in the all-black uniform identified him as a Courier.

"Yes?" Jason crumpled the newsletter in his fist and stuffed it into his pocket. "I'm Jason."

"I have come to escort you to the governor's side." His voice was formal and monotone. "Please follow me." He began to swivel but stopped abruptly, his gaze locking on Jason's wadded clothes. His tone became inquisitive. "You have a Courier's tube?"

Jason snatched it from the bureau along with his discarded shirt. "Yes," he said as he opened the genetic key hatch, hiding his movements with his shirt. "It was addressed to my brother. He asked me to bring it with me."

The Courier extended a rigid arm. "You are not allowed to have a tube that has not been sent to you or by you. Section three of the communications protocol expressly forbids it. Your brother should know that."

"Really?" Jason fumbled for the erasing switch on the side. "I guess that's why he asked me to erase it."

"I will erase it." The Courier marched toward him. "Give it to me immediately."

Jason pushed the button. He would have to hold it down for five seconds, and the genetic key would have to stay inside during the process. "Too late." He turned, dodging the Courier's grasping hand. "Do you ever watch the messages before you deliver them?"

The Courier stepped back. "Of course not. That would be a violation of section two of the protocol."

"That's what I guessed." The tube clicked, signaling the end of the erasing procedure. Jason slid out the hair and enclosed it in his fist. "Here you go." He extended the tube to the Courier. "I'm sure the governor is pleased with your rigidity."

The Courier snatched it out of Jason's hand. "Now," he said coolly, "if you will please follow me. Mortimer will see to your *peasant* clothing."

As he followed, Jason glanced at his pile of clothes. The Courier wasn't happy with Jason's appointment as bodyguard; maybe others in the elite class wouldn't be pleased with this new peasant in their midst either.

They emerged into the palace's main entry vestibule, a chamber enclosed by marble-coated walls and high ceilings.

Above, sunlight vents near the apex allowed the fading orange rays to filter in and illuminate their surroundings. Soon the attendants would light the lanterns that lined the walls and put flame to wick in the candelabra that hung from the ceiling. Although most of the guests had already arrived and entered the cathedral, a few stragglers might venture in. Without energy channels in the walls in this section of the palace, anyone walking through after sunset would need the more primitive lighting fixtures.

The Courier opened a door at the rear corner of the chamber and bade Jason to follow. While they hurried through a narrow corridor with wood-planked floors and plaster walls, Frederick's image—his anguish, his fear—burned in Jason's mind. Why hadn't Adrian told him? Why did he allow the secret to be revealed after he marched away into the woods?

The answer broke through like a gushing flood. Because Adrian wanted to go alone. If he had revealed the truth, Jason would have insisted on joining him. This meant that Adrian hadn't told everything to Father or Mother. To them, this was likely just a foray into the wilderness, yet another fruitless journey in search of the elusive gateway to the world of dragons. Yet Father seemed to suspect something more. Otherwise he wouldn't have reacted so strongly.

And there was something more. This time Adrian had a priceless clue. Someone had intentionally left the hat and a video message. Surely the messenger, whoever it was, would have left other clues, and Adrian would never give up the hunt. He would take greater risks than ever before. He would not come back without Frederick.

As they passed through a second rich chamber, the main living room in the governor's private quarters, Adrian's words filtered back into Jason's mind. *There is a cryptic puzzle in the words. When you hear it, you'll recognize it. I need you to solve the puzzle.*

Jason touched the hilt of his sword. Only he could provide the help Adrian needed. It was time to perform, not to worry. He had to find the bear and the key that rested on his heart.

The Courier stopped at a square entryway and nodded toward the room beyond. "You are to enter now." His tone was still cold and condescending. "We Couriers are not *privileged* enough to step within the governor's private bedroom."

Jason kept his face lax. Without giving the Courier another glance, he strode through the open door and into a chamber every bit as large as the living room. The polished marble floors reflected the light of four energy channels, one embedded in each of the surrounding walls. The four-poster bed, adorned in purple velvet, was big enough for a family of six.

Governor Prescott stood near the far wall. Short, chubby, and dressed in silky purple breeches and a black satin vest over a frilly white shirt, he looked like a beaten and bruised penguin. "Come here, Masters," he said, waving. "I am late, and we have much protocol to discuss."

Holding his sword in place at his hip, Jason marched ahead as quickly as decorum would allow, mimicking the stride and posture he'd seen Adrian adopt so many times as he kept pace with the always-hurried governor.

Prescott set a hand on Jason's shoulder and looked him over. "You're scrawnier than your brother."

Jason straightened his body, trying to appear taller. "He's eight years older."

"To be sure." Prescott pulled away and folded his hands behind his back. "You have probably divined by now that I chose you for one reason and one reason only—your brother's recommendation." As he spoke, his pale cheeks shook, and his watery blue eyes gleamed. His voice was higher and squeakier than the low tones he used during his speeches and proclamations. "There were many aspiring young warriors who longed for this position, so you should be wary for two reasons. One, if you fail me in the slightest way I will replace you without warning. Two, one of my trustworthy counselors has told me of murmurings against you. You should watch for conspiracies that might bring harm to your person or injury to your reputation. Not everyone in my court is as virtuous as I am."

Jason wanted to add, "Or as humble," but he held his tongue. Getting replaced during his first minute of duty would ruin everything.

"Come." Prescott walked toward the entryway. "While I am moving, stay three steps behind me at all times. This way you are able to guard my left and my right."

Jason kept pace. "If I am to guard you, then wouldn't it be easier if I were walking in front of you?"

With a graceful spin, Prescott stopped and faced him, a condescending smile on his lips. "Why, no. Of course not. First, you cannot know where I will choose to turn. Second, those whom I am about to meet will not be able to see my person, which is crucial with regard to the decorum of diplomacy. And third, I am not able to see behind me, so that is my more vulnerable side."

As warmth flowed into his cheeks, Jason nodded. "That makes a lot of sense. I apologize for my ignorance."

Prescott again looked him over from head to toe. "Ignorant or not, your abilities will suit my purpose."

Jason nodded again, unsure of how to reply. "Uh, I hope I can—"

"We have no more time for chatting," Prescott said as he turned and strode away. "Remember, I hired you for your presence, not for your voice. Keep silent unless you are addressed directly. You have seen your brother work with me. You will have to do the best you can."

Jason leaped ahead and followed, staying the required three steps behind. After they hurried through the narrow corridor, they emerged in the rear of the vestibule, now much darker than before. Although shadows blackened the walls and floors, Prescott never slowed.

Staring into the darkness, Jason reached for the hilt of his sword. Something was wrong. It didn't make sense that the governor would so carelessly stroll through an unlit chamber. Shouldn't someone meet them with a lantern trimmed for evening? Why hadn't the wall lanterns been lit?

As they passed by the parlor, something clicked near the wall on the opposite side. Someone was out there, hidden in the shadows. Jason quietly drew his sword. Ahead, a tall statue loomed near an intersection with a hallway.

Jason grabbed Prescott's arm and pulled him against the statue's cubic base. "Someone is hiding out there," he whispered.

Even in the dimness, Prescott's wide eyes were easy to see. "Impossible. Everyone should be at the invocation."

"That's what I was thinking." Jason eased away from
Prescott. "Please stay here. I'll check it out."

"Very well."

While Prescott ducked low behind the statue, Jason
soft-stepped toward the middle of the chamber. Darker
than ever now, the room seemed smaller, as if the walls
were closing in. Adrian had taught him how to overcome
tricks his mind might play. Focus on one sensory input at
a time—first sight, then sound, then smell, then touch,
and finally, that quiet voice inside, a warrior's instinct that
danger troubled the air around him. With that approach,
competing channels of data wouldn't be able to fool his
mind. He would be ready for anything.

Shallow breathing entered his ears. The faint odor of
human sweat drifted by. This attacker was nervous, not
a professional. Soon he would take a deeper breath. That
would be the sign of attack.

Jason stared into a void between two shadowy columns
in the wall. The intruder had to be there. Every sensory
input pointed in that direction.

Flexing his fingers around the hilt, Jason turned ninety
degrees away from the void and waited. Better to let the
attacker believe he had the advantage of surprise. When
he learned otherwise, he would crumble like the rookie
he likely was. Then, instead of killing him, Jason could
take him prisoner and learn where this conspiracy led.

A hooded figure leaped from between the columns,
swift and silent. Jason ducked, allowing the attacker's
swinging sword to sweep over his head. With a leg thrust,
Jason tripped the man and sent him tumbling. The sword
flew from his hand and slid across the marble floor.

Jason leaped up and ran to the sprawled body. He pressed his sword's tip into the attacker's hood and whisked it off. A wide-eyed, square-jawed young man gaped at him.

"Randall?"

Gasping, Randall stared at the sword. "Don't kill me. I was just—" He clamped his mouth shut and closed his eyes. "Just don't kill me!"

A cold chill ran across Jason's skin. *The governor's son. A loyalist. Too unskilled to be an assassin. A sacrificial lamb? Could there be another?*

Turn!

Jason whipped around, his blade up. Another blade clanked against his, the speed like lightning and the force like a charging bull. Grunting under the weight, he crouched. The attacker flew overtop, but after a deft flip landed on his feet and charged again.

Still crouching, Jason lunged to the side. As the attacker's sword swiped past his face, Jason thrust his own blade, but the nimble, hooded figure leaped over it just in time.

Jason jumped to his feet. The attacker spun toward him and pointed his sword, waiting silently.

Flexing his muscles, Jason stared at his opponent. He was good, very good. Shorter than average and lithe, his speed and agility were superb.

Jason stepped to the right to get a better look at his opponent. The dark attacker stepped to his own right at the same pace, making it look like the two swordsmen were orbiting a central point on the floor. Jason watched the attacker's graceful movements. This man had been inside the tournament ring many times. His range was exactly the size of a battle circle. But that could be used against him.

Jason backed against the wall. If this attacker was familiar only with school training, he wouldn't recognize this strategy. Without a passing lane behind Jason for his opponent's escape, a lunge on the opponent's part would be far more dangerous.

The hooded man stalked toward him but halted abruptly several steps away. In an oddly strained voice, he said, "Are you a coward? Come out and face me in a fair, head-to-head battle."

"You talk about fair," Jason said, pushing a tone of challenge into his voice. "You sent a scared puppy ahead of you and attacked me from behind. It seems that *you're* the coward."

"I see." The attacker stripped off his hood. Long auburn locks fell out, and an angular female face appeared.

Jason gawked at her. "Marcelle?"

She smirked, and her normal voice flowed softly and sweetly. "You should teach your brother some of that bravado."

Jason swung his head toward the statue. Prescott emerged from his hiding place, clapping his hands as he approached.

"All three of you performed with excellence!" Prescott said. "And Marcelle, you were right, as usual."

Jason glanced between them. Both the governor and Marcelle carried triumphant expressions. Behind them, Randall rose to his feet, his head low.

Prescott laid a hand on Jason's shoulder. "Merely a test, young man. Adrian recommended you, but, because you are so young and inexperienced, I wanted Marcelle to take his place at my side. Yet Marcelle assured me that you would be a fine bodyguard."

Jason looked at Marcelle. Her smirk softened to a friendly smile, and she offered an approving nod.

"I suggested the test," Prescott continued. "And you have passed brilliantly. Both Randall and Marcelle knew not to harm you, so there was no danger."

Jason held back a rising growl. *Stay calm and polite.* "Not to question your idea, Governor, but I could have hurt your son." He wanted to add that Marcelle was also vulnerable, but that might not have been true.

Prescott reached for Randall's tunic and pulled the shoulder back, revealing a tough sheet of metal. "He was well-protected, and the suit made him heavier, which explains your easy victory over him. Marcelle, of course, required no such protection.

"We needed Randall to distract you in order to test your warrior's sense and your reflexes. My son, of course, is just as qualified to be my bodyguard as you are, but since he is so dear to me, if he were captured by an enemy, he could be used to bend my will."

Still clutching his sword tightly, Jason fumed inside. Randall was good, but they had already proven who would win in a battle of swords and wits.

"Fret not," Marcelle said as she touched Jason's arm, her voice again sweet. "Your skills have been approved. You will make a fine bodyguard for His Lordship."

Jason relaxed his grip and nodded. A strained "Thank you" was all he could muster.

"Now," Marcelle said, turning to Prescott, her smile a bit tighter, "you will adhere to your part of the bargain."

"Of course. Of course." Prescott reached into his tunic's breast pocket and withdrew a set of keys on a metal ring. After pulling a long brass key away, he handed it to her. "You will find what you are looking for in the weapons cache. After you secure it, you may keep the key. I have another. Do you know where the cache is?"

"I do." Marcelle took the key and turned toward Jason, a look of sincerity bending her tawny brow as she whispered, "I meant no insult to your brother. I made this bargain to save his life."

With that, she sheathed her sword and ran into the shadows.

Jason stared after her. What could she have meant by that? Asking Prescott might bring an answer, but she obviously wanted her comment to remain a secret.

Prescott stooped and picked up Marcelle's hood. "The ceremony began long ago, but they will not be able to install Counselor Orion without me. Let us hurry now to the cathedral."

"What do you want me to do?" Randall asked.

Prescott gave him the hood. "See to it that all traces of the battle here are wiped away, and then retire to your quarters. You may get something from the bakery first."

"As you wish, Father." Randall bowed. Then, after shooting an angry glare at Jason, he shuffled toward the battle area.

Prescott strode toward the statue. "Come!" he ordered, his tone becoming agitated. "The people will begin to stir if I am not there soon."

Jason followed. He glanced back at Randall, who was now on hands and knees wiping the scuff marks with Marcelle's hood, a mournful expression on his face. This was the first time he had seen Randall like this—humble and hardworking. Although he had been born in the elite class, this posture gave him a nobler appearance somehow. He had always been a boastful sort during lessons, not mean-spirited or a bully, just overconfident and self-centered. Now he seemed ... well ... peasant-like.

As he slid his sword into its scabbard, Jason kept pace with the swift governor. New revelations swirled in his mind, especially Marcelle's words about saving Adrian. This would be a long evening. Somehow he had to find out the truth, and maybe solving the strange puzzle from the Courier's tube would provide the answers.

four

Koren strained against a pair of ropes as she hauled a cart up a rocky hill. The slope's steepness and the many rocks forced her to keep her eyes on the path, so she couldn't monitor the honeycombs in the dilapidated four-wheeler. At least this cargo was sticky enough to keep it inside the cart. Last week, the olive oil sloshed back and forth, spilling a third of the load.

When she reached the top, she swiped her sleeve across her brow. Despite the relative coolness of winter and the twilight air, the hard work was enough to make anyone sweat. Even with her hair tied up in the back, her neck and collar were soaked.

She hiked up her skirt's waistband and pulled the cart toward the grottoes. No dragon anywhere on Starlight would ever sweat, even if one did lift a claw to do anything more than point at her and complain. The scaly beasts had no pores in their armor. They were impervious, proving

the chants of the other slave girls as they played with spin-
ners before bedtime.

A dragon can't huggle.

A dragon can't snuggle.

A dragon's scales are hard and cold.

The dragons make us struggle.

Koren smiled. The words were silly, but the song made
the younger kids laugh. They didn't have much else to
laugh about, especially during the other three quarters
of the year when hot winds from the swamp brought
mosquitoes and the diseases they carried. Only the very
few kindlier dragons would put up with the frailties of
the younger humans, giving them cooler tasks like fetch-
ing water from the forest stream. The grouchier dragons
would send ill humans to the Separators. There they
would be transferred to an Assignment in another grotto
or to a human herd in the Traders' cattle camp, where
they would have to fend for themselves and fight for food
among the dozens of other children.

Yes, the cattle children were the true paupers in the
land. Earlier that day, after climbing to the top of the fence
surrounding the camp, she had dropped a quarter of a
loaf of nut bread to a small boy on the other side. The boy
looked both ways, scooped up the bread, and tore it in
half.

"Thank you," he had whispered. Then, as he gobbled
down one half, he ran to a little girl in the distance. When
he reached her, he gave her the other half and pointed at
Koren, still hanging on to the top of the fence.

Even now, the boy's whispered voice continued to bathe her mind in sweet comfort. *Thank you.* Those simple words would be a soothing balm every time sad memories scratched a new wound in her soul.

When she passed under the arch of Arxad's grotto, her home now for more than a year, she hurried to the back of the cart and pushed it from behind. She might already be late, and Arxad wouldn't be happy if his sweetener wasn't ready in time for his evening meal.

Now on the entry tunnel's smoother terrain, familiar after such a long Assignment, she jogged quickly. Ahead, a lantern light illuminated the kitchen area. Madam Orley and the other girls had probably finished preparing and serving the meal. Madam had killed four sheep earlier in the day, and butchering them had been quite a chore for her and the girls. Now that the girls had left to take their exams, Madam Orley would be working alone, tired, as could be expected, and probably unwilling to listen to excuses about stinging bees.

Koren wheeled the cart to a stop next to a table with an oak surface and four granite legs. Madam stood on the other side, her hands flat on the table as she propped her stocky body. A weary smile dressed her face. She was obviously tired, but not cross.

Koren picked up a sticky comb the size of her hand and set it on the table. "Will this one be enough for Arxad? I can put the others in jars."

Beneath the light of a lantern hanging from the high ceiling, Madam Orley looked at her, two circlets of gray hair hanging out of her white bandanna and dangling in front of her eyes. With every feature in her wrinkled face sagging, she sighed. "It will be enough." Her voice sounded as tired as she looked. "But you had better hurry. I served the lambs a moment ago, and he is waiting for the sauce to be sweetened. Then you can come back and store the other combs."

Koren grabbed a metal pot hanging from one of many hooks that held cooking utensils on the stone wall and put the honeycomb inside. Kneeling, she inserted the pot into a shelf above the fireplace. With the spit for roasting the lambs still in the fireplace's main compartment, the shelf they used for keeping food warm would have to do. There was no time to move the spit and then wash her hands. All she needed was to warm the comb a little bit.

When enough honey pooled, she pulled out the pot and marched farther into the tunnel. The dining area was in the next chamber. It, too, was well-lit, making it easy for Koren to follow the glow.

She paused near an opening to the right and peered inside. Unlike humans, who shared a community table, each dragon perched on his haunches in front of an individual stone pedestal, Arxad near the left side of the rectangular room, Fellina at the opposite wall on the right. Xenith, their female youngling, perched behind her table near the wall across from the entry door. The room was small compared to the main living quarters, allowing them to speak without shouting, but the cramped space made it difficult for a servant to maneuver around the tables while carrying heavy serving platters and filled goblets.

All three seemed to be in a good mood, each one tearing meat from various portions of the roasted lamb and slurping macko berry wine. With their noisy chewing, their growling conversations were muffled, but Koren's experienced ears picked up every word. They spoke in their own language, of course, but she and the other slaves had heard it so often, translating it wasn't a problem.

"The Separators are promoting three humans," Arxad said. "I will have to prepare them for the ceremony."

Koren held her breath. They were talking about Promotions, a topic they always avoided when she was nearby. Maybe they would let some information slip. She had often dreamed of being one of the promoted humans. It was the only way out of the hotter regions.

Fellina stopped chewing. "Will these duties never end?"

"I will not be long." Arxad looked at Xenith. "And you already know what I will say if you complain that you should be allowed to go. The book of the law forbids it. Someday you will be old enough to see what we do with promoted humans."

Xenith crunched a bone and spoke loudly while grinding it. "Good. I hope Koren gets promoted someday. I think she is—"

"Quiet!" Fellina scolded. "A human is in the kitchen."

The room fell silent. Koren counted to ten, hoping that was enough time for the dragons to believe she had not heard their conversation. Taking a breath, she marched in, gave the three dragons a quick bow, and hurried with the pot to Arxad's table.

"You are late," Arxad growled in the human tongue.

"Yes, I am." Koren poured some of the honey into a bowl of herbs and drippings from the lamb. Using a spoon from the table, she mixed the concoction into a thick sauce.

"If you care to hear the reason for my tardiness, I will tell you."

"I want to hear it," Xenith said. "Koren's stories are always amusing."

Arxad gave Koren a nod. "Very well. Amuse us."

"One moment." Koren poured the sauce over the remainder of Arxad's lamb, set the pot down on the floor, and wiped her hands on her apron. "I am ready."

Giving the dragons a theatrical grimace as she turned slowly in place, she bent her body into a skulking pose, raised her hands as if ready to claw an enemy, and narrowed her eyes. The dragons loved a good show, so she would give them one. Maybe someday she could earn the elusive Promotion.

"The hives are filled with bees," she said in a breathy, overly dramatic voice. "Since you are protected by your impenetrable scales, you dragons cannot fathom the torture we humans suffer when the needle-sharp barbs prick our skin. The sting is worse than a spear piercing a dragon's underbelly. Venom courses through our bloodstreams. Our bodies swell like rotting cadavers. Our throats constrict, and we gasp for just a swallow of air."

She wrapped her fingers around her throat. Sticking out her tongue and gagging, she staggered from one table to another. Finally, she collapsed in a heap and peeked at the dragons. Xenith gawked at her, mesmerized. After a few seconds, Koren spoke in a groaning lament. "Though we beg for death to come and end the torture, the dark predator stalks slowly, laughing at us as we strain to breathe. Then, just as we realize we want to live after all, he thrusts his jagged sword into our chests, deflating our lungs and the last gasping prayer for precious life."

She rose to her feet and posed as she had at the beginning, again using a dramatic voice. "In order to avoid the stings, I wore a robe I constructed out of acorn caps. The hard surface made me feel like a powerful dragon — brave, strong, and invulnerable to the pesky bees. Armed with nothing but a sharp stick, I attacked the hive, and although the wicked bees swarmed around my body, buzzing and driving their stingers into my robe, I managed to pull out the finest honeycombs in the land, dripping with gooey, delicious honey."

She lifted a finger and lowered her voice to a raspy whisper. "But, after I loaded the combs into my cart, a hundred squirrels attacked me." Raising her hands, she ran around the area enclosed by the tables, acting out her story. "I fought them off, stripping each one from my acorn robe and throwing them into the river until I was finally rid of the furry rats."

Koren halted in front of Xenith, panting. "I took off my robe and hurried back to my cart, but my escape had already delayed me too much. I knew I would be late, though I strained with all my might to run up the hill with a cart dragging me back."

Her draconic mouth hanging open, Xenith turned to Arxad. "Father, she risked her life to get your honey. I could almost see the squirrels and the bees. Have you ever heard such a story of courage?"

Arxad chuckled. "No, I cannot say that I have. It was quite a tale indeed."

The male dragon eyed Koren. His pulsing red pupils told her what she needed to know. Although he realized the story was really a tall tale, he was pleased.

"You may wash and retire to your quarters," he said. "Your entertainment has earned an early rest."

Koren smiled and bowed. "I trust that my service to you will continue to demonstrate the loyalty due you and your household."

"You see," Xenith said. "If any human deserves Promotion, Koren does."

Arxad glared at her. "You speak that which you do not understand. The Separators know about Koren and her talents, so it is up to us to be silent and trust their judgment." He glanced at Fellina briefly before turning to Koren with a kindly smile. "Go to your quarters now. Madam Orley will clean up in here."

Koren bowed again and walked out of the room, her back straight and her head high. When she reached the tunnel and its concealing shadows, she leaned against the wall. Her heart thumped. Her legs trembled. *The Separators know about me!* Maybe Promotion was more than just a dream. Maybe she would finally be able to go to the mountain spas and the cooler climate.

Closing her eyes, she wrapped her arms around herself. There she could serve the King Dragon and be with the other promoted humans. The tasks were so much easier there, a few hours of food preparation and cleaning, and the rest of the day could be spent wandering in the hills, picking flowers, singing prayers, or just sitting in the green grass doing nothing at all.

Koren looked back toward the kitchen. At least that's what Madam Orley and the other women always said. The men, of course, told different, though equally wonderful stories. They focused on the ease of lighter outdoor labors, certainly easier than slaving with pickaxes in the deep pheterone mines. And they could enjoy hunting, fishing, and tending bountiful gardens. It was truly Paradise.

After taking a final peek into the dining chamber, Koren scooted toward her sleeping quarters. She passed through the enormous living room, empty now except for the thick mats the dragons used for resting and recreation. They would return here after dinner to talk and play their usual games, most involving quizzes and brain teasers. Once in a while Arxad would bounce with Xenith on the mats and wrestle with her, though such episodes had grown infrequent since she had, as the dragons put it, "come of age."

When Koren reached the far end of the living room, she turned left into another corridor, barely illuminated by widely spaced lanterns. Its lower ceiling made it much harder for dragons to enter, which was a blessing. The girls could talk about the day and complain about their labors without worrying about an eavesdropper listening in. Madam Orley would often tell stories about their origins, starting with the humans' version and telling how dragons kidnapped a group of families from an alien planet called Darksphere. Starlight had begun to lose pheterone, a gas in the air necessary for dragon survival, so one hundred years ago they sent an explorer dragon to Darksphere in search of an alternative place to live.

The new planet had even less pheterone in its atmosphere than did Starlight, but the dragon noticed how nimbly the creatures there used their hands and tools. He stole a group away and enslaved them, forcing them to procreate so they could grow in numbers and dig the deep mines that would release the gas from beneath Starlight's crust and thereby replenish the atmosphere.

Ever since, humans have used picks and drills to dig deep holes in pheterone mines, and dragons have grown stronger because of the replenished atmosphere.

The dragon version of the legend, of course, differed in two details. Indeed, a dragon did go to Darksphere to search for a habitable planet, but he found that humans there were brutally treated by slave-driving mountain bears and often used as a food source. He rescued all he could carry on his back, and in exchange for their safety, humans have worked for dragon survival all these years. The labor was still forced and often torturous, but it was better than being eaten by bears.

Koren trembled. The thought of a huge bear gnawing on her limbs curdled her stomach. At least the dragons never did that. Of course, some of the meaner boys would swear they had seen a dragon eat a human, but they were just trying to scare the girls.

She continued down the corridor until it widened into a dead-end chamber about half the size of the dragons' dining area, barely adequate for Madam Orley and the three girls. Their thick mats lay side by side against the adjacent wall, and a desk sat against the opposite wall. The girls took turns at the rickety pinewood desk, studying their evening lessons—mathematics, geography, politics, theater, and history. With their labors requiring mainly physical exertion, the lessons often seemed meaningless. From time to time, however, a human would be chosen as an accountant or an engineer, so the dragons trained all the younger slaves, hoping they could identify the most intellectually talented humans for further education.

Koren sat on the desk's stool and touched the history book, open to their latest lesson on heroic dragons of the past. The dragon in the drawing, barely visible in the room's dimmed lantern, was a gigantic red beast named Magnar. With wings larger than most, he was the very dragon who once flew to the alien world and brought back the first humans. Now, older than anyone in the world, he presided over the Separators. The few living humans who had ever seen him said he was still as powerful as ever.

Koren, of course, had been in the Separators' Basilica, but only when it was time for a new Assignment. The dragons always made her drink a syrupy potion before taking her there, and that kept her in a daze throughout the process. Only the faintest images remained—a fire, a book on a pedestal, and dragons shouting in their gruff language, sounding like bidders at the Traders' auction. It was all so strange.

Koren closed the book sharply. These stories often didn't match those told by Madam Orley or the poems sung by Tamminy, the dragon bard. Who could tell what was true and what wasn't? Maybe Magnar? If he was that old, surely he would know every story in this world's human history.

She stooped and poured water from a pitcher to a basin they kept near a corner. With the lantern hanging close by, her reflection in the basin looked pale as it wiggled within the ripples. Still, her red hair was obvious, the same red hair that gave her such an advantage over most of the other slaves. The dragons considered it a sign of great intelligence and talent, and her green eyes added to the effect.

"A pair of emeralds shining under a cap of fiery brilliance," the Trader had called out again and again as he paraded her in the courtyard. "She will be a trophy slave for the noblest dragon in the land."

Koren remembered trying to look intelligent that day, though it was hard to keep from glaring at the Trader, a human male who kissed up to the dragons in a nauseating manner. He would be quick to betray any of his kind who tried to escape to the wilderness or anyone who dared to speak against dragon authority. He wasn't a Trader; he was a traitor.

After washing her hands and splashing her face, she dried off with a hand towel from a shelf built into the wall. A full bath could wait until tomorrow.

Sitting on her mat, she crossed her legs and leaned against the wall. Soon, Natalla would come in. Since she was only twelve, the youngest of Madam's orphans, her exams were easier than those of her fourteen-year-old sister, Petra, enabling her to finish early.

Koren looked at the weak flame in the wall-mounted lantern. It illuminated another built-in shelf that held their meager clothes — a thin nightgown for each slave and a single pair of boots in case any of them had to venture into the swamp. They were too big for Natalla and too small for Madam, so Koren and Petra were always chosen to wade out among the serpents to harvest the swamp grains.

She pulled a nightgown from the shelf, sat again on her mat, and straightened her long skirt over her legs. She had shorts on underneath, but it made sense to wear both. The skirt's warm material always felt good during the cool months.

Sighing, she gazed at the lantern again. Now was a good time to make up a prayer song. She had listened to the girls singing anti-dragon chants all day. As usual, they were funny, especially the one Natalla loved.

Dragon, dragon, stinky breath,

Choke on bones, and choke to death.

Wrap your whip around your throat,

Strangle, die, you scaly goat.

Koren sighed. For some reason, when she was alone in her room, the songs seemed stupid, just stones hurled by ignorant children. She couldn't laugh now. If the stories were true, the dragons kept them from being enslaved to the cruel mountain bears. Sure, the dragons also enslaved them, but for humans, slavery was the only option, so it seemed better to be here than in the other world. At least she would never be the main course at a meal.

As she watched the wavering flame, a stream of words entered her mind. Composing prayer songs had always been easy, and now that her hopes for Promotion had been kindled, a surge of emotions painted her verses with a blend of joy and sadness.

I dream of long walks without a command,

The freedom of mind where dragons are banned.

I dance with the girls in meadows pristine;

We splash in cool ponds of aquamarine.

But when I awake from my visions of hope,

I'm bound by a chain; I am pulling a rope,

And dragging a load of sweet honey or oil;

My dreams and my longings all crumble and spoil.

O could it be true, Creator of All,

You'll lift from my coffin this heavy dread pall?

And send me to freedom, to Northlands so grand,

To bask in cool breezes and sing in that land?

I ask you tonight, to hear my lament.

I have no real parents, no family descent.

This orphan cries out to Father above,

O grant my request, O send me your love.

Allow me to know the next step I should take

To learn how to wrestle the chains I must break

And rescue my friends from the shackles that bind

Then fly to real freedom, and not just in mind.

She released the final note with a sigh. She had to hold on to hope. So many other humans had given up and were just going through the motions, especially those who faced beatings every day from the crueler dragons.

After a few silent seconds, Natalla walked in. With her dark hair tied back, her tired eyes were easy to see. She plopped down on her mat and folded her hands in her lap.

"What's wrong?" Koren asked. "Were the exams difficult?"

With her gaze locked on her hands, Natalla firmed her jaw. "I'm being promoted."

"Promoted!" Koren slid over and gave her a strong hug. "That's wonderful!"

Natalla turned toward her. A skeptical frown bent her lips. "No, it's not. A Separator was at exams, and he chose the two girls with the lowest scores. I was one of them."

"The *lowest* scores?" Koren sat back. "How strange!"

"I think Stephan was right all along. The dragons don't send humans to the Northlands. They eat them."

"Oh, nonsense. He's just trying to scare you. You've seen him laugh when you get the shivers."

"How do you know it's nonsense?"

"You've seen the letter from my aunt. She's in the Northlands. I could never mistake her handwriting."

"I know." Natalla crossed her arms over her chest. "But she hasn't written since then."

"Of course not," Koren said. "She explained that. They're allowed to write only once to give comfort to those left behind, but any further correspondence makes us daydream too much about going there ourselves. It's a fruitless desire, considering the odds of getting promoted." Smiling broadly, she patted Natalla on her knee. "But you beat the odds! You get to go!"

Her arms still crossed, Natalla shook her head. "One letter isn't enough. The dragons could have forced her to write it before they ate her. I'm going to try to escape."

"Escape!" Koren looked at the corridor. Sometimes Xenith managed to squeeze in to talk to the girls, but not so much lately. "Even if you get away, you'll be alone in the wilderness, and you would never make it past the great barrier wall."

"Stephan said he would go with me. He's been studying survival skills. We can manage, and we're not going to try to pass the wall. We can set up a new community near the swamplands and steal some of the cattle children away. It will be hard, but at least it'll be better for them than where they are now."

"I can't argue with that." Koren looked at Natalla's determined eyes. "Okay, what if I learn that the Promotions story is true, and you can go to the Northlands? Would you go? Or are you set on escaping?"

"I would go. If the king there is as kind as people say he is, maybe I can persuade him to help the cattle children."

Koren stared again at Natalla. She was too thin and frail to survive the wilderness. Of course Stephan would do all he could to help, but even a brother's love wasn't enough to prevent illness or injury. The only way to keep her safe was to learn the truth.

"Okay," Koren said. "I'll go to the Basilica tonight after the dragons are asleep."

Natalla's voice rose. "But how? You'll be captured for sure. And what kind of proof will you be able to find?"

"Shhh!" Koren glanced at the tunnel again and lowered her voice to a whisper. "You must not let Madam know what I'm doing. I hope to sneak into the Separators' courtroom and see what I can find."

Natalla grasped Koren's hands. "Let me come with you!"

"No!" Koren pulled away and rose to her feet. "Better for one of us to get caught than two."

"They'll send you back to the Traders ... or worse."

"Nothing is worse than that. That's why I'm going instead of you." For a moment, a memory of her weeks in the cattle camps flashed in her mind, but she shook it away. Those days were too awful. She had to keep those thoughts trapped in the dungeon of forgetfulness. "I'll risk it. Anything to keep you from trying to escape."

"Okay. But if you don't come back before Pariah sets, I'm leaving. I might not have another chance."

"If I don't make it back by then, that means trouble." Koren pulled her nightgown over her head, covering her labor tunic and shorts.

"It's third day," Natalla said. "Aren't you going to take off your clothes for Madam to wash?"

"They might not get dry in time. I'm not going outside in just a nightgown."

"Madam will ask questions."

"I'll tell her I'll wash them when I bathe tomorrow. The river's warm enough in the middle of the day."

"But the boys—"

"The boys will be out in the fields. They work so late, they can't take their baths until past girls' curfew."

Natalla shrugged. "If you say so, but I'm using Xenith's pool. It's always warm … and it's private."

After Natalla left to bathe, Koren lay down and drifted in and out of sleep. Soon Madam Orley's laughter jolted her to full wakefulness. Sitting on her mat, Madam leaned back against the wall, a lantern at her side. Natalla and Petra sat cross-legged nearby, both staring at her with identically braided dark hair. Obviously Madam had just told one of her tales, and her eyes shining in the lantern's light hinted she was ready to tell another.

Stifling a yawn, Koren sat up and stretched. Madam Orley and the two girls were dressed in nightgowns, all three clean and smelling like the incense in Xenith's pool room. Petra, as always, stayed quiet. Since her previous

owner ordered her tongue cut out, she never uttered a
word, just an occasional quiet groan when she grew tired.

"So the favored princess is awake," Madam said, smiling.

Koren squinted at her and mumbled, "Favored
princess?"

"As if you didn't know." Madam's smile wilted, but she
seemed sad rather than angry, as if weary of keeping a
gleeful countenance. "Arxad has taken a liking to you,
and that has caused more work for me."

"I'm sorry. I'll make it up to you. I can sweep the cave."

Madam sighed. "You do not need to. Hard work is my
lot in life. I was born a slave. I will die a slave."

Koren scooted closer. With Madam in a melancholy
mood, maybe she would reveal some secrets. "I read
in the history book today about Magnar and how he
brought humans to our world."

"I have told you that tale several times." Madam gave
Koren a skeptical squint. "Why are you bringing it up now?"

Koren reached over and grasped Madam's hand.
"Because I need to know if it's really true."

"True?" Madam's eyes took on a faraway look. She
seemed to stare right past Koren. After a few seconds,
she shook her head. "No, child. That story isn't true—
neither the human nor the dragon version. We tell it to
the younger children so they can learn to have some
affection for the dragons. Working with a spark of love in
your heart is better than stewing in hatred."

"So there is no other world? No bears? No Magnar?"

"Magnar is real, to be sure, but that story and the others
are fables and wishful thinking, and all three of you are
old enough to learn the truth. The elders have documents

written by humans that date much further back than when we supposedly arrived here. There is no doubt about it. Humans have always lived here under the enslaving claws of the dragons. We did not come from another world."

"What about promoted slaves? Do they really go to the Northlands?"

Madam chuckled. "Have you been listening to the boys' teasing about dragons eating humans?"

"Well … " Koren glanced at Natalla briefly. "I have heard the rumors."

"Don't you fret," Madam said, patting her hand. "Dragons despise human meat."

"Really? How do you know?"

Madam pulled her head back. "How do I know? Why, everyone knows that."

"Do you know a dragon who has tasted human meat?" Koren asked. "If no dragon likes it, wouldn't they all have had to try it to know?"

Madam scowled. "You're asking nonsense questions."

Natalla piped up. "It isn't nonsense. I was wondering the same thing."

"Well, then," Madam said, "I suppose you have to eat goat manure before you'll know if you like it."

"Ewww!" Natalla and Koren said at once. Petra grimaced.

A triumphant smile spread across Madam's face. "You know it's bad because of its smell and where it came from. The same is true for humans. To them, we smell like manure, and the very thought of eating one of us will cause their younglings to say, 'Ewww!'"

Koren looked at Natalla again, this time waiting for her to notice. She still seemed skeptical, very skeptical.

"But why would I get a Promotion?" Natalla asked. "Wouldn't the Separators choose someone smarter?"

Madam waved her hand. "Nonsense. They just think you're hatched from the black egg."

Koren let those words sink in. Someday, or so the prophecy said, the queen dragon would lay a black egg, and although the youngling would begin its life encumbered with physical disadvantages, it would grow into the greatest of dragons. And that legend gave birth to the idiom "Hatched from the black egg," which even humans have used to encourage children of lesser intelligence or physical abilities.

"The king of the Northlands," Madam continued, "wants pliable girls who won't talk too much. That's why Koren will never see that great king. She's too smart and too valuable. Have you ever seen a redhead get a Promotion? I haven't."

Koren's heart sank. Now that she thought about it, Madam was right. Only the dark-haired girls were ever chosen. Her "cap of fiery brilliance" would keep her in the hot regions forever.

Madam clapped her hands. "Time for sleep, girls. Tomorrow is another day of sweat and tears."

As Koren laid her head down, Madam's words echoed within. She had repeated that bedtime call every night for months, but this time it pierced Koren's heart. She formed the words on her lips. *Sweat and tears.* It was true. Every day brought both the sweat of hard labor and tears of loneliness whenever she allowed thoughts of her parents to break through. Only fleeting images of her mother's face whisked by, more like a phantom than a living person. Still, she remembered enough to know that Mother was kind. In Koren's memories, her mother's lovely brow was always smooth, never wrinkled in a scowl or frown.

No matter how hard she tried, no image of Father ever appeared. Only his voice ever made its way into her sad memories, a bare few words that she sang to herself before going to sleep every night.

"I love you, little K."

As Koren let the usual tears flow, Natalla slid a hand into hers and whispered, "I'm still going. I don't think Madam knows what's really true."

For a long moment, Koren said nothing. Although the denial that they had come from another world was disappointing, it made a lot of sense. How could a dragon fly beyond the sky? And if the elders had documents that disproved the tale, that pretty much sealed its fate as a myth. Yet the explanations about the Promotions weren't as convincing. She would have to help Natalla learn the truth.

Giving Natalla's hand a gentle squeeze, Koren whispered, "My plans are the same. If I'm not back before Pariah sets, then you and Stephan should go ahead and try to escape."

five

*J*ason fastened the clasp on his new cloak and sat on the marble steps in front of Prescott's castle. With darkness blanketing the hill, walking home would be a lonely journey, especially in the forest. He had lost his fear of the woods long ago, but after being humiliated by snide remarks from several of Prescott's friends at the Counselor's invocation, he felt small and weak.

Only an hour ago, the former Counselor, an elderly man who had reached mandatory retirement age, walked up to Prescott and said, "I see you have chosen another peasant for your bodyguard. I suppose if he dies defending you, it will be no loss. There are many more rats in the sewers who can handle a blade."

Not only that, the new Counselor, Viktor Orion, still dressed in his ceremonial silk, stopped by and looked Jason over, a smirk on his face. "He is a handsome lad, to be sure, Your Lordship. Perhaps he will help us find the Diviner. It is said that the sultry witches are always on the lookout for a callow catch."

And Prescott just laughed at both comments, not offering a single word of defense. He should have known how stupid his silence was. A wise governor realizes that the warrior who watches his back is the warrior who keeps the daggers from flying there.

Jason pondered Counselor Orion's odd words. They seemed practiced, as if scripted for that moment. Was he trying to communicate a message that he didn't want Prescott to understand? If by "the Diviner" he meant Elyssa, why would he mention her unless he thought she was still alive?

None of that mattered now. While the speeches at the invocation droned on, the solution to the puzzle became clear in Jason's mind. Prescott was the bear, and the key was on the ring that he kept in his tunic's pocket, close to his heart. During the ceremony and afterward, he frequently reached into the vest pocket and fingered the keys, as if worried that they might have jumped out and run away.

As thunder rumbled in the distance, Jason rose. One way or another, this would be his last day as that fool's bodyguard. He would either quit or be fired. Considering what he planned to do now, there weren't any other options.

Jason marched back to the castle's main entrance and approached Drexel, the door's guard. "I forgot to give something to Governor Prescott," Jason said. "It's very important."

Drexel, a tall, thin man with a black handlebar moustache, scowled. "What could a peasant have that

His Lordship would want at this time of night? Bodyguard or not, it had better be urgent."

"Oh, it's urgent." Jason pulled his copy of the
Underground Gateway newsletter from his pocket and
smoothed out the wrinkles. "I took this from someone
in his inner circle. It appears that one of those crazy
conspiracy theorists is within his ranks. Of course, I
couldn't interrupt the ceremony, but I forgot to tell him
afterwards."

"You forgot? What kind of bodyguard are you?"

"A new one," Jason said, bowing. "I beg your
indulgence."

Drexel reached for the page, but Jason pulled it back.
"I must speak to him privately. It is up to His Lordship
to decide what to do with this information. It would be a
shame if I had to tell him tomorrow who prevented my
access to him tonight."

"For a new bodyguard, you are a quick student of
political maneuvering." Drexel pushed a key into a hefty
iron lock and released the door's bolt. "Take care that you
don't maneuver yourself into a dangerous corner. There
are people in the governor's employ who are far craftier
than you realize."

Jason brushed off Drexel's condescending tone and
gave him a friendly nod. "I will leave through the rear
door. It's closer to my path home."

"Very well." Drexel almost smiled. "You will find a
lantern in the vestibule."

Jason hurried in, picked up the lantern, which was
already trimmed and lit, and marched across the vast
lobby. Since he had visited Prescott's bedroom earlier,
finding it again would be no problem.

After passing through the narrow corridor and entering the massive living room, he turned down the lantern as far as he could without extinguishing the flame. The bedroom lay only a few steps ahead. From here, a closed door was visible, but no guard. Would someone be stationed inside? If so, wouldn't Drexel have mentioned it? With armed guards at every exterior door, maybe Prescott wasn't paranoid enough to create a gauntlet of soldiers within the castle.

When he reached the bedroom, he set the lantern on the floor and lifted the latch. A quiet click sounded, not enough to wake any but the lightest of sleepers. Pushing the door open a crack, he peered into the dim room. The energy channels in the walls had been turned down to their nighttime setting, just enough light to keep someone on a washroom journey from bumping into anything.

Prescott slept on the huge bed with his wife, Lady Moulraine, who was snoring loudly at his side. That helped. Obviously Prescott had grown accustomed to sleeping next to a human sawmill.

As Jason pushed the door open the rest of the way, the hinges squeaked, but not loudly enough to overcome the snores. After easing the door back in place without allowing it to latch, he walked on the balls of his feet until he stood at the bedside. Prescott clutched his key ring against his silk nightshirt, open in front and exposing a hairless chest that rose and fell with his steady breathing.

Jason wrinkled his nose. Prescott's breath reeked of garlic, but it wasn't as bad as usual. Extending his hand slowly, he reached for the ring. This would take the skill of a thief, and he hadn't stolen anything since the time he snatched a cookie from his mother's baking sheet when he was eight years old.

He curled a finger around the ring and began to pull ever so slowly. It moved a fraction of an inch. Prescott's grip relaxed, but his meaty hand still weighed down the keys.

As Jason pulled again, the ring slid a bit more, uncovering a raised patch of skin on Prescott's chest. Jason stared at it. The size and shape of a finger, the patch throbbed with yellow light, its luminance pulsing between dim and bright.

The bedroom door's hinges squeaked, pulling Jason's attention away. A lantern pushed through the gap, and a man's head appeared.

Leaving the key ring on Prescott's chest, Jason ducked and slid under the bed. The guard, probably a lone sentry who made regular rounds through the castle, walked in. Extending his lantern, he moved it slowly from left to right, sweeping its glow across the bedroom.

Peeking out from behind a dust ruffle, Jason studied the guard's unfamiliar face. He didn't seem worried. If this check was part of his normal rounds, he would probably leave soon. Then again, if finding the door unlatched raised a question in his mind, he might conduct a more thorough search.

As the light drew nearer, Jason slid farther under the bed and held his breath. The guard's boots came into view, the toes pointing directly at Jason. With Lady Moulraine's noisy buzz still drowning out all sound, it was impossible to tell what was going on. A few seconds later, the guard walked away. The lantern's light faded and disappeared.

Jason slid back out and rose to his feet. The door was closed; no sign of the guard. Now he had better hurry and grab the keys. Who could tell when the next bedroom check might be?

As his eyes adjusted again to the darkness, he turned toward Prescott and reached for the key ring, but his fingers struck something else, something long and thin. He squinted. Soon the object took shape: a long dagger protruding from Prescott's chest. Blood covered his night clothes and dripped to the sheets.

Jason gasped. He staggered backwards, barely catching himself before he fell. While Lady Moulraine snored on, he grasped the hilt of his sword. *A murderer was in the castle!*

Drawing his blade, Jason rushed to the door and jerked it open. A man stood there, blocking his way. Lifting a lantern, the man cast a light across his face.

Jason gulped. *Drexel!*

Drexel's cool voice rose and fell in a mocking sort of way. "Have you finished delivering your message to the governor?"

Showing his sword, Jason hissed, "I have to catch a murderer! Someone has killed the governor!"

His face stoic, Drexel let out a sarcastic moan. "Oh, dear! The governor has fallen! And it seems that the only person who entered his bedroom was a certain peasant boy who spoke petulantly to the palace's sentry. He must be an Underground Gateway conspirator who sought revenge on the great governor who forbade his nefarious practices."

Jason set the sword's point against Drexel's chest. "You're the murderer!"

"Oh, not I." A smirk rising on his lips, he gestured with his head. Another guard appeared in the light, the keys in one hand and a sword in the other. "I have already entered my suspicions in the official log," Drexel continued, "so killing me would only double your crime. Perhaps you would like to reconsider your offensive posture and join us."

"Join you?" Jason lowered his weapon. "What do you mean?"

Drexel turned to the other guard. "Bristol, show us what you retrieved from our dear governor."

The other guard extended the key ring and a short, bent cylinder that pulsed with a bright yellow glow.

"Take them," Drexel said, his voice calm and smooth. "You will find what you're looking for in the lowest level of the dungeon, at cell number four."

Jason opened his hand. Bristol laid the key ring and cylinder in his palm. The two bends in the cylinder made it look exactly like a finger. As it continued to pulse, Jason's mind flashed back to Prescott's chest. Bristol must have cut this out of the governor's skin!

"Before today," Drexel continued, "we dared not take this bold step, but now that you have come, we have the means to proceed. You see, when you leave, we will blame you for the murder, and you will be forced to carry out the mission. We have both a warrior and a scapegoat."

Jason's cheeks flamed. He was trapped. Maybe he could fight past both guards and run, but he would still be branded a murderer, and two "eyewitnesses" were ready to send him to the gallows.

"And your answer?" Drexel prompted.

Jason slid his sword back into its scabbard. "It seems I have no choice."

"Ah! Very good! You *have* learned the art of political maneuvering." Drexel pulled Jason into the hall and closed the door. "You have two hours to flee before I alert the new Counselor of your deed. The dungeon guard is one of us, and he will allow you to enter. When you find her on the lower level, you will learn what you must do."

"Her?"

Drexel pushed him down the hall. "Just go!"

Clutching the keys and the finger, Jason hustled toward the rear of the castle, slowing as he approached the door. He nodded at the sentry, glad the guards recognized his uniform and allowed him free range.

Ahead, the tall gallows post stood in the moonlight, casting a long shadow over an expanse of bare ground where onlookers gathered for hangings. As the rope swung in the breeze, the noose's oval shadow swayed eerily.

Jason shivered. Never in a thousand years would he have expected to fear that sight. The noose was for murderers and thieves, not for a son of Edison Masters.

When he spotted the dungeon's night guard standing next to the gate under the glow of a pole-mounted lantern, Jason waved to signal his approach. The guard unhooked the lantern and held it out.

"Jason Masters?" he whispered.

Jason's heart began thumping again. He slid the glowing finger into his trousers pocket and held up the key ring. "I understand that you're expecting me."

"I am." The guard pulled a key ring from his belt, produced a long brass key from the midst of several shorter keys, and turned a lock in the gate on the ground. Grabbing an iron bar, he swung the gate upward and nodded toward the descending stairwell underneath. "You will find a torch and flint at the bottom. We have no energy channels down there. Stay on the center path."

"Thank you." Jason descended the steep, narrow stairs. As the moonlight faded, the steps darkened, forcing him to slow his pace. Above, the gate closed, and the lock clicked.

He looked up. The jailer wasn't in sight. Realizing he'd just walked into the dungeon as an accused murderer, Jason stifled the urge to panic. *Locking the gate is just a precaution. He's one of us. He'll let me out when this part of the mission is complete.*

Now in darkness, Jason ran his hand along the wall, searching for a torch mount. When his fingers touched metal, he ran them up the bracket and grasped the torch. If the jailer followed normal practices, the flint stones would be in a box on the floor immediately underneath.

After finding the stones, he lit the torch's oily rags. As the orange tongues of fire crawled over the top, he dropped the flints into his pocket and guided the flame from left to right. He stood in an anteroom with stone-and-mortar walls and a wood-beam ceiling. Three corridors led into the darkness, one angling to the left, one straight ahead, and one angling to the right.

Again waving the torch, Jason marched down the center path. The air smelled of mildew and human waste, and the sound of dripping water echoed from somewhere in the distance. Heavy wooden doors lined the sides of the corridor, each one with a small, barred window at eye level and a thick crossbar wedge in iron brackets blocking escape.

Jason glanced briefly at a window, but the darkness inside made it impossible to see anything. At this time of night, any prisoners within would likely be asleep. Even if they noticed his passing, wouldn't they think he was a guard making the rounds and not an accused murderer searching for someone to set free?

As soon as the thought entered his mind, a movement caught his eye. Three doors ahead on the left, probing fingers reached between the bars. Easing to the right to avoid them, Jason stopped and looked at the gray-bearded face pressing against the window's grating. Long strands of greasy hair spilled down the sides of his head, and his smile revealed wide gaps between sparse teeth.

"You are finally here," he said with a cackle. "I knew you would come! I knew it!"

Jason set the flame closer to the door and read the number on a metal plate just above the crossbar. Cell number twenty. "Who are you?"

"They call me Tibber the Fibber, but my real name is Tibalt Blackstone. I survived the Great Plague, I did."

"The Great Plague! Then you must be over ninety years old."

"Oh, yes. As old as the hills and older than rust, my bones are all brittle, and my brain's full of dust." He cackled again. "My pappy locked the gateway to the dragon world and founded the resistance against the plucked chickens who still hide its presence. I can help you find it."

Jason stifled a laugh. This man was trying to talk his way out of prison, but how could he have known to mention the dragons and the gateway? "You said your name is Blackstone. Are you related to—"

"Uriel Blackstone. He was my pappy. He showed me the gateway before they locked him up, but I remember where it is. Yes, I do!"

Jason gazed at the old man's wild eyes. "Tibber the Fibber, huh? Does the name fit?"

Tibalt winked. "Oh, yes. I am a liar, to be sure. It keeps things interesting for me. Even if they catch me in a lie, what does it matter? I am already locked up, you see."

"Yes … I see. But how do I know you're not lying to me now?"

"You don't!" Tibalt pointed at Jason with a long, bony finger. "But you are the chosen one, and you will release me. I can help you on your great mission."

"The chosen one? What are you talking about?"

"You bear the litmus finger."

"Litmus?" Jason withdrew the finger from his pocket and set it in his palm. "You could see it?"

"Not see it. Sense it. But it will do you no good in your pocket. It must be embedded in your skin. My pappy told me stories about it, so I know. I know very much. He told me that I would need it to find the gateway, but since I am in here, and you are out there, you will have to be the one to embed it."

"I don't have time to get a surgeon to—"

"No need for a surgeon." Tibalt snatched the finger. "Open your shirt."

"Hey! Give that back!" Jason swiped at the finger, but Tibalt jerked it away.

"Unbutton that fancy shirt, and I'll give it back in a place you can use it. You want to find the gateway, don't you?"

"Well, yes, but—"

"Then pop those buttons, boy, and I'll give you a personal pointer to truth."

Jason set the torch down and unfastened his shirt's top three buttons. When he pulled the plackets apart, exposing his chest, Tibalt whispered in a hypnotic cadence, "Come closer … closer … "

Jason glanced at his sword as he inched toward the old man.

Suddenly, Tibalt thrust out both arms, grasped Jason's neck, and pressed the finger against his chest and held it there.

It burned, sizzling like a hot poker drilling into his chest.

"Augh!" Jason's cry echoed from one end of the corridor to the other. He tried to pull away, but Tibalt's wiry arms held him in place.

Finally, Tibalt let go. Jason staggered back and slammed into the cell door on the opposite side, then slid to the floor. A string of smoke rose from his chest and brushed his face, smelling hot and foul. Pressing his chin against his chest, he looked at the throbbing finger under a patch of cauterized skin. Still glowing yellow, it burned with every rhythmic pulse.

Jason blew on his skin to cool the fiery sting, but it did no good, though the sizzles were dying away.

Looking again at Tibalt, Jason scowled. "So now what?"

"Now you can go on your great mission."

Jason climbed to his feet and buttoned his shirt. "What do you know of my great mission?"

The old man's words breezed like a solemn chant. "A hero comes to rescue those who flew to realms afar. With sword in hand and youthful heart, he slays the dragon star."

"Star?" Jason repeated.

Tibalt nodded vigorously. "It was my pappy's rhyme, not mine, but it works, don't you think?"

"Uh ... sure." Jason picked up the torch. This poor guy was obviously addled, but maybe his experience in the dungeon could help. "Can you direct me to the lower level?"

Tibalt's eyes grew wide again. "If you take me with you, I will show you how to use the litmus finger. It is a guide to truth and direction and wisdom, but if you don't know how to use it, it is worthless, and you will never find the gateway. When I first laid eyes on you, I knew you were a dragon believer, so I know all about your quest. No, you can't fool an old fooler like me. And I can handle a blade with the best of them. Take me along, and the litmus finger and I will lead you to the gateway."

Jason looked at Tibalt's pleading face. Obviously he knew something about the gateway and the finger. Then again, he *was* a liar; he could be an old Underground Gateway member who murdered someone and would spin any lie he could to get out. "I'll tell you what," Jason said. "You direct me to the lower level, and if my contact there says I am allowed to release you, I will."

Tibalt stared at him for a long moment, his gray eyebrows squeezing together. "Well, then, young man, since I'm locked up, I don't have much choice, do I?" He pointed down the hallway. "At the end, you will find stairs to the left and to the right. Beware of the left! Oh, yes, beware of the left, for you will become lost in a maze of crooked halls and rat-infested rooms. Not that I mind the rats, you see. Some of my best friends are rats, but without me guiding you, you might never find your way back."

"So I turn right," Jason prompted. "And then?"

His cadence became singsong. "Beware of the left and descend to the right, or forever be lost in the dead of the night."

"Thanks. I get the picture."

"When you reach the end of the staircase, turn right again. That path will lead you farther downward to a corridor like this one. There you will find the forgotten ones, the deserted ones. Governor Feedor wants no one to know they exist, but he still keeps them alive, locked in heavy chains, for they hold valuable information. Oh yes, very valuable. He wishes to extract it through torture or deprivation."

"Governor Feedor? He was two governors ago."

Tibalt rolled his eyes. "Well, thank you very much for that information. The heralds never come here with the latest news." His head tilted to the side. "Who is the governor now?"

Jason almost said, "Prescott," but the image of the dagger protruding from his chest snatched the word away. "It doesn't matter," he finally said. "I have to go."

As he hurried toward the far end of the corridor, his torch leading the way, he looked back. Tibalt's hand waved frantically. "Beware of the left!" The words bounced around, fading with each echo.

When Jason reached a wall, he turned right and descended a long flight of stairs. The stench increased. The dripping water grew louder. The air felt wet and oily.

Again finding a wall, he turned right. A faint aura of green surrounded the torch's flame, sometimes sparking, as if flint stones were trying to light it. As he marched down the path's slope, he kept glancing at the torch. Could flammable chemicals be hovering in the dank air? Maybe. The corridor seemed to be filled with something unusual, but he had to risk keeping the torch ablaze. It would be impossible to find cell number four without it.

After another minute, doors appeared on both sides. Jason read the plate on the first door on the left—cell number one. On the right was cell two. He hurried to the second door on the right. This was it—cell number four.

Lifting the torch, now sparking wildly in green and orange, he peered into the window and called, "Is anyone in there?"

A female voice sounded from the back of the cell. "If you know what's good for you, you'll extinguish that torch immediately."

Jason looked at the flame. The sparks were popping and dancing. "Then I won't be able to see."

"If a pocket of gas drifts by," she said calmly, "and the entire mining tube explodes, you won't be able to see for the rest of your life, if you survive at all. If that's your choice, then so be it."

Jason dropped the torch. After stamping out the flame, he peered in again, but the darkness made it impossible to see past the bars. "I've come to get you out."

"What?" Her voice spiked with excitement. "Why? Who are you? Your voice is familiar."

"Jason Masters." He fumbled through the keys on the ring. "Your voice sounds familiar, too."

Her voice quivered. "It should, Jason. I am Elyssa."

"Elyssa!" His heart pounded. "So the bear story was a lie after all!"

"Unless you think a bear brought me here for safekeeping," Elyssa said with a tremulous laugh. "How did you find me?"

His fingers shaking, Jason singled out a key and pushed it toward the lock. "I'll explain later." After clinking it against metal twice, it finally entered the hole. He tried to turn it both ways, but it wouldn't budge. "I have the key ring," he explained, "but they didn't tell me which one is the right key, and it's too dark to see them."

After a pause, Elyssa replied, her voice now composed. "When they first brought me here, Prescott unlocked the door with a silver key. It had a round butt end, and the key itself had three square notches at the front and one triangular notch behind them."

Jason began feeling for a key matching that description. "Your memory is amazing, as usual."

"It's important to remember details that might help you later, even the shape of keys."

"I'll try to remember that." Jason ran his finger along a promising key, but it wasn't quite right. "How could you see it if they didn't have a torch?"

"They used a portable lamp. It has no exposed flame."

"I've heard of those. We still don't have them in the commune." Jason unbuttoned the top of his shirt and let the glow of the finger wash over the keys. It wasn't much, but it helped. "I think this is it."

As he pushed the key into the lock, Elyssa spoke again. "Just a warning. I have been in chains ever since I arrived, so I have not bathed. I likely smell worse than the bears that supposedly stole me."

"That won't bother me." Gripping the circular end tightly, he turned the key. Rusted metal screeched, and a loud click sounded. He buttoned his shirt, then lifted the crossbar from its brackets, tossed it to the ground, and jerked the door open. Total darkness masked the interior, and a foul odor assaulted his nose.

"I'm over here, Jason."

Crouching, he scooted toward the sound of clinking chains. "How did you survive?"

"A sentry named Drexel brings me food and water each morning. He told me yesterday of a plan to rescue me. Did he send you?"

"You could say that." He touched a hand and grasped it. "Ah! Here you are."

Elyssa's other hand joined in the clutch, a tight, trembling grip. Chains again clinked as she moved. "Jason, since Drexel sent you, I assume you know about the Underground Gateway."

"I know about the society, if that's what you mean."

"Do you believe the stories about dragons stealing humans and taking them to another world?"

"I didn't until today." He pulled his hand away and fumbled with the keys again. "Do you know what the key to the lock on your chains looks like?"

Like a scientist describing a chemical formula, she rattled off the description. "Square end, two triangular notches in the front, one square notch behind them."

After checking a few keys, his fingers paused on a good candidate. "I think I've got it."

"Good." Elyssa pushed a metallic object against his fingers. "Here's the lock."

Jason slid the key in and turned it. Something clicked. The chains clinked loudly, as if falling to the floor in a heap.

A hand grasped his, and he pulled her up. For a moment, she wobbled in place. "Are you okay?" he asked as he tried to steady her.

"I will be. Just give me a minute."

Jason kept his hand in hers, ignoring her painful squeeze. As she took several deep breaths, each one came back out as a stifled sob. Soon, she settled down and loosened her grip. "Now we have to find our way out of here," she said, her voice assuming a take-charge tone. "Drexel told me that if a rescuer came, we shouldn't use the main dungeon entrance to escape. The guard there is our ally, so we must make it clear that we exited another way. If not, he will be punished severely for not guarding his post."

"I understand. Where is another exit?"

"On the lower level at the opposite side. If we go up the stairs, we should find another descending staircase straight ahead. After we get through a maze of tunnels down there, we'll find the exit gate."

"I heard about that maze. Do you know how to get through it?"

Her voice sharpened. "How would I? I have been in chains ever since I arrived."

Jason sniffed the air. Her comment about not bathing was clearly true. "There's a prisoner on the upper level who says he's here because he's a believer. He says he can help me find the dragon gateway, and he also knows his way through the maze."

"Tibalt?" she asked.

"How'd you know?"

"Drexel mentioned him. He is a believer, but he's as crazy as a loon. He's more likely to stumble over a garden rake than to find the gateway to the dragon world."

"Did he do anything wrong to get locked up in here? I mean, something besides being a gateway believer?"

"Maybe. Drexel didn't say."

"Well, I'd rather have an experienced loon with us than no one at all. Getting lost in a maze wouldn't be a great start."

"Suit yourself, but we'd better get going."

Jason groped for her wrist and pulled her hand against his back. "Hang on to my shirt."

"Got it."

He led the way out of the cell, grabbed the darkened torch, and marched up the sloping corridor. "What's causing the fumes in the air?" he whispered.

"I overheard that one of Prescott's friends found a cavity under the castle that's rich in extane, and they believe it branches out into a matrix of reserves. You know how much our people crave it."

Jason imagined the energy channels in the walls within the castle, a recently invented luxury only the rich could afford. A greater supply would mean cheaper prices for the people and bigger profits for the supplier.

"Anyway," Elyssa continued, "Prescott allowed them to mine it, but only if he got a hefty share of the revenue. Obviously they're doing a messy job, and it's leaking into the dungeon. I hear it's even worse on the other side's lower level."

"So no torch there, either. That'll make the maze even more exciting."

When they reached the top of the stairs, Jason lit the torch and held it close to Elyssa. Dirt smudged her face all the way from her small, rounded chin to her high cheeks to the matted hair covering her forehead. Her longer tresses had twisted into oily brown knots that draped one shoulder, making her look like a beggar in the streets. Her skin had paled from her normal tanned and rosy complexion. Yet her green eyes shone like verdant meadows, giving Jason a glimpse of the fertile mind within. Mother had always said that green-eyed girls were the brightest. The Creator painted their orbs with the color of life.

Elyssa crossed her arms and shifted nervously. "Why are you staring at me? Do I look as wretched as I feel?"

"No, that's not it at all. Considering what you've been through, you look great. I didn't mean to stare. It's just good to see you again."

As she offered a timid smile, he looked at the clothes hanging loosely on her emaciated frame. Her long-sleeved tunic was torn, revealing skin along one shoulder and arm, but her thick riding pantaloons seemed intact. "Are you cold?" he asked.

She rubbed her upper arms. "A little, but it's warmer up here."

"This might help." He pushed the torch into her hand. "You hold it while I find the right key."

When they reached cell twenty, Tibalt pressed his face against the bars, again showing his gap-filled smile. "Ah!

You have come back to old Tibber, have you? You need me to dodge the rats, I'll wager."

Jason tried a key in the lock. "We can't take the torch down the stairs because of a gas leak. Do you think you can find your way through the maze in the dark?"

"Not I, but the rats know the way. I will ask them to lead us. Oh, yes, the rats know the way."

"We'll have to test your rodent-guide theory." After the first key failed, Jason pushed in the second. It turned easily. He lifted the crossbar and leaned it against the wall.

Tibalt shoved the door open and danced on the stone floor with his dirty bare feet. "Old Tibber is free!"

"Shhh!" Elyssa warned. "You'll wake the others."

"No matter," Tibalt said with a laugh. "They're inside, and Tibber's out. They can weep while Tibber shouts."

Jason grabbed Tibalt's elbow. "You'll be quiet, or I'll throw you right back in there."

"And face the rats in the dark? Tibber thinks not. They will eat you for breakfast, be sure of that." He pointed at Jason's nose. "You need the old geezer. Yes, you do."

"Old geezer or not ... " Jason pulled him along as he strode toward the back stairways. "If you want to help us," he whispered sharply, "you'll have to cooperate. We can't have you dancing and singing while we're trying to escape."

Elyssa followed close behind. "I could make a gag, if that would help."

"It might." When Jason reached the stairway, he looked back at her. "Ready to douse the flame?"

"We'll use it while we can. If I see extane sparks, I'll extinguish it."

As they descended the stairs, Tibalt sang out, "Ratty tails and ratty heads, and little ratty noses, watch your feet, or we'll step on your ratty little toeses."

When they reached the bottom, they met a bare wall, black and wet. A dark corridor led to the left and to the right. Jason inhaled deeply through his nose. Nothing except the perpetual mildew and the aroma of two dungeon dwellers. Of course, since extane was odorless, they wouldn't detect it by sense of smell.

"Which way?" Jason asked.

"To the right," Tibalt crooned. "Always to the right. Beware of the left."

Still behind them, Elyssa spoke up. "If that's true, then the maze should be easy."

Tibalt lifted a gnarled finger. "There is one rule that is greater than 'Beware of the left.'"

"What's that?" Jason asked.

Tibalt pointed at a large gray ball of fur in the hall to the right. "Trust the rats."

SIX

The rat scurried into the darkness. "Stay close!" Tibalt called out. The old man crouched low and shuffled away.

Jason gestured for Elyssa to join him, and they walked abreast. Still holding the torch, Elyssa waved it from side to side. Green sparks popped at the edges of the flame, growing louder and more numerous with every step.

"I can feel the extane on my hands," she said.

Jason rubbed his thumb and finger together. "It's kind of oily, isn't it?"

"Yes, it's oily, but I feel its signature. Every element has a fingerprint of sorts, and I can sense it on my skin."

He lowered his voice to a whisper. "Then you really *are* a Diviner."

"You say that like it's a bad thing."

"No, not at all." He glanced at Tibalt, who stooped so low his nose nearly touched the stone floor. "Well, I mean,

I don't think it's the result of a demon seed, but it's not something you'd want everyone to know, especially the priests."

"Trust me. I am well aware of the dangers." She smacked the torch against the wall, killing the fire. "Okay, now it's up to the rats."

Ahead, Tibalt made a chittering sound, as if speaking in a ratty language. It sounded ridiculous, but the noise was easy to follow as he led them through various twists and turns, never pausing for a decision.

Jason opened his shirt again, exposing the finger embedded under his skin. Its glow was dim, painting the air around it a muted yellow, but it provided enough light to illuminate Elyssa's wide eyes.

"You have a key!" she whispered.

He looked down at it. "A key? Tibalt called it a litmus finger, a pointer to truth, or something like that."

"I've never heard it called a litmus finger. I just know that it's part of the history of the Underground Gateway. Ever since I heard Adrian talking to you about the legends, I've been researching it. After I was hired as a laundry maid in the castle, I was able to snoop around and learn a lot. I noticed that every one of Prescott's shirts had a patch of soft velvet sewn in where the material would touch the skin over his heart. I thought it must have been to prevent irritation, so I—"

"The key to the gateway is filled with pure light," Tibalt said in singsong. "It guides you by day and glows in the night. A man who digests it from under his skin can unlock the gateway and venture within."

"That's the Blackstone prophecy," Elyssa said. "Where did you hear it?"

"My pappy taught it to me." Tibalt continued his chittering while blending in words. "Turn left, my ratty friend? Are you sure?"

"Anyway," Elyssa continued, "one day I delivered Prescott's clean laundry to his bedroom. No one was around, so I searched through his private desk and found all sorts of documentation about the Underground Gateway. I got so immersed, I lost track of time, and the head maid found me. She pretended not to care about my snooping, and I went home at the normal hour. But that night, some guards came to our commune and dragged me away." She shrugged her shoulders. "I've been in the dungeon ever since."

"And Prescott faked the bear claw marks," Jason said.

"Drexel told me about that. He's a double agent. Prescott thinks Drexel's infiltrating the Underground Gateway for him, so Drexel couldn't tell people about what happened to me. If that secret got out, Prescott would know who spilled the information."

"Why would Prescott be so interested in the Gateway?" Jason asked. "He's been persecuting its members—it doesn't make sense."

"On the contrary. It makes perfect sense. He's obsessed with finding the gateway. Don't you think having a finger sewn under your skin proves some kind of obsession?"

Jason looked into her sincere eyes. She was still speaking about Prescott in the present tense, as if he were still alive. Maybe it was time to tell her what happened. He touched the edge of the glowing skin. "It's not sewn. It's burned in there. But it wasn't my choice. You see, it was in Prescott's—"

"Explain later," she said, waving a hand. "So I think Prescott is persecuting the fellowship because he doesn't want anyone to find the gateway before he does."

"But why? He can't rescue the Lost Ones by himself. If there really are dragons on the—"

"Treasure!" Barely visible in the finger's glow, Tibalt straightened for a moment. "The dragons collect the delights of their eyes, and silver and gold they pile up to the skies." He crouched again and resumed his slow shuffle through the maze.

"Okay," Jason said. "Prescott's greedy. I can believe that."

"The extane mining already proved his greed." Elyssa rubbed her thumb and index finger together. "And this maze is thick with the stuff. With all the turns, there's no ventilation, so the gas collects in pockets. We'll have to detoxify when we get out of here."

"I thought extane was harmless."

"In small quantities," Elyssa said, "but if you get too much, it can make your heart race so fast it could eventually fail. It's a metabolic intensifier."

"How do we detoxify?"

"We eat the bark of the manna tree. It's a slow healer, but it should work."

Jason licked his lips. A bitter taste coated his tongue. Although extane was odorless, it definitely carried an acrid taste.

"Aha!" Tibalt pointed at a faint light in the distance. "I told you! I told you the rats were our friends!"

"The rear exit?" Elyssa asked.

"I'll find out." Jason drew his sword and skulked toward the light. The air freshened, and the film on his tongue faded. Soon, the source of light became clear, a gate with solid wood bars instead of iron. No guard stood on either side. Had he been called away by Drexel? Or was the security lax here? After all, who would try to break into a dungeon? And any prisoners who escaped from their cells would likely never make it through the maze.

Jason grabbed one of the bars and gave it a hefty shake. Solid. He found a lock and tried a key, but the lock was already disengaged.

He slid his sword back into its scabbard and stared at the gate. Why would they leave it unlocked? It didn't make sense. He quickly tried each key until he found the right one. Taking note of the key's notches, he left the gate unlocked and hustled back to Elyssa and Tibalt. "That's the exit, but it was unlocked."

Elyssa's brow dipped low. "Unlocked? Is Drexel helping us again?"

"I was wondering that, too. And the guard's not there. Drexel's really smoothing the path for us."

Tibalt crooned again in singsong. "A path too smooth is a path to avoid, neither trail nor tongue should you trust. To choose the easy when the path is greasy will turn your lives into dust."

"He's got a point," Jason said. "Could Drexel the double agent be double-crossing us?"

Elyssa's skeptical look deepened. "Why would he lead us this far only to ambush us now? And he knew you had the keys, so he wouldn't have to unlock the gate."

"Another good point. Whoever wants us to march out of here without a hitch must not be associated with Drexel, so we shouldn't take the bait."

"We could set a bait of our own," Elyssa said. "Just to see what's afoot."

"I can hear your brain churning. What do you have in mind?"

She nodded toward Jason's chest. "Does anyone else know you have a litmus finger? Based on my research, it's a key that many greedy people would kill to obtain."

"A few know by now." Jason looked down at his glowing skin again. "So what makes it a key?"

"According to Prescott's notes, it's some sort of genetic material container. It slowly spills the material into someone who puts it under his skin. Over time, that person will become a human genetic key that will allow passage through the Underground Gateway."

"The gateway is genetically locked?"

"Apparently. At least, that's what Prescott's notes say."

Tibalt slapped his leg. "My pappy's a smart one! Oh, yes, he is! He locked that gate, and ain't no one can open it but Pappy himself."

"That was a smart move," Jason said. "But what I can't figure out is why Prescott left papers like that in his desk where any snoop could find them."

"Not just any snoop, Jason. The drawer was protected by a combination lock." Elyssa flexed her fingers near his nose. "I had no trouble sensing the movement of the tumblers."

"Okay. One mystery solved." Jason looked at Tibalt. "You said the litmus finger was a guide to truth and direction. Can we use it now to decide what to do?"

"Not yet." Tibalt rubbed his hands together. "Oooh, it's all coming back to me now. First the finger must be energized. It makes an attachment with you and learns the quality of your character. The more acts of wisdom and heroism you carry out, the more it trusts you. With each act, the color of the light will change, from yellow to orange to red and finally to bright blue, and with each change you will feel its guidance more easily."

"So it was still yellow for Prescott, because—"

"Because he never did a heroic thing in his life," Elyssa said. "He's a selfish egomaniac."

Jason nodded. That was probably true, but it still didn't prove that the litmus finger really worked. "You mentioned setting some bait. What's your plan?"

She took Jason by the arm. "Both of you come with me." She led them back two turns in the maze, ducked into a dark, dead-end corridor, and pushed the torch into Jason's hands. "The extane was densest back one more turn. Light this and throw it around the corner."

"But it might explode before I can throw it."

"That's why you're doing it and not me." In the near complete darkness, the grin on Elyssa's gaunt face made her look like a smiling specter. "It's your code of chivalry, Jason. I know you wouldn't want me to risk lighting it, so I'm skipping the steps where I tell you what I want to do, and then you stop me and insist on doing it yourself."

"Is that a Diviner's trait?"

She nodded. "It annoys my father to no end. I'm always cutting straight to the bottom line."

"Okay. I'll try to remember that." He dug the flint stones from his pocket and strode back toward the dungeon. When he reached the next turn, he stopped and lit the torch. Hundreds of green sparks leaped from the flame and arced to the floor, popping and spitting. With a heave, he launched the torch around the bend and sprinted back toward their hiding place.

A loud *foom* sounded behind him. As soon as he ducked into the alcove, a rush of flames burst past and then shot back, like a dragon's tongue zipping out and in. A loud crash followed. Sand and pebbles fell from the ceiling and pelted their heads.

"Sounds like a collapse," Jason said. "We could get a chain reaction and get buried here."

Elyssa reached up and touched the low ceiling. "No. It's stable."

Loud footsteps echoed, then three men dashed past, too fast to recognize.

"Hurry!" Elyssa grabbed Jason and Tibalt, and all three rushed down the corridor and through the open exit.

Jason slammed the gate. A key ring dangled from the lock, a long, thick key still inserted in the hole. He turned the key, jerked it out, and peered between the bars for a moment. Too bad he couldn't stay long enough to see who had been waiting in ambush. They might have photo guns, and the locked gate wouldn't be enough protection.

After attaching the key ring to his belt alongside the other, he drew his sword and whispered, "Quiet. There might be more."

Now in the forest on the hill's gentle northern slope, Jason led the way down a narrow path illuminated by dappled moonlight. Pine needles silenced their steps, and wind whistled through the swaying trees, further masking their footfalls.

Jason halted and raised his hand. Someone was out there, waiting, watching. No. Two someones. Although they made no sound, Jason's keen warrior's sense raised prickles on his skin. The odor of a man's perspiration drifted in from his left. A slight rise in temperature passed across his skin. A pocket of space in the woods deadened the breeze, an area too big to be filled by one man.

As he lowered his sword and pretended to slide it back into his scabbard, he turned his head but kept his eyes on the spot in the woods. Suddenly, two men leaped out. With swords swinging, one aimed high while the other swung at Jason's legs.

Jason leaped, tucking his body into a ball as he flew between the attackers and slashed the legs of the man on his right. The attacker cried out, and a loud thud punctuated his fall. After a quick somersault, Jason leaped to his feet and flew at the other man. When their swords met in a loud clang, Jason looked at the attacker's face—Bristol, the guard who had stabbed Prescott!

Bristol thrust a knee at Jason's groin, but Jason leaped to the side and sliced into the attacker's calf. He staggered for a moment, apparently not badly hurt, but then suddenly crashed to the ground.

Tibalt took off down the slope like a jackrabbit, while Elyssa stood with a hefty branch clenched in both fists, the top half dangling.

"Thank you," Jason said, bowing.

Elyssa dropped the branch. "Trust me. It was my pleasure."

As the two attackers writhed on the pine needles, Jason stepped toward the first one and pushed him with his foot, shifting his face toward the moonlight. The dungeon guard?

"Why did you attack us?" Jason demanded.

After a pitiful groan, the guard spat out his words. "You know why, you murderer!"

Elyssa's brow knitted. "Murderer?"

"I'll explain in a minute." Jason spun and pointed his sword at Bristol. "So you haven't let your partner in on all the facts, have you?"

With a hand on the back of his head, Bristol scowled. "You will hang from the gallows! We will see to that!"

"Jason Masters!"

Jason turned. Three men stood behind the dungeon entrance, illuminated by a torch. One man shook the bars and yelled, "Don't go with that witch! She will lead you into a trap!"

Jason took a step toward the gate. Viktor Orion? The newly seated Counselor? His usually neatly brushed white hair had flown astray and blew back and forth across his steely eyes and sloping nose. Anger blazed in his red cheeks.

A luxuriously dressed cathedral guard stood on either side. One drew a photo gun and pushed his hand, gun and all, between the bars. A ball of blue flames shot out and blazed by Jason's ear. Like a comet, it streaked into the woods, letting out a shrill whistle until it struck a tree and burned a hole into the bark.

"You fool!" Orion jerked the gunman's hand back through the bars. "I told you he is not to be harmed, and he has our keys!"

Jason pulled the ring from his belt and lifted it. "What am I offered for this means of escape?"

Orion clenched the bar. "I will beg the judge to let you live, and you can have a front row seat to watch the Diviner swing from the gallows."

"Wrong answer." Jason slung the keys into the woods and grabbed Elyssa's hand. "Let's go!"

"Perfect," she said as they ran down the path. "Instead of getting hung, we'll get shot in the back."

"It takes time for the photo gun to recharge, and they'll probably try to shoot the lock first. We need to get as far away as possible."

"Let's hope there's only one gun." Now puffing, Elyssa swung her head from side to side. "Where did Tibalt go?"

"Don't worry. I can find him—after Orion and his guards go back for help. I hope he has the sense to stay hidden."

He slowed his pace and guided her off the path. After trudging into a rain trench, he found a spot where the roots of a huge tree overhung a low, shallow cave. They ducked inside and sat behind the curtain of spindly roots. The moon cast a dark shadow over them, while illuminating the path about a stone's throw away.

Elyssa leaned forward and watched the path. "They'll bring dogs," she whispered.

"No doubt. That's why we have to take off as soon as they leave for the castle. While they're getting the dogs, we'll get the best head start we can."

A peal of thunder rumbled somewhere behind them, and the moonlight faded. The wind picked up and whipped the fallen leaves and needles into a swirl. Light rain pattered the canopy above, and large droplets splashed the ground here and there. Nestled in their cubbyhole, they stayed reasonably dry, but the breeze swept through with a swath of cool, moist air.

Shivering, Elyssa unclasped Jason's cloak, pulled it down his shoulders, and draped it over herself.

"Skipping steps again?" he asked.

Giving him a smile and a wink, she pulled the cloak in close. "I wouldn't be so forward with just anybody, Jason. Just you, Adrian, and my brothers. Remember how I followed you and Adrian like a little puppy until I was eight?"

Jason grinned. "I remember. We didn't mind. We needed a fair maiden to rescue whenever we stormed the sand castles."

She lifted her index finger, barely visible in the dark hideaway. "Do you remember this?"

"How could I forget?" He looped his finger around hers and chanted the verse she had taught him years ago. "We're hooked by these fingers together, as brother and sister forever. Like gander and goose, we'll never break loose, no dagger or dragon can sever."

She pulled her finger slowly away and whispered, "I put *dragon* in there for a reason."

"Because Adrian was already talking about them and getting me interested."

She nodded, and her words floated by like a sad song. "You went the way of the warrior, and I heeded the call of the scholar. We couldn't be more different."

"I guess it was my fault. I should have noticed we were drifting apart. I liked having a sister."

"Well, I always knew you'd be a warrior. Remember what I used to say when we were getting ready to wade across the Elbon?"

"I remember. 'Lead the way, warrior.' And I knew you'd be a scholar. You liked speaking with a formal air. Whenever I asked you a question, instead of 'yes,' you always said, 'By all means.'"

"Those were good days." She hooked her arm around his and sighed. "I feel like they're back. I'm a little girl again, a maiden rescued from a witch hunter."

He looked at her eyes, barely visible in the dimness. "What's that witch talk all about, anyway?"

"Orion is the priest who interrogated my mother and me about my gifts. He was waiting for my sixteenth birthday so he could legally take me and have me examined without my parents' permission."

"Let's see. You're three months younger than I am, so you turned sixteen while you were in the dungeon."

"You have a good memory. It's almost a blessing that I was taken prisoner. Orion must not have known where I was until tonight."

"Right," Jason said. "With Prescott's death, he probably got access to the records and set up the ambush."

"Prescott's death!" Elyssa clapped a hand over her mouth. "Sorry," she whispered. "I get too loud sometimes, but you didn't tell me. Is that what the guard meant when he called you a murderer?"

"Yes, but I didn't kill Prescott. I tried to explain where I got the litmus finger, but you said to tell you later."

"I think now's a good time."

Jason quickly told his story, including details about the excised finger and Drexel's warning that he could never return home without facing prosecution.

"So Drexel wanted the governor dead for some reason," Jason concluded, "but there are too many unanswered

questions. Why the unlocked gate? It gave Orion away.
And when we went out, there was a key in the lock. Why
would they put it in if they knew it was already unlocked?
My guess is that Drexel got wind of Orion's ambush, and
he unlocked the rear gate. It was the only way he could get
a signal to us."

"I recognized the dungeon guard," Elyssa said, "but
who was the other goon who attacked us when we came
out?"

"Bristol, Drexel's henchman, the guy who actually
murdered Prescott. I think attacking us was a ploy to convince Orion that I was the murderer."

"Yes, I see." Elyssa leaned her head against Jason's
shoulder. As she moved, a pendant necklace slipped from
behind her torn shirt.

"I don't remember seeing that," Jason said, pointing at
the swinging pendant.

"It's something my mother made for me." She set her
fingers under it and pushed it closer to Jason. Embedded
in a background of black coral, it looked like a pair of ivory
hands clasped together as if hiding something in their
grasp. "When the priest started questioning me, she was
worried that I would be incarcerated. The hands represent
a prison, and the captive is smothered, unable to taste the
breath of freedom."

She turned the pendant to the other side. The hands
were now open, and a bird was taking wing and flying away.
"This side represents the release of the captive. It signifies
liberty. My mother says that liberty is the Creator's greatest
gift—freedom from slavery to any and all things that keep
us from reaching out to him. So I wear it to remind me that

no matter what happens, even if I have to go to the dungeon, someday I will be free."

She caressed the pendant with a finger. "And it's true. You came and set me free."

Jason gazed at the bird, a white dove with feathery wings spread wide, then looked into Elyssa's eyes. "It's the best thing I ever did."

They leaned their heads together and listened to the sounds of the night—birds, falling leaves, and the sighs of the wind as it passed through the trees. After a minute or so, Orion and his two guards appeared on the forest path. With light rain still falling, Orion waved his arms around and griped at the guards for a few seconds before marching back toward the castle. The guards followed, and soon, the path was clear.

Jason ducked under the roots and, keeping his head low, watched the three men until they disappeared in the darkness. He reached into the alcove and helped Elyssa to her feet. "Now to find Tibalt," he said, "and outrun the dogs."

After hustling back to the path, Jason and Elyssa jogged down the moistened slope and plunged deeper into the forest. Now that they had descended into the valley, the trees were more closely crowded, with lower, thicker branches that blotted out the moon's glow.

Jason stopped, sniffing, listening. "I smell Tibalt," he whispered. "I'm trying to pick up the direction."

Elyssa rubbed her fingertips against her face, smearing the dirt as raindrops drew lines through the smudges. "I sense water."

"Uh … yeah. It's raining."

She shoved him playfully. "I can see that. I mean we're close to a lake or stream."

"You can still sense a body of water, even in the rain?"

"It's more difficult, but, yes, I know there's one around here somewhere."

"Well, your gift is on the mark. Nelson's Creek runs through this valley. Once we find Tibalt, we can use it to our advantage." Jason closed his eyes. Vision wouldn't help now, so it was time to concentrate on the other senses. With the din of pelting raindrops and the swirling wind rustling the trees, hearing Tibalt's breathing or detecting a block in airflow would be impossible.

He took in a deep draw from the cool dampness. Tibalt's odor came from somewhere left of straight ahead. Even in the shifting air, the smell stayed constant, so he wasn't moving. Could he be hiding? If he wasn't hurt, wouldn't he jump out and make himself known?

Drawing his sword, Jason stepped into a stand of thin underbrush, angling away from the path and toward the odor. "Tibber?" he called in a whisper. "Are you out there?"

A quiet moan sounded from beyond a thick tree trunk. Jason dashed toward it and found Tibalt sitting on the other side. The old man had pulled up his torn pant leg and was rubbing his ankle. "Old Tibber can't run like he used to. I was a fox, I was; I could outrun any hound in the kingdom, but now my old legs are as thin as twigs. I tell them to run, but I might as well be asking a crow to sing a lullaby."

Jason touched Tibalt's ankle. "Is it broken?"

"I think not. Twisted, to be sure, but I think I can walk. I thought it better to hide until you showed up. Didn't want Orion to sniff me out with that ferret's nose of his."

Jason helped Tibalt to his feet. "Do you know Orion?"

As he limped back toward the path, Tibalt cackled. "He visited me so often, I accused him of being a door-to-door merchant. I had no money to buy his brooms and no place to sweep the dust." His voice lowered to a tone of mystery. "He asked me questions, many questions about my father and the gateway. He knows, I tell you. He knows it's all true."

"What did you tell him?"

"Why, I told him lies, of course. But I told him many truths, too, just enough to make him believe me. Now he thinks that I am not the son of Uriel Blackstone, but that I still might truly know how to find the gateway. He was to come to see me again today. That's why I was awake when you came through the dungeon. I was working on a new story to tell him. Would you like to hear it?"

"Maybe later."

Tibalt's countenance fell. "It was a doozy. It would have convinced him to let me out for sure."

"And lead him to the gateway?"

"That's what he would think!" Now back on the path with Elyssa, Tibalt pointed at Jason. "But make no mistake. Old Tibber would lead Orion into a pit, and Tibber would be free!"

A hound bayed in the distance. Jason looked toward the castle. The governor's dogs were about a mile away. They would be there in moments.

He touched Tibalt's shoulder. "Do you know the way to Nelson's Creek?"

"Of course. Back in my day, we called it Hornets Creek because of all the hornets—"

"Never mind that." Jason unfastened his cloak from around Elyssa's neck. "Sorry. Safety before chivalry." He rubbed her face and arms with the cloak and did the same to Tibalt. "Now go to the creek, wade into it, and walk downstream in the water. It's shallow enough until you get to where it flows into Elbon River. Another creek runs into the river just a little ways to the left. Walk upstream next to that creek until you see a lumber cabin on the right. You'll have to cross again to get to it, but it should be shallow, too. The workers won't be there at this time of night, so it'll be safe. I'll meet you there."

Elyssa pushed her shoulder under Tibalt's arm. "I'll help you."

As the baying drew closer, Elyssa and Tibalt quick marched down the path and faded into the darkness.

Jason rubbed his cloak on the leaf-strewn path and dragged it to a maple tree. After shinnying up the branches and stopping at a dizzying height, he tied the cloak to a limb and crawled out toward an oak that mingled its branches with those of the maple. The limb bent down, and the wind blew every branch into a tempest.

A thick branch from the oak hung close by, but with both nearly leafless trees swaying, the branch shifted constantly, first jerking up and down and then back and forth.

Jason reached for the oak branch, but it slapped his palm and slipped away. The baying dogs drew closer. Soon he would be in range of a crossbow or a photo gun. He had to make his move.

He stood on the maple limb and leaped for the oak's branch, closing his eyes to protect them from the twigs. As clawlike scratches dug across his forehead and cheek, he grasped the branch with a two-armed vise. It swung down and then back up again, but the swaying soon eased.

He opened his eyes. Below, two bloodhounds sniffed the rain-dampened trail, followed by two men, each holding a leash and leaning back as the dogs strained to break loose. They veered from the path and headed straight for the maple tree. One dog let out a low howl and bared its teeth as it looked up into the branches.

"Can you see anyone?" one of the men shouted.

As the dogs' howls reached a crescendo, both trackers scanned the treetop. The rain increased, forcing them to shield their eyes. Lightning crashed nearby, and an earth-shaking thunderclap rocked the maple.

"Something's flapping up there," the other man said. "Is it a cloak?"

Jason's hands began to slip. He swung his legs up, climbed to a prostrate position, and embraced the branch, now underneath his body. The strengthening gale continued to buffet the branches, tossing him in all directions. Driving rain soaked his clothes, making him heavier and the branch as slick as ice. With his feet pointing toward the trunk of the oak, and his head aiming at the maple, all he could do was hang on and hope.

The first man pointed at Jason's cloak. "Take a shot. He killed your father. You should have the honor."

The other man raised a crossbow to his shoulder, trembling. "But he has had no trial!"

Jason squinted at the two dark forms. *He killed your father? Is one of them Randall?*

"Did he give your father a trial?" the man barked. "Just shoot him! One arrow isn't likely to kill him anyway."

Randall's arrow zinged into the tree and disappeared. "I hit the cloak," he said, "but I can't tell if I hit *him* or not."

The other man pushed a gun into Randall's hand. "Then use this. That'll light up the target."

Randall extended the gun and took aim. A ball of blue flame shot out, its streaming tail wiggling behind it. The ball splashed against the cloak, and, with a loud snap and whoosh, the material burst into flames.

His whole world jumping in rhythm with the branch's dance, Jason hung on and watched. In the midst of fire and loud sizzles, an aura of blue and yellow lit up the tree and the flapping, burning cloak. The dogs, now silent, backed away from the flickering light.

"It's just tied there," Randall said.

"A diversion." The other man pulled his dog farther from the tree, though the rain had nearly doused the fire. "Let's go. It'll be hard to pick up the trail now."

The two trackers lugged their dogs back to the path. With their wet ears flopping as they strained against their leashes, they resumed their desperate howls. After they passed under the oak, the dogs returned to sniffing, apparently picking up a new trail farther away.

As they faded out of sight, Jason slowly pulled his arms from around the branch and grasped it with his fingers as he tried to scoot backwards toward the trunk. Suddenly, lightning struck the oak. Like a blast from a photo gun, a streak of fire shot through the network of branches and sent a jolt through Jason's body. His limbs stiffened. His fingers grew rigid, and he rolled off the limb and dropped.

Branch after branch slowed his fall until he thumped against the ground and rolled sideways to his back, his limbs still rigid and horrific pain shooting from head to toe. Huffing in shallow breaths, he pushed his hand down to his sword, forced his stiff fingers around the hilt, and drew it out.

Needle-sharp raindrops stung his face and drained into his eyes. Mud streamed around his saturated body, so hot from the lightning that vapor rose from his chest. With almost total darkness blanketing the area, he tried to look down the path. Had Randall heard him fall? Or had the thunder and rain drowned out the noise from his plunge?

Blinking away the water, Jason rolled his body to the side. That was better. The wind was now at his back, keeping the rain out of his face, and he could see if the two trackers were returning. At this point, it might be better if they found him. At least Elyssa and Tibber would be safe, and he could get some medical care and maybe escape later ... if they didn't hang him first.

A new streak of lightning flashed, for a brief second providing a glimpse of a lone silhouette coming his way. Lurching again, Jason sat up. His limbs continued to loosen, but every bone felt like it was on fire.

Once more lightning shot across the sky, this time lasting longer as multiple streaks branched out from cloud to cloud. A man drew closer. He seemed to be alone, but it was impossible to tell who he might be.

Bracing himself on one side, Jason pushed himself to his feet. His legs shook like the tree branches, and his heart thumped erratically. Running was out of the question, and fighting didn't seem much better, but it definitely beat swinging at the end of a rope.

In the midst of a series of lightning flashes, the figure finally came into view. It was Randall, his cloak drenched and dripping and his scowl displaying a determination he had never shown before.

"You're alone," Jason said as he raised his sword, fighting to keep the blade steady. "You know you can't beat me."

Stopping out of reach, Randall pulled a photo gun from underneath his cloak and aimed it directly at Jason's face. "Drop your sword."

seven

Koren tiptoed out of her room, leaving the gentle snoring of her fellow slaves behind. Carrying a lantern turned to its minimum setting, she padded through the main living chamber. All was silent. Arxad and Fellina had always been quiet sleepers, not like wicked old Yarwen, Koren's mistress during one of her previous Assignments. She had blasted like a crimped flooter horn all night. And with all the fire she spewed, waking her up for breakfast had been a dangerous game of dodge-the-flames. Yet she had always flown into a rage whenever Koren failed to get her up on time.

After scooting through the exit tunnel, Koren emerged into the cool night air and took in a deep breath. That was the easy part. Now she had to walk into the center of the village, break into the Separators' domain, and look for clues that would reveal the answers to all the mysteries. And she had to do it all without raising any suspicions.

It wasn't unusual for humans to skitter from place to place at night. Some village slaves performed various nighttime duties, like baking bread for morning meals, sharpening axe and saw blades for the next day's lumber cutting or drill bits and chisels for the mines, washing work clothes in the community laundry, and taking care of patients of both species in the village infirmary.

Koren shed her nightgown and wadded it into a loose bundle. The best plan would be to walk confidently, as if she were one of the normal nightshift workers, but would her nightgown be enough to convince anyone that she was hauling a load of laundry? Probably not.

She pulled off her skirt, leaving her with shorts that covered her legs down to her knees, and piled it on top of her nightgown. That should be enough, especially considering how dirty the skirt was.

Since Arxad's cave lay near the edge of the main village, she had to walk up a stony path that led to the massive rocky plateau, the foundation for the enormous structures that housed various dragon functions. The buildings and their entrances had to be big, of course, for dragons to walk or fly through without banging their heads or wings against the doorframes, walls, and ceilings. And the towering structures might be helpful to her cause. Maybe no one would notice a human girl sneaking into a smaller entrance somewhere.

When she reached the plateau, the path smoothed out and widened. Tall buildings loomed in front as well as to her left and right, while one-story edifices nestled in between. A human walked from the butcher shop, carrying a dressed lamb over each shoulder, but he paid her no mind.

As she passed by the Zodiac Cathedral, crisscrossing shadows from its twelve spires darkened her path, cast by the three moons. She shivered. Even though Arxad served there as Priest, and he had always been kinder than most dragons, that place never failed to bring a chill. Every now and then, screams from within its gold-plated walls pierced the night. Sometimes they sounded draconic, sometimes human, but Arxad explained that these were cries of ecstasy from "spiritual transformations."

When she asked for more details about the transformations, he would never answer with anything but "That is not for you to know."

Fortunately, the "transformations" never occurred during triple moons, only on the nights when Trisarian, the single moon with three dark craters, ruled the skies.

A light flickered from somewhere within the Zodiac's deep recessed portico. Someone was at work, studying the stars, their positions, their movements. Was it Arxad? Had he been unable to sleep? It wouldn't be unusual. He often wandered the corridors of his cave and sometimes journeyed back to the Zodiac if something troubled his mind.

She skirted the semicircle garden that acted as a gateway to the infirmary and glanced at the red and yellow flowers, which replaced the usual cacti during these cooler days. Such plants were a pleasant diversion for sick or injured humans staying there. Dragons never kept living plants in their caves. Most didn't care for anything green, except emeralds and green-eyed slaves.

Soon she arrived at the black iron bars that bordered the courtyard leading to the Separators' Basilica. Unlike the

Zodiac, where dragons conducted religious ceremonies, this building housed judges and law enforcement officers, the secular authorities in the land.

She pressed her forehead against two cool bars and peered in between. A semicircular apse lay at the far end of the high-roofed building, the Separators' meeting place where, according to the theories of some slaves, they determined Promotions and many Assignments. Behind that, a lofty dome with a central belfry towered over the rest of the building. The bell inside rang at midday and also whenever a Promotions ceremony had ended. Now it was time to find a way in to see all these mysteries for herself.

"Excuse me, Miss."

Sucking in a breath, Koren spun toward the voice. A tall man stood in front of her, so close, his long scratchy cloak brushed against her bare legs. She looked up at his face, a stern, gaunt face, yet not menacing. Moonlight shone on his bald head, revealing several purplish age spots and a scar along the right side of his scalp.

"Yes?" she said.

"I have not seen you out here before. Have you recently changed Assignments?"

She tried to back away, but the bars kept her in place. "No. I have dirty laundry and—"

"Oh, you are from the slums. I will help you." Before Koren could protest, he slid his arms under her load and pulled it away. "Only two items?" he asked as he lifted her skirt from the pile.

She touched her shirt. "This is dirty, too, so—"

"So you cannot take it off until you get there." His friendly, formal tone glided from his pursed lips. "I understand. Many of the poorer folks have to do the same, which is why males are forbidden to enter the laundry room after dark. I can carry it only as far as the vestibule."

Koren nodded. "Thank you, but I can carry it myself. I—"

"Nonsense. I am the night keeper. It is my duty to help wherever I am able." He walked parallel to the iron bars, away from Koren's home. "My name is Lattimer, and I am on duty thirteen nights and off one, so you must be new, or else I would have seen you." He chuckled. "Unless you go to laundry only once every two weeks."

Koren followed the kindly man. He seemed polished, certainly possessing more education than one might expect from a night keeper. It made more sense to play along than to try to avoid him. She could always return later. "I'm not new. I had a difficult day, so I didn't wash them earlier at my Assignment's cave."

"So you are not from the orphan pool."

Koren cringed. Those words revived so many bad memories. Fortunately, her days in that place were few. There was no way she would ever go back. She would escape to the wilderness first. "I am an orphan," she replied. "But Arxad bought me."

"Ah! I see. But that is no surprise. It is well known that Arxad has a soft spot for orphans. He is the most ... well ... *human* dragon I know."

As they passed by the main gate of the Separators' Basilica, she slowed her pace and scanned the locking mechanism and the dragon guard on the other side of the bars. The keyhole set in the middle of a black metal plate seemed normal, but the dragon was far from normal. With bright, flashing red eyes that followed her as she passed, and powerful wings stretched out to fly, he seemed ready to transform her into a human torch at the slightest provocation.

Lattimer turned. "It is best to march quickly past that gate, young lady. The guardians here are not to be trifled with."

Koren hurried to catch up. When they passed the iron bars and entered a side courtyard, she whispered, "Have you ever been in there?"

"When drugged," he said without looking at her. "I hear that only promoted humans are allowed while in their right mind."

"Have you ever seen a promoted human come out?"

Lattimer stopped and bent over to look at her eye to eye. "Why do you wish to know? Are you on the Promotions list?"

She shook her head. "A friend of mine is."

"I see." After staring at her for a long moment, he looked at the load of laundry in his arms. "You have not come to wash your clothes, have you?"

Pressing her lips together, Koren shook her head. "I'm trying to help my friend." She studied his kind gray eyes. Would he understand? Could she trust him with her story? Maybe if she told it with all the passion in her heart, she could raise some sympathy for her cause. After all, storytelling was her greatest gift, and this night keeper might know some of the secrets of the Separators.

She folded her hands at her waist and rocked back and forth on her feet, altering her voice to that of a little girl. "Can I tell you a story?"

"Most certainly." He nodded toward a bench at the far end of the courtyard. It sat next to a low hedge that encircled most of the yard's stony red surface. "Come. We will talk there."

He strode to the bench and laid Koren's clothes at his side. "Now," he said, setting his hands on his knees, "tell me your story."

Koren took the skirt off the pile, wrapped it around her waist, and fastened it in place. Her legs were chilled, but the real reason for putting it on wouldn't be apparent to Lattimer. It was a crucial prop. Not only would its twirls help with the story's captivating effect, a kind man would be no match for an orphaned waif in a dirty skirt.

She looked up at the three moons. Although their distances from Starlight differed greatly, they arced across the sky in a straight line from one horizon to the other. They seemed to aim three beams right at her, a perfect stage for her tale. As the details raced into her mind, she sighed. This wouldn't be a tall tale. Every word would be true.

She spread out her skirt and offered a curtsy. Lattimer smiled, gave her a nod, and folded his hands in his lap. Apparently he recognized her formal presentation and her position as a raconteur. He was ready to absorb the glow.

Looking him in the eye, Koren stretched out her arms. "I was born to Orson, a stone-mover of courage and integrity, and Emma, a woman of purity, compassion, and inner beauty, who helped him cut the timber to make the rafts upon which the stones would ride. They worked side by side, always in love, and always with patience, even during the hottest of days and under the cruelest of whips."

With a half spin to the side and a twirl of her skirt, she hugged an invisible person. "Orson was my beloved daddy. We played together, sang together, and even danced in spite of the wounds and scars he earned from his labor." As she let her imagination run wild, she saw a man appear in her arms—tall and strong, yet dirty and bloodied. Could this be a long-lost memory of her beloved father?

She pulled back, releasing him, and he faded away. "But, alas, I knew him for only five short years. After losing both legs under a felled tree, my father could no longer move stones, so the dragons cut his rations, and he soon died. Later, the dragons made lovely Emma a ... a ... "

Tears spilled from Koren's eyes as she lamented. "I cannot even say the word. No, no, I cannot. It is too tragic ... too terrible." After wiping her eyes, she took in a deep breath and continued in a steady voice. "Two years later, my dear mother died in childbirth, and I was left an orphan. At the age of seven, I was transferred to a cattle camp where I was put in charge of ten children even younger than I."

She interlaced her fingers and looked at the dark sky. "Oh, Lattimer, it was so awful! The squalor! The hunger! Every night I prayed for help, but every morning I rose from my bed of stone and straw to a new day of torture."

Koren went on, again raising her tone to a lament. "Each day, we gathered smooth stones from a river raft and hauled them in pails while the raft floated along. Then far downstream, we would deposit them back on the raft—useless labor designed to exhaust us. Those stones would then float to the dragon village so the builders could use them for decorating the more opulent homes." Bending over to pluck imaginary stones from the ground, she imagined small children working with her. Like ghosts, they faded in and out as they scooped up stones and threw them into pails. She could hear the sounds come to life in her ears—the flowing river, the plinking of stones in the pails, the grunts and cries of tired children.

She wiped her sleeve across her forehead. "After a brutally hot day, we would be exhausted and hungry. As the blistering sun sank beneath the horizon, the cattle keeper would throw out a few loaves of bread, and like starving rats, the children would rush to the spillings and take what they could, grabbing and clawing, and bigger children would shove the littlest ones away."

As she continued, she acted out every movement, and the characters and scenes appeared to come to life all around her. "Although I was the oldest in our herd, I was neither the biggest nor the strongest, so I was unable to prevent the big boys from stealing the morsels the little ones found at the end of the fracas. I gave them my own scraps and then took a small boy named Wallace into the village, sneaking through a hole in the wall so we could beg for more. Since this little boy was missing an eye, he helped me gain pity for our plight as I told of our woes. I embellished nothing. I merely told the truth with passion and tears, and we were able to gather enough food to survive for another day."

Raising a finger, she lowered her voice to a dramatic whisper. "But my lot in life soon changed. You see, the dragons intentionally fed us too little. Survival depended on size, speed, and cunning. The dragons hoped that the weak and crippled would swoon from the hard labor and lack of food until they perished, leaving the strongest and cleverest among us to thrive so we could be sold to the Traders at a high price."

She shook her hair and opened her eyes wide. "Since I am a green-eyed redhead with a glib tongue, I was sold on the next auction day, so I spent barely a month in the cattle camp."

After letting out a long sigh, she gazed at Lattimer. As he stared at her, entranced, a tear trickled down his cheek. Continuing in a whisper, she looked at the sky and curtsied again, paying homage to the Creator of All. "I prayed for Wallace every night, and I hope that somehow he survived and that my feeble efforts to fill his belly did something more. Perhaps my love applied salve to that wounded orphan's heart and brought light to the darkness in his miserable life.

"And the One who hears my prayers has now given me a great opportunity. As I told you, the Separators have granted that I serve in Arxad's domicile. There I have studied many arts and sciences, including theater and diction, thereby enhancing my gift of storytelling. Yet my newly gained knowledge ignited my curiosity and an insatiable thirst for truth. The legends of our origins now seem no more than mindless chants we sing to toddlers to console their fears at bedtime. Dreams of Promotions have transformed from cool breezes and green meadows to scorching dragon breath as our limbs are broken between the crushing teeth of our masters."

She turned back to Lattimer and lowered herself to her knees. "So here I am, dear night keeper. My friend is being promoted, so I am compelled by forces unseen to find the truth." Closing her eyes, she folded her hands and pressed her lips against her knuckles. "May the Creator of All guide me as I seek the path to enlightenment and the succor that a girl of my age needs in this dark and dangerous world."

She breathed in deeply and stayed quiet, peeking at Lattimer as she waited. For a moment, he sat motionless, his mouth agape. Tears streamed from his wide eyes. "I saw them!" he whispered. "Even as you spoke of your trials, I saw each of your fellow sufferers—your mother, your father, Wallace, the other children. They were like phantoms, transparent, no more visible than a night fog, but as real as love itself, as troubling as pain, and as heart-piercing as a mother's cry of lament."

She straightened her torso but stayed on her knees. "You could *see* them?"

"Like a dream, a mist, a fleeting shadow." As he clenched his hands together, they trembled. "My dear, you are no ordinary girl. You are a Starlighter."

"A Starlighter? I have never heard of that."

He waved a hand at her. "Oh, no, of course you haven't. We haven't had one since long before you were born. Such a person is named after our planet, because he or she is able to tell the tales of history and bring them to life, even as this planet gives rise to history and its soil gives life to the seeds that fall therein. Perhaps it is the pheterone, but something in this world gives shape and color to the vivid thoughts of the Starlighter. Several dragons have possessed this gift in the past, but I have known of only one human Starlighter. The dragons thought her to be dangerous, because her tales enabled her to entrance them, putting them into a hypnotic state."

He reached out a hand and helped her up. "Arise, my dear girl. We will see what succor we can offer."

He picked up the nightgown and looked at the guardian dragon back at the Basilica. "I have seen Maximus scorch a human passerby for simply putting a hand between the bars. He is watchful, and he never sleeps while on duty. During the day, he is relieved by two other dragons of lesser skills, but daylight is a poor time to try to enter with stealth."

Koren looked at Maximus. Even from a hundred paces away, his eyes seemed to pierce her own. "Is there another way to get in?"

Gazing up at the roof of the Separators' building, he shook his head and murmured, "None that I would want to try."

"Maybe *I* would." She took her nightgown back from Lattimer and wadded it under her arm. "I don't want to put you in danger. I'll try to do it myself."

"No, no, that is not my meaning. I was merely thinking about the various possibilities and the fact that the potential openings have access points that would require someone far more athletic and limber than I."

"You mean, the roof?"

"Yes, there are a number of openings up there the dragons use for coming and going, but I cannot imagine how you would scale the walls." Setting his hands on her shoulders, he stooped and glanced around before looking

her in the eye. "Do you understand the consequences if
you are caught?"

"I suppose they would kill me on the spot." She
shrugged. "Then I could be with my parents again."

"No, my dear. You are too young to remember this,
but Cassabrie, another young lady not much older than
you, entered a dragon domain without permission. The
dragons tied her to a crystalline stake within the Zodiac
and commanded people to pass by to watch her suffer.
Barely out of reach of the sympathizers, she stood with
her hands and feet bound, baking in the sun. The dragons
gave her just enough water to survive, but not a scrap of
food. Day after day, she moaned in pain. She begged for
death to come and end her agony. After thirteen days she
finally died, literally cooked in the brutal heat of our hottest
season."

Koren shuddered, and her bravado wilted. Even
though the punishment couldn't be the same during the
cooler season, such a cruel mind could easily think of an
equally painful way to put a new intruder to death. She
swallowed and looked into Lattimer's sincere eyes. "I'm
willing to risk it. I have to ... for Natalla."

"Natalla?" He cocked his head to the side. "Natalla, the
girl at exams this evening?"

"Yes! Yes, she was there!"

Lattimer pointed at himself. "I was the examiner for
this evening's students. I am quite fond of Natalla. She is
far more intelligent than the results of her exams would
indicate. I was hoping to be given permission to tutor
her."

"But she's getting promoted."

"Oh, yes, of course. Back to your purpose." He stroked his chin for a few seconds before continuing. "Why would they promote an underachieving student?"

"That's exactly my question! I have to find the answer."

"The answer might be quite simple. They could be thinking she is hatched from the black egg."

Koren pointed at him. "And that's another mystery I want to solve. Is that prophecy really going to happen?"

"The black egg?" His brow wrinkled tightly. "Dear child, let us hope not!"

"What's wrong with a weak hatchling turning into a great dragon king?"

He patted her on the back. "I suppose your textbooks never quoted Tamminy's rhyme. It is frightening, so I hesitate to tell you."

"If I'm going to risk getting past Maximus, I think I'm ready to hear a bard's tale."

"Very well, but this will not be an exact rendering. I took the liberty of translating it to our language, so the rhyme, meter, and lyrical choices are rather suspect. In fact, *dreadful* might be a better description." Lattimer cleared his throat and spoke the verse in singsong.

An egg of ebon, black as coal,

Will bring about the dragons' goal.

The dragon rising from its shell

Will overcome a deadly knell.

Though weak and crippled at the start,

Its strength begins within its heart.

Above all others it will soar,
And dragonkind will all adore.

Its virtue, might, and crown will rest
Upon a head of nobleness.
Then humans far and wide will flee
In fear of coming jubilee.

For paradise begins that day;
All labors cease and turn to play.
And slaves become like needless mites,
Unfit to stay within our sight.

So drown the vermin, cook their meat
And scatter bones upon the street.
When every human life is spent
The age of vermin truly ends.

In honor of this treasured hour,
We celebrate this dragon's power.
The dawn of paradise will bring
An age of peace beside our king.

Lattimer shook his head. "I told you it was dreadful."
"It *is* awful, but I doubt that you had much to work
with." Koren let the verses flow through her mind again.

As a lover of words, she had always been able to memorize almost anything in an instant, and bringing back lovely songs was usually a pleasure, but these lyrics were different. Although most of the prophecy seemed virtuous and promising, at least to dragons, the fifth quatrain spewed venom and malice, as if the bard had transformed from a seer of sunlight to a diviner of doom.

"How old is that prophecy?" she asked.

"Oh, I do not know exactly. Does it matter?"

"Some legends say humans came to Starlight from another planet. If we were brought here only a hundred years ago, the prophecy can't be older than that."

"And that is one reason to dismiss those legends about our origins. The black egg prophecy is at least a thousand years old. The truth is humans were created here on Starlight many centuries ago, and we have been slaves to dragons ever since. There is no other world. It is a myth designed to provide hope for deliverance from our suffering."

Koren looked at the ground. Lattimer's words stabbed deeply, the truth a sword that punctured hope.

Not a day had passed without a thought about someday escaping to Darksphere—the human planet—and living at peace with the progeny of her ancestors. But now those dreams had been dashed forever. Lattimer and Madam Orley had shown they really were hopeful myths she would have to leave behind.

Trying not to cry, she turned toward the Basilica. "So how do I get in?"

"I will tell you where to find all the access points, but after all you have learned are you still willing to take the risk?"

"If I'm caught, maybe I can use my gift to hypnotize them."

"A reasonable idea. I can provide some words that should help you charm Maximus." He raised a pair of fingers. "Yet there are two problems. First, you have barely learned how to use your talent, and second, the other Starlighter attempted a similar hypnotic scheme, and her execution was brutal."

"You mean … "

"Yes. Cassabrie was the other Starlighter."

eight

Jason forced his limbs downward, lowering his sword. He couldn't let Randall know that the lightning had practically frozen his joints in place. "You'll get only one shot, Randall. If you miss, you're dead. If you let me go, we'll both stay alive."

As rainwater dripped from the photo gun's barrel, Randall spat out his words. "You killed the governor! My father!"

"No!" Jason shook his head. "He was already dead when I found him! Drexel and Bristol conspired to kill him and blame me!"

"Bristol?" Randall lowered the gun a notch. "He's the one who told me *you* did it. He came out here with me and the hounds. He showed me an ugly cut on his head where he says you hit him. He couldn't have put it there himself."

"Elyssa hit him with a branch just a little while ago, while we were trying to escape."

"Elyssa? I thought she was—"

"Kidnapped by mountain bears. That story had a lot of holes, and you know it."

Randall stood still. Lightning flashed, framing his drenched body. "I ... I don't know."

"Think about it, Randall! As much as you hate me, you know I'm not a murderer."

The gun eased down another fraction, but Randall kept a finger on the trigger, saying nothing.

"Where is Bristol now?" Jason asked.

Randall gestured with his head. "He said he'd meet me at the river. Told me to come back and check the dungeon gate. He thought it might have been left unlocked."

Now yelling through the heightening storm, Jason took a slow step forward. "He's not worried about the gate, Randall. He just doesn't want witnesses when he executes me without a trial. He and Drexel set me up—they wanted to cut the genetic material out of your father's skin, but they needed a scapegoat who would be blamed for the murder, someone Elyssa would trust and who would spring her from the dungeon so she could use her knowledge and gifts to divine her path to the gateway."

"So Elyssa really is a Diviner? Orion was right?"

Jason nodded and blew rainwater from his lips. "Elyssa is on the run. If I don't show up, she'll just keep searching for the gateway, thinking I'll eventually meet her there. So Bristol will follow her. Drexel thinks he can use the genetic material to get through—"

"Aaugh!" Randall lunged forward and fell on his face, an arrow protruding from between his shoulders.

Another arrow zinged past Jason's nose. Ignoring his still-protesting joints, he hunched low and searched for the source. Bristol had to be close by. Since Randall had failed to carry out the execution for him, he likely planned to terminate Randall as well and pin the blame on the scapegoat.

A third arrow flew well over his head. Apparently Bristol didn't know where his target lay hidden.

Crawling on his belly with his sword in hand, Jason eased up to Randall and whispered, "Are you all right?"

Randall heaved a breath. "That no-good scoundrel. I'll have him disemboweled!"

"Shhh! Don't give him a target." Jason wrapped his fingers around the arrow's shaft. It wasn't deep at all, maybe only an inch or so. He sheathed his sword and whispered, "I'm breaking it off. We can take it out later."

Clenching his teeth, Randall nodded, his cheek flat on the water-logged path.

Jason snapped off the shaft and grasped Randall's arm. "Let's get under cover. I'll help you."

The two crawled off the path and into the forest under-growth. Pulling on Randall's arm, Jason had to claw the muddy slope to make any progress. After a minute or so, Jason hoisted Randall to his feet, and, still clutching his arm, led him deeper into the forest.

When they were well out of Bristol's earshot, Jason stopped and looked at Randall. Only the occasional flash of lightning allowed him to see the young man's wet and muddy face.

"Listen," Jason said. "I'm really sorry about your father, but I had nothing to do with it."

His face a knot of emotions, Randall nodded. "But what do we do now?"

"Find Elyssa before Bristol does. Now that he couldn't kill me, he might try to kidnap Elyssa instead of just following her. The dogs will probably track her down, so we have to hurry."

"I didn't hear any barking when he sneaked up on us," Randall said. "He must have tied them up somewhere, but he'll have them again soon. We'll never track Elyssa better than those hounds, especially in the rain."

"Except that I know where she went." Jason lifted the point end of his scabbard. "Hang on to this. I'll try not to go too fast."

Another flash of lightning lit up Randall's determined face. "Just go. I'll keep up."

Jason marched across the slope. This wasn't exactly familiar territory, but he and Adrian had worked on positional reckoning for so long they both had become virtual human compasses. All he had to do was keep heading northeast, and he would eventually meet the stream, probably just before the point where it fed the river. For some reason, in spite of the cold, lack of sleep, and a lightning strike, strength flowed through his muscles. His limbs were still stiff, but they were strong. Maybe the extane had affected him after all. His heart was thumping so fast it seemed almost out of control.

The slick mud made for slow-going, but soon the rain eased, and the moon peered through the thinner clouds. With gusts still bending the treetops, the forest looked alive—branches shaking, leaves and needles flying around, and droplets sparkling in the moonlight. Running through the gaps felt like a dash through a gauntlet. Flashes of lightning in the distance added to the effect, providing split-second glimpses of grabbing fingers and spinning debris.

When they finally reached the creek, Jason stopped at the edge and looked around. With the moon now fully exposed, various landmarks came into view—a familiar boulder in the creek bed, a gall on a tree trunk, a fallen log covered with moss. Their location was clear. The Elbon River flowed only a few hundred paces downstream.

Dogs bayed somewhere in the darkness, maybe twice that distance in the opposite direction. Jason pulled Randall and waded into the creek. Although it was swollen well above normal and running swiftly past his feet, they would have to do something drastic to outrun the dogs.

"Can you swim?" Jason asked.

"Normally, yes." Randall flexed his back and grimaced. "But I haven't done much swimming with an arrowhead in my back."

"We can ride the current. When we get near the Elbon, I'll try to signal you. We have to get to the bank on the left, or we'll get swallowed alive. The Elbon will be wild after this storm, and if we get swept into it, we won't stand a chance."

"I understand."

"It's tough swimming with boots on." Jason pulled off his boots and tossed them into the woods. Maybe that would delay the dogs a few extra seconds. Besides, tying them to his belt would make them too much of an anchor.

As soon as Randall shed his boots, Jason waded in up to his waist. The water was freezing. It knifed into his rigid muscles. When Randall joined him, Jason turned to float on his back with his feet pointing downstream and let the current pull him along.

Within moments he and Randall were hurtling downstream side by side. Water splashed over Jason's face, sometimes covering his mouth and nose, but, waving his arms for balance and sucking in air whenever he could, he managed to stay afloat. Randall flailed at times, but he kept his face above the surface.

Looking ahead every few seconds, Jason caught glimpses of the countryside—mostly rolling hills with forested tops. The old hangman's tree would be the best place to start moving to the bank. Since it was at least two hundred paces from the Elbon, they would have plenty of time before reaching the river, and if the rope was still attached, he might be able to grab it and use it to swing toward the bank.

Soon the long branch of a gnarled tree came into view, hanging over the creek with the old rope dangling near the end. Jason held his breath. Could he grab Randall and the rope at the same time?

He grasped Randall's wrist and lunged for the rope, but as he wrapped his fingers around the wet line, Randall slipped away and continued hurtling toward the Elbon. Ahead, the creek turned into a raging torrent, and Randall disappeared beneath the white-capped water.

"Randall!" Jason jumped back into the flow and swam with all his might. Surging waves pummeled his body and shoved him from side to side, but, fighting both the current and his own stiffness, he pressed on. Again, his muscles responded to the call, an unnatural explosion of energy.

He soon bumped into something and grabbed hold. It was a body, cold and limp. Jason wrapped his arms around Randall's chest and stretched his stiff legs downward. Nothing but water—the creek bottom was out of reach. Time to swim for it.

Holding Randall as high as he could, Jason thrashed his free arm against the current, thrusting his body toward the bank with all his might. Finally, his toe touched bottom. Digging in with both feet, he trudged ahead, lugging Randall through the torrent. When he slogged up to the muddy shore, he laid Randall on his side, dropped to his knees, and pressed his fingers against Randall's neck, feeling for signs of life.

Rapid thumps throbbed against Jason's fingertips. *A pulse! He's alive!*

Randall shivered hard. He opened his eyes and choked out, "I hear the dogs!"

"Let's move!" Jason helped Randall to his feet and pulled him away from the raging stream. "We have to get into the woods. They probably can't swim across, but we're in arrow range."

Stiff-legged, they lumbered across a grassy expanse and into a forested area. Although the trees were relatively sparse, a thick trunk would likely shield them from Bristol.

Jason chose a hefty tree and helped Randall lean sideways against the trunk. "How's the arrow wound?"

Randall took in a deep breath and let it out slowly. "Pretty numb right now. I think cold might kill me before that arrow will."

"It's freezing." Jason peered around the tree. Although there was no sign of Bristol, the baying of hounds drew closer. "I know a place where we can get warm, but I have to be sure you believe me, that you're on my side."

Randall shivered harder than ever. "I know you didn't kill my father. The arrow in my back is proof enough."

"There's more to it than that." Jason looked into Randall's eyes. He was in a lot of pain, both physically and emotionally. Only a couple of hours ago, he lost his father to a cowardly murderer, and now he was running for his life. Although he wasn't a friend or even a great guy to be around, it didn't make sense to hide the truth from him. He needed to know why his father was killed.

Taking a deep breath to ward off his own chill, Jason whispered, "Do you believe in the Underground Gateway?"

"That old fairy tale?" Wrinkling his brow, Randall shook his head. "Of course not."

"I know what you mean," Jason said, laughing under his breath. "I didn't believe it for a long time."

Randall squinted at him. "*Didn't* believe it?"

"Right." As the hounds drew closer, Jason pulled open his shirt, revealing the patch of skin, now glowing orange. "Bristol cut this out of your father's chest."

Randall's eyes shot open. "What?"

Glancing back and forth between Randall and the flooded creek, Jason related the story in rapid-fire fashion, trying to include enough to make Randall believe him without dragging out every detail. They had to hurry to the cabin and find Elyssa.

As Jason finished, Bristol came into view on the opposite bank. The dogs howled and strained at the leash, but he held them in check as he surveyed the churning water.

Jason crouched and lowered his voice to a whisper. "He's here, but I don't think he's going to cross. Are you with me or not?"

"If you'll get me someplace warm, I'll believe anything."

Jason helped him up. "Slowly and quietly." Staying low, he tiptoed deeper into the forest, but when he looked back, Randall was standing at the tree looking at his photo gun.

Jason hustled back to him. "Don't be an idiot. Just put it away and we'll worry about it later. We have to—"

An arrow whizzed by Jason's chin. He jerked Randall's cloak. "Let's go!" Pulling Randall along, he hurried into the woods as fast as his frozen legs would carry him. He veered right. The other stream had to be in that direction. It was normally shallow and calm, but what would it look like after this storm?

With the moon giving them plenty of light, he followed a narrow deer path. Sounds of running water coming from various directions competed for his attention. The loudest sound was likely the Elbon, so that provided a point of reference. *Just stay to the left of that rush and follow the quieter one that seems to be coming from somewhere straight ahead.*

He looked back. Randall followed, quiet as a whisper. They had both been trained in stealthy travel, but this was the first time either had put that instruction to use in real life. Failing this exam might be deadly.

After breaking out of the forest again, Jason stopped at the creek. Although it flowed much faster than usual, it seemed shallow enough. He gestured for Randall to follow and charged across. The water rose to his knees, as frigid as Nelson's, but tolerable.

When both splashed up to the creek bank, Jason cupped a hand around his ear. The dogs howled, but they were now far away. "There's a cabin somewhere nearby. If I know Elyssa, she's already started a fire."

"Won't that signal Bristol?" Randall asked.

"Eventually. I doubt he can cross. He'll be back when the water ebbs, but we should have time to get warm and dry before we get going again." Jason sniffed the breeze. A hint of wood smoke flavored the air. "We're still downstream. Not far, though."

After a few minutes, the cabin came into view, a one-story log structure with a steeply angled tin roof. Smoke curled from a brick chimney, and lantern light glowed from a single window.

As Jason approached, a pair of shadows moved within. An old wooden door creaked open, and Elyssa appeared in the gap. She leaned out and stared into the darkness. "Who's out there?"

"It's me. Jason."

"Jason!" She ran out and embraced him. "I thought you might have been caught!"

"Careful," Jason said, pulling away. "I'm soaked."

Elyssa shook water from her hands. "I see that."

"And Randall's here, too," Jason said, nodding toward the darkness behind him.

Randall emerged from a shadow and smoothed out his wrinkled, wet clothes. "Hello, Elyssa."

"Oh!" Elyssa averted her eyes. "Well ... I ... I assume Jason has convinced you of the truth."

"I know he didn't murder my father, if that's what you mean."

She looked at Jason. "What have you told him?"

"Pretty much everything."

A flash lit up the sky, and thunder rumbled loud and long. Elyssa lifted a hand and rubbed her thumb and fingers together. "More rain. Maybe a lot of it."

Jason set a hand on Elyssa's back and guided her through the doorway. "Give us a chance to get dry, and I'll tell you what's going on. If another storm's coming, I don't think Bristol will be able to find us anytime soon. We also have to get an arrowhead out of Randall's back. It's not a deep wound, but it needs care."

Inside, the logger's cabin was warm and well lit. Tibalt knelt close to a blazing fireplace, poking the flames with a long stick. With his eyes wide and his mouth open, he seemed hypnotized.

Knotty shelves lined the log walls and held a variety of basic supplies—bags of potatoes, dried fruit, two old axes, ropes hanging on hooks, bandages, soap and towels, and several lanterns with vibrant flickering wicks. A gray towel hung from a hook, and bubbles coated a bar of white soap.

Jason looked at Elyssa. Her face and hair were clean, as were her clothes. She wore an oversized lumberjack shirt with dark blue squares outlined in black, and men's black work trousers tied at her undersized waist with a rope.

Since there were no chairs in the single-room cabin, Jason knelt next to Tibalt. He, too, was much cleaner. Even his shoulder-length gray hair was brushed back neatly, revealing a bald spot on top of his head.

"We have shirts and boots," Elyssa said. "I'll get them for each of you. And I found a manna tree. Tibalt and I have already eaten some bark, so our bodies have settled down."

Jason felt his chest. His heart still raced, thumping erratically. "I think the extane helped me escape, but I don't think my heart can stand much more."

Randall stood close to the fire and warmed his hands while Tibalt muttered, again using his singsong cadence as he watched the flames.

"A storm beyond the norm, a flood of mud, a flood of blood, the traitors swarm. To flee the tide, see the guide, find the gate and fly inside. The storm transforms, the key is thee, depart this land and set them free."

When Tibalt's murmurings faded, Jason touched his arm, now covered with the sleeve of a dark green shirt. "What were you chanting?"

Tibalt looked at him, his face and eyes somber. "A prophecy. My pappy's words."

"What storm? The rain we're getting now?"

"Oh, no, not that. The rain brought back the memory. It is a storm of oppression, I think. Elyssa told me the story, and what a story! The governor's murder is just the beginning. You'll see, I tell you. You'll see. His killers don't want to end Prescott's folly — his control of the people and his lust for money. They mean to usurp his seat of madness and extend his reach. Oh, yes, that they do. They will tighten the talons around the throats of the citizens and deepen the pit of despair."

Jason glanced at Randall. His jaw tightened, but he kept his stare on the flames and his voice silent. What might the governor's son be thinking now? Did he know deep down that his father was a tyrant?

"What can we do to help?" Jason asked.

Tibalt's familiar grin returned, missing teeth and all. "Tibber knows only the songs, not the solutions. My pappy made puzzles, and the pieces are scattered."

Elyssa tossed a shirt and a pair of boots each to Jason and Randall. Jason set his on the floor while unbuttoning. When he peeled off the wet material, the glow of the litmus finger was obvious over his pectoral as it pulsed reddish-orange.

"Ah!" Tibalt said. "You have completed a heroic act. You will soon feel the litmus finger's guidance."

Elyssa stared at Jason but said nothing. He threw on the dry shirt and quickly buttoned it. "Guidance is good," he said softly. "I'll be watching for it."

"I think I saw a medical bag somewhere," Elyssa said. "We should get that arrow out right away."

Elyssa used a carving knife to open Randall's wound just enough to withdraw the arrowhead. He bled, but not dangerously so. Although he grunted and tightened his fists throughout the procedure, he stayed calm. Obviously his warrior training had paid off. Elyssa placed a towel over the wound to soak up the blood, wrapped a long bandage around his chest, and tied it in place.

Once all four had settled on the plank floor near the fire, Jason munched on manna bark while relating their escape story, including what he knew of Drexel's scheme to kill Prescott. When he finished, he looked at Randall, who had listened quietly.

"So," Jason said, "what do you think Drexel is planning?"

Randall stared at the floor, his face tense. "He's such a smooth talker, I had no idea he was involved. He took me to my father's body and showed me the bloody knife. He said, 'Jason cut a holy relic out of your father's chest, something that will lead him to the Underground Gateway. We have to catch him and bring him to justice before he escapes to the dragon world.'

"With all the blood around and with my mother crying her heart out, I was enraged, so I didn't think to ask him to prove it. I just thought about the trick you pulled in the tournament and that you'd do anything to get what you wanted."

Jason fidgeted. "Yeah, well, about that trick—"

"Let me finish." Randall's voice took on a hardened edge. "I didn't hear much of Drexel's speech after that, but Bristol spilled more information later. He kept mumbling about following Elyssa, so after what you told me, I think he and Drexel were using me to kill you and chase Elyssa to the gateway. Once they found it, they planned to kill us both."

"But why kill you? You believed them."

Randall looked straight at Jason. "According to the law, because of my father's death, I would become governor when I reach eighteen. Counselor Orion would rule as a steward until that time."

"Aha!" Tibalt said. "They waited until Orion's invocation night to do the deed. I should have guessed that old fox was behind the scheme."

Elyssa shook her head. "I don't believe it. Orion's a crusader, not a politician."

"She's right," Randall said. "It's Drexel's plan. If you had been there listening to him, you would know. He's definitely the mastermind."

"How could he benefit?" Jason asked. "He's not in any line of succession."

Tibalt raised a finger. "Power. Influence. Stature. He is a believer in the portal, and Jason and Elyssa were his tracking hounds. If Drexel could rescue the Lost Ones, he would be the hero of heroes. And you know what happens to the law when a crowd gets worked up to a fevered pitch."

Jason gestured with his thumb. "They pitch the law out. Then Drexel would humbly and reluctantly accept leadership."

"And Orion wouldn't fight it," Elyssa said, pointing at herself. "He's in this to get me. Drexel knew where he and Prescott were hiding me, so he relied on Orion's obsessions and set up this deal. Once Drexel returned with the Lost Ones, Orion would step down and give Drexel the office."

Jason nodded. "And Orion watches you burn at the stake while you rave about a portal to the dragon world. Almost everyone will believe you're bewitched, and Drexel and Orion both get exactly what they want."

As a new downpour pelted the tin roof, the group fell silent. It seemed that a dark blanket had smothered their souls. They were animals being tracked, yet they couldn't run. Rain, wind, and darkness would be deadlier enemies than Bristol's dogs and arrows.

After a while, they doused the fire and the lanterns, leaving the glow of dying embers as the only light in the room. Using towels as pillows, the four lay close to each other for warmth and tried to sleep. Jason woke at every unusual sound—a branch falling on the roof, an ember popping in the fireplace, and Tibalt's occasional snore or indecipherable chanting. With each awakening he clutched the hilt of his sword, still at his hip, and opened his shirt slightly to try to pierce the darkness with the finger's glow. Fortunately, the pattering on the tin above drowned out the lesser noises.

The constant din of rain felt like a blanket of protection. As long as the creeks ran high, Bristol would be unable to find the cabin. Of course, he could travel on horseback to the bridge at the Tersot commune and double back upstream. But then he wouldn't be able to bring the dogs, unless he used the covered buggy and walked after crossing the bridge, but that would take him all night.

Soon a dim light eased through Jason's eyelids. He blinked them open. The glow of a cloudy dawn filtered into the window, and the comforting sound of rain on tin continued to drum through the cabin. He rose to a sitting position. Elyssa lay next to him, curled in a fetal position with a towel clutched to her chest. Tibalt and Randall now slept nearer the fireplace, though it had lost its heat hours ago.

Jason shivered. Something was wrong, and not just the chill of a rainy morning. Something stalked nearby. An odor hung in the air, an odd smell—foul and earthy. It wasn't unusual to sense these subtle clues, but they seemed stronger this morning, as if every smell and sound—every sense—had been magnified.

Windblown rain pelted the window and plastered a wide leaf against the glass. A shadow crossed a tree trunk, no more than ten paces from the cabin.

Rising slowly, Jason hissed. "Randall! Get your gun ready."

Randall struggled to his feet, wincing as he raised his photo gun. "What is it?"

"I think it's a mountain bear." Jason nodded at Randall's shaking arm. "The pain must be pretty bad."

"I can handle it." Randall used his thumb to turn a dial on the gun's grip, watching it expectantly. After a second or two, he shook his head. "It's not energizing. I have to take it apart and dry everything out."

Jason drew his sword. "No time for that. Get Elyssa and Tibalt up. We might have to make a run for it."

Randall crouched and nudged Elyssa and Tibalt. "Why can't we stay here? That door's too small for a mountain bear to get through."

"Trust me," Jason said. "He can make it bigger."

Whispering the danger to Elyssa and Tibalt, Randall helped them to their feet.

"A mountain bear?" Elyssa asked. "Jason, how many have you fought?"

"Exactly zero." Lowering his head, Jason skulked toward the door. "A few weeks ago, Adrian and a friend were in a cave looking for you, and a bear trapped them inside. It's a good thing they were together. Adrian says one swordsman is no match for a full-grown mountain bear."

A rough grunt sounded from outside, followed by a loud growl.

"We should escape through the rear door," Elyssa said, "but which way should we go?"

Tibalt pointed at himself. "I know the way to the boundary from here, but my legs are too old to outrun such a beast."

Jason nodded at the axes propped on a wall shelf. "Tibber, get an axe for Randall. We can try to wound the bear and then make a run for it."

Tibalt leaped for the axe and pushed it into Randall's hands. "Here you go, young'un."

Randall shook his head. "I've never used an axe before. I'm better with a sword."

"Did you miss axe class?" Jason asked.

"I thought I wouldn't need it."

"You thought wrong!" Another growl erupted from outside, deeper, closer. With a glare, Jason shoved the sword at Randall and snatched the axe out of his hands. "Okay," he said, waving at Elyssa. "You and Tibalt get to the rear door."

A loud thud shook the cabin. The window shattered. Rain and wind rushed in, brushing back Jason's hair with a wet slap. He set his feet. Randall did the same, both with double-fisted grips on their weapons.

Another thud sounded, then a crash. The door burst into a thousand splinters. Jason lowered his head to avoid the shards but kept his axe high. A bear stood at the doorway, but only the lower two-thirds of its body were visible. As it tried to squeeze through the door, its powerful body cracked the frame, revealing its shoulders and head.

Jason waved at Elyssa. "Go! Now!" He charged with the axe, ducked low, and swung at the bear's legs, but it slapped him with a claw. Jason flew to the side and slammed against a wall. The flat of the axe blade struck his forehead and slid down his cheek.

The bear burst through and, still standing on his hind legs, let out a guttural roar that sounded like, "Fool! I stronger!"

Randall raised the sword. "We'll see about that!"

"No!" Jason shouted. "He's too—"

Randall lunged, but the bear dodged, knocked the sword loose, and wrapped him up with its massive forelegs. As it squeezed, Randall's eyes bulged, but he didn't cry out. He probably couldn't breathe at all.

Gripping the axe again, Jason stood, but a wash of dizziness made him stagger. He sucked in a breath and set his feet. "Let him go!" he yelled.

As the sound of baying dogs drifted in on the rainy breeze, the bear let out a throaty laugh and a new sequence of growls that sounded like, "Or what?"

Jason glanced at the open rear door. No sign of Elyssa or Tibalt. Would the dogs track them down? He trained his stare again on the huge beast. "Or I'll crack your skull open with this axe."

The bear's forelegs clamped down. Randall's face turned from red to purple, and his legs dangled limply. "My prisoner," it growled.

Jason glanced from Randall to the bear, to the sword next to its foot, to the rear door, then finally to one of the shelves. Maybe he could throw one axe and attack with the other. He scanned the shelf, but the other axe was gone.

A scream pierced the air. The bear lurched forward, an axe protruding from its back, the blade deeply embedded. It dropped Randall to the floor, and, as it roared and staggered around, it swatted futilely at the axe handle.

Jason leaped up and hacked at a foreleg, but the bear spun away and slapped him again, sending him flying toward the broken doorway and into Elyssa's arms.

With water dripping from her hair, she propped him up. "We have to help Randall!"

"I'll get him!" Tibalt called from outside. He slipped past them, grabbed Randall's ankles, and dragged him to the doorway. Randall sat up and leaned against the wall, groggy but apparently okay.

The barking drew closer, probably only minutes away. While the bear continued to bellow and reach for the axe, Jason picked up the sword and shouted, "I can relieve your pain in one of two ways. If you agree to help us, I will remove the axe and help you bind the wound, or I can stab you through the heart and end your suffering forever."

The bear stopped and glared at him. His growl-speech seemed clearer now. "What help do you need?"

"Get the dogs off our trail. Take our clothes and drag them on the ground to a place far from the creek."

With blood dripping down its back, the bear studied Jason for a long moment before nodding. "Pull axe."

"Can you trust a bear?" Randall asked. "He could just turn on us."

"Trust the bear!" Tibalt said. "They're mean, ornery, and bloodthirsty, but they're as honest as the day is long."

Jason nodded at Elyssa. "Get another bandage ready."

She scurried past the bear and scooped up a towel and the remaining bandages from the shelf. As she tied the strips together, the bear dropped to a sitting position.

Jason grasped the axe handle and yanked it out. The bear let out a wordless roar. Blood drained in a network of channels down its hairy back.

Elyssa pressed a towel on the wound. "Jason, hold this here while I tie it in place."

As he held the towel, Jason listened to the approaching dogs. They were definitely getting louder. "Better hurry."

"We have to make sure this fine bear survives," Elyssa said as she stretched the bandages around the bear's chest. "I think he came here looking for shelter from the storm and assumed we were hunters."

The bear looked at her. "Woman not hunter. Men hunters."

"Not these men," Elyssa crooned. "The man with the dogs is the real hunter."

A menacing growl emerged from the bear's throat. "Hunter die."

When she finished, she wadded the discarded clothes and set them in front of the bear. "If you rip these and drag them away, perhaps the hunter will think you killed us."

The bear picked up the clothes in his nimble forelegs, rose to his hind feet, and walked through the door. Blocking the wet breeze for a moment, he looked back and nodded but said nothing.

As soon as he left, Jason sheathed the sword and grabbed both axes. He gave one to Tibalt. "This might come in handy. I'll carry the other one."

Elyssa helped Randall to his feet. "Can you walk?"

"Yeah. I think so."

"He has no choice," Jason said. "He's a warrior. He can handle it."

Tibalt raised a finger. "Shall I lead the way?"

Jason glanced at his chest. The battle had opened his shirt, revealing the glowing patch of skin. "It's completely red now. Does that mean I can find the gateway?"

"Maybe," Tibalt said. "I'll take us to the boundary. From that point, it will be up to you and the litmus finger."

All four hurried out of the cabin. To their left, the creek surged in the opposite direction. Higher and faster than before, it drowned out all other noises, even the tracking hounds.

Jason looked at his fellow travelers. Elyssa walked to his left in silence, while Randall limped to his right.

And out in front, a strange old man marched confidently forward with the axe propped against his shoulder, a self-proclaimed liar who made many odd claims that had yet to be proven.

Again Jason glanced at the red glow on his chest. At least this part wasn't a lie. It had changed color, just as Tibalt had predicted. Saving Randall's life in the creek and risking his own neck while fighting the bear had apparently pleased the litmus finger. But by what method would it guide them? And how would an inanimate object know how to find a secret gateway that had remained hidden for decades?

Marcelle's words came back to his mind. *I meant no insult to your brother. I made this bargain to save his life.*

What could she have meant? What dangers awaited them? And where were his brothers now?

He settled into a more relaxed gait. The answers would come soon, maybe too soon.

nine

Koren walked slowly back to the Basilica's gate, quoting Lattimer's words in her mind, words of philosophy and mystery that might capture Maximus's interest. The night keeper's strategy seemed simple enough—try to charm the dragon and enter the easy way, and if that didn't work, go to the rear of the building and find a rainwater drainpipe that led to the roof. She would recognize the correct pipe because of the cornerstone next to it. The stone bore an inscription with the building's construction date, "Starlight—2465," five hundred thirty-four years ago.

As she drew close to the gate, the dragon's eyes trained on her. Her legs trembled, and her arms wilted along with her confidence. She stopped in front of the iron bars, well out of range of a burst of fire. Using the sweetest voice she could muster, she called out in the

161

human language, "Good evening, great Maximus. You are certainly the most magnificent dragon I have ever seen."

Maximus peered at her between the bars, his head bobbing. A low growl permeated his reply. "A flatterer's tongue is one to be torn out, and its bearer flogged and made to eat it."

Steeling her muscles, Koren took a step closer. "Is it flattery to give a sincere compliment?"

"It is not, but the flatterer's tongue will deny its own intent." His eyes flashed bright red. "The tongue wears a mask, yet pretends its face is bare."

"Well spoken." She took another step. "With such wisdom guiding your discernment, how would you ever know if someone bore a true compliment in good will?"

"I would not, and I care not. It is better to decline an honest compliment than to be deceived by a flatterer's guile."

"Ah! I see why they put you at this station. A dragon who cannot accept a gift of love will never be deceived. He sacrifices love for vigilance. It is a sad exchange, is it not?"

Maximus thumped his tail on the ground. "It is most reasonable to reject love when you have learned that it is a myth. A fool believes that his lover is self-sacrificing. He always learns later that loving gestures are all pretence, ploys to receive something in return, usually something greater in value than what was sacrificed. Vigilance is the only answer, the only life to live. No one has ever been wounded by being too vigilant."

Koren eased her foot forward again. "Oh, you are so right, Maximus. When we guard our hearts, they are never wounded. But, alas, the consequences are devastating, for a guarded heart is never believed."

"Never believed?" He snorted a jet of flames. "You are within my range now, you silver-tongued witch. State your meaning quickly and begone, or feel my wrath."

Again forcing her muscles to obey, she slid forward another step. "A heart with a closed door is protected from pain, to be sure, but anyone who raises a shield blocks not only deception that tries to enter, he blocks sincerity that tries to escape. A heart that is not vulnerable is never believed, because it wears a mask of its own."

"Then, pray tell, thou of the fiery cap and glib tongue, how can one see the intent of the heart, even an unguarded heart? For words are the most talented mask-makers. Every word is a potential lie."

"So true, Maximus." She added a gentle laugh. "What would your superiors think if you merely told them that you were a most excellent guardian of the Basilica? Should they rely on your testimony?"

"Of course not. The great Magnar respects only deeds, not words. He knows well the deceitfulness of the tongue. Deeds remove all masks."

Koren stepped forward again, so close the dragon's breath warmed her cheeks. She locked gazes with him and eased into her silky, storytelling voice. "Have you ever seen me before, dear dragon?"

His brow bent low. "You do look familiar. Your red hair and green eyes are quite distinctive."

Nodding, she folded her hands at her waist. Maximus was ready. She ached to glance at Lattimer who watched from the shadows, but she dared not break the stare. "Since you say," she continued in her alluring voice, "that deeds remove masks, perhaps you remember my deeds and what I was doing when you saw me."

"Refresh my memory. I am listening."

"But if I merely speak of my deeds, I would be like a guard at the Basilica telling Magnar of my vigilance with no ability to prove it."

"You make a valid point. Do you have a solution?"

"I do, Maximus." She spread out her hands, allowing her sleeves to ride up and expose her forearms. Her slave's brand, a series of seven black characters in the dragon language, revealed her family line, and an eighth character would tell Maximus that she was an orphan. "When my parents died, I was sent to the orphan pool and soon thereafter to the cattle camps ... "

As she told her story, she visualized every detail—the rocks, the pails, Wallace, and every strike of the whip that drove them harder. With every twirl of her skirt, the images appeared around her, each one moving independently as her voice brought them to life and infused them with animation. Taking one-eyed Wallace by the hand, she knelt with him and begged, reaching out to ghostly passersby who ignored them more often than not. One old lady even spat at them and kicked dust in their faces.

Maximus jerked, and his eyes flamed as a low growl emanated from his snout.

Koren brushed the dirt from Wallace's face, kissed his cheek, and waved him into oblivion. She rose and faced Maximus, her hands again folded at her waist. "So you see, mighty dragon, my heart is open. It is vulnerable. It wears no mask. If I protected it with the shield of vigilance, you would never have seen the deeds or the passion behind them."

Maximus stared at her. His eyes had glazed over. With a low voice, he murmured, "What do you seek from me?"

"Passage." Koren offered a respectful bow of her head before regaining eye contact. "There is no guile in me, Maximus, so I speak only the truth. I seek passage into the Basilica so that I may seek further truth. Surely you can see that I am not a danger."

His murmurings transformed into an echo. "Not a danger."

"So this orphan begs you to heed my words, believe my sincere heart, and open the gate."

"Open the gate." Maximus blew a weak stream of fire at the lock, altering the flames' color and width in a coded sequence. Something clicked, and, as if jolted by the sound, Maximus shook his head. His eyes began to clear. As Koren reached for the gate, the growl in his throat deepened, and words in the dragon language rumbled forth. "Why am I letting you in?"

She swung the gate open, curtsied, and replied in his guttural language. "Because I asked you to let me in."

"You did?" His eyes clarified further. "This is strange."

Koren switched back to the human tongue and her silky voice. "I am an orphan, and you saw my deeds played out before you. I have requested access to the Basilica, because I wish to learn the fate of one of my friends, for she is frightened of the future. You approved, I assume, because of compassion and sympathy for those weaker and less fortunate than you."

His eyes turned glassy again. "Proceed."

Shifting her gaze to the ground, she walked slowly by the dragon's hot snout, careful not to make any sudden moves. Once she had passed, a tingle crawled up her back. Would he suddenly snap out of the charm and roast her? Her legs begged to run, but that would surely wake him up. Just slow and easy. If she could keep from jumping out of her skin, this would work.

She walked under a yawning arch, high enough for the biggest dragon to fly or walk through, and a shadow covered her body. Ahead, a dim lantern glowed in a massive circular chamber, perhaps a vestibule that would lead to other rooms.

"Come back here!" Maximus roared.

Koren broke into a mad dash. She tore into the vestibule, knocked over a lantern sitting on a stone table at the center, and ran into a dark corridor on the left, one of eight that exited the chamber. With the lantern extinguished, darkness prevailed, the walls blocking the barest glow from the moon. She tiptoed. Even a sliding of her foot might give her away. Maximus had also quieted, likely wanting to keep his position hidden as well.

Keeping her hands in front of her, she continued forward on her toes. The sound of a crackling fire came from somewhere ahead, but there was no light. A tingle rode up her spine again. Something was behind her, something hot and angry. Was Maximus really there? Could he see her? Or was it her imagination conjuring up ghosts again?

"Hey, Maximus!" someone shouted. "You left your post! Another human is getting in!"

The human voice came from the entry gate. She turned that way and peered into the darkness. Was it Lattimer?

A loud huff sounded only a few steps away. Something slid on the floor, and a stream of sparks flew to the side.

Wings spread out in the sparks' glow, and whipping wind sent Koren's hair streaming back. Soon, all was dark again.

Koren laid her palm against her chest, trying to calm her thumping heart. That was close! Too close!

She ran toward the circular room she had just passed through, halted at the end of the corridor, and pressed her back against the wall. Moonlight shone over the central table and the toppled lantern. In the distance, Lattimer's shouts continued, intermixed with roars from Maximus. He was trying to buy her some time. She had to go for it now.

After taking her skirt off, she leaped out, grabbed the lantern's top handle, and tossed her skirt as far as she could into one of the other corridors. Then, she ran into the original passageway, confident that this section was clear of obstacles.

She slowed down and listened. That fire had to be somewhere—she needed light for the lantern. Following the crackling sound, she kept a hand on the smooth wall. A breeze dried her sweat, cooling her body. With her legs now bare, chill bumps covered her skin. How long could Lattimer keep Maximus occupied? Would he get burned? Arrested and punished?

Finally, her hand reached a void. She turned toward it and, again feeling with her hands, inched along another corridor. The crackling sound grew. Soon a glow appeared that strengthened with every step she took.

She emerged into a massive chamber. The breeze swirled, troubling a log-fed fire that burned with waist-high flames at the center of the room. Above, two of the three moons peeked through a large ovular hole in the ceiling. A spattering of red and white stars also appeared, though the firelight almost washed them out.

Near the fire, a large book lay open on a stone pedestal that faced a stage, as if whoever would read the book might address an actor on the elevated platform. Open floor space lay behind the pedestal, big enough for at least twenty dragons to rest comfortably.

As Koren gazed at the area, images filtered into her mind, memories from a drug-induced daze. She had seen the book before, and the fire. This had to be the Assignment room, the very place the dragons had brought her for placement into a new slave position.

Koren listened for any sign of movement. Nothing stirred. Lifting the lantern's glass, she ran to the fire, used a thin firebrand at the edge to light the wick, and turned to hurry back. But the book's open pages caught her attention, and she stopped and stared at the black script. The text was in the dragons' language, of course, but she had long ago learned its written form. She often had to read and obey the hastily scrawled notes Arxad left behind when he went to the Zodiac earlier than usual.

The first line read "Promotion Protocol."

Koren tightened her grip on the lantern. This was it! Exactly what she was looking for. The dragons did Promotions here as well as Assignments.

She glanced around. Could she afford the time to stand out in the open and read it? Probably not.

After making a mental note of page number 209, she slid her hand under the book to close it, but a strange noise made her pause.

She tried to quiet her thumping heart and listen.

"Bring her forward!" A throaty growl spiced the draconic words, spoken with the ardor of a prophetic bard, yet so quiet it barely rose above the sound of the breeze blowing past her ears.

Koren searched for the source. It was close, so close.

"Set her on her knees before me."

Koren bent closer to the pedestal. The voice came from the book, as if buried somewhere beneath the pages. As the muffled words continued, she rifled through the volume's thick leaves. The voice grew clearer and clearer until, on page 576, it resonated throughout the room.

"She has red hair and green eyes. Who is worthy to take this gifted human into his custodial care? Since she is now of age, if no one offers an appropriate bid we will match her with a suitable male and begin her childbearing. Then, perhaps, we will be able to propagate more humans with her features."

As if forced by an invisible hand, Koren dropped to her knees. A huge red dragon stood on the stage before her, its wings spread and its eyes like fountains of fire.

Another draconic voice sounded from behind her. "Great Magnar, this girl is not one of the usual redheads. We gave her an extra-strong drug and examined her thoroughly. Her eyes reflect images that do not exist in reality, and her tongue and vocal cords are far more nimble than other girls'. We believe she could be a Starlighter, but we cannot be sure until her gifts are manifested."

Koren looked behind her. At least fifteen dragons sat on their haunches, most with their necks extended to get a better look at her, all with eyes that shone like burning phosphorescence. A few mumbled the word *Starlighter*, low and whispered, as if uttering a macabre curse.

She then turned to the corridor that led her in. No one darkened the entry. Could others see and hear this display, or was it going on only in her mind?

The dragon who had been called Magnar stalked from one side of the stage to the other before returning to the center. "Then she is too dangerous to transfer to the breeding rooms. She must be destroyed."

The other dragon bowed. "Very well. We will put her on the list of—"

"Wait!" The third voice rumbled from somewhere among the watching dragons. "Even if she is a Starlighter, she is harmless at this time, and she could be valuable to me someday."

Magnar's brow arched up. "Valuable, Arxad? How so?"

Koren turned again. Indeed, her master stood nearby, his head lifted higher than those around him. "When her gift begins to manifest itself, I could use her in the Zodiac."

"As a speaker for the stars?"

"A *real* speaker, great Magnar, not one of the pretenders."

Magnar laughed. "Spoken like a true believer."

Arxad's brow dipped, but he showed no other signs of anger. "We all believe what we choose to believe."

"And I choose to believe that your trade is one of chicanery and charlatans. I keep you and your fellow priests around only to entertain me with your absurd prophecies and to appease other superstitious citizens."

Arxad lowered his head. "With respect, great Magnar, you know full well that I and my fellows are not at all alike."

"True. With all your prophecies of doom, you are far less entertaining."

"I speak only what I see. If I had a Starlighter, I could—"

"You could misinterpret her doggerel prophecies and continue painting the skies black with your dark sayings." Magnar laughed again. "An invasion is coming! An invasion is coming! The humans will overtake us!"

The other dragons laughed with him, their coarse guffaws sounding like barking wolves.

Arxad lowered his head and glared at the floor. "If you will grant me this one grace, my lord, I pledge that I will use her expeditiously. If she causes any trouble, let her punishment be doubled upon me."

"Kill you twice?" Magnar stretched out a wing and slapped Koren's face.

She sucked in a breath. Her cheek stung!

Magnar's expression softened. "This little one is not worth risking your own scales."

"I beg you to allow me to be the judge of that." Arxad approached the stage and looked Magnar in the eye. "You know that I do not fear death."

"And you know that your position already rides on the edge of a precipice."

"Yes, I know." Arxad touched Koren gently on the head. "This one might well help me hear the song of the stars. I am willing to risk anything for that."

"Then so be it. If she causes any trouble whatsoever, I will kill her and banish you to the Valley of Bones."

Something twinkled in the corner of Koren's eye. She turned toward the passageway she had entered. At the far end, firelight flashed across the opening to the other corridor.

Koren leaped to her feet. Every dragon vanished. The breeze blew, rattling the book's leaf and lifting the bold text, Promotion Protocol. It was back on the original page. She glanced at the letters. No time to read. It would have to wait.

She hurried to yet another corridor at the far side of the chamber. With the lantern lighting her way, new options appeared. Above, the top of the corridor walls gave way to a bigger chamber with a ceiling that blocked the moonlight. It seemed that her passageway was merely a wide trench in the floor of the room above. But there was no stairway or even a ladder. Yet why would there be? The dragons needed only to fly to access the upper room. Humans could never go there without help; maybe the lower chamber was the only place they were allowed.

She looked back across the Separators' assembly room. A dragon-like shadow in full flight appeared in the opposite corridor. It had to be Maximus!

With a quick jerk, she lifted the lantern's glass and blew out the flame. She leaped into a sprint, the flames behind her guiding her way. Soon, the walls curved and blocked the assembly room's firelight.

Once again probing the dark air with her hands, she slowed. Her fingers struck something solid, a flat wall. A dead end! Yet something fibrous brushed her face. It moved easily from side to side. A rope?

She set the lantern down and grasped the rope, a braided cord too thick to wrap her fingers around, but a series of knots helped her get a grip. With her first pull, the rope descended with her weight. A loud gong sounded above. Then, the rope jerked her upward, and another gong reverberated all around.

Koren grimaced. A bell! She scrambled up the knotted cord. If she could just—

A gust of wind blew her hair. As a third gong sounded, something sharp clawed the back of her shirt and yanked her away from the rope and into the air. She flew into the upper chamber and fell to the floor on her backside. A dragon landed next to her and shouted, "Fool of a girl!"

Koren pushed with her feet and slid away, but when the dragon's face clarified, she stopped. "Arxad?"

"Yes, of course!" He looked down into the trench at the floor far below. "Climb on my back! Hurry!"

She scrambled up his tail and, dodging a ridge of spines, settled in near the base of his neck. In a flurry of wings, he took off.

Koren clenched her eyes shut and wrapped her arms around the dragon's neck. The sudden lift took her breath away. As Arxad flew, Koren forced her eyes open. She couldn't keep a smile from stretching across her face. Had any human ever ridden on a dragon before? It was so amazing!

Arxad flew toward the underside of the dome above. A cylindrical room was attached under the very top, like a jar screwed into the ceiling. Pulling in his wings slightly, he glided through a narrow doorway and settled on the floor inside.

"Down!" he ordered. "Now!"

Koren scrambled to the smooth marble floor. A wooden stand sat next to her that supported a metallic tube pointing toward a wedge-shaped hole in the ceiling.

Arxad's voice stayed sharp and angry. "What are you doing in the Basilica?"

"I'm ... " She stared at his fiery eyes. It would do no good to try to charm Arxad. He knew her all too well. "I'm trying to learn about Promotions. I was worried about Natalla. She thinks dragons eat the humans who get promoted."

His voice became sarcastic. "Oh, she does, does she?"

Koren nodded. "The humans who go to the Northlands never write letters after the first one. What happens to them?"

"That is not for you to know. You will never be a promoted human, so it is not your concern."

She let his words filter in. They sounded so strange. Never be a promoted human? Just hours ago that thought would have broken her heart, but now it was a relief. "Natalla wants to know. It *is* her concern."

"She cannot change what the Separators decide. It is her fate. She must accept it."

Koren pushed up to her feet and brushed her hands against her shorts. "So what do we do now? Will I be punished? More labors? Missed meals?"

Arxad peered out the open entryway. "If only it were that simple."

Following his gaze, she caught a glimpse of another dragon flying at a lower level, just a shadow, but its beating wings and sparks in its breath gave it away. The sight sent a chill through her body. "They'll want to kill me, won't they?"

His head shot forward, setting his blazing eyes directly in front of her. "You should have thought of that before you broke into the Basilica!"

"I didn't break in. Maximus let me in."

"Let you in? If you think such a lie is going to keep you from the cooking stake, you had better invent another one."

"Invent? Do you mean you think that I—"

"What I think is irrelevant." He pointed a claw at her. "What matters is that your foolishness has already caused one human death and will—"

"Death? Who?"

"The night watchman, Lattimer."

"Lattimer is dead?" Her throat caught. Heat raised prickles on her skin, and tears welled. She barely choked out, "How?"

"It seems that Maximus discovered your presence, and Lattimer was trying to distract him. Maximus is easily riled and has been given authority to kill any human who appears to be involved with a Basilica breach. Lattimer raised such a ruckus, I heard it in the Zodiac and flew out to investigate, but I arrived too late. Maximus had already engulfed him in flames. When Maximus told me what happened, I asked him to allow me to find you. That is the only reason you have not suffered the watchman's fate yourself."

Koren gasped for breath. *Poor Lattimer! He sacrificed himself to save me!*

Arxad nodded at her. "I see that you are appalled, perhaps even repentant, but it is too late for such emotional displays of penance. You are the reason for his death, and now you seek to shield your guilt with a lie."

She swallowed hard and tried to steady her voice. "But it's true. I just told Maximus my story. I guess he felt sorry for me."

"You told a story?" he asked, his glare softening.

She gave him a quick nod. "It's a pretty sad story, you know."

Looking away, he mumbled, "Every human has a sad story."

"True, Arxad ... " Koren hesitated. "I know little of the plight of most of my brethren, but when I tell the tales now, I feel the cries of my people's hearts. Like when I told Maximus about Wallace, one of my friends from the cattle camp, I felt his pain so strongly he seemed to come to life. I could see Wallace begging with me in the streets, and Maximus looked right at him, as if he could see him, too." She paused and took a breath. "Could that be why he felt sorry for me and let me in?"

Arxad fixed her with a piercing stare, his red eyes seeming to probe her mind. Koren held her breath. The urge to look away was overwhelming. She hadn't told him everything. Kind though he was, Arxad was still a dragon, still a slave owner, still a keeper of the secrets about Promotions. And if dragons really ate humans, even Arxad was an enemy.

After what seemed an interminable stare-down contest, Arxad pulled his head back. "So it *is* true."

"What's true?"

"Never mind. At this point, it does not matter. If you had not acted so foolishly, you could have done great things for everyone, both dragons and humans."

"Do you mean it's true, me being a Starlighter?"

His brow dipped so low, it shaded his eyes. "Where did you hear that name?"

She swallowed again, barely able to squeak. "From Lattimer."

"Oh, yes." Arxad set a wing tip on the metal tube. "Well, he would know about it. As part of his Assignment, he sometimes came into the Zodiac for sky observations, and we talked about that and many other issues. Most dragons have no idea how powerful a Starlighter can be."

"Sky observations?" Koren nodded at the tube. "Is that what this thing is for?"

"It is." He used his wing to swivel the tube's lower end toward her. "You may ease your curiosity."

She set her eye in front of what appeared to be a glass disk and looked through it.

"We call it a lightcatcher," Arxad said, "for it collects and magnifies light. We are able to see much more than without it, but it is a crude device compared to what we have in the Zodiac."

Koren took in the view—dozens of tiny specks of light, some red, some yellow, some so small and tightly packed together they looked like a glowing cloud. Keeping her gaze locked in place, she said, "Why is it here?"

"To watch for signs of the black egg."

She jerked away and looked at Arxad. "The black egg? Do you mean like what they say about being hatched—"

"Yes, but it is much more than an idiom." Arxad extended his neck and looked out the entryway. As his head swayed from side to side, he made no sound at all. Finally, he nodded at her. "Get on my back again. I will show you. But you must ride low and stay completely quiet. When we arrive in a chamber lit by fire, I will hide you with my wings. It is crucial that you not be seen."

Koren scrambled aboard and seated herself again, this time pressing her chest and cheek against his neck. "I'm ready."

Arxad shuffled out the opening and dropped. Koren gasped but quickly stifled the sound. He spread his wings, caught the air, and leveled out. Shadows zipped past, and an occasional lantern or small fire appeared, but due to the darkness and the wind beating against her eyes, Koren could see little else.

After flying through a wide corridor, Arxad entered a brightly lit oval-shaped chamber. Arrayed in a circle, fountains shot jets of fire that splashed against the stone ceiling. The jets were thin and set close together, making it impossible for anyone to pass through.

When Arxad landed, he sat on his haunches and kept his wings up. Now sitting almost vertically on his back, Koren hung on tight, not daring to peek around his neck. What wondrous object might the fountains be protecting? Who would be there at this time of night to ensure the object's safety? Heat from the fountains drew sweat from her pores, making it harder to hold on. She couldn't slip off. Not now.

"Greetings, Arxad. What brings you to the nest at this hour?"

Koren cocked her head. The voice was that of a female, higher and more refined than any dragon she had ever heard.

"I have news," Arxad said. "As I suspected, Koren is very likely a Starlighter. Her gift has already been manifested in a powerful way."

"This is a pleasant surprise. Have you taken her to the Zodiac?"

"Not yet. I discovered her gift only moments ago, so I thought it best to inform you immediately."

"A wise choice. Take her to the Zodiac as soon as possible. If she proves her mettle, then bring her here to me."

Arxad bowed his head, but not enough to expose Koren. When he lifted off, he rose high before banking, thereby blocking any view of his passenger from ground level. Yet when he headed back the way they had come, he had to dive to clear the top of the entryway. The sudden drop made Koren rise slightly, and when she tried to regain her grip, her fingers slipped. She slid down the scales and fell two body lengths to the floor, landing on her backside with a loud thump.

"Who is there?" the female bellowed.

While Koren lay still and tried to regain her breath, Arxad wheeled around and stormed back into the chamber. After sliding to a stop, he looked at the circle of flames and spoke quickly. "This is Koren, the Starlighter. I did not tell you she was with me, because I thought—"

"You thought I would kill her." The fountains suddenly stopped. For a moment, darkness flooded the room, and cool air washed over Koren's face. Then, as if summoned by individual commands, lanterns mounted on the wall sprang to life one by one.

From the center of the room, a woman walked toward them, crossing the barrier the fountains had once guarded. Tall and sleek, she was wrapped in a form-fitting black garment that looked more like a bed sheet than a dress, tied in place at the shoulder. She kept her head perfectly erect, a posture unlike any human Koren had ever seen.

When she reached Koren, she leaned over, letting her slick black hair slide in front of her shoulders, and extended her free hand. "Rise, child. Let me feel your presence."

Koren rode the woman's strong pull and stood in front of her. She tilted her head up to look at this strange human. Blue paint covered her eyelids, highlighting her black-as-coal eyes with oval pupils that seemed unable to focus, as if she might be blind, or at least nearly so. She smelled of oil and wood smoke, and dark pink blushed her high cheekbones, making her appear as one who had been working in the fields during the hottest part of the day.

Giving the woman's hand a quick glance, Koren mentally shook her head. No. This woman had never worked a day in her life. Her skin was smooth and ivory white. Maybe the heat from the fire had flushed her face.

When the woman drew her hand back, Koren gave her a curtsy. "As my master, Arxad, told you, I am Koren, and I am pleased to meet you."

"Is that so?" The woman's voice dripped with poison. "Perhaps you will think otherwise in due time."

Koren folded her hands behind her back and shifted from foot to foot. What could she say now? Nothing at all would probably be best. Just wait for this owl-eyed woman to decide what to do.

"I am Zena, and I tell you that only for the sake of convenience. You will learn nothing more about me for the rest of your days, which will be few if you are not a true Starlighter." She gestured with a finger. "Come. I will show you something."

Zena turned and, with her head stiff and erect again, walked toward the center of the room. As Koren followed, she tried to see what was in the circle of the now-inactive fountains, but Zena's black-cloaked frame made it impossible. When she crossed an arc of holes in the floor, the output vents for the fountains, Koren looked back. Arxad approached, but slowly. His eyes darted, and his wings trembled. Was he anxious? Scared?

When they arrived at the center, Zena stepped out of the way and extended her arm toward a circular marble basin on the floor, big and deep enough to serve as a human's bathtub. A black dragon egg sat within, padded underneath and at the sides with enough white sheets to make it sit as high as the top rim of the basin.

Koren stifled a gasp. The prophecy was coming true!

"This," Zena said, caressing the egg with her long fingers, "is the hope of the world. When the dragon inside hatches, he will become the ruler of all and will usher in a time of unprecedented prosperity. He will locate deposits of pheterone that are so rich, the dragons will have enough to thrive for millennia. And there will no longer be a need to enslave anyone. We humans will be free to congregate in the Northlands and build our own society."

Koren ached to ask, "What other lies did the dragons tell you?" But she dared not. Still, that and other questions dogged her mind. Why would a human be so dedicated to a dragon egg? Had she never heard Tamminy's rhyme? Did she really believe that the dragons wouldn't kill every human once the pheterone was located? And it seemed that Zena probably lived within the circle of fire, guarding the egg night and day. Why would the dragons put her in charge of such a crucial task?

"So," Zena continued, "if Arxad judges you to be a true Starlighter, you will receive a new Assignment with me, and I will explain your duties at that time."

While Zena was speaking, a soft voice sounded. "Are you all right?"

Koren glanced at Arxad. It couldn't have been his voice. The call was too soft, too weak. And it couldn't have been Zena's. She was talking already. Koren rose to her tiptoes and looked behind the egg. No one was there — only an empty goat-hair bag with a long strap lay near the egg.

"Shall I take her to the Zodiac now?" Arxad asked.

While staring at Koren, Zena nodded. "If she is a Starlighter, the sooner she begins her duties, the better."

"And if she is not?"

A blend of a frown and a smile twisted Zena's face. "Then terminate her. She knows too much."

ten

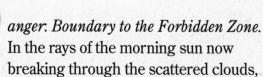

anger. Boundary to the Forbidden Zone.
In the rays of the morning sun now
breaking through the scattered clouds,
Jason stared at a wooden sign nailed to the wide trunk
of an old oak. The black-lettered words felt like pinchers
that drew dark sayings from his mind. The older men in
the commune often quoted sages and warned about the
evils that lurked in the forbidden zone. Misty ghosts called
snatchers stalked the forests, waiting for unwary travelers
in order to suck out their souls. Invisible doorways led to a
domain of darkness where demons would hang intruders
from a tree and slowly dip their heads into pots of boiling
oil. Carnivorous plants abounded. Like expert archers,
they would shoot poisonous thorns at passersby and use
crawling vines to drag them into their clutches.

An old song one of the gardeners used to chant came to mind.

Evil weeds, disguised as flowers,

Keep away your stealing powers.

Treasured thoughts are mine to hold;

Take them not within your fold.

Jason clutched his axe more tightly. Even though he had long doubted these stories, just thinking about them brought a chill. Every tall tale had some seed of truth, and they would soon learn what mysteries gave rise to such grave terrors.

He looked at Elyssa. Now clean and dry in her lumberjack ensemble, she glanced around, as if taking in every iota of data. Was she noticing the way moss hung from low-reaching branches? The thickness of autumn debris on the narrow path? Or was she taking in the variety of reds in the few remaining leaves, each hue so slightly different that only she could tell them apart? Even as a little girl, she had chattered about the subtle changes around them. Back then he had thought she was just playing make-believe, but now he knew better. A Diviner noticed everything.

Randall yawned and stretched his arms. "So what now?"

Tibalt tapped the sign with his axe handle. "This is as far as my old noggin remembers clearly. The last time I went to the gateway, I was just a little tyke, and the dungeon spiders spun cobwebs in my brain over the years. I could try to lead us, but we wouldn't want to fall into any bottomless pits."

"Bottomless pits?" Elyssa repeated. "That's not possible."

"Is that so, little lady?" Tibalt raised a finger. "My own pappy told me about them, and he never told a lie in his life."

Elyssa winked at Jason before shifting back to Tibalt. "Can you tell me who fell into one of these bottomless pits and then came back to report that there was no bottom?"

"Well … " Tibalt's head drooped. "I suppose someone fell clean through to the other side of the world and popped out a hole there. He would have to learn to walk upside down, but you can get used to almost anything."

Elyssa grinned. "I'll accept that, Tibber. Let's try to avoid the bottomless pits."

Tibalt pointed at Jason. "Our next step is up to you. Which way is the litmus finger pointing?"

Jason glanced at his shirt and unfastened two buttons, revealing the odd mark over his heart. The patch of skin pulsed. "I'm not sure what I'm supposed to be feeling."

Elyssa laid a hand on his shoulder. "You're better at finding your way through the forest than anyone I know, even better than Adrian."

"Not better than Randall." Jason nodded toward him. "He won the open division of the tracking tournament."

Randall waved a hand. "Adrian was sick that day. I think he's the best."

"In any case," Elyssa continued, sounding exasperated, "maybe the finger will enhance the gifts you already have. Just start walking and trust your senses. I'll be right behind you, Tibalt can come next, and then Randall can guard our backs."

Randall pulled his photo gun from the holster. "That suits me. I just hope this will dry out soon."

Jason looked down at the path, which ended abruptly at the old oak and was replaced by sporadic gaps in the browning underbrush. After heaving a sigh, he marched ahead. Maybe Adrian had passed this way. But what map did he have? Who had told him how to follow in Frederick's steps? Had Frederick left a clue somewhere?

With every footfall, Jason concentrated on the sensory input. As usual, the scents of the forest—drying leaves, rotting logs, and pine—drifted in, as well as the subtle indicators the gentle breeze delivered—lower humidity, indicating clearing weather; wildflowers, a hint that a meadow of grasslands lay nearby, which would be a good place to get a better view of the land; and something new, something powerful. Was it emotion? Intrigue made into a potent entity? If mystery could ride the air, then this breeze carried it on a galloping horse.

He followed the sensation. With each turn, the lurking mystery either heightened or lessened, allowing him to adjust his direction and aim for the source. He pressed on through the forest, sometimes plowing through thick brush and sometimes clambering straight over low, flat boulders instead of going around them. Now it seemed that the finger's pulse pressed against his skin from the inside, as if trying to break free. Was it really pointing the way?

"Jason," Elyssa whispered, "I sense … "

He stopped and turned. "What?"

Squinting as she glanced around, her voice stayed low. "I'm not sure. Confusion, maybe? Someone or something is watching, and it doesn't understand why we're here."

Randall turned on his gun and spoke over its low hum. "I'm ready."

"Don't be too quick on the trigger," Jason said. "Confusion's not usually a sign of an enemy." He scanned the dense collection of skinny birches and sweet gums. A human wouldn't be able to hide behind any trees in this area, and certainly no mountain bear could. Above, the branches held few leaves, far from enough to veil a predator ready to pounce, at least not one of significant size.

With his gaze locked on the next gap in the underbrush, he trudged forward. "Let's just keep moving. If our confused onlooker really wants to learn why we're here, it will ask."

Soon the forest thinned out, and they emerged onto an endless field of tall green grass and yellow wildflowers—so many blossoms it seemed that someone had scattered wide yellow ribbons on a green canvas.

As if signaled by a musical conductor, the guiding call of mystery suddenly ceased, leaving behind only a fading echo. Jason stopped abruptly. Elyssa collided with him from behind with an "Oomph."

"Shhh!" Jason turned and faced the woods. Tibalt and Randall had just walked onto the field, both wide-eyed as they joined Elyssa at Jason's right.

"What's wrong?" Elyssa whispered.

"Do you still sense someone?" Jason asked.

She shook her head. "But I did until just now."

"And I felt guided by the litmus finger until just now."

Tibalt spoke in a low, mysterious tone. "A guide who hides when a path divides is not a friend but a foe. He laughs when you're lost, he cares not the cost. His plan is to bring you to woe."

Jason nodded. "I get your point."

"So what do we do?" Elyssa asked.

"There are other ways to find guidance." Jason scanned the ground, searching for tracks, bent grass blades, or fragments of broken twigs. If Adrian wasn't being pursued, he would never venture out into the unknown without leaving some kind of trail, either to be followed by someone who recognized the signs or to be retraced in the unlikely event he became lost.

Finally, he grabbed a stalk of grass and broke it off. Nothing. Not a sign that Adrian had come this way.

A hissing voice shot from the forest, as if spat out by a man with sand in his vocal cords. "Turn back or die!"

Jason searched for the source, but nothing moved in the woods. "Turn back?" he called as he raised the axe. "Someone guided us here. Why should we turn back now?"

"The meadow conceals death. Many have trod there, but few have returned."

Randall lifted his gun. "Who are you? Show yourself."

"Indeed," Tibalt added, brandishing his axe. "Why should we trust the faceless? A man who hides his eyes hides his purpose."

The hissing returned. "Very well."

Just inside the forest boundary, thick gray mist gathered on the ground and flowed out to the meadow in a rolling wave. Jason readied the axe. The litmus finger pulsed again, so hard his skin felt like it was on fire.

The mist began gathering into a human-shaped column. Without face or features, the foggy apparition was too indistinct to allow a determination of its gender or expression. It was more shadow than substance.

Soon the shape rose to Jason's height, and the mist swirled and boiled within its nebulous body in concert with its renewed hiss. "Now that you see me, are you more apt to heed my counsel?"

Tibalt gasped. "A snatcher!"

Randall pointed his gun. "Get back before I blast you!"

"Put your weapons away," the snatcher said. "They will have no effect but to anger me. Fear is your enemy, but not I. The only souls I take are those who have already been purchased by my master—the cowardly, the fearful, the spineless members of your race—and they give their souls freely. Only those who display fear need fear me."

Jason let the axe rest on the ground. "Why should we turn back?"

"No human who has ventured into the meadow has ever returned. The flowers are deceivers, and the grass is a devourer. I have seen many brave and strong warriors absorbed like water from the sky."

Jason looked at the meadow and imagined Adrian crumbling into dust, consumed by the innocent-looking grass. He turned back to the snatcher. "I was guided here, and my guidance stopped as soon as I left the forest."

The snatcher stared at him for a moment, as if contemplating his answer. "The only guidance here is provided by the keeper of the gateway, and it can be heard only by the bearer of the key."

Jason glanced at Elyssa, hoping for a bit of silent counsel. Should he tell this ghost what their mission was?

Elyssa bowed to the snatcher. "We appreciate your warnings, kind ghost, but we must be on our way." She hooked Jason's arm with her own and pulled him toward the meadow. "Lose the axe and run."

Stumbling with her forceful tug, Jason dropped the axe and went along. "What are you doing?"

"Skipping steps! Just trust me!"

Randall jogged along at their side while Tibalt followed, high-stepping to avoid the flowers. "Nice buttercups!" Tibalt called. "I wouldn't hurt you. No, not old Tibber!"

As their feet brushed through the flowers, a sickeningly sweet aroma rose into Jason's nostrils. Dizziness swam through his mind. His throat tightened, and his legs grew weak. "Poison!" he gasped.

"Exactly!" Elyssa yelled. "Run!"

She let go and sprinted straight ahead. Jason held his breath and charged after her, glancing back to check on the others. Randall had hoisted Tibalt over his shoulder and was carrying him as he ran, Tibalt shouting all the way. "I can run, you big ox! Put me down!"

Jason pulled on Elyssa's shirt, signaling her to slow down. When Randall caught up, he set Tibalt down and all four ran together. How long could they hold out without breathing in the noxious fumes? The meadow seemed to have no end, and the flowers only thickened as they waded out into the green and yellow sea. Did Elyssa really know what she was doing?

Suddenly, Jason tripped over something, and the ground dropped away. He, Elyssa, and Tibalt plunged into a gaping void. From above, Randall shouted, loud and long, "Grab the rope!" but his voice quickly faded.

Jason caught sight of a rope near the side of the cylindrical pit, close to Tibalt. "Tibalt!" he yelled. "Grab it!"

Tibalt lamented in singsong. "The bottom is never, we plummet forever. No water, no meat, no ground for our feet."

Elyssa nudged his body, sending her own body into Jason's arms. Tibalt grabbed the rope, and, with a loud scream, shot upward.

Holding Elyssa in one arm, Jason flailed with the other, but the rope stayed out of reach. Soon, it vanished in the darkness.

Jason cringed. A bone-crushing collision surely awaited, but nothing happened. He looked at Elyssa, now barely visible, though they were nearly nose to nose. "The bottomless pit?" he asked as the wind stripped away his voice.

"Impossible!" she yelled. "It's a myth!"

Soon, a wet sensation brushed Jason's cheek. It felt warm and slippery. "What is it?" he asked.

"Some kind of foam, like soap bubbles."

Moment by moment the foam grew thicker, slowing their plummet. Seconds later, they splashed feet first into water and knifed into its depths. The cold shock nearly paralyzing him, Jason fought as a strong horizontal current swept them into the icy water's flow. Keeping a grip on Elyssa, Jason thrust his body upward until his head broke the surface.

He sucked in a double lungful of air and pulled Elyssa until she, too, could breathe. With complete darkness all around and nothing beneath his feet to allow for a foothold, he paddled with his free arm, swimming perpendicular to the current. "There has to be a bank to this river some-where!" he shouted.

"Make sure we stay together!" Elyssa's voice was broken by her shivers and clattering teeth. As they held hands, they swam in sync, using their clenched hands as a single arm.

Jason's fingers struck rock, scraping his knuckles. "I'm at a wall. Just float." He and Elyssa stopped swimming and rode the current again, Jason letting his palm rub the sheer face as they floated by. "We can't climb out!"

"We'll just have to see where it carries us. It can't go on forever."

Jason nodded, though Elyssa wouldn't be able to see him. She was right, of course, but the water was too cold; they would soon die of hypothermia. Which would last longer, the river or their heat reserves?

As if again guessing his thoughts, Elyssa wrapped her arms and legs around Jason's body, chest to chest, and pressed her cheek against his. "You keep us afloat," she whispered in his ear. "We'll share body heat."

Now using both arms, he paddled to keep their heads above water. With her hanging on, shifting their combined center of gravity, the effort was as awkward as swimming with a bag of melons tied to his chest. Yet, as he worked, heat flowed from his elbows to his knees, especially at the points of contact between him and Elyssa. The river slowly warmed, and now only his fingers and toes stayed cold, but how long could he keep this up? He couldn't fight the current forever.

She seemed to read his mind. "You can do it, Jason. I believe in you. You are strong. Your arms are like bands of steel."

On and on, she whispered, repeating the same phrases again and again. Yet one phrase penetrated more deeply than the others. *I believe in you.*

He closed his eyes and concentrated. His arms burned. Every muscle ached. But he couldn't give up. He had to get her to safety. Elyssa believed in him, and that was all that mattered.

Keeping their heads above the surface, he paddled on. At times, when the flow eased, he rested his arms, using only his legs to stay afloat. Even then, however, darkness wrapped around them like a crushing serpent, and with its tightening coils, a new wave of bitter cold penetrated his saturated clothes and seeped into his bones, frigid, numbing, stiffening. Soon even the weakest current would be too much to fight.

Elyssa's voice sharpened. "Jason! I sense light. Maybe we'll come out into the open air. Just a little while longer."

"I'm … I'm trying." Jason demanded new strength from his tortured arms but to no avail. Spasms wrenched his biceps, sending new pain from his knotting muscles. Water rose past his nostrils and splashed into his eyes.

Elyssa pulled his arms around her torso and shouted, "Just hang on!"

As his joints locked in place, she battled the strengthening current. Jason rested his chin on her shoulder, blinking away the splashes. The surrounding blackness faded. Walls came into view, dark and rocky.

"I see a shoreline!" Elyssa called. "Keep hanging on!"

With his joints feeling like rusted hinges, Jason wanted to say, "I don't have much choice," but even breathing seemed too much of a chore. Just clinging to her sapped his energy.

Seconds later, new weight dragged his body down. As the ambient light strengthened, he took in the scene. Elyssa was hauling him onto a pebbly riverbank, staggering backwards with his arms draped over her shoulders.

She pried his arms away and set him down gently on his side. He looked up at her, barely able to breathe as he flexed his fingers and tried to unlock his joints. "Are you all right?" he asked.

"I think so." Dripping from head to toe, she set her fists on her hips and looked around. "We're in a cave of some kind." Her voice seemed weak, frail, almost inaudible as water rushed along nearby. "Be glad I didn't have to do mouth-to-mouth resuscitation. The cabin had no toothbrush."

Jason pushed against the ground and rose to his knees. His arm still cramped but not as badly as before. He reached out with his stronger arm, and Elyssa helped him the rest of the way up.

As he swiped gravelly dirt from his pants, he scanned the chamber. A gray ceiling loomed overhead with a few stalactites just out of reach, each one dripping cloudy water at the rate of a slow heartbeat. Three brackets hung on a side wall, two holding antique swords and scabbards and the other empty.

Behind him, the river flowed swiftly past a sheer rock wall. Dim radiance emanated from somewhere, but there seemed to be no hole to the outside world.

He looked at the river—dark and deep with islands of white foam speeding by. "I hope Tibalt was able to hang on to the rope."

"And Randall was able to pull him up," Elyssa said. "Though staying in that poisoned field might be worse than coming down here."

Jason turned to the wall on the opposite side, a rock face about ten steps away. "Any idea where the light's coming from?"

"Maybe." Elyssa strode to the wall and laid a palm on the uneven gray stone. "It's brighter over here."

He pushed his stiff legs into a hobbled walk and joined her. "I can't tell the difference."

As she ran her hand along the damp surface, her eyes following the touch, she whispered, "I can."

"So ... " He kicked a pebble toward the river. "Did you plan that all along? I mean, holding on to me so you could keep your strength?"

Her fingers probed a series of dark circular recesses. "It seemed like the only way."

"How did you know we would get out before you ran out of strength, too?"

She turned and stared at him as if he had asked how she knew water was wet. "It's a feeling, nothing more, nothing less."

"Well, you were right, as usual." He tapped a finger against his head. "I just wish I could know ahead of time what you have cooking up there."

She offered a tired smile. "You'd better get used to it. I'm not going to explain everything I do. There just isn't time."

His legs still heavy, Jason shuffled closer to the wall and squinted at the recesses — eight finger-sized holes in a horizontal row at waist level, with a gap between the first four and the second four, too dark to investigate by sight. "What are those?"

"I'm not sure. I sense energy coming from within, like there's a powerful force on the other side."

"And this wall is emanating light from that source?"
She shrugged. "Your guess is as good as mine."

"I doubt that." Jason pushed his left index finger slowly into the leftmost hole. A slight buzz tickled his skin, but he kept sliding up to the base knuckle until his fingertip touched solid rock, wet and far tinglier. A click sounded, loud enough to echo, and the light in the chamber grew brighter.

Elyssa pushed a finger into the rightmost hole, but nothing happened. "Strange."

"Do you feel something tickly at the back?"
She nodded. "But maybe this one doesn't work."

"I have a hunch." After withdrawing his index finger, he slid his left pinky in, but it wasn't long enough to reach the barrier at the back. He turned his hand palm up, switched back to his index finger, and inserted it again. Then, he slid his middle finger into the second hole, his ring finger into the third, and so on until he had filled all eight holes. Each hole was the perfect depth.

Every time a fingertip touched the end of its hole, another click sounded. Pinpoints of light appeared on the wall, the hundreds of colors creating a mosaic from floor to ceiling—two roaring dragons facing the center where Jason stood, each one with clawed hands open below the holes, as if carrying them. Lettering across the top of the design read, *Where only courageous hearts may brave the river's flow.*

Red light emanated around Jason's fingers and pulsed in time with his heartbeat, making his skin tingle more than ever. Now the chamber looked like a courtyard of rainbows. Bright colors rippled on every surface. Even the river seemed tinted with glowing dye. Warm air breezed in from hidden vents, further drying their hair and clothes.

"Okay ... " Elyssa said slowly, "this is interesting."

Jason basked in the summery breeze. "I guess there's no doubt. We found the gateway."

"True, but how do we open—"

The ground rocked, nearly toppling Elyssa. As a crackling rumble sounded all around, Jason hardened his stance but kept his fingers in place. "Are you all right?"

"I think so." She grasped his sleeve and rode out the trembling ground. "If this is a quake, we're in big trouble."

The sound of rushing water diminished. The river's current eased to a stop and began flowing in the opposite direction, slower than before but definitely in reverse. The trembling suddenly ended, but the lights continued to wash the walls with vibrant colors, and the river stayed on its backwards course.

Elyssa's eyes widened. "Okay, that's even more interesting."

"Have a look around," Jason said. "Maybe the light will reveal something that will open the gateway."

As Elyssa searched the chamber, Jason twisted his body to watch. She looked at the river, scanned the floor, and studied each wall before returning to the holes.

"Nothing obvious," she said. "Just bare rock, pebbles, and sand. They're beautiful in this light, but I didn't see anything useful."

As he kept his hands in place, a gentle throbbing made him glance at his chest. The litmus finger pulsed harder than usual, as if filling the holes had energized it as well. Tibalt had said something about the finger, once absorbed, enabling someone to open the gateway, but since the skin overtop was red and not yet blue, maybe the absorption hadn't been completed yet. The insertion was energizing the portal but not opening it.

Using his eyes, he gestured toward the red skin. "Do you think the holes worked for me and not for you because of the litmus finger? It seems more active now."

"Of course. That's got to be it." She studied the wall around Jason's hands. Her brow scrunched, and her head tilted to the side. "Wait just a minute."

She slid between Jason and the wall, her back against his chest, and brushed dirt away from a spot just above and between his hands. As grit fell away, a glassy surface appeared at eye level, round and dark, about the size of a human head. She set her face close to the glass and peered in.

"See anything?"

"No, but I feel something. A presence. Dark. Mysterious." She swiveled her body and looked at him face-to-face. "Dangerous."

As their eyes met, a sense of warmth flooded his body. For the first time since they escaped from the dungeon, she seemed unsure, even frightened. And since she stood so close, her shivering body sent trembles into his own. Whatever this feeling was, it was powerful.

He cleared his throat and forced a tone of confidence into his voice. "Let me have a look. Maybe the litmus finger will make it show me something it wouldn't show you."

Elyssa's warm smile returned. "Good idea." She slid out of the way and crossed her arms. "Be sure to let me know what you feel as well as what you see."

Keeping his fingers in place, Jason edged closer and looked into the dark glass. Inside, only vague shadows appeared — black ghosts on a charcoal canopy. Too indistinct to decipher, they moved like curtains swaying in the breeze. "Just dark shapes."

"And how do you feel?"

He concentrated on the scene. Soon, images came to mind — his brother Frederick as he spoke through the Courier's tube, Tibalt reciting his strange poetry, and the litmus finger glowing yellow within Prescott's chest as he lay in bed, not suspecting that a murderer would soon take both the finger and his life.

"I think … " He licked his lips, now dry in the warm flow. There had to be a connection between Frederick, Tibalt, and the finger. Prescott had the finger, but he obviously never got to the gateway. Yet Frederick didn't have it, and he made it to the other world. There had to be a key that didn't require the litmus finger, a secret code of some kind, something that only certain people, trusted confidantes of Uriel Blackstone, would know.

"You think what?" Elyssa prompted.

"You mentioned it before. A genetic key."

She set a finger on her chin. "That's what Prescott's documents said. But whose genetics?"

"The son of the man who locked the gateway?"

"Tibalt?"

"Sure." Jason withdrew his fingers. The pinpoints of light blinked out, dimming the area. As his eyes adjusted, another rumble shook the chamber. The sound of rushing water returned. When the shaking eased, Jason looked at the river. It had resumed its earlier direction, from left to right, and its rate of flow.

Elyssa marched in place, as if testing the stability of the ground. "How could one man have put this entire foundation on a balancing pin?"

"Let's concentrate on opening the gateway," Jason said. "We can figure out the rest later."

Elyssa crossed her arms again, but not in a confrontational way. She seemed perplexed, curious. "Okay. What's your genetics theory?"

Jason raised a finger. "If Frederick knew about the key, he could have easily taken some hair from Tibalt. As Prescott's bodyguard, Adrian could have granted Frederick access to the dungeon."

She pointed at him. "And the litmus finger itself is a clue that you have to use your fingers in this wall."

Jason nudged her with an elbow. "You're way ahead of me again."

"No need to waste time," Elyssa said, grinning. "It does seem clear that Uriel wanted no one to come through the gateway without his son being involved. Tibalt knew a lot about the finger—Uriel must have taught Tibalt about the secrets before he died. But that was decades ago, and now Tibalt doesn't remember everything."

"How are we going to get him down here?" Jason asked. "Swimming upstream is impossible enough, but climbing back up that hole would be worse. We don't even know if the rope comes down that far."

She glanced between the river and the wall. "But maybe I could swim to the pit we fell into if the current changed direction."

Jason nodded at the holes in the wall. "You mean … "

"Exactly. Put those enhanced fingers of yours back in there and reverse the river." She pointed at the current.

"The flow wasn't so turbulent going the other direction, and it will be a lot easier knowing there's an end."

"Okay. I can't argue with that, but what about scaling the walls of that pit? I can't even guess how far we fell."

"No one would hang a rope without making sure it went all the way down. Obviously Uriel planned this thing out pretty well."

Jason let out a sigh. "I guess we have no choice."

Elyssa wiggled her fingers and smiled. "Get to work, litmus boy!"

Smiling back at her, he turned to the wall. "Just remember I'm down here. Don't let those flowers drain your brain."

Her eyebrows lifted. "Oh, don't be silly. I would forget my own mother before I'd forget you." She blew him a kiss, gently, tenderly. "I will be back, Jason Masters. I promise."

The motion brought back the memory of an eight-year-old girl performing the same offering. This time, stringy, dripping hair replaced the girlish pigtails, and a mature feminine form replaced the preadolescent frame, but the rest was exactly the same—eyes of love, a spirit of virtue, and a sister's promise.

Jason caught the kiss and applied it to his cheek. "I know you'll be back. I'll be waiting." He reinserted his fingers. The colorful dual-dragon design sparkled once again, and, after another brief quake, the river reversed its course.

Elyssa waded in. "It's warmer now," she said, pointing toward the river's new source. "Maybe there's some kind of geothermal heat in that direction. That would account for both the warm air and the water."

"Great. At least you won't freeze to death going that way."

"Just don't pull your fingers out. If the river switches while I'm in the water, I doubt I could survive." She began swimming with the flow and disappeared from sight.

Jason turned again to the wall and stared at the embedded dark glass. Ovular in shape, it seemed to be a black egg hovering above his hands. Now it made sense. The dragons weren't carrying the finger holes; they were supporting this floating egg-shaped object, as if ready to catch it.

Now, with his hands in place and his skin tingling, he felt as if he, too, were supporting the egg. It seemed that the buzz of energy created a force field that kept the dark sphere aloft, and if he withdrew his fingers it would crash to the ground.

As he waited, he studied the details in the stunning, colorful display. Each dragon had a pair of outstretched wings, each wing at least as long as its body. Their eyes flashed red. Fire shot from their mouths, orange light shimmering across the flames, making them appear to move. Smoke spewed out from the fire's orange pinpoints, a mist so real it seemed to expand.

He sniffed the air, but no smoky odor entered his nostrils. Still, the smoke really was increasing. What was it? Part of the thermal energy source?

He looked at the other dragon. Smoke poured from its flames as well and drifted down to floor level, piling up in a swirling column. Soon, twin columns of smoke twirled at each side. They shaped themselves into humanlike forms, though no faces appeared.

Jason froze. New shivers crawled along his skin. "Snatchers!" he whispered.

The phantom on his left spoke with a raspy voice. "You heeded not my warning. The creator of this conundrum designed the gateway to be opened by one man, and you are not he."

"We figured that out," Jason said. "We had Tibalt with us before, though. Why did you warn us not to come?"

Darker smoke swirled around the snatcher's head. "The gateway's lock has a precise combination of steps to take, with many perils along the way, and you are attempting them in the wrong order."

Jason studied the misty phantom. Should he ask questions? Could he trust it to tell the truth? Maybe. It was worth a try. "If we perform all the steps, will we open the gateway, even if they're out of order?"

The snatcher leaned to one side, as if looking at his twin. Jason swiveled his head. The other snatcher returned the look with a nod but said nothing.

"It is possible," the first snatcher said, "but success is as unlikely as rain reversing its course and regenerating the clouds. You have already reversed the river, but can your friend defy gravity and ascend to the surface where Tibalt slumbers among the flowers of forgetfulness? Gravity is a law with an unmerciful penalty, and the river makes no stops to allow its passengers to dismount. If your friend fails to terminate her ride at the entry pit or falls back to the water when the slippery sides give way, the river will sweep her to an airless tunnel and a watery grave."

Jason stared at the snatcher. His stiff legs ached. His arms burned. What could he do? If he jerked his fingers out, Elyssa might drown in the reversing surge and colder water. If he left them in place, she might drown anyway. And how could he know when to reverse the flow to bring her and Tibalt back? They hadn't talked that part through. Had she already decided on a plan of action on her own, once again skipping steps and assuming he would know what was going on?

He took in a deep breath and let it out slowly. Elyssa had been right so far. Her instincts were sharp, and he could trust her once again. For now, his job was to keep the river flowing backwards and watch for a signal to do otherwise. But what would that signal be?

The second snatcher spoke up. Lower and clearer, his voice carried a hypnotic cadence. "Your mind is awash in confusion. I see it in your eyes. Release your grasp on this illusory quest. It holds nothing for you but sorrow and death, for the souls you seek will not believe that you have come to rescue them. They will perceive you as enemies, troublemakers, liars motivated by selfish interest."

Jason gazed at the snatcher's nebulous face. A pair of black eyes formed. Or were they just darker rings of mist? Everything seemed warped, out-of-focus, dizzying.

"Withdraw your fingers," the snatcher continued in his mesmerizing rhythm, "and we will take you back to the surface. You will return home in peace, and those who seek your life will grant your pardon. No one need ever know that you found the gateway. Let the portal remain closed so that no dragons will ever again stalk this world in search of slaves for their quarries. Let the Lost Ones be few, and let the number of free humans not diminish by even one unfortunate soul. Why should you expend so much energy when you will gain nothing but slavish strife and lead yourself and your friends into chains?"

Jason absorbed the words. The snatcher's tone was like a song, a mournful ballad that penetrated his mind and weighed down his heart. It seemed that his will to go on drained toward his wet boots and leaked onto the floor. Maybe this creature was right. Surely it knew more than he did about the gateway and dragons. Perhaps he should leave well enough alone and not risk losing the blessings of freedom. The idea made sense, a lot of sense.

Water swirled around Jason's soles. The river was spilling over its bank and flooding the chamber floor. But how far would it rise, and how fast? Could Elyssa make it to the top of the pit and somehow signal him before he had to withdraw his fingers to keep from drowning?

"It is time to decide," the snatcher continued. "Give up this foolish mission or die."

Flexing his arms, Jason glared at the apparition. "Get out of my sight!" Heat surged through his cheeks as his voice rose to a near scream. "You snatchers are good at draining a man's will. Is that how you steal souls? Do you first rob them of the will to fight?"

"There is never a struggle." The snatcher's voice stayed calm and alluring. "Every man gives us his soul freely. Even the will to fight is surrendered without the slightest—"

"Shut up!" Jason shouted. "Maybe every man has given up without a fight, but I am not every man. I am Jason Masters, son of Edison Masters, and we will never … *never* … allow a slave to toil in misery while we live at ease. That would be hateful, the heart of the godless." He took a deep breath and let his voice settle to a low growl. "I will never give up. I will stand here until I rot if I have to. Elyssa and I will find the Lost Ones, their children, and their grandchildren, and we will not rest until every last one of them is safe in our world."

"Safe?" The snatcher let out a scratchy chuckle. "What do you know about safe?" Its smoky arm pointed at the floor. "The water rises. We will see how long your resolve lasts." With that, the snatcher and its twin dispersed and vanished.

eleven

Koren hugged Arxad's neck, staying low on his back as he flew in tight circles toward the Basilica's ceiling. He had warned her to stay quiet and out of sight. The ride to the Zodiac would be rough but quick, so she just had to hang on.

Arxad shifted upward and zoomed in a near vertical angle through an opening to the starry sky. Koren tightened her grip to keep from sliding down his scales. Then, when he whipped back to level out, she lifted from her seat for a moment before snapping down and banging her chin against his armor-like skin.

Seconds later, Arxad dropped suddenly, making her rise even higher. Interlocking her fingers, she barely kept her body from being ripped away before they entered a hole in the Zodiac's roof. His plunge eased, and as she settled to his back again, he sailed along a corridor, his wings rising and falling with only the slightest sound of whipping leather interrupting the silence.

Flaming torches lined the walls. As Arxad passed by, each oil-filled cresset flickered, making the dim orange light waver along the stony passage. The fuel-tinged air tickled her nose and pinched her throat. She held her breath, willing herself not to cough or sneeze.

Soon a massive set of double doors swung open, and, dipping under an arch, Arxad glided through and landed in a flurry of wings. "You may get off now," he said in a low tone. "You are safe here, but keep your voice level at a minimum."

Koren slid down. Her legs wobbled for a moment, but, as she took in a deep breath from the cleaner air, her muscles strengthened. She looked around. Exposed to the sky, the room was like a courtyard—at least five dragon-lengths wide, bordered by river-stone and cactus beds, and floored with dark slate. Stars spread out over the black canopy above, and the three moons shone clearly, but the cathedral's spires were nowhere in sight, nor was the belfry at the Basilica.

"We are in the Zodiac's observatory," Arxad said. "The ceiling is a dome that projects the heavens for us, so I can watch the nightly dance under any weather conditions."

She squinted at the display. Now the scene came into focus. It was, indeed, a curved ceiling, several times higher than Arxad's body length. Clear and crisp as the sky itself, it seemed too real to be a copy. "How do you get the image up there?" she asked.

"With the Reflections Crystal." Arxad set a clawed hand on a sphere sitting atop a head-high crystalline column embedded in the floor. The moment he touched it, a shadow darkened the room, as if a cloud had drifted overhead. "We have a series of scopes on the roof, similar to the one you saw at the Basilica, that sweep the sky and send their images to this sphere. It puts those pictures together into one blended view of the heavens. As you can see, when I touch the crystal, I block the projection, and if I move away … " He took a step back, and the shadow disappeared. "The ceiling above us is also retractable, so I can get a direct view if I wish."

Koren gaped at the sphere. How could it possibly perform such a miracle? And how could these dragons create such intricate objects, especially considering the fact that they needed humans to do something as simple as drill for pheterone?

She reached out to touch it but quickly drew back again. With a sigh, she just breathed its name in a whisper. "The Reflections Crystal."

"Knowing you," Arxad continued, "you probably want to learn how it works, but we do not know. Magnar brought it to us long ago without much explanation. He merely said it had magical properties and that I should experiment with it. Because our prophecies are filled with sayings about the black egg and similar objects of ovular or spherical shapes, my curiosity was piqued. You see, nearly every object like this, including the black egg itself, has the ability to provide a view beyond the physical realm. Of course, I discovered quickly that this was not an egg, and I learned of its prowess in collecting light images and projecting its input in an orderly way. It has many beneficial properties … " He averted his gaze from the crystal. "Among other things."

"So it's the smartest sky scope on Starlight." Koren reached for the sphere again, but Arxad grasped her wrist and pulled her back.

"Wait. Before you touch it, I want to prepare you for the test."

"To see if I am a Starlighter?"

Arxad's voice turned somber. "Good. I am glad you remember." He held up a claw. "Stay here while I move out of the way. I will tell you what to do in a moment."

As he slid into the shadows, a knot formed in Koren's stomach. Even though the test hadn't left her mind, the thrill of the dragon ride and a host of new discoveries had pushed aside the gravity of the situation. Whatever this test was, if she failed, she would be terminated, and if she passed, she would be in Zena's service, whatever that meant. No matter what, her Assignment with Arxad would be over, the best Assignment she had ever had.

"Please place both palms on the sphere." Arxad's voice penetrated the darkness, as did his scarlet eyes. It seemed that the shadow itself had spoken, dark and mysterious in its tone.

She obeyed. The second her skin came into contact with the glassy surface, her whole body tingled. She gasped, though there seemed to be no reason for the sudden surge of emotion and the need for a drink of air. She exhaled and quickly drew in another gulp. "What … " She swallowed through a lump. "What's happening?"

"Settle your mind." Arxad's voice seemed to come from a distant room, quiet, yet echoing. "And your breathing."

As she inhaled slowly, the shadows around her melted away, and the floor disappeared. She floated in the midst of the sky, weightless, free from all burdens of body and mind.

"Now, Koren, probe deeply into the heavens and tell me what you see."

She cocked her head. That voice. So quiet. So far away. Who was it? Someone familiar.

"Tell me with your heart, Starlighter. Relate the tale as only you can tell it."

As the voice faded, the blackness around her altered to a detailed skyscape filled with millions of stars interspersed with darker objects, and the crystal, sparkling white, pulled her up into the sky. The objects floated past her until one of the shadowy forms came into focus. Somehow, its name flowed into her mind and through her lips. "Darksphere."

Like a flood, dozens of images flew through her thoughts, but, just as the crystal had collected and projected its massive array of input, the images straightened and marched past her mind's eye in order. Words flowed, and the images combined into a single animated scene, as if commanded by each phrase she spoke.

"Darksphere," she said in a deep, rumbling voice, "I have found you at last. You are a planet of knights and knaves, so I must avoid the courageous hearts in your midst and deal with the fools, for they will be easy to overcome and allow me to take what I need. When they see my mighty wings and fiery breath, they will cower like frightened curs and give me even their own sons and daughters, for such is the heart of the timid."

The crystal, still in Koren's grip, turned smoky gray, as if contradicting her boast.

Suddenly, the dark planet brightened until it became as dazzling as one of the stars. The scene abruptly changed. She stood in front of ten humans, five men and five women, each about the same age, perhaps their early twenties. Bearing torches and wearing chains around their wrists and ankles, their eyes sparkled in the firelight. Tears streamed down the cheeks of men and women alike as they hunched in fear near the bank of a rapidly flowing river. One man, however, stood tall, his shoulders back and his jaw firm. Instead of a torch, he clutched a book in his hand.

Koren related each detail, even the words the man said as he spoke boldly. "No matter how distant your world, I swear to you that I will escape and return here. We have courageous men, and we will mount an army you cannot withstand. We will not rest until every soul you have stolen returns to its homeland."

Now the crystal turned clear and sparkling again, casting a glow over the speaker.

Koren laughed and replied with a deep, throaty voice. "Uriel, you are a fool. No one in Darksphere knows of the portal, and I will be back to take more of your kind, for we need many to dig deep in search of pheterone."

Again the crystal darkened in her grip, turning almost black.

"You are the fool!" Uriel shouted. "When I return, I will lock this portal so that no one can pass through from either side, and I will not unlock it until our army is ready to invade and destroy you slavers."

"You overestimate your comrades," Koren said. "I have half a mind to release you to prove your error. You are one of the few who care for more than his own bread and porridge. Your fellows would not believe you, and even if one could be persuaded, he would be frightened, unwilling to risk being thought of as insane. Even if you escape, no one will join your army. No one."

She waved her arm, but, instead of her skin, a dragon wing passed in front of her eyes. "Enough of this prattle. Move to the wall."

The men and women shuffled toward a bare wall, their chains clanking with every slide of a foot.

"Keep walking!" Koren touched a dark ovular window embedded in the stone barrier. Instead of a hand and fingers, a scaly dragon's claw covered the glass. A light appeared behind the claw, first yellow, then red, and finally blue. It pulsed, brighter and brighter, spreading out and flooding the area with radiance. The blue brilliance washed away the walls, the river, and the prisoners as they marched past the former barrier. After a few seconds, the light faded.

Koren pulled back and looked at the humans. "Now halt."

Most crouched and covered their faces with their hands, but Uriel stood tall, his stare riveted on Koren.

"You are now on Starlight," Koren said, "and here you will stay. If you work for us, we will treat you well. In order to provide us with more labor, you will populate our world as quickly as possible. If you fail to obey, we will kill you and return to your world to capture others."

Again the crystal turned gray.

She scanned the group, reading the teary eyes and trembling bodies, save, of course, for Uriel. His fiery stare never faded. "This one is strong," she said, though her voice seemed more of a thought than a spoken statement. "We will break him soon enough."

On the floor, a row of crystalline pegs made a line from one side wall to the other. She plucked the middle peg, and the river disappeared. With a wave of a wing, she turned and pointed at an upward sloping tunnel where light poured in. "Come. You will no longer need your torches."

As the prisoners marched toward the exit, Uriel trailed them, now fixing his stare on Koren. Defiant and fearless, he said not a word, though his fiery eyes communicated volumes. He would escape ... somehow. And he would return with his army.

A voice penetrated her mind. "It is time to end your voyage."

Suddenly, the people shrank. She floated backwards, away from the planet, which dimmed as she drew into space, again among the stars. Like a spinning top, the stars whirled around her head. She grew dizzy, oh, so dizzy. She staggered to the side until something caught her and propped her up.

"Koren, you must gather your wits. It is imperative that we fly immediately. If you are found out, I can no longer protect you."

In the midst of the swirling lights, a dragon's face orbited with them. She murmured, "Found out?"

"You are a Starlighter, and you are far more powerful than the one Magnar executed."

"How ... " She licked her dry lips. Her throat felt parched. "How do you know?"

"You made Darksphere brighten and come to life. The previous Starlighter did the same, but she revealed the humans' origins with only a little detail."

"You mean, you knew we came from Darksphere?"

"Of course I knew, but the tale you told differs greatly from Magnar's version."

With the spin slowing, she pulled away from his grasp. "How so?"

"He claimed to have rescued a few survivors from a dying planet. According to him, his was a noble gesture, and we have cared for you all these years in exchange for your labors." Arxad's brow wrinkled. "Magnar's definition of caring for humans, however, is not universal."

She concentrated on his face, trying to make it stop in the center of her vision. "Do you believe him?"

"I believed his story about rescuing survivors." His eyes seemed to erupt in flames. "Until now."

"What are you going to do?"

"If you are able, you must climb on my back. I will take you to the Northlands. There lives someone who might be able to help."

"The Northlands?" A shot of excitement worked to focus Koren's brain. "So there really is such a place? Promoted humans really go there?"

"There is such a place." Arxad lowered his head. "Now mount quickly."

She stepped up to his neck and, bracing herself with her hands, crawled to his back. Grasping a protruding spine, she whisper-shouted, "I'm ready! Let's—"

A new low voice interrupted. "Ready for what?"

Koren swiveled her head. A dragon stood by the entryway, larger than Arxad. With two beats of his enormous wings, he scooted closer. "I assume, Arxad, that you are bringing the Starlighter to me for my judgment."

Arxad bowed his head and shifted in front of the Reflections Crystal, blocking the other dragon's view. "Of course, Magnar. Why would I do anything else?"

"Perhaps your words confused me. I heard something about fleeing to the Northlands."

"A plot to fly to a mythical land?" Arxad let out a chuckle. "It was merely a tale to gain the girl's cooperation. Did I not deliver the previous Starlighter to you?"

Koren gulped. Cold sweat moistened her back. She looked at the Reflections Crystal. For some reason the sphere had turned black.

"You did, in a manner of speaking." Magnar's brow dipped. "Yet why do suspicions keep rising in my mind?"

"I am sure that I cannot answer that for you." Arxad snorted a stream of smoke. "It seems that my record of loyal deeds should erase your suspicions."

Magnar glanced toward the door. "Shall we go directly to the cooking stake? I see no reason for a formal trial."

Koren eased to the side, ready to jump down and run.

Arxad lifted a wing and wrapped it around her body, keeping her in place. "Have you spoken to Zena?" he asked. "She has indicated her desire to have a Starlighter in her service."

"Has she?" Magnar's eyes pulsed crimson. "I thought she had abandoned that idea. The black egg has not created a portal as she once suggested."

Koren struggled to free herself, but the wing held her fast. With the webbing covering her mouth, she could let out only a muffled grunt.

"I spoke to her this very night," Arxad said, "and she seemed quite insistent."

Magnar stretched out his wings. "Then let us visit her together. I want to hear this for myself."

"Your trust in me is not exactly inspiring." Arxad glanced back and forth between Magnar and Koren. She licked her lips again. Her master seemed strange — angry, threatening.

"When you earn my trust," Magnar said, "I will give it freely."

Arxad unwrapped the webbing and shouted, "Stay on my back, Starlighter, or I will make a torch of you!"

Koren stiffened. Her mouth grew so dry, she couldn't speak. What could she do? If she tried to escape, one or both of these dragons would turn her into a heap of ashes. What had happened to her master? He had never been so menacing before.

Magnar beat his wings. Arxad did the same. They rose in wide circles toward the ceiling's projected sky, once again filled with pinpoint stars and three glowing moons. As they flew by Pariah, its sad, cratered face stared at her. Constantly battered by sky rocks, Pariah's expression changed from time to time. Tonight, he seemed melancholy and frightened, lost and alone as the other two moons cast scornful glares at him. Soon he would set below the horizon and escape from the tyranny of those greater than he.

As the Zodiac's ceiling opened at the top of the dome, tears welled in Koren's eyes. She was Pariah. She had messed up everything. Because of her, Lattimer was dead, and Natalla would run away to the wilderness. All was lost.

When Arxad flew through the opening, Koren grasped a spine with both arms and wept. Now she would be executed or perhaps enslaved by that strange Zena woman. In either case, the best Assignment of her life was over. Arxad, Fellina, and Xenith had never been cruel, while Zena's black eyes spelled cruelty. She stared from dead orbs, a heart of soul-lessness, a living cadaver who would inflict suffering without compassion. Her obsession with the egg seemed to stretch beyond the bounds of sanity.

Koren would lose what little freedom she had, and Natalla would never learn about Promotions. She and Stephan would live with the daily threat of starvation and exposure or be captured by a slave hunter and executed, especially if they tried to rescue the cattle children.

And Koren could do nothing to stop them.

Or could she?

She slid up high and called out, "Arxad!"

The great dragon curled his neck and brought his head close. "You are to be silent!"

"Please!" Koren cried. "Please, let me speak!"

His brow loosened. "Very well, but make your words few."

"Natalla plans to escape. She fears Promotion. Can you stop her?"

Arxad stared at her for a moment. "She deserves what-ever befalls her." With that, he straightened his neck and looked ahead.

Koren let her head droop. It seemed that every ounce of energy drained away. But she had to hang on, some-how escape and keep Natalla from going through with her plan. She just had to!

When they arrived again at the Separators' Basilica, the circle of fiery fountains assaulted her cheeks with stinging heat and her eyes with blinding light. The flames' *whoosh* sounded like a gusting breeze rattling dry leaves on creaking old branches.

Magnar landed first and shouted, "Zena, Arxad and I have brought the Starlighter. Extinguish the wall."

As Arxad alighted on the marble floor with Koren, the towering tops of the spewing fountains descended, pulsing in a fast cadence. Seconds later, they revealed Zena, standing in front of the black egg and gripping a pair of chains and manacles. Her voice boomed over the dying *whoosh* and the clinking chains. "If she is truly a Starlighter, then we will allow her to decide if these bonds are necessary."

"If the Prince wants her," Magnar said, "he is welcome to her, but when he no longer needs her, then she must be destroyed." Magnar reached to Arxad's back, snatched Koren's shirt with his teeth, and slung her toward Zena. Koren tumbled a full somersault before falling flat on her chest. A warm, slender hand slid under her chin, lifting her face. The two chains in her other hand came into view, each one tethered to an iron ring on the floor.

Her silky voice crooned. "Magnar is not the gentlest of the Separators, dear girl, but if you are a true Starlighter, you need have no fear of him. You will be assigned to me. Yet if you fail my final test, you will perish at the stake."

Koren rose to her knees and stared at the chains, avoiding Zena's vacant eyes. She tried to speak, but only a rasping reply came forth. "What are the chains for?"

"If you are antagonistic regarding our mission," Zena said as she fastened a manacle around each of Koren's wrists, "then they are for you, but I wager that you will learn to love your new Assignment, so they will not be needed for long."

Koren rose to her feet and looked back at Arxad. With his scaly brow low, he seemed conflicted. Did he really care about her at all? Or was he just worried about his standing with Magnar? Obviously the Separator was suspicious, and Arxad didn't want to do anything to anger his superior. Maybe he cared only about himself.

"Come." Zena gave the chains a gentle pull, yet with enough authority to communicate the reality of the situation. Koren was a prisoner, and there would be no escape.

With hot, dry air still baking the area, Koren followed Zena toward the egg, but as they drew close, the chains tightened, forcing her to halt. The egg, just out of reach, seemed dull in the chamber's ambient light, more like dusky soot than the polished obsidian it appeared to display earlier.

Zena waved her hand toward the dragons. "Stay beyond the barrier. She is mine now, and I will administer the final test."

Magnar shuffled back, but Arxad was already gone. Zena slid a floor panel to the side and turned a dial. The fountains of fire erupted again, creating the wall of flames and a symphony of whooshing sounds. Instantly, the air grew hotter and began to swirl. Koren flinched at the scorching breeze. Her eyes dried out, and her cheeks felt like fireplace embers. Would this be her destiny, living in a baking oven until she turned into the corpse-like woman who had enslaved her?

As soon as the fountains reached their full height, the sounds abated, and the rush of scorching wind eased. Although the air remained hot and stifling, it seemed bearable, more like the heat of a summer day than the inside of Madam Orley's bread oven.

Above, a narrow vent had opened in the ceiling, allowing much of the torrid air to escape. Apparently this entire setup was an incubator of sorts, as well as a way to safeguard the prophetic egg. No one, except perhaps small birds, could get in, and no one, especially human slave girls, could escape.

The egg regained its shine, once again glossy black. Koren stared at her reflection. Every detail emerged in vibrant color—red hair, green eyes, and tanned furrowed brow. In spite of its blackness, the dark shell proved to be a better mirror than the glass in Xenith's room, an echo of more than images; it seemed to reflect emotions. Koren felt her own fear and anguish bouncing back at her.

In spite of the dry air, tears glistened in her eyes. Natalla appeared and stood next to the black egg, transparent, yet as detailed as if she stood there in reality. Stephan's ghostly image came into view. He and Natalla joined hands and walked into a dense forest, each one carrying a hefty knapsack.

"No!" Koren cried out. "You can't go! It's too dangerous!"

Soon a dragon confronted the pair of humans and blew a burst of fire at Stephan, setting him ablaze. As the splash of flames dispersed, the scene disappeared, leaving only the egg in her field of vision.

Koren thrust out her arms, so hard the manacles tore her wrists. "Natalla! Stephan! No!"

The clanking chains held her fast. Koren drooped her head and smeared blood on her cheek as she wept. "Oh, Natalla! Your poor brother! What will that dragon do to you?"

Zena's warm touch combed through Koren's hair, pulling out the band that tied it back. As the red locks fell past Koren's shoulders, Zena crooned, "I have no more need of tests, Starlighter. You are very powerful indeed."

Koren clenched her fists and swung at Zena, but the chains restrained her again. "I don't want to be your slave! I need to save Natalla!"

"Oh, I am afraid that will be impossible. She will likely suffer the same fate that her escort suffered. The same fate Lattimer suffered. The same fate suffered by all humans who dare oppose our masters." Zena let out a *tsking* sound. "It seems that your rebellious acts of late have resulted in tragedy."

Koren lashed out with both arms. Her skin tore again, and blood dripped to the floor. "You she-devil! Let me go! Let me save Natalla!"

Zena shook her head sadly. "As I feared, the use of your gift has ignited a powerful emotional outburst. That is why you are in chains. Until you get to know the egg, I must protect it from you."

"Get to know it?" Koren relaxed her knotted muscles. "What do you mean?"

Zena tilted her head. "Have you not heard its voice yet?"

Koren stared at Zena. Indeed, she had heard something from the egg earlier, a weak "Are you all right?" call. But she didn't want to let this slave mistress know, at least not now.

"Hmm … " Zena pressed a finger against her chin. "Your reticence proves that you *have* heard from our dragon prince."

Koren avoided her dark stare and focused on the egg. "Prince? How do you know it's male?"

"Because the last Starlighter prophesied its gender long before Magnar's mate produced it." Zena ran a hand along the smooth shell. "When you get to know him, you will love him, and you will tell me what he has to say. All of Starlight, including humans, must know how to prepare for his arrival. Every life on our planet depends on it. Until you learn this love, you will have to remain in chains. Yet when your gift is fully awakened and you are ready to serve him as I do, not even the strongest chains would be able to drag you away from him. Only at that time will I reveal what you must do to serve as the egg's surrogate keeper."

Koren glared at her chains, then again at the egg, still barely out of reach. If this prince, whoever he was, charmed wicked women like Zena in order to have sycophant servants, he couldn't be noble.

"You are hurt." The tender, whispered voice emanated from the egg. "There is no need to torture yourself. Resistance will result in pain, while submission will bring you rest."

Koren kept her face in the same scowling pose, not wanting Zena to know that she heard something. She searched the shiny surface. The more she stared, the more it seemed like a deep, dark hole, as if she could reach into a void.

Suddenly, the fountains diminished. Zena had stooped at the controls and was sliding the panel access back into place. "I must acquire an appropriate vestment for you," she said. "Those dirty peasant clothes simply will not do. The prince's attendant must be adorned properly for his imminent arrival."

Zena rose, strode from the protected circle, and stopped at a column. "Anyone can turn the fountains on from outside the nest, but they cannot be turned off from here without a specific voice command that only I know." She pressed a button on the column, and, as the fiery geysers began to rise once again, she offered a crooked smile. "I will return with suitable clothing. It will be up to you whether it becomes a festival gown or a funeral shroud."

The fire streams rose above Zena's head. Now only slices of Zena's form were visible as she glided away and disappeared into the shadows.

Again scorching heat brushed past Koren's face. New whooshing sounds assaulted her ears. The vent in the ceiling reopened and ushered the rising air into the night sky.

Sliding on her knees, Koren edged as close to the egg as the chains allowed. Now free to experiment, she gazed at the reflective shell and whispered, "Can you hear me?"

The lips in her reflection moved as a soft reply floated from the egg. "I am able to hear you."

Koren touched her lips. The girl in the reflection touched hers. She hadn't moved them, had she?

Keeping her hand to her mouth, Koren spoke between her fingers. "What is your name?"

She pressed her lips closed and watched the reflection. As the voice returned, mumbling now, she could barely decipher the words.

"Release my mouthpiece and I will answer. The first time you heard me, I spoke to your mind. Now I prefer to gain experience speaking through your lips."

Koren jerked her hand down. "My lips? You mean, you're talking through me?"

"I have no voice of my own, at least not yet."

Koren stared again at her reflection. Her lips had moved along with the unborn dragon's words. She leaned back and looked away. She couldn't let this slave-driving prince have control over her body.

Slowly, ever so slowly, she turned back to the shell. Maybe the prince could provide information. Even though he had never seen the light of day, he was obviously intelligent, and maybe Zena had taught him the history of Starlight.

She cleared her throat and leaned close. "Are you ready to tell me your name?"

"I am ready, but you are not."

"What do you mean?"

"Only when you learn to love me will I tell you my name."

Koren shook her head. This might be a lot more difficult than she had expected. "Okay, how about this? Do you know where the passageway is to the world of humans?"

For a moment, her anxious face continued staring back at her. Then, as if painted by a meticulous artist, a new image slowly formed on the shell. A male teenager, maybe close to Koren's age, appeared. With water glistening from his brown hair, small nose, and square jaw, he looked like he had been swimming. The area around him was dim, though light enough to reveal a rushing river behind him. Had he waded to shore after an evening dip in the water?

She strained against her manacles and looked closer. His arms were stretched toward her as if he were holding something, but his hands stayed off the screen. His eyes, too dark to discern their color, riveted on hers.

She gasped. He could see her!

His lips moved, and a voice thrummed in her brain. *"Who are you?"*

"Koren," she whispered. She wanted to shout, but letting Zena know about this boy wasn't a good idea.

When she looked again, fog had formed in front of the boy. An angry glare bent his features, and he seemed to shout, but no words came through. Soon the fog vanished. Behind him, the river overflowed its previous bank, flooding wherever it was he stood.

She leaned closer and whispered a little louder, "I'm Koren. Who are you?"

twelve

Breathless, Jason glanced between the rising water and the wall. A light sparkled just above his fingers. The glass in the black egg grew brighter, as if someone had wiped a coat of dirt from the other side and allowed light to pass through. Inside, a redheaded girl stared at him. Her green eyes shone brightly, reflecting the same black egg in her irises. As she reached for the egg with both hands, she lifted chains attached to manacles on her wrists. Dried blood surrounded the metal rings, obvious signs that she had struggled mightily attempting to free herself. Blood smeared one cheek, and a tear tracked through the redness, drawing a thin line as it made its way toward her chin.

Jason stared at her. Could she be one of the Lost Ones? Was she a slave on the dragon planet, somehow drawn to this viewing portal between the worlds? Her pain, her sadness, her longing expression combined to draw passion back into his heart.

"Who are you?" he asked.

Her lips formed a word that looked like "Koren," but no sound came out. Could she see him? Was she trying to communicate? If only he could call to her, tell her he was trying to rescue her. Yet now it seemed that he was the one needing rescue.

His own words echoed in his mind. *I will stand here until I rot if I have to.* But now they seemed a prideful boast, nothing more than the bravado that had intimidated his opponents within the tourney ring.

He looked again at the floor. The water had climbed to his ankles. This was no tourney ring, and this river would not be intimidated by mere words. Without compassion for its opponents, the river would leave no survivors.

❧

Elyssa swam with the current. Although darkness shrouded her vision, the walls on each side appeared in her mind as vague shadows, her Diviner's gift painting an image of abrupt changes in density and moisture in her surroundings. As the river washed her to one side, she pushed the wall with her hands, giving her an extra burst of speed.

And speed was crucial. How long could Jason keep his fingers in place? As usual, she hadn't let him in on her plan. This time, it could cost her her life.

As she pushed off a curve in the left wall and jetted into a frenzied swim, she bit her lip hard. Why couldn't she trust Jason enough to tell him everything? Why was she so hard on anyone who couldn't see beyond the physical? He was smart. And wise, too. But being surrounded by fools at the governor's palace had long ago ripped away her trust in others. One traitor after another had violated a promise, even to the point of revealing her gift to the Counselor. If not for Adrian's intervention, she would have been tied to the heretic's stake and burned to death.

Even in the water's increasing chill, heat from the fire's image sizzled across her skin. No heretic had been burned in years, but memories of the last victim still blazed in her mind.

At the age of seven, she and Jason had gone to the village to buy yeast, and a crowd was funneling toward the pillory. Being inquisitive children, they followed and arrived just in time to see the previous Counselor setting a torch at the feet of the widow Halstead. As the flames took hold of the bundles of sticks and straw, she writhed in front of the tall wooden stake, her eyes clenched shut. She cried out, "Creator of All, have mercy on these ignorant people! They know not when a prophet is in their midst!" Then, her head lolled to the side. She was dead long before the fire should have killed her.

As soon as flames began eating the widow's dress, Jason covered Elyssa's eyes and hustled her away. "It'll be all right," he had whispered. "She must have done something really bad."

But they both knew better. The widow had been kind to every child in the village, telling stories from days gone by, even tales of the dragon world and the Lost Ones, which, she and Jason had later concluded, were the stories that probably got her in trouble. Yet Elyssa knew more. When she and Madam Halstead were alone, the kind old lady would teach her how to use her Diviner's skills, constantly warning her not to let anyone know about either of them. The Counselor wouldn't understand that these talents were not evil, but gifts of foresight provided by the Creator to a chosen few who would be prophetesses, and were certainly not the result of dark magic that arose from the powers of the wicked one. At those moments of warning, when the widow spoke with such caution, the image of fire always ignited in her mind, warming her skin now as it did then.

Fueled by the memory, Elyssa swam on, kicking and paddling even harder. Every few seconds, she glanced ahead, using her eyes as well as her inner vision to search for the rope, the foam—any sign she was approaching the hole.

Soon, subtle changes pricked her senses—a slight deepening of the water and a slippery feel. Although no foam islands drifted nearby, something was injecting a soapy ingredient. She reached to the right, grasped a rocky projection, and hung on, her face and chest pointing toward the wall. The river rushed by behind her, but not so fast that she couldn't hold on.

She looked up. Yes! Light! It was a tiny circle, far, far away. This had to be the bottom of the bottomless pit, and the rope was probably hanging nearby, concealed by the pervasive darkness.

Unable to search for the rope without letting go of her handhold and risk being swept into the river's flow, Elyssa closed her eyes and concentrated on the walls around her. To her right, the channel leading back to Jason was tall and wide. To her left lay a narrow tunnel with just enough headroom for her to be sucked into a much swifter flow. Her heart thumped. A death hole. Too close for comfort.

As she pushed the fear aside, she continued her inventory. In front and behind stood bare walls with only a few rocky projections. Climbing them would be impossible. A strange object protruded just above the mouth of the narrow channel to the left, something long and narrow. Hanging on to her wall with her right hand, Elyssa stretched to reach for the object with her left. She grabbed hold. It felt like a metal rod, and it moved with her weight and shifted slightly toward her.

A sudden gush swept her off her perch and toward the smaller tunnel, but, keeping her head high and holding fast to the rod with both hands, she propped her feet on the wall on each side of the opening and straddled the channel.

Water splashed against her back, a crushing pressure that pushed and pushed, each second bending her toward the wall's consuming mouth. Now closer, she could see the mouth more clearly in her mind's eye. Sharp stones protruded from the top, making it look even more like a gaping maw ready to crunch her body if she gave in to the raging current.

Her legs cramped, but letting go was out of the question. How long could she stay like this? Sooner or later she would have to give in.

She pressed her lips together. The rod had to be there for a reason. She gave it a push toward the right. It moved, but again only slightly. Flexing her muscles, she pushed it once more with all her might.

It jerked fully to the side, nearly slipping from her hand.
A low rumble sounded. As she continued watching with
her Diviner's vision, the "teeth" receded, and the upper
half of the mouth descended, cutting off the river's exit.
The water level began to rise, buoying her body and lifting
her higher and higher. Soon, a hint of light clarified her
surroundings and allowed her to see with her physical
eyes. The rope came into view, its end dangling above. She
would be able to reach it within seconds.

She squinted at the odd sight. Why would it hang down
only this far? That didn't make sense at all. What good was
a rope that could neither lower someone to the bottom nor
allow someone to climb from below?

Seconds later, she grabbed the rope and pulled. The
rumble sounded once again, this time muffled by water.
The river's level steadied before slowly descending.

Elyssa thrust the rope away. The rumble stopped for
a moment, then returned. Again the water rose, and as
she lifted with the flow, the sounds of the river's shutoff
valve faded. Above, the circle of light slowly grew larger.
Treading water with one arm, she reached for the rope
and let it pass through her fingers. Better to keep it close
in case she had to open the channel again. Apparently,
sliding the metal rod to the side passed control of that
gate's open-and-close valve over to the rope.

Soon the water lifted her to the top and spilled her onto
the field of grass and yellow flowers. Still loosely grasping
the rope, she found its attachment point, a small hole in a
rocky slab. She knelt beside it, water flowing all around,
and gave the rope a pull. It slid out a hand's breadth and
stopped. The water receded toward the hole, and the
ground soaked up the remnants.

Elyssa dropped the rope. A click sounded near her feet, and the water slowed its descent. Perhaps it would now rise again, but she couldn't hold on to the rope indefinitely. Breathing out a long sigh, she looked around. Not far away, two bodies lay on their bellies amidst the flowers. Randall and Tibalt.

She jumped up and ran toward them. Reaching Tibalt first, she knelt and tried to turn him over, but tiny roots attaching themselves to his skin kept him in place. With a quick jerk, she pulled him free and laid him on his back, his face toward the warm sunshine.

A satisfied smile lifted his features, but his eyes stayed closed. Blood stained his ratty shirt, so shredded now it exposed a nest of gray chest hairs.

She lifted his hand. A makeshift bandage was wrapped around it, obviously hastily fashioned from his shirt. His other hand bore a similar wrap.

"Tibalt!" she called, shaking him. "Wake up!"

He let out a snort and slept on, oblivious.

Shifting on her knees, she turned Randall to his back, again breaking skinny roots that had attached to his skin and clothes. "Randall!" She patted his cheek with her cold hand but to no avail.

As the meadow's fragrance drifted into her nose, dizziness flooded her brain, and her vision grew fuzzy. What was she doing here with Randall? And who was the strange old man?

She glanced from side to side. What was this place, anyway? Where was Jason? Didn't they come here together? And why was she so wet?

Moisture seeped in around her knees. She jumped to her feet and looked for the source. Dizzy, she spread out her feet to keep her balance. Water rose from a hole in the ground and spread out across the meadow.

She squinted at the sunlight's glare on the water as it bubbled up. How strange! It couldn't have been doing that for very long. Otherwise the field would have been covered long ago. She stooped and touched the flow with her fingers. Stranger still. It felt slippery, soapy.

Lifting her fingers to her nose, she took in the odd odor. It was sharp, penetrating. Her dizziness suddenly eased, and her vision clarified. The meadow, now a thumb-length deep in water, took on a new aspect.

Danger!

She dipped both hands in the water, splashed her face, and shook her head to sling away the drops. Her confusion flew away with them.

"Jason!" She jumped up and ran to Randall and Tibalt. They both stirred, apparently aroused by the invigorating flow.

Tibalt sat up and blinked at her, his stringy hair dripping. "Was it really a bottomless pit?"

"I must admit," she said as she grasped his wrist to help him rise, "I never found the bottom."

"Hee hee!" He stamped a foot in the mud. "I knew it! I just knew it!"

Randall struggled to his feet and stretched out his arms. "I thought I'd never get that crazy old man up here. He's not that heavy, but it was a long way—"

"Who's crazy, you big oaf! I was climbing like a spider monkey, and your pulls just slowed me down!"

"Quiet," Elyssa said, waving her hands at them. "We have to get back to Jason."

Randall pulled the photo gun from his holster and examined it. "Where is he?"

"At the gateway," she said absently as she stared at the hole. "But I can't figure out how to get back. I can make the water level drop, but I have to signal Jason to switch the underground river's flow. We'll never be able to swim against its current."

"Switch the flow?" Randall shook his head. "You'd better start from the beginning."

For the next minute or so, Elyssa rattled off what had happened, but only enough to provide the basic picture. They had no time to waste.

When she finished, Randall stroked his chin. "I'm no expert on hydrology, but it sounds like you've put Jason in a lot of trouble."

"Trouble? How?"

He pointed at the hole. "Water follows the path of least resistance. It probably backed up into Jason's chamber."

"Oh, no!" She ran to the edge of the hole and searched for the rope, but a layer of muddy water covered everything around the rim. "He'll drown!"

"I wouldn't worry about that. He'll pull his fingers out of the wall first."

Elyssa searched through the water frantically. "Oh, Randall, you don't know Jason like I do. He thinks switching the flow would kill me. He'd rather die than do that."

Randall and Tibalt joined her, but it seemed hopeless. While her brain was under the influence of the flowers, she had lost track of where the rope was attached. Even if she did find the it, would she be in time to open the channel?

※

With water now rising to his waist, Jason kept his hands in place and called to the girl in the viewer. "My name is Jason Masters. Are you one of the Lost Ones? Are you on the dragon planet? And what was your name again?"

The girl in chains cocked her head. She leaned forward as far as she could and mouthed her words carefully.

Jason read her lips. *I am Koren, and I am on a dragon planet. I am a slave here.*

His heart thumping, he shouted his reply. "I'm trying to open this portal so I can rescue you! But the chamber's flooding! Do you know how to stop the water from rising?" He glanced at his hands. He knew one way to stop the water, but withdrawing his fingers was a deadly option.

I have no idea, Koren mouthed. *Can you run away?*

Jason shook his head. "It's complicated. I think this is a portal, and I activated it somehow. Maybe the viewer I'm seeing you through is the way to get from here to there."

If only I could pull you out. Koren extended a hand, grimacing as the cruel manacles tore into her skin. *I ... can't ... reach ... any farther!*

"No! Don't hurt yourself!" Jason looked at the water, now level with his chest. Cold and swirling, it took his breath away. At this rate, he would be completely underwater in less than a minute.

What can I do? Koren asked.

"I don't know. Is there a code? A secret word?"

She shook her head, obviously frustrated. *Are you alone? Is there no one you can call to rescue you?*

The water rose to his neck. "I wasn't alone earlier. Elyssa was with me, but I can't leave or the river will reverse course, and she might drown."

Elyssa? Tell me about her. Maybe I can find her for you. I can see what most people can't.

With the water now to his jaw, he lifted his chin to keep his mouth above the surface. "She's three months younger than me, maybe two inches shorter. Long reddish brown hair, green eyes, pretty face."

As Koren closed her eyes, her brow furrowed. *I think I see her. Is her face oval shaped?*

"Yes, I would say so."

She looks wet.

"Yes! That's Elyssa!" His words bubbled in the water. "Is she all right?"

Koren's face scrunched tightly. *She is kneeling on a carpet of muddy grass and yellow flowers.*

Jason stood on tiptoes to spit out his reply. "Kneeling? Not swimming?"

Yes. Kneeling. She is with two men, one old and one young, and they are searching for something.

"Are you seeing the past? The future?"

Koren opened her eyes. A morose expression dragged down her features. *I don't know. This is all new to me.*

Now holding his breath as the water rose past his lips, Jason stared at Koren. Could she be trusted? Might she be a figment of his imagination, planted in his brain by a snatcher? Or was she real, a true Lost One who begged for his help?

As if summoned by his thoughts, the smoky ghost returned, swirling above his head. "Release the portal, Jason Masters, or you will die."

Jason glared at the phantom. It wanted him to fail, so why should he listen? Maybe this was all part of the gateway puzzle. Maybe filling the chamber was necessary to get the portal to open. Could that be what the inscription meant? *Where only courageous hearts may brave the river's flow.* Someone had to have the courage to stay put while water rose to the ceiling. If he could hold his breath long enough, the opening of the portal might rescue him.

Maybe.

The litmus finger began throbbing against his skin. He begged for guidance, but it seemed that the special powers the finger had given earlier had faded. And why not? He had found the portal. Maybe that was all the finger was good for.

Now submerged, Jason looked at the viewer once more. Koren stared back at him, her hands folded in entreaty. The current warped his view, making her lips difficult to read, but she seemed to be shouting "Jason," again and again. As her chains rose with her clenched hands, she looked so sincere, so pitiful, so lovely.

He closed his eyes. The image of Elyssa diving into the river's flow came to mind. Maybe she was safe and kneeling in a field, as Koren had seen, and maybe not. At this point, even if he withdrew his fingers, he probably wouldn't find a way to escape anyway. Keeping them in the wall seemed to be the only way to survive. The opening of the portal was his only hope.

With his lungs feeling ready to explode, Jason tried to peer at the water's surface, now up to the ceiling. No air remained in the chamber. All hope of survival seemed to wash away. Even if the portal opened, he might not have the strength to go through it.

He looked again at Koren. She had buried her face in her bloody hands, crying bitterly. With her image firmly implanted in his mind, Jason closed his eyes again, and everything faded to black.

❈

Elyssa snatched up the rope. "I found it!"

"I'll hold the gate open," Randall said, taking the rope from her. "But how are you going to fight the current all the way back to Jason?"

Elyssa shot to her feet and stared at the water. Although it began receding immediately, it seemed slow, far too slow. "If the flow goes down enough, I'm hoping to find a footpath alongside the river. If I can't, you'll have to close the gate again so we can rise back to the surface."

"How will I know? I can't see down that far."

Elyssa kept her gaze on the hole. "Tibalt will have to hang on to the rope while I work. He'll give it a tug."

Tibalt set his toes at the edge of the pit. "This is familiar, like a story my pappy used to tell me."

"A story?" Elyssa asked.

"He told me about a river that changed direction." Tibalt lifted his hands. "And you can make it change by using your fingers."

"Yes, I know." Elyssa kept her focus on the water as it drained toward the pit. In only seconds it would be time to jump in and float down with it. "There are holes at the gateway, and when Jason put his fingers in them, the river switched course."

"Pappy didn't say anything about that." Tibalt lowered his voice and spoke in a growl. "The hero reaches for the gate by touching dragon's teeth of eight. But enter not the dragon's cave, or the dragon's throat will be your grave."

Elyssa shuddered. "I saw the dragon's teeth."

"So you can reverse the flow?" Randall asked.

"We'll soon find out." Elyssa jumped into the hole and paddled to keep her head above the surface. "Tibber will let you know if I get the flow reversed. If I succeed, I can lock the gate open with a lever I found down there. When I slide the lever back to where it was before, the rope won't control the gate at all."

"Why don't you just let me close it after you reverse the flow? Then the river will be trapped behind that gate and dry up. You could walk to Jason."

"The teeth were there only when the lever locked the gate open, so I have to take control down there. Besides, if it was dry, you wouldn't be able to jump in and join us."

"Join you? By jumping from way up here?"

Elyssa shrugged. "It's up to you. If your courage is lacking, feel free to go home."

"Courage?" Randall's grip tightened on the rope. "Diving into an underground river to nowhere isn't courage. It's crazy!"

"You only live once!" Tibalt leaped into the hole. He submerged but soon bobbed to the surface and spat out a stream of water. "It tastes like soap!"

As she descended with the water, Elyssa looked up at Randall and gave him a smirk. "I understand. Tibber and I will be the crazy ones, an old man and a girl. Go back to the palace and put on some clean silk stockings and the satin underwear you keep in your top left drawer."

"What? I don't have any—"

"I used to do your laundry." Elyssa blew him a kiss. "I'll see you at the gateway."

The rate of descent increased, and the water began a slow spin. Tibalt grabbed the rope and fed it through his bandaged hands. "When do you figure I should hang on?"

"I'm not sure," Elyssa said. "I'll just have to guess." Swirling faster now, she closed her eyes and imagined the dragon's mouth. Now open, the water would be flushing through it. How far down was it?

As she concentrated, the scene below took shape in her mind: the outline of the mouth, the bubbles in the current, and the lever, but no teeth.

The mouth drew closer and closer. At this rate, she would be there in seconds. "Tibber!" she shouted, opening her eyes. "Hold the rope!"

With light from above quickly diminishing, Tibalt tightened his grip and rose out of the water, dripping like a captured fish. "Don't leave me hanging too long!"

"I won't!" Elyssa gazed at the brave old man. His hands had to hurt, and fresh from his escape after a lifetime in the dungeon, here he was, ready to risk his life to help them find something he remembered like a storybook tale. His courage was amazing.

Soon a current began to pull on Elyssa's feet. In almost complete darkness, she let her mental vision expand, hoping to find the mouth again. There it was, only two body lengths down. Water rushed through, creating a downward sucking action that would soon grab her body and sweep her into its vacuum.

She pressed her hands and feet against the wall, slowly letting them spread apart as she descended. With nothing more than smooth irregularities in the stone to grip, she fought against the downward pull.

With a loud slurping noise, the water's surface fell below the top of the gaping mouth. The river rushed through, pulling her clothes and straining at her body. She let the pressure slide her farther down until she braced one foot on each side of the hole. Then, inch by inch, she moved one hand toward the protruding lever, now in front of her. She grabbed it and jerked it back to its original position. Eight stony teeth slowly pushed from the top of the opening and locked in place.

The water stopped its descent. Now a smoothly running river once again, it continued its never-ending flow, pushing against her lower back, as if trying to shove her into the throat. In her mind's eye, the dragon came to life with eyes of red glowing just above the hungry maw.

"Randall can let go now!" she yelled.

The river's tumult drowned out her voice. Had Tibalt heard her at all? And the force was incredible. Her legs wavered. The friction stung her skin mercilessly, but she had to hang on. For Jason's sake, she just had to.

She let go of the lever and slid her right hand down a conical tooth and touched the sharp point at the bottom with a finger. Then, spreading out her hand, she touched three others.

Now for the other hand. But with her right no longer bracing against the wall, her legs and other arm began to buckle. Could she resist the wet onslaught at her back with just her legs?

As she slid her left hand down, her calf cramped. Pain knifed through her muscles from her ankle to her thigh. Any second they would give way and—

"Aaugh!" Her body lunged through the mouth feet-first, but she grabbed on to a tooth, flipped over to her belly, and looked straight out the dragon's maw. Water surged into her face and blasted into her mouth and nose. She couldn't breathe. She had to let go, or else drown in a matter of seconds.

She strangled the tooth and pulled with all her might. She couldn't let go! She had to get back to Jason.

Her fingers slipped. They were numb, frozen digits petrified by cold water and pain. The current beat against her face. Trickles forced their way through her nostrils and into her lungs. But she couldn't cough them out. She would drown for sure. Only one choice remained: let the river take her and see what lay at the other end of the dragon's throat.

Clenching her eyelids tightly, Elyssa loosened her fingers and let go.

thirteen

Koren buried her face in her hands and wept. "Oh, Jason! What have you done? Oh, Jason!"

She peeked between her fingers. Should she look? Would he be dead?

The egg's black shell came into focus, but no scene of a flooded chamber returned, just her own reflection.

As she lowered her hands, her lips moved, unbidden. "Why do you lament for this human?"

She choked out her reply. "He was trying to come here to rescue me."

"Rescue you? Why do you need rescue? You have been granted the most glorious Assignment in this realm."

"Glorious?" Koren shook her chains. "Do you call this glorious? Shackled to the floor to serve a dragon in an egg?"

"The chains are necessary only until you learn to love me. Then you will be ready to serve me without bonds, as Zena does."

Koren scowled at her reflection. "I don't ever want to be like Zena. She's a walking corpse. And, besides, if you force someone to love you, that's not really love at all. Love has to be a choice. Chains can never bind a heart."

"Are you saying that you would choose to love me? In your current condition of aggression and doubt, would you ever be convinced that I am worthy to be served from the heart?"

She shook a chain again. "If this is your idea of being worthy, then no, I would never learn to love you."

"Yet if you stay in chains long enough, you will love me, so the chains must stay. It is better that you love me by force than be given freedom to choose and not love me. You see, as a slave, you have no capacity to love me yet, so I must force love upon you. At the end, your heart of devotion is all that matters, not the path you take in getting there."

Koren glared at her torn skin and blood-stained wrists. "I beg to disagree."

The strange voice again emerged from her lips. "I understand your doubts, but you do not know me well enough yet to trust me. When you learn, you will then understand."

She closed her eyes. Watching herself speak the dragon's words was beyond confusing.

After waiting a few seconds for her thoughts to come together, she replied in a firm tone, "And you don't know me well enough to trust me, either. If you prove yourself worthy of love, I won't need chains."

For a moment, silence ensued. Koren barely opened her eyelid and peeked out. Somehow, her expression mimicked the feelings she projected on the dragon—perplexed, caught in a trap.

Finally, her lips moved again. "Since you are a Starlighter, I should have expected such an interesting proposition. Shall we make a deal?"

Koren closed her eyes again. "What kind of deal?"

"You will be released—free, no longer a slave. Roam the chambers of the Basilica to learn what you may. I will ensure that no one here accosts you, and I will instruct Zena to provide meals for you whenever you wish. Visit me each evening, and we will talk. If you have not learned to love me before I hatch, you may return to your previous Assignment."

She opened her eyes fully. In the reflection, her face took on a skeptical slant. "What's the catch?"

"Nothing burdensome. You must wear the Starlighter's cloak, for that will let every dragon in the Basilica know that you are under my supervision. They will think that you have submitted to me and have been allowed freedom. You must also stay in the Basilica. I cannot protect you outside these walls."

Koren looked at her chains. They felt as heavy as pails of rocks from the cattle camps. Getting set free would allow her to escape the Basilica and find Natalla, but that would break the agreement, the deal that would sever the manacles. Was it a violation of the Code to lie in order to save a life? The Code was clear that lying for selfish reasons was not allowed, but this was different. Natalla needed her. Could she make this deal with the dragon and then break it? Risking her own life to save an innocent one was the most unselfish act possible, wasn't it?

Yet, this wouldn't be like one of her tall tales, designed to entertain rather than to deceive. Maybe she could make the promise, fully intending to keep it, and just pray that the solution would become clear later.

She lifted her hand, her palm toward the egg. "I agree to your terms."

"Excellent." Once again, her lips moved to give voice to the egg's occupant. "Zena should return soon with your cloak, and I will command her to make the arrangements. For now, you must stay here and rest. Your freedom will come in the morning."

⇒·⇐

Elyssa braced herself for a plunge into darkness and death, but she didn't move. In the midst of the sound of rushing water, a voice rang out. "I've got you! Try to push with your feet and free hand."

Tibber's voice! Did he have a grip on her wrist? With all the water pelting her skin, she couldn't feel his hand.

While kicking with both feet, she clawed the rocky side. Like a fireball, her body slung forward and out of the dragon's mouth. Then the current reversed her momentum and kicked her back toward the dragon, but Tibalt wrapped an arm around her waist and held her fast while bracing his feet against the rocky wall.

"If we don't work together," he said, "we'll be dragon bait. I'll hold you while you touch that rascal's teeth."

Now shivering with relief and cold, Elyssa reached for the sharp points and pressed the pads of her fingers against them. As she held them in place, she spoke into Tibalt's ear. "Notice any changes?"

He shook his head, slinging droplets into her face. "Nothing yet. Maybe it needs more body heat."

"If I have any left." Elyssa pressed harder—so hard, the points pierced her skin, but it was too dark to tell if she had drawn blood. The pain was awful, but she clenched her teeth, determined to keep pushing until the river changed course.

After a few more seconds, the ground shook and seemed to tip slightly. The water slowed to a halt and sloshed against their faces. Elyssa pulled away from the teeth and sucked on the most painful finger, the salty taste of blood sharp on her tongue.

Soon the river began to flow again, this time toward the gateway.

Tibalt shouted, "I think we're about to go for a ride!"

Elyssa wrapped her arms around him. "You keep us afloat for a while. When you get tired, I'll take over."

"Are you sure?" Tibalt began to paddle. "I can try to swim all the way."

"Trust me. I've done this before."

The rush slung them into the tunnel leading toward Jason, the water now warmer than last the time but still uncomfortable. Elyssa gritted her teeth, trying to keep from shivering or thinking about the possibility of finding Jason lifeless at the gateway's entrance.

As they rushed along, she penetrated the darkness with her mental vision. At times, she kicked against the walls to keep from smashing into them. Soon a hint of illumination entered her mind. The chamber was near. Would Jason still be there?

She probed further and searched for signs of life. Nothing. No warmth. No movement. Not a stir.

After a few seconds, light rushed into her vision. She opened her eyes and groped for shore, shouting, "We're here, Tibber. Swim!"

Her hands slapped the riverbank, and her feet scraped against the bottom. She trudged out and scanned the area, her heart pounding. Jason lay on his stomach near the wall, motionless.

Dripping and sliding, she ran to him, laid him on his back, and checked his pulse. Nothing.

She lifted her head and screamed, "Tibber!"

"I'm coming." Tibalt sloshed to Jason's side and dropped to his knees. "He looks as dead as a fence post."

Elyssa pushed on Jason's chest with rhythmic thrusts. "Can you do this for me?"

When Elyssa slid her hands away, Tibalt put his in their place. "Like this?" he asked as he copied her motions.

"Perfect! Keep it up!" She tilted Jason's head back, opened his jaw, and covered his gaping blue lips with her mouth. Her body shaking all over, she blew. Then, after taking a quick breath through her nose, she blew again and repeated the process several times, listening for any sign of recovery and mentally probing his body for the slightest change.

Finally, Jason coughed and spat. Elyssa jerked away and waved for Tibalt to stop. She helped Jason rise to a sitting position and patted him on the back while he continued hacking. "Just keep coughing it up. Get all the water out. You'll be fine soon."

Tibalt took one of Jason's hands and rubbed it briskly. "Better get some blood flowing, boy. You're as blue as a baby bonnet."

After several more heaves, Jason shook his head hard before staring at Elyssa with wide eyes. "What happened?"

Elyssa grinned. "You drowned."

He looked up at the wall. "Oh, yeah. I kept my fingers in the holes until I blacked out. Pretty stupid, I guess."

"Not at all." She kissed him on the cheek. "I'm sure you did it for me."

Jason's eyes shot wide open again. "Koren!"

"Koren? Who's Koren?"

"The girl in the portal." Jason climbed to his feet and staggered to the wall. Touching a dark glass oval, he looked back at Elyssa. "We talked through this window. She's on the dragon planet."

Elyssa rose and, rubbing her wet arms, shuffled closer. "You talked to one of the Lost Ones?"

"Well, not really 'talked.' I read her lips."

"She told you she was a slave?"

Jason rubbed his wrist and nodded. "She was in chains, bleeding. It was really sad."

"Can you see her now?" Elyssa tried to peek past Jason. Had he really seen someone, or was it all a dream?

"I don't see her now." Jason reinserted his fingers into the holes. "I'll try again. Maybe—"

"No!" Elyssa jerked his arm back. "You might reverse the river again."

"What's wrong with that? You're both safe. Besides, we need to turn on the warm air before we freeze to death."

"Randall might come. He was supposed to follow us."

"*Might* come?" Jason repeated.

"Well, he never said for sure, but I think he will. He just has to summon the courage to jump."

"Oh, he'll come," Tibalt said, cackling. "This pretty young lady shamed him down to a toadstool. If he's half a man, he'll be here."

"Speaking of which … " Elyssa walked to the river's edge, hugging herself and shivering harder. "We'd better watch for him."

Jason's voice spiked. "What's more important? Watching for a guy who might come, or trying to get in touch with the girl on the dragon planet?"

Elyssa spun back toward him. "Get the water out of your brain, Jason. The girl you dreamed about might not be real."

"She's real. I'm sure of it. She responded to me."

"Then she's safe for now. She can wait a few more minutes."

"Wait for what? Koren is a slave in chains. Randall is a trained survivor. After we go through the portal, the river will probably turn back our way. He'll be fine."

They stared at each other, neither flinching. Tibalt glanced at them in turn. "Well, this is all a bunch of fish feathers! If Jason's fingers came out of those little worm holes when he fainted, then he wasn't the one who changed the flow to what it is now. Whatever you did back there with those dragon fangs, this river is now a one-way paddleboat stream, at least until your blood drips off those teeth." He marched to the wall and inserted his fingers, pushing his bandage back and exposing his raw wounds. "You watch for Randall. I want to see the slave girl."

The moment his fingers slid to the back of the holes, the lights flashed on again. As before, warm, dry air swirled throughout the chamber, and the dragons pulsed, but this time, the firelights from the dragons' mouths changed direction and breathed on the window. Like oil spreading across a pond, the oval expanded and covered the lights, as if a dense cloud had shadowed every speck of radiance.

Tibalt's eyes widened, and he drew his head back, but he kept his feet and fingers locked in place. "It's my pappy's story!"

As the glass stretched out, it brightened, turning from black to gray to white. Soon it became transparent, as if no barrier stood between them and the scene on the other side. The new room appeared to be an extension of their own chamber, yet with sunlight flooding in from a passageway at the far side and a staircase that sloped up and out of sight.

Tibalt looked at his hands. "I can still feel the tingle, but there ain't any holes."

"It looks safe enough," Jason said as he reached a hand into the new chamber.

Elyssa clutched a fistful of his wet shirtsleeve. "If that's the dragon world, it's not safe."

"This is what we came for." Jason touched the sword hilt at his hip. "I'm ready."

"No use standing around," Tibalt said. "A door that opens is bound to close, and this one might slam shut in our faces."

Elyssa looked back at the river. "What about Randall? If he comes, he'll be trapped here."

"We can't afford to wait." Jason let out a huff. "I feel bad for Randall, but we have to save the Lost Ones. This might be our only chance." He pointed at the sword brackets. "If he comes, he can grab a sword and wait for us."

"I'll stay," Tibalt said, shivering as a draft blew in from the new opening. "It looks like I'm the only one who can open this door, so if he shows up, we'll find you. Randall's a good tracker."

Jason nodded. "And we might need his photo gun." He grasped Tibalt's shoulder. "Thank you."

"Don't thank me. That's not cold making my bones shake. I want to delay meeting any dragons for as long as I can. You know what the old song says. When you offer a hand, make sure he's a friend, or when you draw back your arm, it won't have an end."

Jason nodded at Elyssa. "And what's causing your shivers? The cold or the prospect of meeting dragons?"

"Both." She resisted the urge to grab his hand and march with him into the other world. That's what would happen anyway, but skipping steps now would be out of line. He needed to make the offer.

As if reading her thoughts, Jason reached for her. "Let's find a warmer place in the dragon world."

"By all means." She smiled and took his hand. "Lead the way, warrior."

—⋅—

Koren opened her eyes. The light of morning filtered in from the air vent in the ceiling, barely visible in the radiance of the fiery geysers. The egg was there, still black and shiny, with her reflection again staring back at her. Yet much had changed since she first came into this new Assignment only hours ago. The chains lay on the floor nearby, the manacles open. A soft pillow supported her head, and a thick pad cushioned her body; gifts from Zena, who had become far more courteous than before.

After climbing to her feet, Koren caressed the elbow-length white sleeve on her silky gown. Thin, loose-fitting, and smelling of desert flowers, wearing it felt like bathing in perfumed water. A cloak of dark blue draped her shoulders, the hem of which swept an inch or two above the floor. With a clasp holding it together between her sternum and throat, and a loose hood hanging at the back, it was more like a hooded cape, sleeveless yet royal.

She touched an embroidered pair of green eyes at the left breast and ran her finger along the raised threads. So this was a Starlighter's cloak. Had Cassabrie worn it? Did she have it on when she died?

With her bare foot, she nudged her dirty old shirt lying on the floor next to the open manacles. It was good to shed that smelly old garment, but she had kept her shorts on underneath the dress, just in case she had to run or climb.

Behind the egg, Zena sat cross-legged on the floor, the goat's hair bag now in her clutches. A half smile adorned her face, making her seem prettier than usual. "I will dispose of that for you."

"Thank you." Koren picked the shirt up and set it next to Zena. A rumble stirred in her belly. When had she last eaten anything? As she set a hand on her stomach, she offered Zena a polite nod. "Where shall I go for my meals?"

Picking up the dirty tunic, Zena rose to her feet and adjusted the bag's strap at her shoulder. "You will dine in the presence of the prince. It is now early morning, so breakfast will be served soon. But the Starlighter slept only a little while. May I suggest another nap?"

"No. I think I'm fine. But I would like some water."

"As you wish." A hint of sarcasm spiced Zena's reply. "Perhaps the Starlighter would enjoy a massage to loosen her muscles."

Koren tried to read Zena's expression. That was the first hint that she might be annoyed at the new arrangement. Koren was tempted to say, "Yes, a massage would be wonderful, and a palm branch to fan me, if you please," but putting more tension on Zena's already strained civility wouldn't be a good idea. Instead, she offered a curtsy. "You are very kind, but that won't be necessary. And I will be glad to help you prepare the meal."

Zena's tone relaxed. "There is no need."

Koren looked around at the wall of flaming fountains. It was time to go and search for answers. Natalla was either dead or in shackles, possibly awaiting transfer to the cattle camps. Maybe a record of her capture existed somewhere, a log book for reassigned slaves. "So may I explore the Basilica now?"

"You may." Zena slid open the floor panel and turned off the fountains. As the fire died away, she nodded at the egg. "Before you leave, does the prince have anything further to say?"

As Koren glanced between the egg and Zena, a new realization dawned. Zena's only means of direct communication with the prince must be through a Starlighter. Earlier, the prince had spoken to Zena through Koren's lips, and he had given her commands with words that only the dragon or Zena would know, thereby convincing her that the true prince was speaking.

Koren drilled her stare into the egg. What about now? Could she imitate the prince and issue commands to Zena? Or would that be an improper means of deception?

The dragon's voice passed through her lips, again unbidden. "Zena, the Starlighter should be on her way now. When she has departed, I will speak to you in the old manner."

"Very well, my prince." Zena touched the bag hanging at her side. "The old way is much more to my liking."

Koren eyed the bag. Obviously Zena carried something within that helped her talk to the dragon. There would be no way to fake a command as long as Zena could learn the truth.

After giving another curtsy, Koren strode beyond the boundary of the egg's circular incubator and hurried out of the chamber.

With sunlight passing through stained-glass windows above and all around, the interior came alive with streams of vibrant colors, painting skewed copies of the designs in the windows—dragons of all shapes and sizes; feasting pedestals covered with slaughtered elk and sheep; and various balls of fiery light, some white and some bright yellow.

Slowing her pace, she stared at the largest ball of light, a white one in the center of a ceiling window pane. It hovered at the left of the largest of several dining pedestals, as if it were ready to devour the meat set before it. What could it be? A representation of a dead ancestor? A deity? Might the dead animal be a sacrifice?

Koren stopped at the edge of a precipice. The dragon meeting hall spread out below, and the book still lay open on the pedestal, but now the fire was no longer burning. From her vantage point directly above the stage, the dragons' seats stretched out in front of her from left to right. Two dragons rested in the back row, one flicking his tail at the design in the window behind him, which depicted a human lugging a cart with two dead goats within.

Although the window was far away, sunlight outlined the human shape clearly, allowing Koren to study the man's slavish strife. How old was this window? The Basilica had been constructed centuries ago. The inscription on the cornerstone proved that. Since the wall surrounding this window looked just as old, and the glass itself seemed ancient, the design meant that humans had been slaves here for a very long time.

Yet the appearance of the young man—Jason—in the egg contradicted this evidence. He knew about the dragon planet, and he had asked if she was one of the Lost Ones.

She let those words trickle off her tongue. "The Lost Ones." If the old fables were true, then captured humans would be considered lost by those they left behind. But was he real? Could he have been a dream, a reflection of her hopeful mind? Something the dragon conjured? Might she be just a scupper, a way for this strange egg to leak its desires and have its schemes carried out?

More dragons filed in, some shuffling, some beating their wings to scoot along the floor. Most were males, their longer spines and glimmering scales revealing their gender, but a few females dotted the crowd. The females were especially easy to see when they flew around at night. Their glittering yellow pupils looked like fireflies hovering in the darkness.

As they gathered, the dragons' low voices sounded like rocks grinding together. Koren picked out a few phrases spoken in the dragon tongue—"unusual trial," "earliest I can remember," and "the wicked girl," but she couldn't connect them together. Could they be talking about Natalla? Might this trial be about her?

Koren searched for Arxad, but, unless he somehow stayed hidden behind the other males, he wasn't there. Without him, Natalla was surely doomed.

fourteen

oon, Fellina and Xenith came in, both glancing from side to side. They appeared nervous, as if they had not been in this room before.

As soon as all were seated, a great flurry of wings sounded from above. Magnar glided down through a hole in the ceiling and settled on the stage in front of the pedestal.

The dragon crowd settled to a hush. Magnar flipped the book's page and spoke a deep, thunderous command. "Bring the accused to the witness altar."

From the door on the left side, a dragon walked in, shuffling on its hind legs while using his front claw to push a dirty little girl. With her hands bound at her waist and a heavy chain connecting iron fetters around her ankles, she could barely walk.

Koren leaned forward to get a better look. It was Natalla.

When they arrived at a bench at the side of the pedestal, the dragon shoved Natalla to her knees and unlocked the fetters. She folded her hands and set them on the bench, weeping.

The bell rope dangled about thirty steps to Koren's right, and for a moment she considered climbing down and trying to help Natalla. No — it would be better to watch and wait for the results. There was no sense in revealing her presence now.

Magnar boomed again. "One of our priests requested to act as counsel for the accused, as is the right of his office. Let him come now and stand at her side."

Another dragon entered, but this one came from a door at the right end.

"Arxad," Koren whispered. *He'll help Natalla.*

The crowd murmured. New phrases punctuated the hushed voices — "doomsayer," "human lover," and "speaks his mind." But soon the buzz died away.

Glancing between Magnar and the gathered dragons, Arxad approached the pedestal and bowed.

"Have you had sufficient time to prepare the escapee's defense?" Magnar asked.

Arxad blinked. "I have. The case is quite simple."

"Indeed. I know." Magnar spread out a wing and gestured toward the crowd. "As we all know. But these noble dragons have joined us as witnesses, I suspect, not to see the routine execution of an escaped slave, but to learn why a priest would risk his reputation to defend her."

Arxad nodded at the book. "You know the law as well as I. Having counsel is her right, and it is my obligation to offer it."

Magnar touched the open page with the tip of his wing. "It is safe to dispense with details when the end result will always be the same. An escaped slave is an escaped slave. No counsel can alter this fact, and you have not answered this obligation in all your years as priest."

A scowl formed on Arxad's face. "While he lay burning to death at her side, her brother begged me to fulfill my duty. I do this because of my office, great Magnar, not because I have any fondness for humans. The law commands that I honor the request, and I must obey the law." He lowered his head and his voice with it. "You know I am not like most priests."

As another murmur arose, Magnar chuckled. "That you are not, Arxad. About the uniqueness of your character, we can agree. You are both dependable and annoying."

Arxad kept his head low. "Since we are in agreement, may we now proceed?"

Koren swallowed through a lump. Stephan really was dead! And Natalla would be next. What could her former master do to stop her execution? He didn't sound enthused about his counselor role at all. Would he just go through the motions out of duty and watch her die at the stake?

"The case is simple," Magnar said, now addressing the crowd. "This slave, assigned to Arxad as a housekeeper, fled into the wilderness with the aid of her brother. It seems that she learned about an upcoming Promotion, and, not wanting to leave her soft position and fearing the unknown, she opted to escape. My guard, the honorable Reeloft, found them while patrolling the perimeter. When the brother drew a sword, Reeloft killed him, as any guard must do when faced with such a weapon. Because of the escapee's unprovoked attack, Reeloft turned to slay the girl as well, as is allowed by law."

Magnar gave Arxad a sideways glance before continuing. "For reasons unknown to this court, Arxad arrived on the scene and prevented the summary execution, appealing to section fourteen, which gives a priest the right to intercede and request a formal trial.

"Reeloft, of course, acquiesced, and that is why we are all gathered here." Magnar looked at Arxad again, this time keeping his stare in place. "Wasting the time of the court and all who are present." After taking a deep breath, Magnar nodded. "You may proceed with your defense, and I trust that it will be a quick one."

Natalla looked up at Arxad. She smiled weakly through her streaming tears, but Arxad didn't bother to make eye contact. He simply returned Magnar's nod and spoke in an even tone. "Great Magnar, as a priest who takes his obligations seriously, I not only offer my counsel to this wretched slave, I do so without prejudice and without heeding the pressures that befall someone who undertakes an unpopular task. Although the rigor that I employ and the thoroughness with which I will defend this creature will likely bring ridicule and persecution, I cannot simply offer a pretense of counsel, for that would be worse than not giving counsel at all. It would be a sham, a black mark on my integrity. It would be a hypocritical hoax to this girl who clings to her last shred of hope—a tenuous hope that a dragon, a member of a race that enslaved her, roasted her brother before her very eyes, and now threatens to apply the same fiery breath to her, might stoop so low as to stand in front of others of his kind and speak for her cause."

Arxad turned toward Natalla and set the tip of his wing under her chin. She smiled again, but he offered no smile in return. "She is human, to be sure. Most see her execution as nothing more than the slaughter of a goat. You see her body as just another carcass that can be butchered and sold for consumption. Yet, as her intercessor, I see her as a creature with an immortal soul."

As the loudest buzz yet drowned out Arxad's voice, Magnar shouted, "You go too far, Arxad! With that statement, you violate the law yourself. You risk arrest and prosecution."

Louder murmurs sounded. Fellina cried out, "Arxad, no!"

Arxad turned away from Natalla, and his voice rose above the others, loud and commanding. "Section three, article seven, states that a counselor for the defense must take the role of the defendant, and as such I am merely stating her beliefs and the beliefs of every human on this planet. The words you hear are not my own, but the cries of every slave that toils under the burden of our collective fiery breath. 'We have souls! We were not created to be enslaved to anyone but our maker. We have the right to be free!'"

"Arxad!" Magnar shouted. "You speak blasphemy! The fire spirit endows only dragons with that right."

"Be that as it may," Arxad continued in a loud voice, "as a counselor for a human, I speak as a human would, so I am not bound to the laws concerning the speech of a dragon. I offer her defense in her words, not my own. When I step back into my office as priest, then you may examine my words however you wish and prosecute me accordingly."

Magnar scowled. "Take care, priest. I might just grant that request."

As the murmur died away again, Arxad turned to the crowd. "This slave, Natalla by name, learned that she received the honor of a Promotion. As you might have heard, rumors have been rampant among the humans as to what Promotion entails. Some believe that promoted humans are eaten by dragons because they are a delicacy that we love but are unwilling to consume frequently due to their value as slaves. We cull the herd of the less bright and able, thereby maintaining a healthier genetic pool, while at the same time enabling us to serve a favorite meal to a privileged few."

Chuckles erupted from the seated dragons. Koren searched for the source. Smiles appeared on many of the younger dragons, but the older ones wore dour expressions.

Arxad mirrored the smiles. "Yes, yes, I know how absurd that sounds, but a girl barely into her pubescent years cannot discern between such fairy tales and reality. Natalla's flight was not the result of rebellion against dragon sovereignty; it was because of fear, fear that the creatures who threatened to scourge her back because of any perceived lack of skill or effort were now ready to devour her flesh.

"You see, Natalla had just scored poorly on exams, and news of her Promotion came in the wake of that disappointment. The fairy tales haunted her. She would soon appear on a dragon's dinner pedestal, and the thought of being ground to pulp by a dragon's teeth drove her to the brink of insanity. Again, hers was not a crime of rebellion; it was an instinctive response to a stimulus.

"The law states that a human escapee is to be tried for rebellion, and the punishment is death. On the justice of this law, we can all agree. But the law says nothing regarding the fate of a girl who has merely flown in fear of death. She is clearly not a rebel. If you examine her service record, you will find it free of any formal reprimands. Her conduct has been exemplary. She is a model slave."

Arxad again lifted Natalla's chin. This time he gave her a smile. "If you believe Natalla is nothing more than a beast of burden, then you must acquit, for as a beast, she merely responded to instinct and ran from those she perceived to be butchers."

Releasing her again, he turned back to the watching dragons. "Yet, if you believe that this little girl is something more than a beast, you still must acquit, for as a creature who bears a soul, she deserves more than the status of a stupid beast whose death no one will remember. If, however, you find her guilty and proceed to melt her skin, roast her body, and cast her blackened bones to the forsaken valley, you will confirm in every human mind in this land that dragons are cruel and heartless, that dragons are bestial, that dragons are without the slightest shred of compassion … " He turned to Magnar and looked straight at him. "And that we are the ones without souls."

Koren leaped for joy, but a new eruption of shouts volleyed toward the stage. "Blasphemy! Heretic! This is a priest?" Yet nearly half the audience stayed quiet, especially the older ones who merely whispered among themselves.

Magnar met Arxad's stare and waited for the crowd to settle before replying. "Your skill in speaking in the human's place is most impressive. If not for my knowledge of your own exemplary record in loyalty to me, as well as my experience in seeing you as an actor on this very stage, I might be persuaded to agree with the accusations of heresy. You have played a very convincing role."

Arxad bowed. "Even my role as a supplicant for the defendant is offered in your service, great Magnar, for I trust that you would want nothing less than strict adherence to the law, and only the most skillful and enthusiastic fulfillment of my duties to you and to our codes of conduct."

As Arxad settled to a seated position next to Natalla, Magnar mumbled, "Yes. Quite." He then surveyed the crowd, his brow dipping lower with every passing second. Then in a rumbling, low tone, he continued. "Your eloquence, however, is no replacement for evidence. If this slave were truly fleeing for her life, she would not have waited for the dead of night, nor would she have enlisted an accomplice. She did, in fact, conspire to do this deed in a premeditated fashion. She caused dissension and fostered rebellion by leading others to follow her, and in so doing, brought about her own brother's death."

Raising his voice, he pointed a claw at Natalla. "These are not the deeds of a frightened little girl. They are the deeds of a rebellious wench who would likely repeat her crimes if given the chance, and perhaps increase them by gathering others into her rebellious fold."

Natalla winced and turned her head away from Magnar. Koren edged toward the rope, ready to leap to her aid if the worst happened.

Magnar turned back to the dragon crowd. "Only execution will show these vermin that we will not allow them to destroy our survival efforts. Such acts are tantamount to slaying us as we sleep, for without their labors we would all soon perish."

"I rise to counter," Arxad called out in an even tone as he rose to his haunches. "You are projecting motivations on the defendant that have been proven false. She has shown no aggression toward dragons, and her service record is spotless. Convict her of escaping, if you will, but adding a charge of attempted murder of a dragon is not a rational act."

Magnar glared at him. "I withdraw that statement and rest my prosecution on the simple fact that the girl escaped with an accomplice. She is guilty. So say we all." He closed the book with a thud. "Now for the sentencing."

Koren gasped. This couldn't be happening!

"I rise to call for a vote." Arxad turned to the audience for a moment, scanning the dragons before refocusing on Magnar. "I realize that this is a formality, but I must complete my duty. The accused is allowed to see which individuals are numbered with those who condemn her."

Magnar gave him a nod. "All those who agree that the slave is guilty of escape and should be sentenced according to the dictates of our laws, raise your right wing to signify."

Nearly every dragon raised a wing. Koren riveted her stare on two dragons who kept their wings down: Fellina and Xenith. But would they be enough to stop an execution?

"We have the requisite percentage, Arxad. I am sure we all appreciate the thoroughness of your defense." Magnar nodded toward the door Arxad had entered. "Having fulfilled your obligation, you are now excused."

"Very well." Arxad lifted his head and shuffled toward the door. Fellina squeezed between two dragons in front of her and followed. Xenith trailed them, her head hanging low.

As they neared the exit, Magnar set his claws on the closed book. "We will not force her to suffer the ultimate penalty and be cooked at the stake. Let her be tied to the bars outside these walls, and Maximus will incinerate her."

Natalla buried her face in her hands. One of the nearby dragons grabbed her wrist and jerked her to her feet.

Koren bolted toward the rope, jumped out, and grasped it with both hands. As she climbed down, her weight pulled the bell. A loud gong sounded, and she shot back toward the upper level. Grimacing, she continued a painful slide down the fibrous rope, enduring the up-and-down ride and the earsplitting bell. When the floor came close enough, she jumped and sprinted toward the gathering of dragons.

Every head had already turned her way. Arxad, now standing at the door, seemed frozen in place. With her fists clenched, Koren marched into their ranks, grabbed Natalla's hand, and jerked her free. "I will take her back to her home now."

Magnar bellowed, "What is the meaning of this?" With a wave of his wing, he gestured toward the dragon who was escorting Natalla. "Take her and tie her to the bars as well."

As the dragon reached for Koren, Arxad shouted, "No! She is the Starlighter!" Flapping his wings, he scooted toward them, waving a foreleg. "You can see for yourself that she is wearing the vestment."

Magnar waved a wing again, and the dragon guard backed away. "If the prince has allowed the Starlighter to roam freely," Magnar said, "he must have deemed her to be suitably acquiescent. Why, then, is she opposing the execution? Certainly Zena would not have flinched at the death of an escaped slave."

"Zena is not a Starlighter," Arxad said. "She cannot see into the heart. Koren, on the other hand, has every gift of the prophetess that has been promised throughout the ages. If the prince has allowed her access to the Basilica, then her insight must be heard and heeded."

Magnar scanned the onlooking dragons. He seemed concerned, perhaps anxious about how they would react to his response. "Heard, yes. Heeded, no. She has earned access to our ears, but not compliance from our hearts." After a throaty laugh, Magnar turned to Koren and took on an amused tone. "What message do you have for us, Starlighter?"

Koren ignored the condescension and watched Arxad out of the corner of her eye. Should she try to use her gift? Would it work on so many dragons?

Giving her a firm nod, Arxad spoke sternly. "The chief of all dragons has asked for a message, Starlighter. Are you going to insult him with silence?"

Koren looked down at her cloak. *Vestment*, Arxad had called it. Longer than her old skirt and far more impressive, it would be perfect. She pulled the hood up over her head, and, gripping the sides of the cloak, she made it twirl. "I have a story to tell you," she said, now spreading out her arms. "A story of courage, of heroism, of sacrificial love that bursts through the barriers of self-centered motivations."

Every dragon trained its eyes on Koren, some mouths already gaping. Arxad kept glancing to the side, as if trying to avoid the hypnotic trance.

She began a slow sway, letting her cape toss back and forth, and she moved her arms in time with the rhythm. As she acted out her words, images of Jason came to mind, and the vision she had seen within the egg expanded, showing her the action as if she were standing at his side. "A human boy was searching for his lost friends, lost for time unknown, captured by a cruel enemy. Oh, how he loved his friends! He would do anything to save them."

She splayed her hands, palms up. "He found a wall, a barrier that stood between him and his loved ones, and inserted his fingers into holes drilled through stone."

A ghostly image of a young man appeared next to her. With his facial features blurred, Koren barely recognized Jason. Maybe masking his identity would be for the best.

Jason performed Koren's story, giving her freedom to sway and twirl her cloak as she glided around him. "Ah!" she exclaimed, pointing at the oval glass in the wall. "It is the black egg! The prince! And this young man honors him by cradling the egg in his palms. Such care! Such devotion!"

Koren raised a hand to her lips and pointed at the floor. "But what is this? Water? A river is rising! What will happen to this brave hero?"

As she continued her dance, water rose to her ankles, and her feet splashed through it. Some of the dragons lifted and lowered their hind legs, but they had no effect on the mirage. Other dragons just stood and stared.

Koren tilted her head upward to address Jason. "Will you brave the waters, my hero? Will your heart of sacrifice be so strong that you will risk drowning, because you believe that caring for the prince's egg will lead you to your friends?"

She turned to Magnar and the nearby guard and dropped to her knees, splashing once again. With her hands clenched, she pleaded. "Oh, can you not see the nobility that this human possesses? Can you not see that he has a soul of great value? Not only is he risking danger to save his fellow humans, he cherishes our prince! Surely humans are more than beasts! Surely they have worth beyond cattle!"

The water rose past Jason's neck. He lifted his chin and called in a spurt of bubbles, "Is she all right?"

"You see!" Koren cried, still on her knees as she looked back at Jason. "Even in his peril, he is asking about the welfare of another! Is there no one who can help this heroic stranger?"

"I will help him!" Arxad turned toward the entrance and spread out his wings. "Koren! Natalla! Climb on my back, and we will fly to this hero. Perhaps we can rescue him before it is too late."

Koren raised her clenched hands again to Magnar. "I am bound by a promise to stay, but if you are truly the chief of all dragons, you have the authority to release me. Will you allow me to search for this young man?"

Blinking his glassy eyes, Magnar nodded. "You are released."

Koren took Natalla's hand, and the two dashed to Arxad. As the other dragons looked on, locked in a hypnotic spell, Koren helped Natalla climb Arxad's spiny tail and settle on his back. When Koren took a seat behind her, she called out, "We are ready, good dragon. Let us fly immediately and save the hero!"

Arxad beat his wings and took to the air. Flying close to the floor, he passed through the wide doorway.

With her hood blown back and her hair flowing freely, Koren looked behind her. The dragons just stared at them wide-eyed and slack jawed. Natalla turned, wrapped her arms around Koren, and kissed her cheek. "Oh, thank you! Thank you for saving me!"

Arxad swung his head toward them. "You are not saved yet, little one. We still have the final dragon guard, Maximus, to deal with. He did not witness the sacrifice of the young hero, so if we are to fly to the rescue, we must get past him."

As they swept through the corridor, Koren pondered Arxad's words. Was he, too, hypnotized? Did he really believe there was a human hero to rescue? If so, why did he specifically call for both of them to go along? Maybe his desire to save Natalla blended with his hypnotic trance.

When they burst out into the open air, Maximus roared a challenge. "Where are you going with those humans?"

With a great flap of his wings, Arxad lifted past Maximus and rose into the sky, calling behind him, "Magnar himself has released this Starlighter and has given her a life-saving journey to undertake."

Maximus shot after them, still roaring, "You carry the escapee. She is not a Starlighter."

Arxad began an orbit around the Basilica, just above the belfry. "Magnar witnessed our departure. Go to the Separators' stage and ask him yourself. I can delay no longer."

"Then be on your way." Maximus trailed Arxad, circling with him. "Since Magnar is inside and my shift relief is at hand, I can leave my post and follow you. We will see whose lives you seek to save, but the Starlighter best not think her spell will work on me again. One word out of her, and I will light her up like a torch."

fifteen

ason and Elyssa crossed the gateway and looked back. The chamber and river appeared to be an extension to the new room they had just entered, and Tibalt stood in the open with his fingers extended, as if he were cradling a pocket of air. On the floor between them, a line of crystalline pegs, no taller than tent pegs, stretched from one side wall to the other. At the middle, however, it seemed that one was missing.

Crouching, Jason grasped a peg and tried to pull it out, but it wouldn't budge. As he rose, Elyssa nudged a peg with her shoe. "I suppose no one can steal them," she said.

"True." He pushed a hand into his pocket. "Now that we're on this side, how do we—"

"Close the portal for twenty heartbeats, Tibber." Elyssa said. "We need to see what it looks like over here so we can figure out how to signal you to open it later."

Jason winked. "That's what I was going to suggest."

"Not exactly. You hadn't thought about how long he should leave it closed before opening it again. I gave him something to count."

"How did you guess that?"

"I just know you so well."

Jason rolled his eyes, but smiled. "Keep it up. That skill is either going to save us or annoy me to death."

"Here goes nothing," Tibber called out as he withdrew his fingers.

Tibalt slowly faded, and the river behind him transformed into a smaller room with a series of three low corridors carved in stone at the rear, much like the network of hallways in the dungeon back home.

Jason knelt and studied the hard, claylike ground. Grooves marred the surface, some as deep as a fingertip and as wide as his hand, and others shallower and thinner. "Something heavy has been carried on wheels, but the ground's too hard for footprints."

Elyssa pointed at one of the deepest grooves. "I'll see where this one goes." Leaning over, she marched into the center corridor and suddenly vanished.

Where Elyssa had been walking, the river appeared, and in front of it, Tibalt and his gap-toothed grin. "This is the fastest mural painting in history. I can make you appear and disappear like magic."

Jason clenched a fist. He couldn't get to Elyssa now, and knowing her, she would track that wheel groove without worrying about safety. Trying to keep calm, he spoke in a low tone. "Maybe you'd better close the portal until Randall gets there."

"Did you figure out how to signal me?"

"Not yet." Jason glanced around. Could there be a way to get a message across the closed portal? If Tibber's father had locked the portal, and dragons had not returned to capture more humans, that meant the dragons were no longer able to use it from their side. There was likely no way to send a signal.

"I have an idea," Jason said. "How good are you at marking time?"

"Time is like the wind. I feel its effects, but I can't see it and don't care to. When you've been in the dungeon as long as I have, it's all just one big breeze that passes by."

"But can you guess when one hour expires?"

"That I can do. That's how long it was between guard patrols. Me and Sammy across the hall used to play scalawags between patrols, and we knew exactly when to quit and wait for the guard to pass."

"Scalawags?" Jason asked.

"Indeedy. You get a handful of straw, and you stick the ends together with—"

"Never mind. Just close the portal and open it again after one hour. Maybe Randall will be back by then. Have him come over here and look around. If Elyssa and I aren't nearby, then wait another hour. Got that?"

Grinning again, Tibalt gave him a wink. "Not a problem, finger boy."

Jason glanced down at the litmus finger, now glowing violet under his skin. His top three buttons had come loose under the weight of his soaked shirt. He refastened the buttons and nodded. "Okay. Close the portal."

Tibalt stepped back. He and the river vanished, revealing once again the triplet of corridors. Elyssa was nowhere in sight.

Lowering his head to keep from bumping into the low ceiling, Jason hurried into the middle tunnel, debating with himself as the light from the entrance dimmed. Should he call? If someone had accosted her, a stealthy approach would be best, and if she happened to be trapped somewhere, calling her name would make sense. But if she were caught, wouldn't she be screaming for help?

As the tunnel dimmed further, Jason slowed to a crawl. "Elyssa?" he said in a whisper.

"Jason!" Elyssa's whisper matched his. "Over here!"

Jason blew out a sigh. She sounded excited rather than frightened. That was a relief. With his hand on a wall, he tiptoed toward the voice. The tunnel curved slightly to the right, and as his eyes adjusted, he spotted Elyssa's familiar form. "What did you find?" he asked.

"Tools." She lifted something that looked like a pickaxe. "And a torch, but I don't see a way to light it."

Jason squinted at the unlit torch in her other hand. "Did you find it in a frame on the wall?"

She set the torch and pickaxe down and nodded. "About three steps back."

"Dragons wouldn't be able to fit in the cavern past the portal. If these humans are from Major Four, then they might use our customs. Flint stones might be near that frame. I had some, but I think I lost them in one of the rivers."

"I suppose the original captives would have passed along their ways to the next generation." Elyssa turned and disappeared in the shadows for a moment before returning with two small stones in her palm. "I found them."

Jason held the torch while Elyssa lit the oily end. With a rush of flames, orange light burst through the corridor. The walls stood about a pace and a half apart and rose to Jason's shoulders, forcing him to stay in a bent posture. Scratch marks and abrupt edges proved that the stone had clearly been chiseled out, and multicolored layers revealed sediments of red and orange—hardened clay that made tunneling easier than drilling through granite or other bedrock.

"Now we can see where this tunnel goes." Jason led the way deeper into the shaft.

"The fuel on the torch was wet," Elyssa said as she followed. "It's been used recently."

"So whoever put it here might be coming back. If we knew what time it was, maybe it would make sense to wait."

After passing an empty bucket, a pair of old boots, and a hammer, Elyssa called out, "It's early morning."

Jason stopped and looked back. "How do you know?"

She rubbed her thumb against her fingers. "A feeling in the air. I can tell the time by sensations."

"But this world might be different."

"True enough." She picked up a child-sized hat with a wide brim and felt the inside. "Damp salt."

"From sweat?"

She nodded. "Humans have worked here recently. If it *is* morning, we might have visitors soon."

"And that would be perfect. We could talk to them without dragon interference."

"Perfect? Maybe. We have no way to prove our story."

Jason touched his chest. "I have the litmus finger."

"That would probably scare them."

He nodded back toward the entrance. "Tibalt's supposed to open the portal again in an hour. That will be all the proof we need."

Jason continued his hunching march deeper into the tunnel. What would happen if the workers arrived just as Tibalt reopened the portal? *Imagine their surprise if they walked straight back into the human world. But then they'd have to get upstream safely, and if children were among the workers, that would be no easy task ...*

Suddenly, a breeze wafted by. The torch's flame sparked green and made a snapping noise, like feet tramping on dry twigs.

Jason wrinkled his brow. "Extane?"

"Feels like it." Elyssa rubbed her thumb and fingers again. "It's oily."

Before long, light shone ahead; a sunray streaming across their path. Jason stopped at the edge of the light. Above, a cylindrical channel had been cut to the surface, and below, a circular pit descended into the depths with two ladders leaning against the perimeter.

As a breeze sucked air from the pit and up into the chimneylike hole, the flame sparked again, this time more fervently. "More extane?" he asked.

She extended her hand into the flow. "A lot of it, but it's escaping into the atmosphere. Maybe they don't know how valuable it is."

Jason looked down into the pit. The light from above illuminated several ladder rungs, but it was impossible to tell how deep they went. He checked the flint stones in his pocket, tamped out the torch, and set a foot on the top rung. "Let's see what we can find."

As he descended, he listened for any signs of life, but the scratching of Elyssa's shoes on the rungs above him ruined any chance of hearing subtle noises. After about thirty steps, his foot landed on something more solid.

He waited for Elyssa to join him, letting his eyes adjust to the dimmer light. The shaft far above still provided illumination, but much less than on the upper level.

They stood on a rocky ledge that encircled a larger pit that was so wide, the ledge on the far side of the pit was barely visible—maybe a full stone's throw away. Using his foot, he nudged a shovel leaning against the outer wall next to a variety of picks and pails standing in a line. He knelt and touched a rope, anchored to an iron bolt. The fibrous line descended into the void, too dark to discern its depth.

He gave the rope a gentle tug. It compressed slightly, as if it were hollow. Could it be an air tube as well as a climbing rope? A weight, not very heavy, held it in place; maybe a tool attached to the end.

After letting the rope fall back in place, Jason smacked his lips. The familiar bitter taste of extane coated his tongue, thicker than in the dungeon. Maybe the slaves needed the breathing tubes while working down below where the gas was more concentrated. Although it wasn't poisonous, it could displace oxygen, making the tubes necessary.

And what harm might long-term exposure to the gas cause? The dragons probably didn't care. These slaves likely worked each day until it grew too dark and would return with the morning sun, unable to decide their hours or take days off because of concerns about their health.

As Jason brooded over the slaves' lives, something thin and brown caught his attention, a wafer lying near the edge of the pit. He picked it up and examined it. Fibrous and light, it didn't feel like stone at all, more like plant material.

Elyssa knelt with him. "What is that?"

"Not sure." He lifted the wafer close to his nose and sniffed it. "Smells sort of like—"

"Manna bark?"

"Good guess again. The gas has to be extane, but they must be mining something else and releasing the gas along the way. If they were really digging for extane, they wouldn't waste it by letting it leak into the outside air."

With her hands on her thighs, she peered down. "I say we wait."

"Wait? What do you mean?"

She looked at him, her green eyes still visible in the low light. "You were going to ask whether or not you should climb down. I think we should wait for the workers to show up. Better to learn from someone who's been there. And since they're slaves, they probably start early."

"I *was* thinking that."

She gave him a wink. "I know."

"You figuring out what's going on in my brain is starting to scare me."

"Good. Now that we're in the dragon world, a little healthy fear might be the best medicine."

For the next few minutes, they sat and talked about what the people here could be mining. Gems? Gold? A mineral unknown in their world? Whatever it was, it had to be of great value to the dragons. Otherwise, why would they bother to keep humans captive and feed them? With the arid breeze circulating, their clothes finally dried to a comfortable level, and, as more light poured in from the rising sun, their eyes fully adjusted.

At the opposite side of the pit, another hole to the upper level came into view. Something snapped, and a light flashed from the top of the hole, further illuminating the chamber. A male human descended a ladder and settled to the ledge with a thump. With his head and shoulders slumped low, his face stayed out of sight.

"If his ancestors came from our world," Elyssa whispered, "he might know our language."

"This is what we came for," Jason said, rising to his feet.

Jason lifted his hands to show that he carried no weapon and called out, "Excuse me, sir. May I talk to you?"

The man jerked his head around and stared, saying nothing. A severe burn scarred the side of his face from his eye socket to the bottom of his jaw, so deep the wound may have nearly cost him his life.

Jason walked toward him, slowing his rate of speech. "Do you understand what I am saying?"

Nodding, the man edged back toward the ladder. His torn sleeves revealed muscular arms, but the fear in his face contradicted his strength. The breeze swept his curly brown locks back, revealing a receding hairline. With a trembling voice, he offered a weak, "Who are you?"

Jason stopped several paces away and gave the man a courtly bow. "I am Jason Masters. I have come from Major Four."

Half closing one eye, the man mouthed the words *Major Four*, but said nothing.

Jason gestured toward Elyssa. She rose and joined him. "Elyssa and I are here to help you escape from the dragons and return to our world ... *your* world. It has taken us many years to find the gateway to this place, but we have finally arrived to rescue you."

For a moment, the man scowled, but soon his tight lines loosened. A smile emerged, and he broke into a low chuckle. "A fine jest, indeed! For a moment, I thought you were serious, that one of the lowland humans had gone insane." Still laughing, he mumbled, "Oh, a fine jest. Harlon will pay for this. Yes, he will."

"A jest? What do you—"

"Who told you to play this prank? Was it Harlon?"

"Harlon? I have no idea who he—"

"Cassandra, then. She knew about my birthday and wanted to tease me. She promised you a berry pie, didn't she? And she asked you to dress in those strange outfits, I'll wager." The man lowered his head, shaking it. "That little sprite. She is always playing tricks on me." With a smile and a wag of his finger, he added, "You tell Cassandra for me that Uncle Allender will get her back."

"Allender!" Elyssa called in a firm voice, her hand held high. "Stop these thoughts of friendly jests from your niece. Jason and I are not pranksters, nor are we insane. Didn't your ancestors tell you that they came from another world?"

"Tales from old women!" Allender picked up a shovel and nodded toward the ladder. "My fellows will be here in a moment. You'd best end this prank now, or you'll have everyone laughing, and we won't make quota today."

"Quota?" Jason asked. "Are you mining gems?"

This time, Allender's finger stiffened as he pointed it. "Now I know you're playing the fool. I don't know which

Assignment you're from, but I suggest you return there before your foreman misses you. If my workers don't make quota, I'll make sure the stripes they get on their backs are doubled on yours."

Elyssa bowed her head before looking him in the eye. "Foreman Allender, it is noble of you to care so much for those you oversee. You must be a good and honorable man. Since this is so, I trust that deliverance from the bondage of slavery would be your highest goal for those in your employ."

"Employ? Your Assignment must keep you ignorant of the real world." As a female child descended the ladder, Allender lifted her to the floor. He turned her around and pulled her collar down, exposing her shoulders and the top ends of three red stripes. "These are our wages. From the littlest and weakest to the biggest and strongest, our masters beat us mercilessly if we come short of quota by even the tare of a pail."

After patting the girl on the head, he pushed her along before pointing at Jason again. "Unless you want to be the reason she earns more of those welts, young man, I suggest that you silence your other-world talk. That myth is nothing but fuel for wagging tongues and added fury for dragons' whips. If you breathe another word of it, I will pump you full of pheterone and use you as a torch."

Elyssa leaned toward Jason and whispered, "Pheterone must be their name for extane."

Jason matched her whisper. "Right. I guessed that."

Smiling and backing away slowly, Jason offered a quick bow. "Give my best to Cassandra ... and happy birthday."

With that, he took Elyssa's hand and hurried to the ladder they had descended. After letting her climb first, he

looked back at Allender. He was handing pickaxes to men
as they dismounted the ladder. The little girl had been
joined by a smaller boy, and both clutched pail handles
with the pails resting on the ground.

Jason sighed and followed Elyssa. She glanced over
her shoulder at him. "What now?"

"Get outside and explore. Maybe we can find the old
women who still tell the tales."

Elyssa nodded. "Good idea." When they reached the top,
they hurried back to the portal chamber, not bothering to
pick up the torch, and climbed up twenty stairs cut in the
stone until they emerged outside.

The sun shone just above low hills in the distance, more
like jutting rocks than the forested hills back home. Although
the rays felt hot, a cooling breeze wafted from the cloudless
sky and brushed against squatty, oak-like trees and tufts of
wiry grass.

Jason shielded his eyes and scanned the area. Near a
creek, a line of people filed into a low opening at the base
of a cliff, similar to the one he had just exited. Standing
with its back to him, a huge scaly creature with wings and
a long neck and tail held a whip in a clawed hand.

Swallowing hard, he whispered, "It's a—"

"A dragon!" Elyssa finished.

The dragon cracked the whip across a lagging boy's
back, making him flinch, but the boy did nothing more
than glare at the cruel beast before tromping back into
the line.

Jason cocked his head. Did that boy have only one
eye? For a moment it seemed that the boy had noticed
them, a half-second pause, but he didn't give any further
indication.

Grabbing Elyssa's hand, Jason pulled her back under the cave's arched entrance, a yawning mouth big enough for that dragon to fit through. He leaned out and watched the boy disappear into the cliff. "Maybe now that they're all inside, the dragon will go somewhere else."

Elyssa peeked over his shoulder. "I see an old woman with water flasks. She's probably stationed outside for the carriers."

"Carriers?"

"They're digging a huge hole, Jason. The rocks have to go somewhere. The men are the strongest, so they probably cut out the rocks and haul them to the top of the pit. The children then carry them in pails to the surface and float them away on rafts."

"I didn't see any rafts."

"Or any piles of rocks, either. The rocks have to go somewhere, and I didn't see any other conveyances, so I just guessed that they have rafts."

He stared at her, wide eyed. "Thinking ahead again?"

She nodded. "You're welcome."

After a few minutes, a little boy emerged from the other cave, carrying a heavy pail. He dumped the contents near the creek and, swinging the empty pail, marched back. He kept his gaze on the ground, apparently not daring to look directly at the dragon that watched his every move.

Soon two small girls did the same — carrying a pail and dumping rocks — but the smaller of the two stayed at the creek bank. About a minute later, a wooden raft floated from upstream, and the girl waded in and pulled it to shore. Then she loaded the rocks onto the raft one by one.

"What a waste of time!" Jason said. "Why don't they dump the pails directly onto the raft?"

Elyssa nodded slowly. "Strength training. Repetitive exercise with small loads for the youngest children."

"You're just guessing again."

"No. Deducing. These dragons are treating them like beasts of burden that they train for manual labor. I'll bet they even breed them, too."

"You mean ... "

"Right. Arranged marriages to produce the fittest. You can bet they forced even young girls to have babies, at least early on when they wanted the population to grow as quickly as possible."

Jason grimaced. "That's disgusting."

"True, but it stands to reason. Once the population rose sufficiently, they probably allowed only the strongest to breed, so these girls are tested for strength while they're very young. The weak or handicapped will never find love."

"This isn't about love." He drew out his sword. "If the dragon stays in that position, I think I can take him out."

She grabbed his sleeve. "Maybe you shouldn't."

"Why not?"

"What if there are more dragons around?"

"Did you see any?"

She shook her head. "That doesn't mean—"

"Look," Jason said, pointing with his sword, "we know he's the enemy. We saw him hit the boy with his whip. We came here to rescue the Lost Ones. This isn't exactly a difficult decision."

"I understand, but how many dragons have you fought?"

He stared at her for a moment. No use answering her question. She already knew the answer—zero, just like with the mountain bear. "Okay, what do you think I should do?"

"Well, maybe—"

The whip cracked. Jason spun toward the sound. The little girl tumbled face-first at the river's edge and spilled her load. The dragon stood over her and whipped her back, snapping up a slice of clothing and a spray of blood.

Jason boiled inside. Strangling the sword's hilt, he showed Elyssa its blade. "'Maybe' nothing."

With his sword extended, he ran on the balls of his feet, trying not to make a sound. He had to get there before the dragon struck again. For now, it just stood over the small slave with the whip raised, as if daring her to move. It spoke, but in a guttural, growling sort of tongue that made no sense at all.

The girl curled up in the dragon's shadow, covering her face with her hands and crying. A woman with a water flask stood nearby, but she just let her shoulders sag and shook her head.

Jason felt no fear, just anger—hot, fuming anger. And why should he fear this monster? He and Adrian had trained to fight dragons. Adrian had set up a furnace and hose combination that spewed fire from the top of a platform mounted on two ladders. It probably wasn't anything close to the real thing, but the moves Adrian taught helped him understand how to fight an enemy that hurled weapons from above.

Yet this would be different. Very different. This beast had a brain and a streak of cruelty. A surprise attack would be his only chance.

As he closed in, Jason eyed the spiked tail. That weapon was another matter. Adrian had mentioned it in passing, but he couldn't fabricate a reasonable facsimile.

Taking a deep breath, Jason raised his sword. Maybe the answer would be to eliminate the problem before it could become one.

With a mighty heave, he hacked down on the tail's midsection. His razor-sharp blade sliced between two scales and amputated half the tail.

The dragon roared and spun on its haunches. Jason dashed past it and sliced across its midsection as he ran, striking the precise spot where Adrian had said its skin would be armored with thinner scales.

Brown blood poured from the sword-length wound. The dragon roared again, this time shooting fire from its mouth and nostrils. Jason dodged. The flames glanced off his arm, but the damp sleeve didn't ignite.

With a lunging thrust, Jason drove the blade deep into the dragon's gut, jerked it back out, and leaped toward the little girl. The dragon coughed. Fire and blood gushed from his mouth, but with no apparent aim. Then, like a falling tree, it toppled to the rocky terrain. A loud thud shook the ground. The dragon wheezed, then breathed no more.

Jason set his sword down and helped the girl rise to her feet. "Are you all right?"

She brushed hair out of her eyes and nodded. "I am."

"What's your name?"

"Tam."

"Well, Tam, you won't have to worry about that dragon again." Jason retrieved his sword and began cleaning the blade on a tuft of grass.

The girl let out a gasp and pointed at the dead dragon. "Look what you did!"

"I did it for you." Jason resheathed his sword and stooped at her side. "Now you can be free."

"Free?" She squinted at him. "Will the Traders give me away?"

He slid his hand into hers. "That's not what I mean. You can go wherever you wish. You can—"

"I have to work." She jerked her hand away. Picking up another rock, she shuffled to the raft and dropped it with the others.

Rising, Jason took a step. "But you—"

"Hey!"

Jason shifted toward the call. Allender stood at the cave entrance, three small children huddling at his feet. He stalked out, his fists clenched and head low.

Extending his arm, Jason hoped for a congratulatory handshake. Slaying that dragon and saving Tam felt good, very good. "Did you see what that dragon was doing to that poor little—"

Allender punched Jason across the jaw. "You fool! Don't you know the penalty for killing a dragon?"

sixteen

Jason reeled back and staggered to stay on his feet. Rubbing his jaw, he stared at Allender. "Why did you do that?"

Allender shook his fist. "If I weren't a praying man, I'd give you another one."

"But I killed the dragon. We can run to freedom."

"To freedom? You really are a cracked pot, aren't you? Where will we run? To the Northlands to visit the fairies? To the wilderness to be eaten by the jungle birds? What old woman's tale do you want us to believe this time?"

Jason tried to draw the portal with his finger. "There's this invisible gateway, and—"

"An invisible gateway?" Allender shook his fist. "I should grind you to powder. Yarlan will be here soon, and when he sees what you did, he will kill every adult among us and send the children to the cattle drivers."

"Yarlan?"

"The patrol dragon. You would do well to tremble at the sound of his name."

Jason pointed toward the cave where he had left Elyssa. She had emerged and was now walking toward them, her arms folded. "Not if we escape," he explained. "All we have to do—"

"Jason!" Elyssa called.

"What?"

"One hour has almost expired. Maybe only a minute or so left. Proof is your best defense now."

Jason lifted his hands in a surrender posture. "Listen, Allender, if you'll just follow me, I can show you. Then if you're not convinced, you can grind me to powder. I think a praying man should at least give me a chance to prove myself."

Allender scanned the skies. So far, the deep blue canopy was free of dragons. He loosened his fist and gave Jason a skeptical nod. "Very well."

Jason waved a hand toward the children. "Maybe they'd better stay in the mine until we get back."

Allender whistled a shrill note, and all but one youngster ducked out of sight. The one-eyed boy stood tall and approached. "I'm going with you, Uncle. I don't trust him."

"Very well, Wallace," Allender said as he rubbed the boy's rag-mop hair. "I welcome your company."

"What do we do with Rittle?" Wallace asked, nodding toward the dead dragon.

"We don't have time to dispose of his body. Our only choice is to hide in the mine and, when Yarlan arrives, negotiate for the most lenient punishment."

Jason gestured toward the portal cave entrance. "Maybe that won't be necessary." Leading the way, he hustled down the stairs. From the point directly above the row of crystal pegs, the antechamber's ceiling descended rapidly toward the rear of the cave, making it unlikely that a dragon could easily pass beyond it. Humans could hide there safely, but standing out in the open, they would be easy prey until Tibalt opened the portal.

"So where is this invisible gateway?" Allender asked as he stood at the bottom of the stairs, Wallace at his side. Elyssa slid past them and hurried to Jason.

Jason guided his hand along the portal plane in a circular motion. "This is like a window ... an invisible cave entrance that leads to another world, the planet where your ancestors came from. Soon my friend in that world will ... " He looked at Allender. The foreman's brow had knitted tightly. It seemed clear that a detailed explanation about inserting fingers in holes would probably incite another punch in the jaw.

After clearing his throat, Jason continued. "He will open this window, allowing everyone to escape the dragon tyranny."

Allender set a hand on Wallace's back. "Come along. We have heard enough of this madman's ranting."

Wallace stood firm. "I believe him."

"What?" Allender stared at the boy. "Even with one eye, you can see as well as the rest of us. There isn't anything there."

"It took me two years to convince the dragons I wasn't bad luck," Wallace said, pointing at his eye. "So I learned a lot about how to tell the difference between superstitions and truth. Being without one eye sometimes makes me see better than most."

"What do you mean?"

"A long time ago, I heard about the other world. Koren said—"

"Oh!" Allender said, adding a condescending laugh. "I should have seen it coming. Another Koren story. That girl was telling old women's tales as soon as she could talk."

Jason stiffened but managed to keep his voice calm. "Koren? What does she look like?"

"A pretty little thing," Allender said. "Red hair. Green eyes. Fifteen years old, I think. But she was born a tale-bearer, I tell you. She will talk the ears right off your head, and I fear that she has charmed Wallace with her fanciful stories."

Jason glanced at Elyssa. Her eyes told him that she remembered the name. "Where is she now?" he asked.

"She serves one of the Zodiac priests," Allender said, "a plum Assignment, to be sure. The dragons favor the redheads, and the priests love stories." His lips bent into a sneer. "The priests spin fables of their own, so Koren likely supplies them with fresh lies."

"They're not lies!" Wallace snapped. "If you would just open your mind you would—"

An earsplitting scream ripped through the chamber.

"Yarlan!" Allender grabbed Wallace's arm and pushed him toward the tunnels at the back wall. "Hurry to the mine and gather everyone at the ledge. I will be there in a moment."

"I can't leave you here," Wallace said. "That would violate the Code."

Yarlan screamed again, closer. Thumps sounded on the entry slope, and the cavern darkened.

"He's coming!" Allender hooked his arm around Wallace's elbow and did the same to Elyssa. "Run!"

They dashed into the central tunnel. Jason followed, instinctively ducking as he neared the opening, but a flash of light made him turn. Fire erupted, but instead of the expected blast of flames aimed at his back, a ball of sizzling blue shot in the opposite direction, toward a dragon standing at the entryway. It splashed against Yarlan's scaly flank and drizzled to the floor.

"Shoot 'im in the belly!" a voice called out.

Jason yelled at Elyssa. "That was Tibalt!"

Elyssa jerked free from Allender and rushed to Jason. "Where is he?"

As they stood in front of the central tunnel at the rear of the chamber, Randall appeared out of nowhere, stalking toward the dragon with a drawn sword and shouting, "He's immune to the photo gun, Tibber. Time for slaying the old-fashioned way."

"Run 'im through!" Tibalt called. "I'll try to distract him!"

Randall half crouched near the left side of the cavern, the photo gun in one hand and one of the antique swords in the other. Yarlan glanced between him and the center of the room, obviously confused.

"I heard Tibber again," Elyssa said, "but I don't see him."

Jason drew his sword. "Stay back." He marched past the portal plane to the right side of the anteroom and shouted, "Hey, Yarlan! Over here!"

The dragon swung toward him and shot a fireball. Jason leaped toward the exit, zipped past the dragon, and stood at the bottom of the staircase. Now at Yarlan's rear, he looked toward the back of the cavern. Tibalt stood with his hands outstretched and his fingers splayed. The river rushed behind him with no sign of Elyssa or the others.

Jason jabbed at Yarlan's flank, but his blade just clinked against the scales. As the dragon turned to face him again, Jason shouted, "Randall! Come with me! Tibalt! Close the portal! Open it again in … in about one hundred heartbeats!"

Jason charged up the stairs and into daylight. Standing outside the arch, he listened.

"Back, beast!" Randall yelled. The report of a photo gun blast echoed. Yarlan squealed. Seconds later, Randall stormed out of the cave, breathing hard. "Next time … next time you want me to run right past a dragon, give me a little more support."

Jason waved his sword. "I tried to stab him. This one seems tougher than the one I just killed."

A roar sounded from the cave along with a tromping march. Randall pressed his back against the wall on one side of the entry and motioned Jason toward the other. "You killed a dragon?"

Breathing heavily, Jason copied Randall's pose and pointed with his sword. "Yeah. Over there."

"Impressive." Randall lifted his sword into ready position. "If he pauses at all, he gets one blade in each eye."

"Got it." Jason held his breath. Less than two seconds later, Yarlan shot out, leading with barrages of fire. Jason hacked at his eyes, but the head zoomed by so fast, his blade missed the target and glanced off the dragon's tough neck. As Yarlan launched skyward, a wing slapped Jason in the face, sending him rolling away.

He leaped to his feet and searched the sky. High above, Yarlan bent into a quick turn and headed their way, fire again blazing. Jason rushed over and helped Randall to his feet. A long bloody gash striped his face. He wobbled, still clutching his sword as Jason pushed his shoulder under Randall's arm and helped him down the stairs.

A blast of fire splashed behind them, close enough to warm their backsides, but Yarlan stayed outside, apparently wary of reentering a dark cave where two sword bearers awaited.

When they emerged into the anteroom, Elyssa helped Jason lower Randall to a sitting position.

"Are you all right?" Elyssa asked.

Randall, his eyes a bit glassy, touched the wound near his cheekbone. "It smarts, but it probably looks worse than it is."

"Woowee!" Tibalt shouted, still standing with his fingers extended. "That's a mark that'll make the ladies swoon!"

Jason stared at him. The river still rushed at his rear but flowed from right to left toward the pit. Maybe the river had washed away Elyssa's blood, and now Tibalt controlled the direction.

"Didn't you close the portal?" Jason asked.

"I did, but I was so excited, a hundred heartbeats didn't take long."

Jason looked at Elyssa. "Are Allender and Wallace still watching?"

"I'm not sure." She nodded toward the river. "I think they're still back there, but who can tell? This is all very strange."

Jason waved an arm, imagining the two Lost Ones watching from behind the portal window at the rear of the chamber. "Come over here, and you can see the other world."

Allender's voice filtered toward them, muffled by the river's rush. "Other world? Stop spewing that nonsense. I'll have no part of it. You saw what the patrol dragons are capable of. The Royal Guard are twice as powerful, and Yarlan will summon them here, you can count on that."

"What's the harm in looking?" Wallace said as he walked through the portal plane and suddenly appeared out of nowhere. He turned back and added, "The Royal Guard won't be here for—"

Wallace's eye shot wide open. "What ... what happened?"

Jason stood and joined him. "You're looking into the other world, and this is my friend Tibalt."

Tibalt grinned. "You can call me Tibber."

Smiling nervously, Wallace gave him a polite nod. "It's nice to meet you."

"Likewise. I'd shake your hand, but I would just disappear. And that wouldn't be a gentlemanly thing to do."

"You see," Jason said as he stepped over the line of crystal pegs, "this is a portal, a gateway between worlds. And in Allender's view, I probably disappeared."

Wallace sucked in a breath. "Uncle! Can you see it? Did he disappear?"

Jason glanced at Elyssa and Wallace in turn. "Did he answer?"

"Not a word," Elyssa said.

"He probably went back to the mine," Wallace said, "to prepare the others for the coming of the Royal Guard."

Elyssa tilted her head. "Prepare them?"

"Let him explain later." Jason stepped back into the dragon world. "Tibalt, we can't risk going outside to get to the mine pit, so you'll have to close the portal for a while. And we can't let you stand there, because a dragon might come in here while we're gone."

"I ain't gonna argue with that. I think I'm allergic to dragons." Tibalt wrinkled his nose. "How long this time?"

"Better not go by heartbeats. Can you guess how long a half hour is?"

"Yessiree. I can figure fractions with the best of them. I can even do thirds if you want."

"Half should be fine. Go ahead and close the portal. When you open it again, if we're not here, and there's no dragon around, just keep it open and wait for us. If there's danger, close it right away and check again in another half hour. Can you do that?"

"I am Tibber the Fibber, lord of the dungeon. I am an expert at being sneaky and disappearing when I have to."

"Great. Then we'll see you soon."

After giving all four a final nod, Tibalt vanished, and the three tunnels reappeared. When the rush of water faded, the silence in the cavern felt heavy.

Wallace's smile spread across his face. "This is even better than Koren's stories!"

"How long before the Royal Guard dragons show up?" Elyssa asked.

Wallace turned and looked up the stairs. "It depends on who is available, but with a murdered dragon, I think we have only a few minutes."

"Minutes," Jason repeated. "I wonder if they're the same length here as they are at home."

Wallace looked up at the ceiling for a moment. "About sixty-five heartbeats?"

"Sounds right." Jason reached down a hand and hoisted Randall to his feet. Now his eyes looked bright and fiery, and his legs seemed stronger.

"I want another shot at that beast," he said.

"Then you can hide out in this room, in case Tibalt has trouble with a dragon. Since Yarlan saw humans with swords here, this is where they'll probably come first."

Randall regripped his sword. "Suits me fine."

Wallace led Jason and Elyssa through the tunnel and down the ladder to the mining ledge. At the opposite side of the pit, six men crouched in a huddle with six or more children standing around them, trying to look over their shoulders.

Tam shuffled on her bare feet and touched a man's shoulder with her skinny roughened hands. He reached back and patted her tenderly. "Don't worry, Tam. Everything will be all right."

A tear inched down her grimy cheek. She nodded but said nothing.

Breathing a quiet shushing sound, Wallace signaled for Jason and Elyssa to follow. When they reached the gathering, a thin man with a goatee held up a pair of crooked fingers and said, "I say we offer them two of us in exchange."

"Not three?" a blond-haired man asked. "The dragon wasn't just attacked. He was killed."

"True enough," a third man said. He pulled a sweat-dampened towel from around his neck and mopped his dirty brow. "After what that boy did, it's better to leave room to negotiate."

"Negotiate!" A wrinkled man with no front teeth bent his brow. "I say it's about time someone stood up to those slavers! If I had that boy's youth and strength, I'd have done it myself." He spat on the ground. "Negotiate, indeed!"

"Listen, Micah," Allender said, "it's pretty easy to get all cocky when you have nothing to lose. But the rest of us have plenty to lose."

"Plenty to lose?" Micah reached for Tam and turned her back toward Allender. The rips in her shirt exposed two long, bleeding welts. "Is this the price you want to keep paying? Are you going to let the little ones take the blows? What will they learn about courage? Will they really believe you love them when you send them out time and time again to cower under the dragons' cruel whips?"

A man who appeared to be Tam's father pulled her into his arms. He spoke in a strained but measured tone, his entire body quaking. "I will *not* let her go back out there. Over my dead body."

"Which might just be the case." Allender crouched with his back to Jason. "It's settled. We offer two, and we will go up to three if we have to, so we should cast the die for all three now."

The men mumbled their agreement. As Allender pulled a small cube from his pocket, marked on each side with a number from one to six, sweat beaded on the forehead of each miner.

Allender placed the cube on his palm. "Highest three are safe. Lowest three will be the offering, with the highest of them on the cusp as the bargaining extra." He tossed the cube on the ground. It spun for a moment before settling. "Three!" He scooped up the cube and passed it to the man on his left, Tam's father.

The man glanced at Tam briefly and cast the cube. When the numeral one came up, the five other men groaned.

Micah reached out and tipped the cube over, exposing the six. "My roll was a six, but I'm trading with Cowl for his one. That's allowed if both agree."

"Micah," Cowl said, "I cannot let you take my—"

"Why not? My children all died in the cattle camps years ago, and my heart died with them. The last time a human killed a dragon, they took every last child in the Assignment to the camps. You know what they do to them there." Micah picked up a towel and twisted it. "They wring out every drop of rebellion by starving them into submission. No rebel is allowed to gain muscle from mining labors, because the dragons are afraid we will figure out that we are strong in numbers. Once we gain a little courage, we will never cast the die again."

"Well spoken," Cowl said. "Yet the dragons have little to fear. It seems that having children keeps us parents cowardly."

"Not cowardly. Protective." Micah pointed at himself. "I will gladly offer my life if it means keeping you and Tam together. I know her poor mother would have wanted it that way. Ever since she passed away, I just ... " The old man shook his head, unable to continue.

Cowl nodded, his eyes wide and wet. "Thank you, Micah. You are a man of the Light."

The remaining men cast the cube. A four, a five, and another six rounded out the lot.

Letting out a sigh, Allender pointed at the blond-haired man who had cast the four. "You are on the bargaining cusp, Mark."

Mark nodded, his shoulders sagging. "Do not fear to offer me if necessary. I am not afraid to die."

Allender rose, nearly bumping into Jason as he took a step back. His eyes flared, and his mouth opened as if to shout, but he lowered his head and sighed again. "I apologize for my harshness. It is not our custom to belittle those who have … " He stroked his chin before continuing. "Deficiencies. In fact, deep inside, every man here has wanted to slay one of those monsters, especially Micah, so I think no one will blame you. Madness could drive any of us to commit such a crime."

Jason raised a hand to protest, but Wallace spoke first, bouncing on his toes. "Uncle, he's not deficient. I saw the gateway. I saw the other world."

Allender stared at him for a moment. "Is madness a disease one can catch?"

"Of course not," Micah said. "Wallace is the sanest person here. Nothing rattles him."

Cowl laid a hand on Allender's shoulder. "What is this gateway? And who is this young man? He has a strange look about him."

Jason bowed. "I am Jason Masters, and I want to show you a way to escape this mine so that none of you has to offer himself to the dragons."

"By all means," Micah said. "What is this way of escape?"

Allender shook his head. "He is mad. He believes in the tales of another planet, and—"

"I tell you I saw it!" Wallace pointed at his eye. "I don't need two to see past my nose. I know what I saw."

Cowl grasped Jason's arm. "Show us, Jason. If it is madness, we will all soon know."

Jason looked at Cowl's tight fingers. His grip was strong but not painful. "The way out won't appear for about ..." He glanced at Elyssa, who held up all ten fingers. "For about ten minutes."

"Does this gateway hide itself?" Allender said, chuckling. "If this story gets any stranger, I will have to withdraw my apology."

Micah frowned at Allender. "For a man who is about to be offered, your risk of offense to the Light seems higher than I would expect."

"Perhaps so, but we might not have ten minutes before the guard comes. Then we will not have the opportunity to test his story."

Wallace let out a huff. "You can just keep ignoring me, but I'm going to the gateway, and if you men don't care about the children enough to see if it's true, then I'll take them all with me."

Jason held up his fingers. "Just give me the ten minutes. You can last that long, can't you? The dragons can't get to you in here."

"If we tried to stay," Allender said, "they would starve us out. If we don't acquiesce immediately, it will be more difficult to get a good bargain."

"I see." Jason looked at the pit. Could the mine's harvest add to the negotiations? "What are you digging for?"

Allender gave Jason a quizzical look. "Pheterone, of course."

"I heard you mention that before. Why are you mining it?"

Wallace waved his hand in the air. "Dragons need it to survive. We dig down to pockets of pheterone and release it into the atmosphere. I say that we should keep digging but make sure we never break into the pockets. That way, the dragons will eventually get weaker and we can rise up and break our bonds."

"You and your political speeches." Allender shook his head. "Your brother would be proud. But where did that get him?"

"Promoted," Wallace said proudly.

Just as Allender opened his mouth to reply, Micah laid a hand over it. "Let us not start the Promotions debate, or we will all die from a gas called hot air."

Jason nodded toward the ladders. "We can hide in the tunnel until the portal appears. Then if it's safe, we can escape."

"How will you know when it appears?" Wallace asked. "We weren't able to see it from the tunnel."

"Good question. I'll have to figure that out when we get there."

This time, Jason led the way, followed closely by Elyssa and Wallace. After climbing the ladder and help-ing Elyssa to her feet in the tunnel, he looked back at the miners. The men were helping the children onto the ladders, whispering to them as they let them go.

When they came within reach, Jason and Wallace hoisted the children to the top and lined them up to make room. Soon, the six men joined them, and Jason squeezed toward the front of the line, whispering "Quiet" and "Shhh" to each child he passed.

Then, leading the way again, he soft-stepped to the end of the tunnel. When he stopped, he lowered to a crouch and peered out. The anteroom was empty. No sign of Randall.

Tam laid her head on his back and whispered, "The dragons can get into that room."

"I know. That's why I'm stopping here." With a smile, he added a quiet, "Shhh."

Elyssa crept up and knelt at Jason's side. "Where's Randall?"

"That's what I was wondering."

"For all we know," she said, "the gateway is open now. It's about the right time. Maybe he's in the gateway room with Tibber."

"Do you think I should call?"

"Not too loud. I sense a shadow across the entryway."

"A dragon?"

"I think so."

"Then I'll have to do it another way." Drawing his sword, Jason tiptoed into the room. A dragon-like voice sounded from the entry, making him freeze in place. It had the cadence of language, but the words made no sense at all.

Elyssa whisper-shouted, "Jason! Tam knows the dragon's language. She says it's coming in!"

Light from outside dimmed, signaling the dragon's approach. Jason ran to the front of the anteroom and turned around, hoping to see Tibalt and the river, but only the three tunnels were there, dark in the muted light. Elyssa, the men, and the children ducked into the shadows.

He pressed his back against the front wall and waited at the edge of the opening to the outside. If he bolted for the central tunnel at the back, the dragon would likely see him and maybe send a volley of flames, endangering the children. He had to stand his ground and either fight or make a run for the top of the stairs with a hope that the dragon would follow him outside. But then he would have to face at least two dragons ... alone.

A barrage of flames flooded the room, blasting all the way to the tunnels. Jason pressed harder against the wall. Heat blistered his arms, though they stayed out of the fire. This dragon had to be three times as powerful as the one he had slain, and ten times as angry. Smarter than Yarlan, too—that fire was likely designed to clear out any adversaries before he entered. The dragon would be storming in at any second, and this one would be tougher than any Jason had yet encountered.

seventeen

s Arxad descended, Koren eyed the strip of grass that abutted the stream below. Two teenaged boys unloaded some of the stones from a raft they had slid onto shore, piling them into a cart, probably for construction material in the village or at the great barrier wall. One of them straightened and stared at the river with his arms crossed over his chest. Another raft floated their way, this one empty.

Koren squinted. That was strange. Why would one of the mining crews let a raft pass their station without loading it? Surely the labor dragon wouldn't have allowed that, would he?

Taking in a deep breath, she shook her head. Something must be wrong, very wrong, but she couldn't let it worry her. She had too many problems of her own.

With bright sunlight reflecting off the water, Koren looked back at Maximus, still trailing. His flashing red eyes were riveted on her, two scarlet beacons of pure skepticism. When she dismounted, would she be able to hypnotize him? Not likely. He wouldn't fall for that again. And would Arxad be able to protect them if Maximus decided to take revenge on her for breaking into the Basilica?

As Arxad beat his wings for landing, Koren wrapped both arms around Natalla and whispered, "Don't be scared. We'll be all right."

"Why is he taking us to the river?" she asked.

"I don't know, but I think we can trust him."

Arxad skidded across the water and ran up onto the shore, finally stopping in a smooth slide on his belly. "Get down quickly," he hissed, "and keep me between you and Maximus."

Pulling her cloak up, Koren slid down his right flank and helped Natalla join her on the shore, a blend of dark mud, green grass, and finger-tall mushrooms. When Maximus landed within dragon-breath range, Koren grabbed Natalla's hand and ran under Arxad's neck to the opposite side. She crouched there and listened.

"Why have you come here?" Maximus asked.

"Koren had a vision of a boy drowning. This is the only place he could be. There is no other abundant supply of water."

"Arxad, you are among the wisest of us all, but you have been taken in by the spells of this sorceress. She concocts dreams from her imagination and uses them to hypnotize us. She did the same to me, but I will not be deceived again.

Koren peeked around Arxad's body to watch, making sure Natalla stayed put.

Arxad shook his head, as if dazed. "I saw great quantities of water. I thought perhaps the river had flooded. Since the young man seemed strong, I could not allow him to drown. We need such slaves. They are the best workers."

"There is no flood. The river runs the way it always has. Your compassionate ways have allowed the witch to take control of you. Can you not see how she has used you?"

Arxad eyed the empty raft. "Yes, I see now. She is a sorceress, indeed."

"It is good to see you coming to your senses."

"What shall we do?" Arxad asked.

"Destroy the escapee immediately, but I want to see the redheaded one die a Starlighter's death." A wicked smile revealed Maximus's sharp teeth. "Her suffering would bring me great pleasure."

Arxad bent his neck and turned back to Koren, scowling fiercely, yet his voice was as soft as a whisper. "Take Natalla to the mine station marked by the bent tree. Run as fast as you can, and do not look back. If you hesitate, you will die."

Swallowing hard, Koren looked at Natalla. "Are you ready?"

She nodded, her chin quivering.

"Then run!" Letting go of Natalla's hand, Koren dashed toward the forest, her cape flowing behind her.

"They are escaping!" Maximus roared.

"I will get them," Arxad said. "You take the two boys to the other side of the forest. We cannot have witnesses to a summary execution."

"No, Arxad! I must stop them now. Stand aside!"

As Koren rushed onto a tree-shaded path, dragon shrieks filled the air behind her. She ached to look back, but Arxad's command still pounded her brain. *If you hesitate, you will die.*

Natalla ran at her side, her eyes straight ahead and her shorter arms and legs pumping hard. She seemed brave, at least for now. Under the cover of the tallest trees in the region, the dragons wouldn't be able to see them, but soon they would have to emerge from the forest and traverse the higher, rockier ground where only a few stubby trees dotted the landscape. Would a passing dragon swoop down and snatch them up with his sharp claws, or would he just cook them as they ran?

As soon as they burst out of the forest, Koren cringed, expecting the worst, but the skin on her back stayed pain-free and cool. She looked up. Nothing appeared but blue sky, the sun, and a lone vulture soaring lazily on the breeze.

They slowed, but Koren dared not stop. "Nice and easy now," she said, puffing as she jogged. "Remember, don't look back."

From the corner of her eye, Koren watched the cloak's cape flap behind her. It slowed her pace slightly, but no matter. Natalla wouldn't have been able to keep up with her at full speed, and since the cloak offered her protection before, it might be useful later. Besides, it seemed to be a part of her now, a symbol of who she was. It felt ... right.

Ahead, the path disappeared, leaving nothing but a field of rocky soil, wiry grass, and a dozen or so stunted trees no taller than the girls. The land sloped upward, not enough to be called a hill, yet enough to make them push harder to keep going.

After several minutes, Koren reached the crest of the rise and stopped to wipe her forehead. Shielding her eyes, she scanned the arid lands ahead. The squatty trees looked like stooped old men, their scant hair flapping in the warm breeze as they searched for morsels of food among the tufts of grass.

To their right, the river flowed back toward the forest, promising Koren and Natalla a drink of water before they reached the mines. Upstream, the river bent slowly to the left until it disappeared behind a mesa in the distance. A tree stood near the mesa, the tallest tree in the area. Yet it, too, had a severe crook in the middle that made it bend toward the rocky uprising, as if bowing in worship.

Koren studied the scene, remembering what she had once learned about this mine. The rock outcropping was ovular in shape, with two entrances on the side facing her—the main entrance near the right side just before the mesa bent away, and a secondary entrance near the opposite bend on the left. The stream flowed within fifty paces of the right extremity, and upstream it meandered until is passed out of sight behind the mesa.

Farther away, near the horizon, smoke billowed from another mesa, the higher yielding of the two mines now in operation. What had happened there? An explosion?

Koren shifted her gaze back to the first mine. At the point where the river flowed closest to it, three dragons stood at the water's edge near two empty rafts and a large unidentifiable lump, partially shielded by the dragons' bodies. After apparently discussing something, one of them flew to the left side of the mesa, landed, and walked into the secondary entrance.

"I see dragons there," Natalla said.

"Three of them. Two Royal Guard and a patrol, I think."

"Did you notice the empty rafts?"

Koren nodded. "I don't see any humans walking around, so something's going on inside the mine. It can't be good."

"What do we do? If we go to the mine, they'll see us for sure."

"I know. I know." Koren studied their movements for a moment before pointing. "One of them went into the secondary entrance, so he might be gone awhile. It's big enough for dragons to enter."

"Secondary? How do you know so much about it?"

"Wallace was once assigned to that mine. The last time I saw him, he was collecting stones at the raft drop-off point, and he told me all about it."

"How long ago was that?"

Koren bit her lip. The memory of Wallace and his handicap pierced her heart. As she replied, her voice trembled. "Four years, Natalla. I haven't heard from him in four years."

"Why not? He could easily send word through the gossipers."

"He ... " She swallowed hard. "He was boasting about his plans to destroy the great wall, and I called him ... " She pulled in her lip again. Even her nasty, busybody tone came back to mind, but she didn't dare mimic it. "I called him a one-eyed swamp puppy, too small for his duck feet and too big for his britches."

"But that was so long ago. You've grown up since then, and you've been studying the Code every—"

"It was stupid, Natalla!" Stiffening her arm at her side, she clenched a fist. "Stupid! Evil! I don't blame him for not forgiving me."

"Did you ever *ask* him to forgive you?"

"In my daydreams, a thousand times, and he forgave me there. But in my nightmares, he just stood and shook his head sadly, as if I had broken his heart forever. If I could just see him again, I'd drop down on my knees and beg him to forgive me."

Koren raised a fist to her mouth, but she refused to cry. Such an emotional upheaval over so small a thing!

"At least you might have a chance someday," Natalla said gently.

Koren looked at her. "What do you mean?"

This time, it was Natalla's turn to pull in her lip. Tears began to flow, tracing the dried tracks on her cheeks. "If … if it wasn't for me, Stephan would still be … " As her voice trailed away, her shoulders began to shake.

Koren hugged her close. Poor Natalla! Her dear brother was dead, and ever since the trial she had suffered in silence. Now she blamed herself, and who could possibly talk her out of it? In so many ways, her accusations were true. But what did that matter now? She was sorry, but Stephan would never come around to whisper the three words she so desperately needed to hear—I forgive you.

"Look!" Sniffing back her tears, Natalla pointed at the mine. The two dragons flew awkwardly, burdened as they dragged a heavy load along the ground. "Are they carrying a dragon?"

Koren squinted. A long neck hung low from the dragons' claws. "No doubt about it."

Natalla raised a hand to her mouth and gasped. "Did the humans kill it?"

"That would explain a lot." Koren waved an arm. "Come on. Let's get down there while they're distracted."

�·ई

As the dragon stomped down the entrance path, Jason breathed a silent prayer. This would be it, all his training rising to the top in a life-or-death battle with the most powerful and ferocious beast he had ever encountered. He flexed his muscles, listening to the silent words Adrian had signaled just before the tourney's final round. *Listen to your heart, but use your brain.*

Giving his brother a nod, he jumped in front of the entryway with his sword straight out. The dragon charged towards him. Jason lunged. The sword struck the dragon's belly, but the blade merely glanced to the side. A swipe from the dragon's claw threw him backwards.

After a slide and a reverse somersault, Jason leaped to his feet. Now his ribs ached, but he couldn't double over. He had to stay ready to strike or dodge.

The dragon stalked into the anteroom and straightened his body. The spiny head at the end of the long neck nearly brushed the ceiling. It wavered from side to side as its red eyes scanned the dim chamber.

Jason glided out of the way and crouched low near its flank. Apparently its eyesight hadn't quite adjusted. Could he take advantage? Did this dragon have a weak spot? It had to have a weakness somewhere, didn't it?

He caught sight of the tail, fully armored with thick spikes and scales. Every inch of this beast seemed impenetrable. Maybe a leaping stab at his eyes would do some damage, but his head stayed so high, that, too, seemed impossible.

Suddenly, the river appeared with Tibalt standing in his usual place and Randall next to him. Tibalt's eyes flared. "A dragon!"

Randall aimed his photo gun. A blue fireball shot out and splashed against the dragon's cheek. It wagged its head and roared. Then, rearing back, it seemed ready to launch a barrage of flames.

His ribs still aching, Jason cringed. It was now or never. He jumped up and dove headfirst through the portal. A rush of fire flashed in the corner of his eye, and heat warmed his legs, but when he rolled to a stop and settled on his back, darkness flooded his vision, and a puddle of water cooled his skin.

Barely visible in the dim room, Tibalt stared at him. "That was a big one!"

"Definitely," Randall added as he extended a hand to help Jason up.

Jason grasped Randall's hand and shot to his feet. "We have to get back there. Elyssa's trapped in the mine."

"In that low tunnel?"

Jason nodded, refusing the urge to wince at the pain. "They're hiding. I'm sure they were watching, so they probably saw me disappear."

"That dragon's too big to chase them," Randall said. "She'll be fine."

Jason pointed at Randall and spat out his words. "What are you doing in here? You were supposed to be guarding the door! I could've used your help!"

"I *was* guarding the door, and Tibalt showed up. I heard a dragon making those growling, barking kind of noises, so I ducked in here for a while. We tried to guess when we could open the portal again." Randall pointed at himself. "I did help you by guessing right."

Jason stared at him for a moment, his teeth grinding. Randall *had* helped. In fact, he had displayed a lot of courage, far more than Jason ever expected. Maybe it was time to give Randall a break and start treating him like a warrior.

Jason hung his head. "I guess you're right." He offered Randall his hand. "Thanks."

Randall shook his hand warmly. "I'm just glad it worked out."

"I'm sorry about the trick I played in the tournament."

Randall clapped Jason's arm. "Forget about it. We have to save Elyssa."

Now holding his side as he limped toward the wall, Jason sheathed his sword. "Right. What do you think we should do?"

"As long as that dragon's there," Randall said, "we can't move a muscle. To him, my photo gun was like an annoying firefly."

Jason touched the viewer. "Maybe we could get another look without opening the portal."

Tibalt winked. "Didn't you say you saw a pretty girl through that glass?"

"Koren?" As Jason looked at the black window, Koren's face came back to mind—sad, wounded ... and lovely.

"I did. But if this viewer just shows her, it won't do much good."

"Maybe she can help," Randall said. "If she's a slave there, she'll definitely know more than we do about dragons."

"A weakness?"

Randall shrugged. "Maybe. It's worth a try."

"We have to make this fast." Jason inserted his fingers. As before, the dragons lit up, as did the inscription and their fiery breath. He gazed into the glass, silently begging for it to clarify once more and show Koren.

After a few seconds, the image of a girl appeared, a younger, dark-haired girl. With tear tracks smudging her cheeks and deep lines digging into her brow, she seemed worried, if not terrified. Well beyond her, two dragons were lifting the body of a third dragon onto a pair of rafts. The dead dragon had only half a tail.

"It's the dragon I killed!" Jason strained his eyes. "It's like I'm standing on the opposite side of the mesa from where I was before."

Randall looked over his shoulder. "If those dragons are so tough, how did you manage to kill that one?"

"It wasn't too hard. It definitely wasn't the same kind of dragon." Jason studied the girl's cracked lips. She was saying something, but she kept licking her lips, making them impossible to read.

"Well," Randall said, "do you see anyone in there?"

"Shhh! I see someone, but I'm trying to concentrate." For the moment, the girl had stopped licking, and as Jason pieced the words together, he spoke them out loud. "What did you say, Koren?"

"Koren?" Tibalt asked. "You found her?"

"Quiet! Just listen." Again Jason drilled his stare at the girl and, copying her lip movements with his own, gave voice to her words. "You're hearing someone? Who?" The girl stared straight at Jason and continued speaking.

This time, Jason stayed quiet as he read her lips. *Jason?* she asked. *The boy you saw in the egg?* The girl looked more worried than before. *That's impossible. You're just upset and imagining things.*

"No!" Jason shouted. "Koren! It's me, Jason! You're not imagining things."

The girl squinted. *Koren? What's wrong?* She stepped closer. *How can you talk to Jason? He's not here.*

"Koren," Jason said. "Listen carefully. I can't see you this time, and I can't hear you, but I can see the girl who is talking to you. Tell her to carefully repeat what you want to say to me, and I'll be able to read her lips."

The girl cocked her head. *Okay, Koren. If you say so.* She straightened and spoke slowly. *My name is Natalla, and I am Koren's friend. We are trying to get into the slave mines, but there are two dragons close to the entrance, so we're waiting for them to leave.*

A feminine hand reached out and pushed Natalla's hair away from her mouth. Wounds marred the girl's wrist, blood still oozing from a raw cut.

Jason sucked in a breath. Was he looking through Koren's eyes? How could that be?

"Koren," Jason said, "it looks like you're near the entrance where the workers go in. Do you know where the other entrance is?"

Yes, Natalla's lips said. *Why do you ask?*

"There's a chamber at the bottom of the stairway, and a huge dragon is there blocking my way out. If it leaves,

I can open a doorway to my world and help the slaves escape forever, so can you tell me when it comes out?"

I will take care of it.

—❊—

Koren grasped Natalla's arm. "Stay here. I'm going to act as bait to get that other dragon out."

"What other dragon?"

"Jason said there's a dragon inside the secondary entrance, blocking his way. Remember? We saw him go down there." Koren pointed at herself. "When the dragons come after me, run into the main entrance. Do you remember where that is?"

Natalla nodded. "And what about you?"

"Don't worry about me. I'll tell a story that should give me enough time to get away from them." Koren set a hand on the mesa and peeked around its curving side. The Royal Guard dragon and the patrol dragon had finished loading the dead body onto the rafts and were now conversing, each one glancing at the mine entrance from time to time. The weight of the rafts combined with the dragon's body dammed the stream, and the water flowed toward the mesa, following a trench with newly dug earth and rocks lining the sides.

A bend in the trench diverted the flow from the main entrance and into a hole at the base of the mesa near her feet, probably an air vent for the miners. She stooped and pushed her hand into the water. Whatever the dragons were up to, it couldn't be good.

Taking a deep breath, she leaped over the trench and dashed around the bend. She passed by the first entrance, a low arch with stone steps descending into darkness, and sprinted toward the second.

"Stop!" one of the dragons roared, but Koren didn't look. When she reached the second entrance, she slowed down and crouched as she negotiated the steps. The dragon came into sight, huge and armored—probably a Royal Guard. He faced the inside, his tail flicking back and forth within reach of her outstretched hand.

With his back towards her, his eyes stayed out of view, but his head's rhythmic swaying from side to side indicated his fixation on something toward the rear of the chamber. Even with all their brains and brawn, these Royal Guard dragons sometimes obsessed beyond reason. It wouldn't be easy to draw him away, and with the other two dragons probably closing in from behind, she would have to use all her skill to get out of this mess.

Koren pulled the hood over her head and called out, "One day long ago, a dragon flew to—"

"Stop!" The dragon swung his head around, revealing his familiar face.

"Ma ... Magnar?" Koren backed slowly up the slope.

"Yes, Starlighter." Magnar hissed as he followed, his head low and his tongue flicking in and out. "I think your storytelling days are over."

eighteen

The dragon's following her!" Jason jerked his fingers from the wall and stepped aside. "Tibalt! Quick! Open the portal."

"Will do!" Tibalt pushed his fingers in place. As before, the glass expanded and brightened, revealing the scene in the anteroom, still somewhat blurry. The only sign of the dragon was the end of his tail snaking up the entry slope.

Jason and Randall withdrew their swords as one. "You check on Elyssa," Randall said. "I'll see what I can do to help Koren."

Jason pointed with his sword. "That dragon's a tough one. It'll take both of us to kill it, and there are two more besides."

"I don't mean to kill it. I'm just going to distract them long enough to get Koren to safety." He patted his photo gun holster. "This will at least blind them for a few seconds. One of us needs to check on Elyssa and the kids."

"Okay, I guess you're right." Jason strangled his hilt. The portal seemed to be taking longer to expand this time.

Finally, the gateway wall disappeared completely. As soon as they leaped to the other side, Randall ran up the entry stairs, and Jason spun around. "Open it again every half hour until you see us. Got it?"

"Got it." Tibalt raised a hand as if to salute and disappeared.

A roar and a sword clanging on scales erupted outside along with Randall's groan.

"Randall!" Jason turned toward the exit. The distinctive pop of a photo gun sounded from outside, followed by two dragon yelps.

"Jason! Over here!"

Jason spun on his heels and found Elyssa waving her arm frantically.

"Hurry!" she called.

He ran to the central tunnel and ducked inside with Elyssa. "What's wrong?"

"The mine pit is filling with water."

"Where is it coming from?"

"The miners had an air vent to the outside. Water's pouring in from that down deep in the pit. Allender thinks the dragons diverted the stream to flush the slaves out."

"I think you're right," Jason said. "I saw the trench they dug. But can't the miners plug it?"

She shook her head. "They were all at the ledge talking, and no one noticed the water until it was too deep. Even if someone dove down there, he wouldn't be able to see well enough to find the hole, much less plug it before running out of air." She pulled him farther into the tunnel. "Come on. You need to talk some sense into them."

"Sense? Why?"

As they hurried through the dark passageway, Elyssa spoke in a low tone. "Allender proposed sacrificing two men, but the dragons demanded either all six men or two children. If they sacrificed the six men, all the children would be given new Assignments instead of being put in the cattle camp."

When they reached the ladders, they descended in parallel. "What did Allender say to that?" Jason asked.

"He countered with four men. Two had to stay alive to make sure the dragons kept their word regarding the children."

"And?" Jason prompted as they stepped down to the lower level.

"The dragons upped it to all six men or three children. Now Allender is trying to get the deal back to the first offer, but I think he's trying to persuade the men to let two children die."

"What?"

"Come and listen for yourself."

Jason followed Elyssa toward the far side of the mine pit where Allender stood in the midst of the other five men, who were sitting with their hands clasped on their laps. Allender waved his arms as he spoke, but his voice stayed too quiet to hear. The children were nowhere in sight, not even Wallace.

Jason looked into the pit. Light glimmered far below, perhaps a reflection on the surface of the water, but it was too dark to discern the rate at which it was rising.

When they arrived, Allender glanced at Jason for a brief second before continuing. "I maintain that it is better for the children to die than to be sent to the cattle camps.

Their suffering would be unimaginable. If they die, they will be in the comfort of the Holy One's arms."

"Only a cowardly man allows a child to die in his place," Micah said, shaking a finger.

Allender gave Jason another glance. "For the sake of the foolish boy who has caused our troubles, I will say it again. I would gladly give my life to save any child. In the casting of the cube, I lost, and I made no complaint. Even now, I would walk into the dragons' fire without flinching if I could be sure that they would keep their word. But as it stands, no one would remain to make an appeal to the priests of the Zodiac if they break their promise."

Mark looked at his wringing hands, sweat dripping onto his fingers. Another man leaned his forehead against his tight fists, rocking as his lips moved silently.

Jason read his unspoken words. *Holy One, O Holy One, grant us wisdom. Grant us courage. Grant the children freedom and peace.*

A ripping pain stabbed Jason's heart. These poor fathers and uncles! They loved their children so much! And there seemed to be no way out of this deadly predicament.

Yet there was a way out, but not for almost half an hour. Would the water rise that quickly? Did they have time to wait for the portal to open? And would Allender and company now believe him?

Cowl rose to his feet, wiping tears from his eyes with his thumb. "I say we give them six men. I trust Wallace to make an appeal if necessary. He is almost of age."

"Almost," Allender repeated. "Almost will not pull the pail. Since Wallace has only one eye, he would be the best candidate for sacrifice. We need to choose only one other."

Jason boiled inside, and his voice erupted unbidden. "You can't be serious!"

"The dragon killer speaks." Allender gave Jason a mock bow. "Now that you have brought us this calamity because of your madness, would you kindly offer us another generous helping of insanity?"

Jason bit his tongue. A hundred retorts flew into his mind, each one nothing more than a combative insult. But that would truly be foolishness, definitely not using his brain. Heaving a sigh, he spoke in an even tone. "How long do you think we have before we're flooded out?"

"Based on the last measurement," Cowl said, "about fifteen minutes."

Jason nodded toward the ladder. "All the way to the upper chamber?"

"We think it will rise to that level by then. It's hard to be sure."

Jason looked at Elyssa. "Tibalt won't open it in time."

"I know what you're thinking. It's probably our only chance."

"You know what I'm thinking?"

She nodded. "It'll come to you. You'll see."

He looked into her eyes, sparkling green and sincere, the same eyes that coerced him into so many brave and daring acts when they were children. Her little-girl voice echoed from the recesses of his mind. *You can do it, Jason!*

Young Elyssa had fallen from a tree and was clinging to a branch that hung low over the fast-flowing river. The current beat against her dangling legs. She couldn't hold on much longer.

Eight-year-old Jason stood on a limb, clinging to a vine. "I'll have to climb down and grab you!"

"You can do it, Jason!" Then, as now, Elyssa displayed no fear, just trust—trust that he would find a way to rescue her.

As the vision faded, Jason let out a long sigh. "Okay. I think I know what you mean."

He returned Allender's bow. "I will go with five other men, and we will be the sacrifice. I suggest that Cowl remain as the survivor so that he can continue to be a wonderful father to Tam."

Allender studied him for a moment. Then, extending his arm slowly, he grasped Jason's wrist. "Very well. I think I misjudged you, young man." He turned to the others. "What say you all?"

Four men spoke. "Aye!"

Cowl shook his head. "I cannot vote for my own survival while you brave men give your lives."

"No need to give us a nay, my friend," Micah said, clapping him on the shoulder. "You are outvoted."

Allender took in a deep breath and motioned toward the ladders that led to the main entrance. "I will go first and tell them, and the rest of you follow. Let Jason be the last, but he will have to leave his sword behind."

As Allender climbed a ladder, Jason detached the sword and scabbard from his belt and looked at Elyssa. "Is this what you had in mind?"

"No. It was what *you* had in mind. I just prompted you to act on what you believe in."

"Then you don't have a problem with me sacrificing myself?"

She kissed him tenderly on the cheek. "You're a hero, Jason, and you have to do what heroes do. But I think you'll figure out a way to survive. And we still have Randall and Tibalt, right? Maybe Randall will show up and—"

"Tibalt's in our world counting his heartbeats, Koren was here to try and stop the dragons, and Randall might have died trying to save her. I think we're on our own."

Elyssa laid her hands on his cheeks and forced him to look at her again. "We're *never* on our own."

Her words sounded so strong, so filled with conviction. "Okay," he whispered. "I get your point."

When she lowered her hands, Jason looked down at the mine pit. The water was now less than a body length from the top. "It's rising fast. Where are the children?"

"Wallace is with them near the main entrance," Elyssa said. "Allender didn't want them to hear the debate."

"Good thing." They walked to the ladder and waited next to Cowl while another man climbed.

Elyssa set a hand on Cowl's elbow. "Would you stay with me for a minute? I have a question for you."

Cowl glanced at Jason before answering. "Certainly, Miss."

"Elyssa, you need to get out of here," Jason said. "This place will be flooded soon."

Elyssa gave him a gentle push. "Go ahead. Don't worry about me."

"You're plotting something, and, knowing you, it's something dangerous."

"Go, Jason. You do your part, and I'll do mine."

He met her eyes for a long moment, then turned, tucked his scabbard under his arm, and grasped a rung. Behind him, Elyssa and Cowl whispered, but he caught only one word: *water.* As he climbed, Elyssa's words reverberated in his mind. *Don't worry about me.* But how could he not worry about her? They were both risking their lives.

When he reached the top, he stepped into a tunnel, well lit by sunlight pouring in from the exit to the outside, perhaps thirty paces away. In the low corridor, Wallace stood between Jason and the exit with six small children huddling around him in perfect silence, each one watching Jason's every move with wide eyes. The other men lined up behind Allender, who was standing at the bottom of an upward-leading stairway, looking out into the daylight.

Wallace soft-stepped toward Jason, his worn-out shoes crunching the pebbly soil. "I heard what you did," he said. "But why don't you just open that door to the other world again?"

"I wish I could, but we have to wait for our friend on the other side to open it. I'm hoping to find a way to delay the sacrifice and make a break for the portal."

"Where is Elyssa?"

"On the lower level with Cowl. I'm not sure why. It's not unusual for her to stay a step ahead without telling me what she's doing."

"I'm going to check." Wallace scrambled down the top rungs of the ladder. "I'll let you know what I find out."

Jason leaned to one side, trying to see around the men and through the exit. Why was Allender just standing there looking up the stairs? And where were Randall and Koren?

Allender suddenly turned and waved with both hands. "Get back, everyone! Give them room!"

As the men withdrew, Randall stomped down the steps carrying a girl in his arms, his scabbard clanking behind him as it dangled from his hip. His face bruised and bloodied, he stopped at the landing and wobbled.

Mark took the girl from him and cradled her. She appeared to be breathing, but unconscious.

Jason weaved through the crowd and grasped Randall's arm, supporting him. "What happened?"

He pointed back to the stairway with his thumb. "She happened."

Bare feet and ankles appeared on the stairs, then a flowing white dress and trailing cloak. As she descended, her entire form came into view, a petite girl with windblown red hair, a blood-smeared face, and raw wounds on her wrists.

When she reached the bottom, she smiled and offered a curtsy. "Hello, Jason. I'm glad to finally meet you."

→·←

Elyssa knelt with Cowl at the edge of the mine pit and began reeling in one of the ropes. "I'm guessing this is an air tube."

Cowl nodded. "Ventilation is poor down there. We made an air vent to the outside, but it wasn't big enough to make much of a difference. Drilling such a long hole through solid rock takes a lot of time, and the dragons thought it was a waste to drill another. This mine has very low pheterone yield compared to the others, so they believe we will not suffocate down there."

"That doesn't make sense. If it's a waste of time to drill another air vent, isn't it a bigger waste to drill in an unproductive mine?"

"We have asked ourselves that question many times, but the dragons tell us to keep following the holes."

Elyssa wrinkled her brow. "Holes?"

"A long time ago, someone drilled three small holes from the top of the mesa deep into the ground. The dragons have told us to dig until we reach the point the holes stop. One day, Allender dared ask Magnar himself why we're doing this."

"And what did Magnar say?"

"Did you see the burn on Allender's face?"

She pulled the end of the tube to the surface and held it. "Yes ... I see what you mean."

"And another reason we're not like the other mines." He nodded toward the exit ladder. "A drone watches every rock and pebble that comes out of here."

"A drone?"

"A male dragon without ... well ... "

"Never mind. I understand."

"They are relatively weak, bad-tempered beasts," Cowl said, "but they are meticulous. If a pail contained even the smallest crystal speck, he would find it."

"A crystal speck?"

"Indeed. Anyone who brings something crystalline to the drone receives double rations."

Elyssa stared straight ahead. "So this mine is really here to find some kind of crystal for Magnar. He believes a crystal treasure exists at the bottom of the three holes."

"We all think so, yes."

She turned to Cowl. "Back to the air vent subject. How wide is it?"

He set the fingers and thumbs of one hand against the others to form a circle. "About so wide."

Elyssa scanned the ledge. "I need a rock to plug it."

"But the hole is down near the bottom. It's so dark, finding it will be impossible."

She set a hand on Cowl's cheek—which was scruffy, warm, and sweat-dampened—and poured her heart in her words. "Trust me, Cowl. I'm trying to save your daughter's life."

New tears welled in his eyes. He picked up a rock and set it next to her. "This is close, I think."

Water spilled over the pit's edge and spread across the floor, wetting their knees. "Okay," Elyssa said, "I'm no expert on fluid dynamics, but … " She set her hand on the surface and pushed down. "I know the water source is much higher than we are, but won't the weight of the water eventually stop the flow way down there and make the feeding hole back up?"

"Maybe, Miss. I have no knowledge of such things, but I can tell you that when we drilled to the surface to make the vent, we detected an air pocket in between. If the water pools there, my guess is the weight of water in that pool might overcome the weight in this one."

"Just thought I'd ask. Obviously the water's still rising." She set the end of the tube in her mouth and breathed in. It worked fine. She slid into the water, oily and warm compared to the river in her own world. "Make sure the other end stays clear. If I tug once on the tube, the rock you gave me is too small. Twice means it's too big."

"Miss, the danger is great. Let me go down there."

Elyssa shook her head. "No time to explain. I'm perfect for this job." She held her thumb over the tube's opening, grabbed the rock, and submerged. Releasing most of her breath, she surged toward the bottom, hoping the loss of air and the weight of the rock would help her dive. Darkness flooded her vision. Water pressure increased in her ears. This wouldn't be easy.

As she kicked and paddled the best she could with her burdened hands, she closed her eyes and probed with her mind. The bottom still lay well beyond her reach.

A flow brushed her cheek. Ah! That was it! Just follow the current, and it would lead her to the hole.

Soon a sense of fogginess numbed her brain, and the pressure grew too painful to go on. Tucking the stone, she pinched her nostrils closed and tried to blow through her nose. That helped a lot. She pushed the tube into her mouth and drew in a long breath. Good. Much better. After plugging the tube with her thumb again, she pressed on.

When she reached the source, the current poured out of the side wall at eye level. She braced her feet against some protruding rocks at the bottom to keep from rising.

Again probing with her mind, she sized up the hole and slid the rock inside. A rush of water pushed back, but not too forcefully. At first, the rock seemed too small to close the gap, but as she shoved it in farther, it lodged in place and slowed the flow to an almost imperceptible trickle.

Had she pushed it far enough? She tried to move the blocking stone, but it wouldn't budge. There seemed to be no choice now but to leave it and trust that it would work.

After taking another breath, she let go of the tube and pushed with her legs to zoom to the top, but one foot wouldn't move. She probed through the inky blackness and assessed the situation. Her foot was caught in two rocky knobs she had used to brace herself at the bottom. She jerked her leg to pull free. No luck. Trying not to panic, she searched her senses for the air tube. Something slender floated nearby in the darkness. That had to be it.

She swiped at it. Missed. It drifted farther away. Stretching her body, she swiped again. Snagged it! She pulled the tube into her mouth and sucked in. One gulp of air came through, then a stream of water.

nineteen

Koren's voice sounded smooth and sweet, yet tinged with pain. After helping Randall sit, Jason walked over to her. "How is Natalla?"

Koren smiled weakly. "I think she'll be okay. She's more exhausted than injured."

Randall, leaning his back and head against the wall, spoke up. "I was fighting the dragons, and … " He winced briefly before continuing. "And I was losing. Then Koren started telling a story. I thought she was mad, but it seemed to work. Two of the dragons turned and listened, like a pair of moths drawn to the light. The third one, a dragon she called Magnar, kept fighting. He seemed slower, kind of confused, but if not for Koren keeping up her story, he'd have killed me for sure. Those dragons are just too tough."

Randall pointed at various wounds. "I took a claw slap to my cheek, a blast of fire to my foot, and a jab from a tail spine to my thigh. That last blow sent me flying, and

I slammed into Natalla. When I picked her up and ran, Koren stopped her story and followed."

A loud growl sounded from outside. "Allender! Come out! The conditions have changed!"

Allender's shoulders sagged. He looked back at his men for a moment before tromping up the stairs in silence.

Koren stooped at Randall's side and dabbed his bloody cheek with the hem of her dress. "You were so brave!"

"It was the least I could do." He winced again and turned to Jason. "Where's Elyssa?"

"Down below." Jason gave Randall and Koren a quick summary of what happened, including the bargain Allender made with the dragons, as well as the rising water in the mine pit. He added some details about the portal room, so Koren would understand the situation.

"I guess Elyssa thought she could help from down there." Jason pointed at the ladder leading to the lower level. "She can't stay for long."

"I saw the redirected stream," Randall said. With a quiet *oof*, he tried to rise. "I could go out there and sneak past—"

Jason pushed him back. "You're too weak. I'll have to do it. Maybe if I could stop the flow, it would buy us enough time to get the portal open."

"Before I came in," Koren said, "I heard Magnar order the patrol dragon to go down to the other entrance. The gateway to your world will be guarded again."

"And if Tibalt sees a dragon, he won't wait for us. He'll close the gateway in less than a heartbeat."

Allender descended the stairs with heavy footfalls, his shoulders sagging more than ever. Everyone turned toward him, each face reflecting his anxiety.

"Magnar knows we have two more young men among us," Allender said, forking his fingers at Randall and Jason, "so he wants both to be included in the sacrifice."

Micah combed his fingers through a little girl's tangled hair. "Will they allow the children to be reassigned?"

Allender nodded. "No cattle camp. But … " He shifted his fingers to Koren and Natalla. "Those two have to stay in the mine."

"And drown?" Jason asked.

"Magnar fears the redhead, so he wants her to stay here, and the other girl is already under a death sentence for escaping."

Randall climbed to his feet and grasped the hilt of his sword. "Well, if I'm scheduled to be on a dragon's dinner menu, I'm going down his throat scratching and clawing all the way."

"If you fight," Allender said, "the children will go to the cattle camp, and you will die anyway. Keeping them out of there is the reason we are willing to die."

"What's so bad about the cattle camp?"

Allender glanced at the other men. Micah heaved a sigh, while two others just shook their heads sadly. "I cannot even begin to describe it," Allender said, "but if a man were ever to see it for himself and still not risk his life to keep the children out, then I say he is not a real man."

The other men murmured "He's right," and "Ghastly place," as well as a few indiscernible words salted with oaths.

Randall echoed one of the oaths as he kicked the wall with his heel. "It's against my training! I can't go down without a fight."

"I have a suggestion." Koren held out her arms, showing her injured wrists. "Bind me hand and foot and take me out to the dragons. Tell them that the great prince wants me back at the Basilica, and they dare not keep a Starlighter from his judgment and the cooking stake. I beg you not to ask what these things mean. Please just trust me and offer me in trade for everyone's lives. They do not fear me as much as they fear my voice. Put a gag in my mouth, and their fears will vanish."

"Can you trust a dragon's word?" Randall asked.

Allender looked at Randall as if he had lost his senses. "Maybe you really are from another world."

"The dragons have a system of laws," Koren explained, "but they are far more concerned about appearance than adherence, and that can work to our advantage. Whenever a dragon has gone against his word in a legal matter, we are allowed to appeal to the Zodiac. Most of the priests there are pleased to start a fight with the secular authorities, so the dragons usually just adhere to their bargains in order to avoid embarrassment."

Allender took one of Koren's hands in both of his and kissed her thumb. "You are a brave lass, indeed, far wiser and more eloquent than I remembered. If we are all in agreement, I will make the entreaty."

With the exception of Micah, the other men nodded and said "Aye," each one adding a word of compliment for the "courageous young lady."

"What do you say, Micah?" Allender asked.

The gray-haired man reached toward Koren with a dirty, gnarled hand and slid it under her wrist. He looked at her wound, then at her face. "You are well-acquainted with grief, are you not?"

Koren gazed at the group of children. "I have worked in a mine, so I know the grief these children have already suffered. I also spent time in the cattle camp, so I know what these children will face if we neglect to do all we can to keep them from that torture." She turned back to Micah. "It is far better for me to suffer death than for one of these to live in unspeakable horror."

Micah gave her a solemn nod. "Well spoken."

"Then what say you?" Allender asked.

"Aye, but I wish to accompany her. No girl should be given over to the dragons without a friend at her side — especially this one. Besides, it would be against our code of honor to allow her to face danger without an escort."

"So be it." Allender walked up the stairs, calling back, "I assume Magnar will accept."

Jason's stomach churned. What could he do to stop this from happening? Everyone here was so noble, so sacrificial. They didn't deserve to die. And now Koren, one of the slaves he longed to rescue, was about to walk into the dragons' jaws. And it was all his fault! If anyone should be offered, it was he, not this innocent girl.

He looked down toward the lower level. Water had risen over the ledge, probably about waist high to anyone still down there. What was Elyssa doing? And with the portal guarded, did it even matter? Was there any safe path back to the portal?

When Micah hooked his arm with Koren's, Jason set his sword down and stepped forward. "Micah, I appreciate your courage and honor, but since I am the one who killed the dragon, Koren's sacrifice is on my head. It is my right to be her escort."

"Ah! That is true," Mark said. "Her blood is on his head."

Micah stepped away and allowed Jason to take his place. "If your story is true, how are we to go to our home world without you?"

"Wait for Elyssa—she knows the way, as do Wallace and Randall."

Allender returned, this time trotting down the stairs with a lighter step. "Magnar has agreed. Bind the girl quickly. We have to hurry before the water drowns us all."

Koren held out her hands and waited while Micah and another man bound her wrists. She smiled at Mark, who sat on the floor, cradling Natalla in his arms. Natalla breathed easily, though her eyelids and arms occasionally twitched.

"You will take care of her, won't you?" Koren asked.

He smiled and brushed back Natalla's hair. "Like she was my own daughter, Miss."

As Micah placed a gag over Koren's mouth and tied it in the back, Jason looked into her bright eyes—sad eyes, filled with depth and wisdom.

What had he done? If not for him, this girl would likely be free on Major Four, along with all the other slaves in this mine. Now she would be sent to her death, and the rising waters might shut down the portal for good.

Jason clenched a fist. Somehow he would find a way to save her and the others. Maybe using his brains for a change would get everyone out of this mess.

◦⋅◦

Elyssa continued pulling her leg and clawing at the stones trapping her foot. Her lungs begged for air. The surrounding water pressed in. Her ears ached, and wetness leaked into her nose.

Something yanked on the breathing tube, and she gripped it tightly. A sleek form darted through the water, and powerful arms wrapped around her waist and pulled, but she stayed put.

She shouted in a flurry of bubbles, "I'm caught!"

Nimble fingers worked around her foot, pressing, squeezing. Pain stabbed her bones, and new throbs pounded her head. Somehow the pain helped her mind draw in the details—her foot, the two protrusions holding it in place, the blocked air vent.

Suddenly, the stone blew out of the vent, and a glittering sliver of light, no longer than her hand, fell in its wake. Although her foot wouldn't move, the vent was within reach. She picked up the plugging stone, jammed it in as far as she could, and scooped up the crystal.

Something jerked her foot free. Bending her knees, she vaulted toward the surface. Again her ears ached, but this time the pressure pushed from the inside, as if her brain were about to explode. Her muscles knotted, and her joints locked. She flailed with her arms, but they felt like stiff boards. Light appeared. The surface couldn't be much farther, could it?

Something grabbed her wrist and jerked her upward. Her head broke through the surface. Ah, yes! Air! She sucked in two lungfuls, then coughed them back out, spitting water. She breathed in again, slowly this time. Once her head cleared, she looked into Cowl's worried eyes.

"Are you okay, Miss?"

"I think so." She looked around. Her feet were planted on solid stone, but she stood chest deep in water. "Wasn't that you who freed my foot?"

"That was Wallace." Cowl held up the end of the rope. "I felt your tugs, but I had to keep this above water, so he dove down to see what was the matter."

"My foot was stuck, and the tube leaks." She scanned the surface, dim and rippling. "Have you seen him?"

Cowl pointed at a ladder leading to the portal exit. "He made sure you were safe and then scrambled up."

Elyssa looked that way. Water dripped from rung to rung before spilling to the flood level. "Maybe he's going to see if the path to the gateway is clear."

"The water is no longer rising," Cowl said. "It seems that you were successful."

"At least for now. I'm not sure how well that stone's going to hold. It already popped out once." She laid the crystal in her palm and showed it to him. Like a tent peg, it had a blunt cap on top as if for striking with a hammer. "Magnar's prize?"

Cowl's eyes widened. "Where did you find it?"

"It came out of the air vent." As she gazed at it, the dim light in the chamber gave clarity to something in the center of the crystalline cap, two tiny dark spheres slowly orbiting each other, like a pair of pebbles in a swirling dance.

"Maybe it was in the air pocket we found," Cowl said, "and the river washed it out."

She rubbed her thumb along the smooth, clear surface. "So Magnar guessed it was here somewhere. It's as if someone buried it, and he was looking for it."

"A fair deduction. Allender's burn injury tells you that Magnar is quite passionate about finding it."

Elyssa pushed the crystal into her pants pocket. "Now that we have time to wait for Tibalt to open the portal, we have more options."

"First we have to stop the sacrifice," Cowl said.

Locking her stare on the miners' entry ladder, Elyssa began slogging through the water, swiveling her hips and arms. "I have to get to Jason. Now!"

⋗·⋖

After Micah tied Koren's ankles together, Jason formed a cradle with his arms and lifted her. She felt light, not much heavier than a child half her age. As he ascended the stairs, she set her bound wrists on her waist and looked into his eyes. Although her mouth had been gagged, she communicated so much with her sad, yet hopeful expression. *Do not fear, Jason*, she seemed to be saying. *All will be well.*

It was so strange. Those words seeped into his mind as surely as if he were reading her lips. And how could it be well? Everything was falling apart. Soon, the mine cavity would be flooded, and every man and child would face the risk of drowning. Choosing death to save the others, who might die anyway, wasn't exactly "All will be well."

Not only that, where was Elyssa? What was she up to?

When he reached the top stair, he blinked. Three dragons stood in front of him, two with thick scales and long spikes from head to tail, along with Yarlan, the patrol dragon.

Jason eyed them in turn. Yarlan was tough enough. These other two would be impossible to slay alone. Somehow he had to buy time. Elyssa, Randall, and Tibalt would come through.

"Lay the Starlighter on the ground," one of the big dragons growled.

Stooping, Jason laid Koren down gently. He glanced back. Randall and Allender stood on a step halfway down the flight, watching. Randall flashed a glimpse of his photo gun hidden underneath his shirt, apparently waiting for a signal from Jason.

Jason shook his head. The blasts from that gun had served only to annoy the dragons, and without his sword, both he and Koren would be dragon fodder. There had to be another solution.

"I am Magnar," one of the big dragons said. "I will take the Starlighter now. You may go back to your fellow slaves."

Jason bowed. As he rose, a barrage of thoughts whistled through his brain. Apparently Magnar didn't know the slaves well enough to recognize him as a newcomer. Had their encounter in the darkness been too short for Magnar to get a good look at him?

"Magnar, may I intercede on behalf of this girl? It is not our way to allow a young woman to face such dire consequences without an escort."

The dragon snorted derisively. "Why would she need an escort?"

"To ease her passage to the next world." Jason gave him a surprised look. "You do believe in another world, don't you?"

"It depends on what you mean by another world." Magnar extended his neck and brought his head close to Jason's. As the draconic eyes stared into his, the dragon's hot breath warmed his cheeks. "You are veiling your words. What is it that you are not telling me?"

"If you allow me to go with her, I will give you more information, but first I want to —"

"So be it." Magnar withdrew his head. "I will carry the Starlighter," he said to the other big dragon, "and you will take the male. Yarlan is capable of dispatching the rabble."

The word pierced Jason's mind. *Dispatching?* "Wait," he called. "What do you mean by 'dispatching'? We had a bargain."

"Shall I carry him by claw?" the other dragon asked.

"It is the only secure method." Magnar flapped his wings, and, with a jump into the air, snatched Koren off the ground with his claws.

"Wait!" Jason called again, but the dragons ignored him. He looked back at Randall, who had drawn his photo gun and sword.

"We won't go down easily," Randall said.

The other dragon launched as well, and with a swipe of his eagle-like talons, he grabbed the back of Jason's shirt and jerked him into the air.

Elyssa ran out of the mine, dripping wet and screaming, "Jason!"

A claw bit into Jason's skin. The shirt pulled tightly against his chest, making the litmus finger throb again. Now well above the top of a nearby tree, he shouted back. "Is the way clear to the portal?"

"It is!" Elyssa paced back and forth underneath him. "What should I do?"

"Just make sure the Lost Ones get home!"

"I will!" As she spread out her arms, her wet clothes clung to her dungeon-thin body. "And I'll bring you home, too! I will find you, no matter how long it takes!"

The dragon shot higher, making it impossible to communicate, but the shrinking bodies of his friends still

said so much. Elyssa let her arms droop. Randall wrapped
an arm around her shoulders and hurried her back into the
mine.

Yarlan sent a blast of fire after them, but it missed well
high of their heads.

When his carrier dragon leveled out, Jason looked over
at Magnar. Koren dangled in his claws, her cloak flapping
in the breeze. She stared at him, peaceful, as serene as a
sleeping child, even with her hands and feet in bonds.

Starlighter. The name kept echoing in Jason's mind.
What could it all mean? Why was she so valuable? And
what caused the dragons to go back on a bargain?

Jason nodded to himself. No witnesses to appeal to
the Zodiac. Yarlan would likely stage a mining accident,
and no one would be the wiser. The only hope for Elyssa
and the others would be to escape through the portal
before the accident occurred. Yet, if anyone could figure
out what to do, she could. Apparently she had already
stopped the flood.

He let out a sigh. It was best now to settle down and
survey the area. Maybe remembering the landscape
would serve him later.

To his left, the stream flowing next to the mine, as well
as three other streams, ran together, creating a substantial
river that ran through a forest that stretched into a massive
wilderness on the opposite side. The green hardwoods
signified healthy, fertile soil, far better than the sanitized
clay back at the mine.

Ahead lay a town, a village of stone. Two of the buildings
stood out—a cathedral-like edifice with a tall belfry, and

a multi-spired structure with a smooth dome cap. Beyond the village much farther downstream, a high wall of stones stretched from left to right as far as he could see. The river ran up to it but disappeared beyond, as if it passed the boundary underground.

After a few more minutes, Magnar glided into an opening in the roof of the structure with the belfry. Jason's carrier followed, and they flew through a marble-lined corridor and into a huge chamber. Inside, dozens of fountains of fire shot up toward the ceiling, making a circle of flaming geysers.

Magnar swooped low and released Koren. Her chin slammed against the marble floor, and she slid several body lengths. Jason's dragon dropped him from nearly twice his height, but he managed to land on his feet in a run.

As the dragons settled to the floor, Jason hurried to Koren and lifted her to a sitting position. He reached for the gag, but Magnar shouted, "Do not take that off!"

Jason lowered his hands and slid one over Koren's. "I will do everything I can to protect you," he whispered.

She looked at him with glistening eyes. Again, they seemed to speak, as if she wanted to say, "I know, but please save yourself if you can."

After Jason's transport dragon flew back into the corridor and disappeared, Magnar stalked toward them, speaking in a gruff tone. "Who are you, little man, and where did you come from?"

Jason glanced at Koren again, then at the flames behind him. They warmed his back beyond the comfort level, and the potential flames in front of him seemed just as dangerous. "My name would mean nothing to you, Magnar, but I think you already know where I came from."

"Do I?" Magnar again drew close and studied Jason from head to toe. "You are too healthy, too well fed to be one of our slaves." The dragon's tongue flicked out and in. "How do you explain that?"

"My mother is a good cook." Jason spread out his arms. "I promised to give you answers, so ask me another question. I, unlike dragons, will not go back on a bargain."

Magnar snorted a plume of smoke. "You emerged from a mine, wearing clothes unlike other miners and with hands not yet broken by the hammer and chisel. You are clearly not a miner. I wonder if you even know where you are."

As the dragon's head swayed from side to side, Jason watched his fiery eyes. Apparently Magnar expected an answer even though he hadn't asked a question.

Jason firmed his chin. This interrogation would be like a sword duel, yet with words as weapons. "Magnar, are you asking me about my location? I'm sure a dragon as wise as you already knows where we are."

A ball of fire shot past Jason's cheek, singeing his eyebrow.

"Do not patronize me!" Magnar roared.

As he rubbed the superficial burn, Jason looked at Koren. A tear tracked down her cheek and into her gag. Her anxious eyes seemed to warn him of something, but what?

He turned back to the dragon and squared his shoulders. "I am from Major Four, the fourth alpha planet from Solarus, and I have crossed into Dracon through an underground gateway."

Magnar's brow lifted. "Ah, yes. Dracon. That is what you call Starlight on your world. I had almost forgotten."

"What do you call our world?" Jason asked.

"Darksphere." Magnar moved a step closer. "How did you open the gateway? Did you find the crystal?"

Jason leaned back to avoid the hot breath. "I don't know anything about a crystal."

Magnar stared at him eye to eye. "We will see how truthful your words are." He called out, "Zena, lower the shield. I want to speak with you."

The fountains subsided, revealing a tall, slender woman who wore a wraparound black sheet. Holding her head high and carrying a shoulder bag, she walked past a dark object that looked like a big egg.

As she neared, her eyes came into view. The pupils were black ovals with no surrounding irises, more like a ghostly cat's than a human's, and they seemed to wander, as if unable to focus. "What do you wish?" she asked.

Jason shuddered. She looked like a risen cadaver who had forgotten to stay planted in the ground. Even her voice seemed to come from the grave.

"Take the Starlighter back to the prince," Magnar said. "She must be chained again. Under no circumstances may she be released until I give the word."

Zena kept her head held high. "And if the prince chooses otherwise?"

Magnar spoke through a low growl. "The prince will *not* choose otherwise."

"As you wish." Zena withdrew a dagger from the bag and sliced through Koren's bonds, including the gag. She led her to the egg and fastened manacles to her wrists and ankles.

Now sitting cross-legged, Koren gazed at Jason with a forlorn look in her eyes. "If it is in your power," she said weakly, "please come for me."

Her voice ripped through his heart, bringing tears to his eyes. He held up a fist. "One way or another, I will set you free. I promise."

Magnar smacked Jason with the tip of his wing. "You make a beggar's promise, bread for your children when you have empty pockets."

With a spin on his heels, Jason faced Magnar again. "What do you want from me?"

The dragon's eyes flamed. "The crystal."

Jason pushed his hands into his pockets and turned them inside out. "Like you said, I have empty pockets. I don't even know what you're talking about."

Magnar extended his neck again and sniffed Jason's clothes for a moment before pulling back. "Perhaps when you see the Starlighter tied to the cooking stake, you will remember where you put it."

Jason resisted the urge to ask about the cooking stake. Whatever it was, it had to be bad. It would be better to probe for more useful information. "Who is Zena, and what is this black egg?"

As if on cue, the fountains of fire began to rise again, veiling Koren, Zena, and the egg. Although all three were still visible in between the columns, the wavering flames distorted the view, making it impossible to know what they were doing inside.

"Your first lesson as a new slave on your new home planet," Magnar said, "is that you do not ask questions of your master unless you are in a submissive posture." He swung his tail and bashed Jason on the side of his head. One of the spikes jabbed his scalp and nearly penetrated his skull. He collapsed and writhed on the floor, holding a hand against the wound. Warm liquid flowed between his fingers.

"Ah! That is better." Magnar let out a low chuckle. "Now you may repeat the question."

Jason pushed up to his hands and knees. Blood streamed across his cheek and down his chin before dripping to the floor. He looked up and glared at Magnar. "This is not my home planet. If you hope to learn anything from me, I advise you to treat me as an emissary, not as your slave."

"Emissary?" Magnar's voice shifted to a surprised tone. "If you are an emissary, why did Prescott fail to communicate your visit to me in the usual way?"

Jason focused on the blood pooling in front of him. *Usual way? And how does he know Prescott's name?* He cleared his throat. "The governor was indisposed."

Magnar stared at him, his red pupils oscillating between wide and narrow. After a long moment, he extended a wing and helped Jason rise to his feet. "If you are really an emissary, I will not insult you any further. Yet, if I discover that you are not, your execution will be instantaneous."

Jason wiped blood from his hand to his shirt. Again, blistering retorts flooded his mind, but any one of them would likely mean death.

"Climb on my back," Magnar said, "and I will take you to the Zodiac's courtyard. There we will find my emissary to your world, and I have some pointed questions for him."

twenty

Koren stared at the black egg. The shell's polished surface reflected everything around—the circle of fountains spewing fire to the ceiling; Zena standing nearby, stoic, as if in a trance; and her own reflection, her downturned features painting a portrait of her feelings— tired, sad, near the point of despair.

She wept. Would Natalla be able to escape the dragons? Would she be sent to the cattle camp? What would Magnar do to Jason? At long last, someone had come from the other world, a promise of rescue, a sign that the stories were all true, and now her hopes were being dashed.

As she cried, a voice drifted into her consciousness. "Koren, if you had done as I asked, your rescuer would not be in peril."

She looked at the egg. The voice continued, and her lips spoke the words. "Leaving the Basilica was a tragic mistake.

Your presence at the mine provided a way for the men to rely on something other than their inner strength and sense of sacrifice for their loved ones. They allowed you to sacrifice yourself, and any man who gives up his duty to protect and defend the little ones, and transfers that duty to someone whom he should protect, has shredded his masculine dignity."

Koren swallowed, but her throat tightened, making her voice squeak. "Do you mean that it would have been better for them to die?"

"In the long run, yes, because now they will never regain the courage they have shorn, and the future of humans on this planet is darker than at any time in history, for the Starlighter will be lost forever."

"Lost forever? Do you mean that Magnar will kill me now?"

"Is that not the sacrifice for which you offered yourself?"

"Yes, but I thought maybe you would defend me. You're the prince, and they do what you say."

"I said you would be safe as long as you stayed within these walls. You violated that arrangement, so your safety is forfeit. If Magnar has his way, you and your rescuer will soon die, and yours will be a most excruciating death."

Tears dripped down Koren's cheeks and fell to her manacles. "Is there anything I can do? Anything to help Jason and the others? Even if I have to die, I am willing, but I want my fellow human beings left unharmed."

"Is that so?" Her head turned unbidden toward Zena, and words spilled from her mouth. "Zena, move the Starlighter close to me so that we may have a more intimate conversation."

A hint of a smile bent Zena's lips. "As you wish, my prince."

Crouching, Zena pushed a key into a lock where the chains attached to a ring on the floor. She reeled out several more links, extending the length between the ring and the manacles, and locked them in place again.

Koren's lips again moved without command. "Come closer, Starlighter. Wrap your arms around me and listen to my inner voice."

She glanced at Zena before shuffling forward on her knees. The chains dragged and jingled as she moved, and the extra links allowed her to reach the egg. She draped her arms over it and laid her ear on the shell near the top. A faint noise, low and rhythmic, sounded from within. Could that be the dragon's heartbeat?

Words entered her mind, but this time without her lips giving them voice.

Listen to my heart, Koren, and I will infuse what you hear into yours. Put away the confusing thoughts in your mind, for they will never lead you to me. And do you remember what I said to you about the chains?

"If I stay in chains long enough, I will learn to love you. It is better that I love you by force than be given freedom to choose."

You remember well. A soft laugh emerged. *How did freedom serve you?*

"Poorly. But I was trying to love, trying to sacrifice. The Code says you will recognize love when you see someone sacrificing himself for the sake of a pauper, and that's what I was trying to do."

Ah, yes! The Code. Now you see that the rigors of the Code are too difficult. You are unable to love, unable to sacrifice, so the Code is useless. Obeying it is out of your reach. You were born a slave, and you will die a slave, so

the only good you can do is to serve me. As I taught you ear-
lier, in your condition of aggression and doubt, you would
never believe me worthy to be served, but now that you have
learned how foolish you really are, and chains once again
bind your ankles and wrists, perhaps you are less certain
than you were before.

"Less certain about what?"

Your notion that love is a choice, that chains can never
bind a heart. Your freedom has led you to seek a breaking
of our covenant. Whether or not Magnar's word superseded
mine is of no consequence. The result has been disaster. So
you can see now that you must be forced to serve me, for that
is the only way you will ever learn to love me. Even now, if
you will acquiesce with heart, mind, and soul, and agree to
these chains for as long as I command, I can save your life.

Koren gazed at her chains. The prince had allowed them
to be extended, not taken off. He had given her permission
to touch, to listen, to embrace, but she still couldn't walk
away if she chose to do so. What did it all mean?

As she pondered, the memory of her recent conversation
with the prince returned to her mind. She had shaken one
of her chains and said, "If this is your idea of being worthy,
then no, I would never learn to love you." And that statement still seemed so true. No one would force love on
someone else. It wouldn't be love at all.

Still, she couldn't argue with him. Not now. Her choices
had proved disastrous, regardless of her motivations.

She looked at the raw skin and oozing blood that
outlined her manacles. He was wrong. This wasn't love.
This couldn't be love.

Koren stared at Zena. She stood erect, a ring of keys
dangling from her fingers, and a sheen of perspiration

making her skin glow. With the fountains reflecting in her shimmering pale skin, she seemed to be on fire. What was she, anyway? Those black, ovular pupils made her look like the egg had imprinted itself on her eyes.

Letting her gaze drift down Zena's arms, Koren squinted to get a good look. The sweat on the slender white wrists highlighted a slight discoloration in her skin. Manacle abrasions? Yes, that had to be the reason. The shape and size of each mark was exactly right. She, too, had been shackled in these irons, and now she served the prince without chains.

Koren stiffened. Was Zena a picture of what she would become if she listened to the voice of the prince? Would she transform into a mindless zombie who believed love was hatched from bondage, that the Code was useless and impossible to obey, that her sacrifice for friends caused the hearts of men to fail?

She fingered once again her cloak's green eyes, embroidered over her heart. Or should she listen to the voice in her heart, the one that sang like a bird whenever she read from the Code, the one that whispered into her mind saying how much the Creator loved her, that he would woo her with grace and mercy rather than with chains?

Loosening her arms, she drew away from the egg. As she slid backwards on her knees, a voice came through her lips. "Why are you drawing back? You are learning so much, and now I need to tell you—"

She slapped her hand over her mouth and pressed her lips closed. Breathing heavily, she concentrated and, slowly lowering her hand, forced her mouth to speak her own words. "No! I will not listen to you or your heart! I have to follow what I know to be true, the Code, that I can do what it says, that love is embodied in sacrifice, not chains! I will never love a despot that demands a kneeling posture while flailing my back with a whip! That's not love. It can't be love! I will never be your servant!"

She closed her lips again, but the voice managed to break through once more. "So be it … Zena, take the Starlighter to Magnar."

❧·❧

Surrounded by Cowl, Allender, and the other men as well as the children, Elyssa pointed toward the interior of the tunnel, water dripping from the heel of her hand. "Where does this lead?"

"To the secondary entrance," Allender said. "It was once the only entrance, but Magnar forced us to dig a new one."

Elyssa nodded. "I was there, and I saw three tunnels. The middle one leads to a hole Jason and I used to come down to the mining level. Where do the other two lead?"

"As you face the tunnels," Allender said, gesturing with his hands, "the one on the right leads here, and the one on the left goes up to the top of the mesa. When the dragons deliver supplies, they land up there, and we use that tunnel to carry heavy objects in the cart. The wheels work better there than on the stairs at the entrances."

Cowl lifted a finger. "We have one dragon guarding us. If my guess is right, he knows by now that a portal is in the secondary entrance chamber, so he will try to stop us."

Randall struggled to his feet and raised his sword. "I'll see what I can do to keep him out of there."

"Any idea how long till Tibber opens the portal again?" Elyssa asked. "I lost track."

"Me, too." Randall nodded toward the recesses of the tunnel. "Just gather everyone over there and wait in front of the portal. If I can keep the dragon out, you should be safe."

Allender let out a sigh. "I am no longer sure what to believe, but I am the leader here. If that little redhead can show such spirit, I can show a little bit more myself."

"And I," Cowl said. "When I saw the emerald fire in her eyes, it awakened something in me I had forgotten, like a flint lighting a torch that had long since been abandoned."

Micah curled his bent fingers into a fist. "Yes! Let it burn!"

"You cannot face the dragon alone," Cowl said, laying a hand on Randall's shoulder. "I will help you."

"But what about Tam?" Elyssa asked. "If you—"

"Then she will always remember that her father was a hero. I should have embraced that legacy when the numeral one came up on the cube. Seeing it made my heart quake, and I listened to my fears. After watching that blessed angel being carried bound and gagged up those stairs, I swore I would never listen to that dark voice again."

"Then I will go as well," Micah said, "I can—"

Randall withdrew his sword. "Cowl will be plenty. If every man suddenly gets the heart of a lion, no one will be left to protect the children."

"Fair enough." Allender marched ahead, side-stepping the hole leading to the lower level. "Follow me."

Three men shadowed Allender. Mark carried Natalla, and another raised a lit torch, while Micah guided the children ahead. Elyssa waited for the others to walk out of earshot and looked at Cowl and Randall in turn. "I think we're in more trouble than we realize," she said.

"I agree." Randall rubbed the hilt of his sword with tight fingers. "I was wondering about that *dispatching* business. Every man and child here knows about the portal and our world, so the dragons don't want to leave anyone to spread the news to the other slaves."

Elyssa laid a hand on the tunnel wall and closed her eyes. She allowed her mind to probe within, feeling the structure as she mentally drilled into its depths. "I sense trembling. It comes and goes in a rhythm."

Randall looked up. "Footsteps? A dragon's footsteps?"

"Could be. There is also another sensation, like a low buzzing noise. Very strange." She flashed open her eyes and stared at Cowl. "At the top of the mesa, is the opening to the third tunnel big enough for a dragon to go through?"

Cowl nodded. "But only for a few steps. It quickly gets smaller."

"Do the dragons have anything dangerous that Yarlan can put into the tunnel, something that would kill anyone below? Poison gas or a wild animal?"

Cowl stroked his chin for a moment. "I cannot think of—" His face suddenly turned pale. "No! There is something!"

"What?"

"Bees!"

"Bees?"

"Yes, in the forest we have beehives that slaves harvest for the dragons. The bees are extremely vicious, and their stings are fatal. Only a few humans have been found who can safely work around them. The dragons, of course, are immune because of their hard scales."

Elyssa touched the wall again. "That would explain the buzzing I sensed."

"For that to work," Randall said, "Yarlan would have to close the exits."

Cowl gestured with his hands, as if going through the dragon's motions. "First he would put the bees in place and close the top opening. Then, while the bees are finding their way through the tunnel, he would likely close the secondary entrance."

"And then this one," Randall said.

"Yes, there is a boulder near each that he can push in place." Cowl picked up Jason's sword. "Come. We must get out before he shuts us in. We have to keep this escape open."

Elyssa ran deeper into the tunnel, calling back, "I have to warn them. If the other entrance is already blocked, we'll come back through this one."

As her path turned darker, she again probed with her mind. The ground was even and the walls were smooth, no obstacles to prevent her from running as fast as her tired legs would carry her.

Soon, light returned. Ahead, the tunnel ended at the anteroom, and the men and children were gathered near the stairs. Natalla, pale, but otherwise recovered, stood holding Mark's hand.

Allender stooped at the lowest stair, looking up at the exit while the man with the torch stood beside him. Wallace crouched in front of the portal plane, staring at the line of crystalline pegs embedded in the floor. "I saw the crystal you recovered," he said to Elyssa. "It must be the missing peg."

She pulled the crystal from her pocket and hurried to his side. Kneeling, she inserted the pointed end of the peg into the hole, but sand and pebbles kept it from going all the way in. "It's blocked."

"I will clean it out." Wallace withdrew a small knife from his pocket. "It won't take more than a minute."

"We might not have a minute." Elyssa left the peg with Wallace, rose, and waved at Allender. "We have to get the children out of here."

Allender looked back at her. "Danger, Miss?"

"Plenty." Elyssa set her hand on Tam's back and guided her toward the stairs. "I don't want to frighten the children, so if we can just get out and—"

"First let me see if the dragon is up there." Allender started up the stairs, but in a rush of flames, he stumbled back down and crashed to the landing. Micah helped him to his feet.

Several seconds later, a distant thump shook the walls.

"I know that sound," Micah said. "Yarlan sealed the main entrance."

"It seems so," Allender said. "At least this one is open. We might have to wait here and—

Elyssa grasped his arm. "No! We can't wait here!"

"Calm down, Miss," Allender said, patting her hand. "You warned of danger. What is it?"

"Shh." She tiptoed toward the passageway on the left, listening. With every step, a buzzing sound increased. There was no doubt about it. Something was coming through that passageway, something angry.

"Bees."

twenty-one

*J*ason stood under a curved black ceiling with hundreds of starlike dots sprinkled throughout its expanse. If not for torches on the perimeter wall, this room would have looked like an outdoor courtyard rather than the central hub within the confines of the building Magnar had called the Zodiac.

He tried to touch his throbbing head, but his arms, bound at his wrists with a rope that wrapped around his waist, could not reach that high. Riding on that monster had been torture, with every jostle sending a new stab of pain into his wound.

Magnar sat behind a crystalline column at the center of the room. As thick as Jason's arm and almost as clear as the air surrounding it, the column stood about head-high and was capped by a sparkling, transparent globe the size of a human head.

Something clicked. A hole opened in the center of the ceiling and grew rapidly. Sunlight peeked through, and a few seconds later, the entire sky, blue and cloudless, came into view.

As Magnar scanned the canopy above, a menacing scowl tightened his scaly face. "Arxad has much to answer for. If his explanation for his actions is inadequate, he will face the same fate as his beloved Starlighter."

Jason blinked at the bright sunlight. "What did he do?"

"He rebelled against my authority, but the details are none of your concern."

"If he knows he's in trouble, maybe he won't come back."

"We have no need to fear that. He will not abandon his precious Starlighter or his family."

For the next few minutes, Jason stealthily studied the room, trying to memorize the locations of escape doors and potential weapons—a broom, a fallen cactus, and a metal rod the length of his forearm—yet nothing seemed adequate.

Finally, Magnar snorted. "You see. Arxad approaches."

High in the air, a dragon flew toward them, but his flight pattern seemed awkward and jagged. Soon, he flew into the roof's opening and settled to the ground, his wings, torn and bleeding, beating the air.

Breathing heavily, he bowed and spoke in the dragon's strange language.

"Use the human tongue, Arxad." Magnar pointed at Jason with a wing. "I want this boy to listen to what I have to say to you."

"Very well." Arxad's rapid breaths continued. "I apologize for my appearance, but Maximus and I had a rather significant disagreement."

"You fought with him?"

"I did. You see, I took the Starlighter to the river where I thought I might find that drowning boy, and when Maximus

joined us, his presence jolted me back to my senses." After
taking a long draw of air, Arxad's breathing eased. "The
river had not flooded. All was normal. So I scolded the
Starlighter fiercely, and she and her friend ran away. Of
course, I could easily have overtaken them, but Maximus
attacked me."

"He attacked you?" Magnar's tail whipped the floor.
"Why?"

"I can only guess, but I think when he learned that I
would so easily scold the Starlighter, he knew that I was
no longer under her spell. As you might know, ever since
Maximus allowed her to enter the Basilica, his motives
have come into question among some of us. It seemed
that he was completely under her spell himself, and he
was pretending to be angered by her trespassing.

"So when I left with her, he followed. But why? Was
it to ensure her safety, thinking that I might punish her
when my mind was restored? Evidence could lead one to
believe that. Because of our battle, she escaped, giving
further evidence that he has been aiding her all along."

"A most interesting story," Magnar said, "but lying
does not become you."

"Lying?" Arxad blinked. "I have spoken no falsehoods,
and the Reflections Crystal shows that every word is true."

Magnar looked at the crystal column. The globe at the
top reflected a gleam of sunlight that projected a barely
visible ray toward Arxad.

"Speak an obvious lie," Magnar commanded.

Arxad glanced at Jason before answering, "I am not
here."

The globe slowly changed from clear to gray, and
finally to black.

"It appears to be functioning properly." Magnar scanned Arxad's body. "Your wounds also corroborate your battle story, but when Maximus arrives, I will hear his account of events as well."

Arxad lowered his head. "Maximus will not be arriving."

"What?" Sparks flew from Magnar's nostrils. "What happened to him?"

"Our struggle took us into the river. Of course I had to defend myself, but after a great battle, he drowned."

"Drowned?" Black smoke shot skyward from Magnar's snout. "How could a powerful dragon drown in a shallow river unless someone held him under the water?"

Arxad glanced at the crystal, a look so brief, Jason thought Magnar couldn't have seen it. The globe had faded, but it was still somewhat gray.

"I held him under, great Magnar. It was not my purpose to drown him. I merely hoped to keep him from killing me. As powerful as he is, my only chance was to use my greater weight to my advantage."

Magnar swung his head toward the globe. It stayed a dull, smoky gray. "If you are still speaking the truth, why is the crystal not growing clear?"

"Neither is it darkening," Arxad replied. "The crystal knows that I speak the truth as I understand it, though I am unsure of my own motivations. You see, I have despised Maximus for many years, and I wonder if my old hatred has clouded my perception. I can assure you, however, that if I had any intent to drown him, I did it only for the future of Starlight, not to save the girl."

The crystal instantly turned clear. Magnar stared at it and nodded. "Your loyalty to our race is undiminished, but you will have to stand trial. Even an accidental death must be investigated thoroughly."

Arxad bowed his head. "I understand."

"I want to ask you about this boy who implies that he is an emissary from another world."

Arxad's brow lifted. "You mean, the crystal is—"

"No. When I checked the portal, it was still closed, and the crystal was not there. Have any of your communications with Prescott provided information that would explain this boy's presence here?"

Jason leaned closer. The conversation was getting much more interesting.

Arxad extended his neck and looked Jason over for a moment. "I have never seen him in my life. I have no idea how he arrived here, so I think it best to maintain silence in front of him about these matters until we learn more."

"Agreed, and the crystal again confirms your words. Perhaps a round of torture for this fellow would induce—"

A squeak sounded. Magnar turned toward a cavernous hallway. Zena emerged, leading Koren by a chain attached to a neck iron. No longer wearing bonds on her ankles, Koren walked unhindered, her cloak flowing behind her and a black gag covering her mouth, a stark contrast to her flowing white gown.

From a strap over her shoulder, Zena carried the same bag from which she had earlier drawn a dagger. That side of her body drooped, proving that something heavy weighed her down, and she glanced at it with every careful stride.

"Chain her to the crystal," Magnar ordered. "And allow her to speak."

Staring straight ahead, Zena set the bag down and pulled her prisoner toward the crystal. As Koren passed by Jason, she looked at him, her eyes imploring. Her green orbs seemed to speak once again, but not with an appeal for rescue. She begged him to run, to save himself.

Jason shook his head. He couldn't run. He had to stay and figure out a way to escape with her. But how? Two fire-breathing dragons could catch him and turn them into a pair of torches with a single puff.

Zena pressed Koren's back against the column and locked the chain to a ring embedded in the stone floor, choosing a link that kept the chain tight between the ring and her prisoner's neck.

With her arms and fingers straining to make the chain tight, Zena wrapped the remaining links around Koren's chest and, using a padlock as big as her hand, fastened them together behind the column. Then, with dramatic flair, she drew the dagger from her bag and sliced Koren's gag at her cheek, nicking her skin in the process. As the gag drooped and fell, a trickle of Koren's blood followed.

Jason's anger boiled. He focused on the key in Zena's bony fingers, a long silver one. Immediately, Elyssa's words came back to mind: *It's important to remember details that might help you later, even the shape of keys.*

He studied the key—three square notches on the shaft and a blunt oval end attached to a metal ring with at least eight other keys of similar size and color. As Zena attached the ring to a strap on her bag, he felt his pockets for his own ring of keys, but it was gone, likely swept away during his wild ride in the river.

"Your spells will not allow you to escape," Magnar said as he walked in front of Koren and looked her in the eye. "Now will you tell us a tale?"

Koren glared at him. With her cheek bleeding, her eyes sparkling, and her red hair blowing in the warm breeze, she looked like a persecuted prophetess ready to announce an oracle of doom, as if dragon's fire might erupt from her lips at any moment and consume her adversaries.

Yet not a hint of bitterness spiced her words as she said with a meek voice, "What tale do you wish to hear?"

Magnar glanced at Arxad before replying. "Take us back to the day when Uriel Blackstone escaped. He hid something that belongs to me, and I want to know where it is."

"Very well," Koren said. "If I may have some water, I am sure I will be able to deliver this tale more clearly."

Jason studied Koren's expression. Why was she being so submissive, so willing to give Magnar what he wanted? Might the request for water be a ploy? Was it a distraction so her rescuer could think of a way to set her free?

Magnar nodded at Zena. "Get a flask, and be quick about it."

"The closest flask suitable for a human's use would be in the Basilica," Zena said.

Magnar's voice sharpened. "Then get it!"

"As you wish." Zena hoisted the bag by its strap and trudged toward a doorway.

"Leave that here," Magnar ordered. "It will only slow you down. I want you back here as quickly as possible."

Zena stared at him with her blank eyes. "But the prince—"

"I know what is in there! Leave it!" Magnar draped a wing over the bag. "The prince demanded attendance, so let him stay. No harm will come to him."

As soon as Zena left, Jason looked at Koren. Her eyes focused on the bag. He spotted the key ring dangling from

a loop, barely visible under Magnar's wing. How could anyone sneak up and remove the key without him noticing?

"Magnar," Arxad said, displaying a grimace. "While we
are waiting, would you mind looking at a wound on my
back? I cannot bend my neck far enough to see it, and it
feels quite deep. I think Maximus's claws were the sharp-
est in all of Starlight."

"I am not a physician," Magnar growled. "It seems to
me that you deserve your wounds. See to that later."

Arxad glanced at the bag before returning his gaze
to Magnar. "Perhaps you should get the boy to put the
prince in position before Zena returns. It will save time."

"Have a resident of Darksphere handle the black egg?"
Magnar pulled the bag closer to his body. "I should say
not! I am in a hurry to find the answer I seek, but not in
that much of a hurry."

Jason looked at Arxad's darting eyes. He was plotting
something, apparently trying to get Magnar's attention,
but the first two attempts, both hasty and desperate, had
failed. Even though the bag now sat closer to Magnar, his
wing was no longer touching the top.

Finally, Arxad bowed his head. "Great Magnar, I have
a confession to make about my battle with Maximus, and
I trust that you will be a fair judge."

"Confession?" Magnar edged closer to Arxad, his wing
still over the bag. "Are you willing to forego a trial?"

Jason tightened his muscles. This was his chance, but
he had to hurry. He tiptoed toward the bag, straining
against the rope that bound his wrists. Just a little slack
would be all he needed.

"I ... " Arxad kept his stare fixed on Magnar. "I am willing to let you decide my fate."

Jason stooped and ducked under Magnar's wing. Using both hands, he grasped the ring, found the correct key, and began threading it off the metallic circle. He begged the keys to stay silent. No clinking together, or he would get fried for sure.

Magnar shifted his body slightly. Jason shifted with him. The dragon's wing brushed the top of his head, but Magnar apparently didn't notice.

"You see," Arxad said, his words coming out slowly, as if each syllable brought great pain, "Maximus and I have never been close friends."

Jason detached the key and slid it into his mouth. Then, he opened the bag and looked inside. The black egg lay in a nest of wadded cloths with the dagger's hilt protruding from an inner sheath.

"Yes, yes, I know," Magnar said. "Go on."

Jason withdrew the dagger and, twisting it in his hands to grip it properly, began slicing the rope.

"But," Arxad continued, "he has respected my wisdom and counsel. He once asked me about a problem he had with his mate."

As he continued sawing the rope, Jason glanced at Koren and the stake. The globe on top stayed clear.

Arxad's voice lowered, as if he were whispering a secret. "I am wondering if his despondency over his marital situation might have led to his initial mistake, his allowing the Starlighter to enter the Basilica."

The globe turned gray, but it seemed that Magnar hadn't noticed. Jason continued sawing. It wouldn't be long now.

"I think I might have taken advantage of Maximus's emotional state, and he surrendered to my strength more easily than a dragon of his stature might have otherwise."

"Are you saying that Maximus allowed you to drown him?" Magnar asked.

Arxad just nodded.

Jason looked at the globe again. It remained smoky gray. Could it detect a nod, or did a lie have to be verbal?

"What kind of confession is that?" Magnar barked. "You are heaping blame on Maximus, not yourself."

When he had sawed through ninety percent of the rope, Jason returned the dagger to its sheath.

"What are you doing?"

Jason snapped his head around. Zena's voice! He shuffled backwards, but not quickly enough to avoid Magnar's swinging tail. It batted his ribs and sent him flying across the room. He rolled like a log, nearly swallowing the key, and stopped next to Koren's feet.

"Be brave," Koren whispered. Her voice trembled ever so slightly. "We are never forsaken."

He looked up at her. In spite of the brutal chains and the bleeding wound on her cheek, she seemed so peaceful, so filled with compassion.

"What trickery were you concocting?" Magnar roared.

Jason shot up to a sitting position and used his tongue to tuck the key between his cheek and gum. "I was trying to escape," he said, showing Magnar the still-intact rope and his empty hands.

He glanced up at the globe. It was clear.

"The prince!" Zena threw down a leather flask, stalked to the bag, and swept it into her arms. Heaving a sigh, she hugged it against her chest. "He is unharmed!"

Magnar glared at Arxad. "Were you trying to distract me?"

When Magnar looked away, Jason spat the key into his hand and enclosed it in his fist.

"I was trying to get your attention, great Magnar, but not for the purpose of allowing the boy to harm the egg. That would be pure treason. I hoped to explain my relationship with Max—"

"Enough!" Magnar looked at the globe. It stayed clear. "Is the crystal still working?"

"Let's find out." Jason fixed his stare on Magnar. "You are a just and noble dragon."

The globe instantly turned black.

Magnar spewed a ball of flames that splashed on the ground near Jason's leg, sending sparks across his clothes. He followed with a bellow. "I will not be taunted with contemptuous blather from a petulant human! I keep you alive for one reason."

Maintaining a scowl on his face, Jason remained seated. "What reason is that?"

"To ensure that the Starlighter tells me the story I request. I will incinerate you if she does not."

Jason looked up at Koren. Her eyes now told him to be quiet. All would be well.

"Set the prince in position," Magnar said, "and let us proceed without further delay."

Zena took the egg out of the bag and laid it in the middle of the cloths about five paces in front of the crystal. She then retrieved the flask and held it to Koren's lips. With her head tilting back, Koren took a long drink, the muscles in her delicate but dirty throat pulsing with each swallow. When Zena pulled the flask away, Koren coughed and took several deep breaths. When she settled, she stared at the egg, her arms limp and her body resting against the binding chains.

Staying in a sitting position, Jason scooted back toward the egg. He kept his hands in his lap. Could he secretly break free from the rope? At this spot, the egg would be out of reach of his bound hands, which would make its corpse-like keeper happy, but once loosed, he would be able to grab the egg easily.

Koren pulled the hood up over her head. She closed her eyes for a moment and took another deep breath. When she opened them again, they seemed to shine like beacons in the hood's shadow, and the globe at the top of the stake began to glow, brilliant and white.

"I am a Starlighter," she said in a clear, loud tone. "I will take you back to a time when Magnar was one of only two dragons who knew of Darksphere's existence."

twenty-two

*L*ight from above streamed into the globe, as if the sun poured radiance into its crystalline surface. The glow spread out like an aura, and Koren's cloak took on a brilliant dazzle. Even the embroidered green eyes shone.

The aura spread across the nearby egg and reflected back toward her with dark light, as if the shell were casting a shadow. When the darkness passed over her, a voice entered her mind, smooth and low. *If you tell this tale to Magnar, he will no longer need the boy. The only reason he stays alive is so that you will use your gifts to reveal the past. Once you have done Magnar's bidding, he will surely kill the alien human.*

Koren looked through the shadow and locked her gaze on the reflective shell. She streamed a thought toward it. *If I don't do this, he will kill Jason anyway. Maybe I can learn something that will stop him. It's my only hope.*

Again the voice spoke in her mind. *Better to let Jason die without revealing the secret, for Magnar will surely use this knowledge to gain more human slaves and eventually conquer their world. Refuse him, and I will keep you safe. All you need do is submit to my chains.*

Keeping her head turned toward the egg, Koren glanced at Jason. He seemed to be working on an escape plan, though Magnar hadn't noticed. If this brave young man had risked his life to rescue her and also managed to survive a flood, maybe he could work another miracle now. Finally, she focused on the egg again. *I will take that chance.*

"What is the delay?" Magnar shouted.

As the aura faded and shrank, Koren swallowed. "The prince interrupted my concentration."

Magnar swung his head toward Zena. "What is the prince doing?"

"I will ask." Zena pulled something from the bag and pressed it against the egg's shell.

Koren squinted. The object looked like a girl's finger!

Jason grasped his shirt, tugging it open. A patch of skin on his chest pulsed with purple light. He bit his lip and grimaced.

After craning her neck for a moment, as if listening to something, Zena nodded and put the finger back in the bag. "The prince is encouraging the Starlighter to submit to him. He wishes to continue speaking to her while she is telling her tale."

Magnar angled his neck back toward Koren. "Was he speaking to you?"

"He was." Koren sagged within her cocoon of chains. "But when he speaks, I am unable to concentrate. I wish to tell this tale, but I cannot do so unless I can stay focused."

"Is this merely the prince's request?" Magnar asked Zena.

She nodded. "A most earnest one, but he will acquiesce to your wishes. This trial is for your benefit, not his."

"Cover him!" Magnar ordered. "I must learn the truth!"

Zena draped one of the nest cloths over the egg, shutting off the blackness.

Koren took in a deep breath and straightened her body. "I can continue now."

"Proceed," Magnar said. "The egg will stay covered."

As Koren continued breathing deeply, the aura strengthened and began spreading again like a widening cylinder of light. A powerful force weighed down her mind, evil, dragon-like. She allowed her face to twist and her voice to deepen into a growl. "Since you will never escape, it will serve you well to obey. Death is the only other option."

Ghostly images appeared within the aura—a dragon resembling Magnar and ten or more humans, all but one groveling on their knees. One man stood tall, and as he strode up to the dragon, Koren spoke his words in the tone of a masculine human. "If given that option, you foul beast, I gladly choose death over slavery."

Koren switched voices as quickly as the characters surrounding her switched speakers.

"Uriel," Magnar's image said, "you amuse me too much. Killing you would be like slaying a clownbird. Even as good as they are to eat, their antics are too amusing to use them as food."

Uriel lifted an arm, revealing a chain dangling from a manacle. "You will see. Someday we will all be set free."

Suddenly, the scene changed. Uriel lay alone on the ground. He sat up and let a key slide from his mouth and into his cupped fingers. After unlocking his chain, he crept on hands and knees.

In the aura, he didn't appear to be moving at all, but the ground passed by his body. After a few seconds, he stood and ran. The aura flashed, and, in an instant, he arrived at a mesa. Kneeling at its base, he dug into loose soil until he found a thin rope. He reeled the line in until a crystalline peg popped out of the mesa's grip and into his lap.

He stared at it and spoke in a whisper. "After this voyage to my homeland, I will return you to your hiding place. Perhaps my plans will fail and my son will be the next human that gazes at your beauty, but I hope no dragon ever looks upon you again."

A whispered voice from behind passed into Koren's ear along with the clinking of metal on metal. "This is Jason. Zena and the dragons are hypnotized. I'm still tied, but I'm loose enough to unlock your chains and the ring around your neck. Try to stay focused on your tale until I can break free."

For a moment, the aura began to fade. Koren took another breath and searched her mind. *Bring back Uriel. Where did he go? Where is he now?*

As she regained her concentration, Uriel materialized, kneeling again and retying the rope to the peg. He picked up a long metal rod and pushed the crystal into the hole as far as the rod would allow. He then shoved the dirt back into place, packing it tightly with the rod.

He set his hands on his knees and blew out a breath. "Must hurry," he muttered. "The portal will not stay open long." Then, he vanished again, and the aura began to fade.

"The lock's open," Jason whispered. "I'll think of something to get those chains unwrapped."

Underneath the aura's diminishing light, Jason crawled on hands and knees back toward the egg.

When the crystal's light disappeared, Koren looked at Magnar and heaved a loud sigh. "I think that's the end of the tale."

Magnar, Arxad, and Zena blinked and shook their heads. Then, with a rising growl, Magnar whipped his tail from side to side. "So it *is* buried in the mesa! The holes Uriel drilled in the center pointed to a deeper burial. The little rodent outsmarted us."

Zena marched toward her bag. "Uriel's method of hiding the key makes me wonder ... "

Koren swung her head toward Jason. He jerked at his bonds, but they still held him fast. It seemed that only a few threads kept him from breaking free.

"Aha!" Zena lifted the key ring. "There is one missing!"

Koren shook off the neck ring and thrashed at her chains. They loosened and slid down her body, but they tangled at her knees. She couldn't break free.

Magnar's head shot toward Jason. "Where is the key?"

Jason broke the final thread and tossed the key high in the air. As Magnar and Arxad followed its flight, Jason leaped toward Koren.

"The Starlighter!" Zena screamed.

As Jason pulled on the chains at Koren's feet, Zena ran and crashed into him, knocking him over.

Magnar roared. "You will now cook, Starlighter!" A streak of fire shot from his mouth and struck the globe next to Koren's ear. The crystal erupted in blazing light. Heat surged across Koren's back. She stiffened. Her body seemed to adhere to the stake as if her skin were fusing to the crystalline surface. She swiveled her head toward Jason and cried out, "Help me!"

With a loud grunt, Jason threw Zena to the side and lunged toward Koren. Setting one hand on the stake and one on Koren's back, he pried her loose and shoved her away. She tripped over the chains and rolled on the ground, her legs now free.

Arxad jumped toward Koren and set a clawed foot on her chest. "I have her, Magnar!"

Koren struggled beneath the pressure, but she couldn't budge. She looked at the crystalline stake. Jason still stood there, his hand apparently stuck in place as the fiery glow wrapped him in its clutches. He moaned, his gaze riveted on Koren's, his eyes wide and anguished. Zena climbed to her feet, smiling as she crossed her arms and stood guard.

"No!" Koren screamed. "If he dies, I will never tell another tale for you!"

"I have no more need for your tales," Magnar said, shuffling to Arxad's side. "The Starlighter will follow him at the stake. Let us be rid of them quickly without a public spectacle." He sent another stream of fire at the globe. Its energy redoubled, sending streaks of jagged light into Jason's body. He arched his back, making more of his body cling to the stake as he let out an elongated cry, "Koren! Use your gift! Save yourself!"

"Silence her wicked tongue!" Magnar ordered.

Arxad shifted his foot from Koren's chest to her mouth and set his head near hers, shouting, "You will be quiet!" He then added a whisper, "Magnar has one vulnerability. If you are wise you will discern my meaning."

His foot lifted slightly, allowing her to turn her head toward the egg, still draped in its nesting cloths. The key Jason had thrown lay on the stone floor in between.

With a mighty thrash, she jerked away and scrambled on hands and knees, scooping up the key as she scuffled toward the egg.

"Stop her!" Zena cried out.

Koren lurched to the egg and jerked off the cover. Wrapping her arms around it, she set the end of the key against the shell and shouted, "If you don't let Jason go, I'll break it and kill him! I swear I will!"

Magnar let out a trumpeting screech. "If you do, I will slaughter you in an instant!"

"You'll still have a broken egg and a dead prince."

For a moment, Magnar just stared, shifting his weight from side to side. Zena seemed frozen in place, her pupils wide and wandering. Arxad's eyes darted, but his expression gave nothing away. Jason moaned. As fiery light encircled his petrified body, his wet, red face continued to twist in agony.

Koren eyed the globe. It remained blazing white. But was that because it had transformed to cooking mode, or was she really telling the truth, that she really would break the egg and kill the prince? At this point, she didn't know, and she didn't care. "I'm not going to wait much longer!" A breeze blew her hair across her face, and sweat and tears kept it plastered there. "Release him now!"

Magnar waved a wing at Zena. "Make it cease!"

Scowling, Zena ran to a support column near the courtyard's doorway and pulled a lever. The ceiling began to close again. As the partition crossed the sunlight's path, Jason's flaming cocoon ebbed. When the dome finally clicked shut, the flames died away, leaving a few surrounding torches as the only lights in the chamber. The globe atop the stake continued to glow, its color now gray.

Jason slumped and dropped to his hands and knees, his head down as he gasped for breath.

"What do you propose to do?" Magnar growled. "You cannot hold this impasse indefinitely."

"I will ... " Koren looked around at all the eyes staring at her, four from dragons and two black orbs from Zena. "I will take the egg and Jason away from here."

Magnar's growl deepened. "We will follow you to the ends of Starlight. You would never have a moment's peace. And when the prince hatches, what will you do? Will you murder him? Or will you, like most humans, consider his life more valuable once you can see him?"

Koren gulped. She hadn't thought that far ahead. And Magnar had a good point. The dragon inside the egg was alive. Could she really kill him? "If ... If you let us go, I promise to keep him alive."

Magnar looked at the globe. As its grayness faded to white, he let out a rumble from his throat. "I see."

Koren stared at him. She had to maintain confidence, but with the globe once again detecting lies, he could easily ask questions that might expose her uncertainty about killing the prince immediately.

The shell began to grow warmer, and its familiar voice penetrated her mind. *You cannot kill me. Yes, you might run away, but deep inside, you love me, and you will return to me. Someday you will gladly accept my chains.*

She sucked in a breath but maintained her stare. She couldn't let Zena or the dragons know that her courage was about to crumble.

Arxad stepped close to Koren and spread a wing toward her. "May I offer a solution?"

"Speak your mind," Magnar said.

"I will take the boy and girl, with the egg still in the girl's possession, to a secret place where they can escape

386

to freedom. She will release the egg to me, and I will bring it back here unharmed."

"And if she breaks the shell or harms the prince?"

Arxad guided his head directly in front of Koren's face and breathed a blast of hot air. "Then I will kill them both."

Magnar and Koren turned toward the crystal in unison. The globe stayed clear. His face still red, Jason rose to his feet and staggered toward Koren. He dropped to his knees next to her and gasped, "Thank you."

"No, Jason," she whispered as she looked into his glazed eyes. "Thank *you*."

Jason turned toward Arxad. "How do we know you'll keep your end of the bargain?"

Arxad spoke directly to the globe. "If the Starlighter honors her word, I will take her and the boy to a place where they can escape to freedom without interference from the dragons."

Again, the globe stayed clear.

"Only if no one follows," Jason said. "Not Magnar, not Zena—no one."

Magnar growled. "So be it. Take the two humans, and let us be done with them forever."

"One more item," Arxad said.

Magnar swung his spiny tail, apparently growing more agitated by the second. "What is it?"

"If I do this great deed for our citizens, then I ask that all charges against me regarding Maximus be dropped. By my willingness to kill these two, you now know that my loyalty ultimately lies with dragons and not with humans."

The globe shone as clear as ever.

Magnar stilled his tail, staring at Arxad for a moment before answering. "The charges are dropped. Let the records show that Maximus drowned in a tragic accident."

The crystal turned as black as the egg's shell. Magnar looked at it briefly before muttering, "This lie will remain. The official records need never know the truth."

"Okay," Jason said reaching toward Zena. "Give me the bag, and we'll get out of here. Arxad needs a way to carry the egg, and the strap should work."

Zena removed the finger and dagger from the bag, and then set the bag at Jason's side. A tiny circle of red blazed at the center of her pupils. "He will hatch soon," she whispered, "perhaps tomorrow, so the egg had better be back in its nest tonight. If he commands me to bring you back, I will hunt for you, and nothing will be able to shield you from my view."

⤜⤛

Elyssa strode back to the bottom of the exit stairway where Allender stood with the children and the other men. "The bees are almost here."

Wallace stayed on his knees, frantically digging with his blade.

Allender hoisted a little girl into one arm and guided a boy with the other. "Come! Everyone into the tunnel. We'll have to hide in the water."

"I almost have it!" Wallace pushed the crystal's point into the hole, but it still wouldn't quite fit. "Just a few more seconds."

After herding everyone into the right-hand tunnel, Allender set the girl down and paused at the entry. The children and the other men waited behind him. "Wallace! You must come!"

"If I open the portal, we can escape!"

A thud sounded from the top of the stairs, then another. The buzzing noise heightened.

"Yarlan is coming!" Allender hissed. "We will try again later!"

A third thud sounded, closer. A line of bees streamed from the left-hand tunnel and flew in an orbit above Wallace's crouching form. Allender ran out and batted the bees with his arms. They pelted his body with sting after sting. Allender grew suddenly still, his eyes fixed on the children huddled in the tunnel entrance. Then, with more bees gathering on his skin and adding their stings, he turned and walked into the massing swarm near the rear wall.

Groaning as the bees enveloped his body, he staggered back into the anteroom and, with a sudden burst of speed, ran up the stairs. "They're dead!" he screamed as he disappeared through the exit. "The bees have killed them all!"

A flash of light appeared, and a horrific scream echoed throughout the chamber. The bodies of twenty or more bees dropped down the stairs, scorched and charred. A few seconds later, a louder, more bestial scream ripped the air, then silence.

Elyssa covered her mouth. "Oh, Allender!"

Wallace jammed the crystal peg into the hole. "I got it!"

"Shhh!" Her legs trembling, Elyssa ran back into the anteroom and spoke in a low tone. "We have to make the dragons think we're dead."

The three tunnels at the back of the chamber faded away, revealing Tibalt standing with his hands in his pockets. The river behind him flowed steadily from right to left. "How did you do that?" Tibalt asked. "I opened it a few minutes ago, but no one was—"

"Quiet!" She waved toward the right-hand tunnel, though it was no longer in sight, and whispered, "Everyone come! Hurry!"

Micah's head appeared through the portal plane, then his arms and legs. Natalla came next, followed by the other children and the men, each one glancing at the exit and the charred bees. Tears streamed down Micah's cheeks, but he said nothing.

"Everyone step into there," Elyssa said, pointing toward the river. "Tibalt, put your fingers in the holes so I can close the portal from this side."

Tibalt withdrew his hands from his pockets, now unbandaged, raw and bleeding. "But I can't see the holes."

"Okay." When every slave except Wallace passed safely into Major Four, Elyssa stooped next to him in front of the line of crystalline pegs and looked up at Tibalt. "When the wall reappears on your side," she said, "open the portal again immediately."

Tibalt flexed his fingers. "I'm ready."

As Elyssa grasped the crystal, another thud sounded at the top of the stairs. She jerked her head up and looked at Micah. "Yarlan?" she whispered.

Micah stooped in front of her, his voice also low. "It likely is, Miss. No human could make such a footfall."

A series of bumps rifled through the chamber. Elyssa raised her splayed hand and hissed, "Open it in five minutes." After jerking the peg out, she grabbed Wallace's arm and hustled to the tunnel on the right. They crouched in the shadow and watched the anteroom.

Grunts erupted near the bottom of a stairwell along with another loud thud. Finally, two male human forms appeared. One had his back turned toward Elyssa, blocking the other from view. Each one grasped the side of a raft and dragged it into the room.

"On three," one of them said. "One … two … three!"

In unison, they dropped the raft on the floor, making something metallic rattle on top of the rope-bound logs. Both men stood with sloped shoulders, their heads low.

"Randall?" Elyssa called out. "Cowl?"

The closer man turned. "Elyssa!" Randall's face beamed. "You're alive!"

She ran out and embraced him with damp arms, but he didn't seem to mind. When Wallace joined them, Randall clapped him on the back. "Who else survived?"

"We all did," Wallace said. Then his smile wrinkled into a frown. "All except Allender."

Cowl clasped his hands, and his voice shook with passion. "I thank the Almighty One for my daughter's life, but how can I celebrate in the shadow of my friend's death?"

A shiver ran up Elyssa's spine, and she pushed back a surge of emotion. "What happened to Yarlan?" she asked.

Randall pointed at the exit. "Cowl and I were watching from the other stairs, hoping for a chance to attack. When Allender distracted him, the dragon dropped his guard. That's when we moved in."

"Did you kill him?" Wallace asked.

Randall picked up a blood-smeared sword from the top of the raft. "No, but he's blind now. I don't think he'll be bothering us."

Elyssa lowered her voice to a whisper. "And Allender? Are you sure he is dead?"

Randall and Cowl looked at each other for a moment. Cowl combed his fingers through his hair and cleared his throat. "Miss, Yarlan burned Allender, and … " As his voice drifted to silence, he turned his head, obviously trying to keep his composure.

Setting a hand on Cowl's shoulder, Randall added, "Let's just say that the myths about dragons' eating habits might well be true."

Elyssa clutched her stomach as nausea churned within. No one said anything for several moments.

Finally, Elyssa stooped and touched the raft. "This is a brilliant idea, but it will be a rough ride."

"I think two adults with each child will work," Randall said. "Since we have to climb the rope and switch the river back and forth, it'll take a lot of time, maybe hours."

Elyssa imagined the process. It would be torturous. "I don't have hours."

"But you know how to operate the mechanism. We need you."

Elyssa pressed a finger into Randall's chest. "So do you. Between you and Tibalt, you can figure it out."

Randall tightened his grip on his sword's hilt. "I should search for Jason. Not to insult you, Elyssa, but he needs someone who knows how to fight."

She grasped his bicep. "You're stronger. That's why you need to be there to haul people up that rope. Besides, if Counselor Orion gets wind that I've returned, my life won't last very long. And Jason needs someone stealthy who can sneak around."

Wallace raised his hand. "And someone to show her how to find him."

Elyssa pulled Wallace to her side. "That would be perfect."

"Okay," Randall said, nodding. "You win."

She stooped and inserted the crystal into the hole. Instantly, the portal reopened. Tibalt stood closer to the plane, his fingers extended. "I was just about to—" His eyes widened. "Randall! Good to see you!"

Cowl spread out his arms. Tam leaped over the line of crystals and jumped into his embrace. With a lively step, he carried her into Major Four and turned back towards Elyssa. "We are ready to explore a new world."

"That's wonderful, Cowl." Elyssa felt a tear welling in her eye. "Just wonderful. I hope to see you again soon."

Randall took Elyssa's hand in his fingertips and kissed her knuckles. "It has been a pleasure, dear lady. It might take some time to get these folks situated. I don't think Drexel and his conspirators will be happy to see me or the Lost Ones, so I'll try to blend them into the communes until I figure out what's going on. If you're not back by then, I will return to search for you and Jason."

Tibalt pressed a fist against his chest. "And so will I. That young buck can't open the gateway without me."

Elyssa laughed. "You two do that. We might just need you."

Natalla strode back into the anteroom. "You have to find Koren and help the cattle children."

Elyssa stroked the back of her head. "I promise you from the bottom of my heart, I will find Koren. And Jason and I will do everything in our power to bring every last human to freedom."

Natalla gave her a sad nod. "When you see Koren, please tell her I love her, and … " Her voice faded away.

"And what?"

A weak smile dressed her lips. "Tell her it looks like I really did get promoted." Natalla walked back across the portal and took Mark's hand. "I think I found a new daddy."

Mark laid an arm around her shoulders and pulled her close. "And when Petra gets here," Mark said, "she will have a new daddy, too."

After Randall helped the men haul the raft into Major Four along with torches and flint stones, he set his sword down at Elyssa's side and joined Tibalt and the children at the river.

"By the way," he said, pointing at the stairs. "Jason's sword is outside. He might need it."

"I'll put it somewhere he can find it." She stooped and grasped the peg, gazing at the flowing river. Might this be the last time she would see her home planet? Would she ever be in her mother's arms again?

As if reading her mind, Randall smiled and said, "Don't worry about home. I'll let your mother know that you're alive and well. No mountain bear could ever be smart enough to outwit that clever daughter of hers."

Tears welling, Elyssa nodded at him and returned his smile, but no words would squeeze through her tightening throat. She pulled the crystal from the hole, and when the other world disappeared, she let out a long sigh.

Wallace stooped beside her. "You'll get home eventually. I know you will."

She swiped a tear away and squeaked, "How can you be so sure?"

"Because of something Koren once said to me."

Elyssa nodded. Although she had seen Koren only from a distance as a dragon carried her away, she could tell from the young woman's determined expression that she was remarkable. Elyssa rose and reached for Wallace's hand. "Tell me what Koren said."

Wallace slid his hand into hers and stared at Elyssa's necklace as he spoke in singsong.

When hands entwine, two hearts in line,

Impossible things come true.

Together we'll hold, together be bold,

As long as it's me and you.

As she gazed at him, more sincerity poured forth from his single eye than any pair of eyes she had ever seen. This young warrior would be a partner she could count on.

She picked up the sword and pressed the hilt into Wallace's hand. "Lead the way, warrior. Let's find Jason and Koren."

⇥⇤

Jason stood on the raft and steadied himself. The logs seemed stable enough, and the anchor at the end of the trailing rope held fast in the riverbed below. Near one corner of the raft, the bag of food—bread, dried fruit, and salted meat—rode the current without a problem. Tree boughs arched overhead and swayed in a cool breeze that carried unusual odors, some sweet and some earthy. Using his tracking skills in this new world wouldn't be easy. Even the shadows fell across the river at odd angles.

Koren looked on from shore, holding a torch that carried a tremulous flame. With night settling in and a moon rising over the trees, the feeble lights barely illuminated her face.

"Ready?" Jason asked, reaching toward her.

"Ready." Koren took his hand, stepped aboard, and tapped out the flame on the side of a log. When the flickering light died away, only moonlight remained, casting them both in near total darkness.

"To the Northlands?" Koren asked, still standing.

As his vision adjusted, Jason took in her sparkling eyes. They seemed excited, yet pensive. Many worries dragged against her sense of adventure. He smiled, trying to communicate a dose of confidence. "To the Northlands. Maybe I'll find my answers there."

"Answers?" Koren sat down and crossed her legs. "What are the questions?"

"I'm not sure I know all of them." Jason knelt and pulled up the anchor, then picked up a pole and pushed it into the water, shoving against the riverbed. The current caught the raft and sent it along at a quick but comfortable rate. Staying on his knees, he looked at Koren. "The biggest question is how to get the slaves off Starlight and back to my world."

"That's why we have to go to the Northlands. Arxad once told me someone is there who might be able to help me. Maybe that someone can tell us how to come back and free them."

"Okay, that's a good start."

Koren spread her cape over her legs. "What other questions trouble you?"

"Let me think … " Jason watched her callused hands as she smoothed out the rich material, an intriguing contrast of slavery and high position. Her blend of confidence and modesty also seemed contradictory somehow, yet oddly appropriate for this mysterious girl.

He sat down fully, copying her cross-legged pose. As he leaned forward, a pendant dangled from a necklace and twirled slowly—Elyssa's pendant. The two sides took turns coming into view—closed hands and open hands, slavery and freedom. Earlier, Arxad had taken them to the mine so they could find out what happened to Elyssa and the others. Elyssa had left the necklace draped around one of the crystal pegs with the open-hands side showing, her sign that slavery had lost the battle. Freedom had triumphed. And finding his bloodied sword nearby proved that Randall had aided the effort heroically.

Jason grasped the hilt of the sword, now safely tucked away in his scabbard. Yes, Randall was truly a hero, a far better man than Jason had given him credit for. They had worked together and risked their lives to free the captives, and now many slaves were in a new world, no longer fearing the punishing whip of the dragons. These Lost Ones were no longer lost.

He tucked the pendant under his shirt and let it rest against the litmus finger. Now bright blue, it pulsed against his skin, though not painfully. Would it become a guide again in the coming journey? Only time would tell.

"Let's see," Jason said slowly. "I was wondering what happened with that black egg. What was it saying to you?"

"Oh, that." Koren dangled a hand in the river. "He reminded me that if I came back to him, even though I would have to wear chains for a while, he would make sure of my safety."

"Came back to him?"

"It's hard to explain. I don't really want to reopen my wounds. Maybe later."

Jason glanced at her wrists. Even in the poor light, the bloodstained abrasions were visible. "Okay, I guess my next question is about Elyssa, but you likely can't answer this one. When will she come back to try to find me? I know she will eventually. And where are my brothers, Adrian and Frederick? I haven't told you about them yet, but I think they're here somewhere."

She drew her hand out of the water and pulled her knees close to her chest. "I think we have plenty of time. Tell me about them."

Jason looked up at the sky. Arxad flew across the face of the moon, his wings flapping slowly and the bag dangling from his claws. What a mysterious dragon he was. At times he seemed to be on the side of the humans. His willingness to take them to the mine and his gift of food for the journey gave them every reason to believe it. Yet, when he claimed that he would kill them if they didn't keep their end of the bargain, his vicious eyes and the clear globe proved that he really meant it. He was a mystery, indeed.

"I'll tell you about my brothers," he said, "but I want to learn everything about you and this place, too … Starlight."

Koren smiled and pointed at a moon setting on the western horizon. "First lesson. That is Pariah, our smallest moon. It is one of three that often rise together. And Trisarian … " She shifted her finger to the opposite horizon where a larger moon peeked above the tree line. "Trisarian is the one that shines brightest, but it's always alone when it rises to its apex. Sometimes I think Pariah needs to be alone as well."

"Pariah is a sad name."

Breathing a sigh, Koren nodded. "It is appropriate. He always seems to be wearing a sad face. It is said that sky rocks constantly strike his surface, and the other moons hurl insults at him."

"Insults?" Jason suppressed a smile. "Do you really believe that?"

Koren laughed. "No. There are many superstitions that I play along with, but I don't really believe them."

Jason laughed with her. Koren seemed so innocent and naïve, yet filled with wisdom at the same time. Maybe her slavish life of poverty and sacrifice had given her more insight during her few years than most get in a lifetime. She might be able to teach him a few things. "How do you separate superstition from reality?" he asked. "Who is to say what's true and what's not true?"

Koren looked up at the rising moon again. "Most of my people can't tell the difference, but I can."

"Because you're a Starlighter?"

She straightened her cloak again, though it was already straight. "No, that's not it."

"Then how can you tell?"

Turning back to him, she slid her hand into his. "I have so much to say to you about our ways here, Jason. If you'll just stay with me, I will teach you, but not all at once."

Jason looked at their clasped hands. Her hand was rough, hardened from her many labors, but it felt cool and good, a touch of friendship that revived memories of his adventures with Elyssa when he and Adrian stormed the castle to rescue her from the clutches of dragons. "Okay," he said. "Not all at once. But can I at least have a second lesson? I was hoping for more than just a moon's name."

"Very soon. I promise." She released his hand and took the pole from him. "You look exhausted. Lie down. I'll guide the raft for a while and sing you a song. The words will be a symbol for our journey."

"A song?" Jason lay down on the rough logs, keeping his gaze on her. "Sure. Why not?"

As the raft continued following the river's gently meandering course, Koren looked out over the water and sang.

When hands entwine, two hearts in line,

Impossible things come true.

Together we'll hold, together be bold,

As long as it's me and you.

When she finished with a sigh, Jason sat up and slid his hand back into hers. "That sounds good to me."

"Yes," Koren said. "As long as we follow the light together, the Creator will help us find our way."